Ordo Lupus II

The Devil's Own Dice

Lazlo Ferran

Ordo Lupus II: The Devil's Own Dice

Lazlo Ferran

PRINTING HISTORY

Second Edition

Printed in 12 point Times New Roman

Published by Future City Publishing, London.

Cover: OmriKoresh.com

Acknowledgments

Thanks to Ash, Derek, Hannah and Gary.

Author's note: The following transcript is taken from a journal. This journal was handed to me by the wife of the author of the tapes which make up the first book in this series, Ordo Lupus and the Temple Gate. In it, you will finally learn his name but I don't want to reveal it just yet.

Chapter One

Trapped! *In a Medieval dungeon with no way out*!
I was in an oubliette.

'Oubliette' is French for a 'place to be forgotten.' An oubliette is a dungeon of extreme darkness and despair. The only way *in* is through a small, locked, iron grate far above the floor of the dungeon. There is no way *out*!

What was worse, I had no memory of being put there. I didn't even know who I *was*.

But I did know I was locked inside an oubliette.

Of course, it took me a little while to work this out. It was pitch-black!

***

Where the hell am I?
When I first became conscious, I groped around me on the damp floor and then felt the wall I had been slumped against.

Rough stone.

I squinted and peered into the blackness. After a while I could just make out a source of light, high above me.

I wanted to retch. The gnawing demon of my innermost fear was trying to grope its way out of my stomach and up my spine.

I am not going to die!

But then my strange ability to sense evil told me that if *I* was not going to die soon, *somebody* close to me certainly was.

I stood up unsteadily and began walking, following the wall with my hands. The wall streamed with cold water, and in places it was slimy. Occasionally my feet would bump into something soft. I soon understood that I was walking in a big circle. I kicked around on the floor for something I could put against the wall as a marker, and after a few uncertain steps my foot met with something soft but quite large. Curious, I bent down to touch it and then recoiled in horror, as if hit by an electric shock.

A body!

What was worse was, it stank. I have never smelled such rancorous fetidness, not even during the War. It was an indescribable distillation of decay. I pulled back against the wall and tried to breathe evenly. It began to dawn on me, if you will forgive the ironic pun, that I was not somewhere that was good for my health. At all! However, I needed to know exactly what I was up against. I pulled off my jumper and laid it against the wall

Much safer.

Then I continued on. I counted the paces as I walked. When I reached my jumper again with my foot, I had counted twenty-five paces.

A quick calculation told me that the circular chamber was approximately eight yards in diameter.

I sat down and looked up to where the ceiling might be. My head was thumping, but considering my predicament, I wasn't surprised.

I will see what is up there!

I willed myself to see, and after straining for perhaps ten minutes, I thought I could make out something like a grate, who knew how far above me.

That's when it dawned on me, if you will excuse the ironic pun again, where I was.

An oubliette! God! What have I done to deserve this? More of my incredible bad luck! But I can't be here! How could this happen?

The question had no answer, and my mind swerved between indignant denial and a blind terror that welled up in waves, until I had to scream, "No!" silently, to stop the voices.

"Help!" I shouted instinctively. Two confused echoes followed the single word.

I waited for a reply.

Nothing!

I cupped my hands around my mouth and shouted as loud as I could:

"Help!"

Two faint echoes followed the single word. Then nothing. For an hour I carried on calling until my voice grew hoarse, and the calls seemed like only abbreviations of the despair.

An oubliette is a place of extreme darkness and despair; a dungeon where a victim the only hope is to die.

I have to do something!

I could still hear my instructor in the Secret Service telling us, "During a disaster or emergency, whatever you can do that might be useful, do it. Think while you work. Later you can form a proper plan. Even seconds can count when it seems you have a lifetime."

I certainly seem to have a lifetime, just a very short one.

I guessed the grate would be man-sized, say three or four feet across. Judging by its nebulous glow far above me, it was probably thirty feet away. Perhaps more. The only possible way out was going to be through it, either by subterfuge or – and I had to take a deep breath here – by ingenuity. The first was out for now.

I had to know what else might be on the floor. Walking in straight lines, I paced out every square foot of the floor. My feet hit something soft, just like the first, twice more, and a quick exploration with my feet revealed two more corpses. Grim as it was, this was something in my favour.

I began stripping off what remaining clothes I had. It was then that I started to wonder about the heavy hoop, stitched into the back of strange belt I was wearing. I had noticed the hoop when first groping for the wall but put it to the back of my mind while I urgently explored my tomb.

Roughly made; probably iron.

As I tore my clothes into strips, I began to ponder more deeply how I had come to be here. I knew who I was, but I had no memory of getting here and only vague memories of my life before. I seemed to be suffering some kind of amnesia. I did know that I lived in the 20th Century and that oubliettes, at least fully operational ones, were not a thing of my time. And yet here I was.

My shirt had plastic buttons, too neatly made to be wood or bone, and the trouser material felt like denim. That all appeared normal. I had some difficulty removing the belt; it was thick, stiff leather with the buckle behind my left hip. I had to suck my breath in to rotate it before I could work at it with my fingers. Even then I tore a few nails and cut my fingers.

The tongue in the buckle will be very useful.

I took off my boots and removed the laces, which I put in the boots. After checking my trouser pockets, and finding them empty, I used the buckle-tongue to pierce the denim so that I could tear that into strips.

I only had my underpants and socks on then. I was cold, but I would die of thirst before I would die of exposure. I guessed it was late spring or early autumn outside, if I was somewhere in Europe.

As I worked, I started calculating. Thirty feet to the grate would mean I would need at least at least sixty feet of 'rope' unless I could find some way to snag the grate. The iron hoop was a possibility: I would make forty feet and give it a try. I soon saw a major problem though; for the rope to be strong, I would braid three strips of cloth together, but this meant I would only get about eighteen feet from my clothes, using each sleeve of my shirt, twisted, on its own.

As I worked I remember that I had a wife called Rose, and that I was a historian; a teacher. And then I remembered something else. An image came into my mind of a pastor, an old enemy of mine, stealing some documents from a museum; the British Museum. His name was Pastor … . Pastor Michel! *Yes*! It was a start.

I worked for hours, tearing and then braiding the rags together to make my first length of rope. The activity calmed me and took the edge off a growing anger.

Whoever put me here is going to suffer! If I get out!

The defiance gave me the strength to work toward a way out.

"Collect water." That was the other thing I remembered our instructor telling us. "Any amount is worth collecting."

As I completed lengths of my makeshift rope and spliced them into the main length, I laid them against the base of the wall where they could collect water as it ran down the walls.

Keeping the cloth wet should help to bind the braids and knots tighter too.

After a few hours of tying and twisting, my hands hurt. I needed a break, and I had to do something else.

Going back to the three corpses, I stripped them of their rotting rags. The putrescence of the bodies had absorbed the cloth in places, and tugging it loose released the most awful smell I have ever experienced with a sucking 'plop' each time. I had to grit my teeth and force myself to complete the task. The pitch-blackness was a blessing.

I piled the rags and two pairs of boots up next to my rope and leaned against the wall to rest. Each time I put my hands near my face I had the impulse to gag.

How can I drink any moisture from the rope now?

Dysentery or worse would be the result. Nevertheless, I had to drink. I took off one of my shoes and tried to twist my home-made rope over the shoe in such a way that water might seep from the section not in contact with my hands. Not a drop could I hear. In desperation I lifted the shoe to my lips, but no water touched my lips.

I threw down the rope in disgust.

In a few days I might have a full cup of water!

I would die of thirst if I didn't get out. But then this was an oubliette. Nobody, as far as I knew, had ever escaped from one.

I swore at myself for thinking about defeat and carried on, stubbornly braiding the rotted rags from the corpses.

As I twisted, I heard myself humming the tune 'The Ballad of Bonnie and Clyde.' I laughed at myself.

Incredibly ironic! Here I am, in jail. Great!

Suddenly a clear image, connected with my memory of Pastor Michel, came into my mind. I gratefully played it over and over, expanding it until I had the whole picture.

***

Rose and I were just going to bed in our Highgate flat, in North London. We bought the flat when I began teaching again so that we could spend my summer holidays there.

It was a first-floor apartment, and on this evening a gentle breeze was rustling the blue curtains through the open windows. The window-glass was leaded, in a diamond pattern. This was one of the features that attracted Rose to the flat; it reminded her of our house in France. I had just poured myself a glass of whiskey to enjoy with a new translation of the Vezelay Chronicle, excellent bedtime reading for a historian. The pubs were emptying – I think it was a Friday night. I was glad to relax after a rather harrowing day.

As often happened, I had experienced that feeling of present evil on my way to the British Library. I had promised to call Rose when I arrived, so I stepped into a telephone box, placed right against the brick edifice of a large building. I reached into my pocket for the only pound coin I had on me and withdrew it. Just as I raised my hand to the slot, the coin inexplicably slipped from my grasp and fell to the ground. It bounced, to my surprise, through the gap vacated by a missing pane of glass, and rolled off, between pedestrian legs.

I dropped the receiver and ran after it. It turned and rolled toward the wall, where I managed to finally get my fingers on it. Knowing what such events usually resulted in, I glanced up, just in time to see a window-cleaners' platform crashing down upon me. I just had time to dive out of the way.

"Jesus! Are you alright man?" a tall, dapper black man said, hauling me to my feet. Already, a crowd of people surrounded me.

"It's quite alright. Happens all the time!" I replied.

"Shit!" he added.

The window cleaner himself had actually been on a lunch break, and once the police arrived to take a statement, I continued on, into the library. These incredible chains of events happened to me every week, so I was no more shaken than if I had cut myself shaving. At first, I considered these the attempts of the Devil to kill me, but since I had become sensitive to the atmosphere that preceded them, I just considered it his attempt to keep me on my toes.

"Could you close the big window dear?" Rose asked from the bed.

As I put the glass down, the telephone rang, and I picked up the black receiver.

"Hello?"

"Ah! Bonjour Monsieur." I heard a lot of background noise, and the voice checked my name, speaking poor English with a very thick, French accent.

"Yes, that's me. What can I do for you?"

"Ah. Sorry. My Engleeshe is not good. You remember Inspector Parcaud, no?"

"Yes. From years ago … ."

"Yes. He is retired now. My name is Inspector Clemenceaux, and he has left a note for me to call you in certain circumstances … ."

"Yes … ?"

"And those circumstances has 'appened. I am sorry to tell you that a prisoner has escaped; Michel Georges. You know 'im?"

I was confused for a moment. "Georges? No, I don't think I know anybody with that name?"

"You may know him as something different; he was a Pasteur, Pasteur Michel?"

At the mention of that name a dread curled around and down my spine like a cold eel down one's gut.

"Sorry, can you say that again. Did you say he has escaped? From prison?"

"Yes. Sorry." The poor man seemed to be apologising for the whole French Gendarmes.

"Do you know any more; where he is or where he is likely to go?"

"I am sorry Monsieur. I don't know these things. I will 'ave to go. All I can advise is that you take extra precautions as you wish. He will probably hide. Anyway … . I will send details and a photograph to your local police station if you will tell me the address please?"

"Err. I don't have it with me right now. It's late."

"Ah. Yes! You can call anybody here and leave the address any time tomorrow. The number is … ."

He gave me the number and hung up.

I put the phone down and rolled over to look at Rose. Her lips were pursed.

"It was a French policeman: he told me that Pastor Michel has escaped from prison."

"Oh, not that awful man from Beauvais Cathedral? Do you think there is a danger … ?"

"Not much I don't think. He is … was, inside for multiple murders. He has no chance for freedom if he's caught. I think he'll go into hiding. The Inspector thought so too." I tried to sound hopeful.

"This doesn't *mean* … ?"

"What? That I'm going to go chasing demons all over again?"

"It sounds like … ."

"Sounds like my past is catching up with me again? I know, but I made you a promise. I'm a teacher now, and that's the way it's gonna *stay*."

I put the book on the bedside-table and leaned over to kiss her bare shoulder. Her skin felt slightly cool to my lips. I could see the curve of her still-firm breast below the neckline of her night-dress, and I stiffened at the familiar but still exciting sight. She breathed more deeply but didn't look up. I wrapped my arms around her shoulder as she turned away from me, and I held her close. I am not sure whether she was more angry or *scared* of the news. We fell asleep soon after.

Two other things happened at about the same time; my son, Edward became engaged for the second time, and I finally gained access to some manuscripts, which wanted to translate, at the British Museum.

Edward's first marriage had been a disaster, but thankfully there had been no kids. After only five years he had divorced Sheena. Rose and I thought he would never marry again, but we were wrong. He met Diane, a beautiful, quiet girl, in the summer of 1990.

The manuscripts had first been discovered nearly forty years before, at the end of the Second World War, in a damaged church in France. The owner claimed they had been penned by Bernard of Clairvaux. Not very likely but possible. The British Museum had accordingly given them a low research-priority, but after persistent requests they finally gave me research-access. One document in particular interested me. Purporting to be a list of descendants of Dagobert II, famous King of Austrasia in the 7th Century, it was a single sheet of parchment about six inches square.

What I didn't know at the time was that the bottom half of the document was missing. It had been removed with a neat tear.

While remembering all this, several other, disparate images came into my head; a car rolling over and over and a thunderstorm. But I didn't understand their connection, either to the documents or Pastor Michel.

In the darkness of the oubliette, I didn't know how long I had been braiding rags. Judging by my extreme thirst, it must have been something like forty-eight hours later when I finally felt that ready.

That will have to do!

I had over sixty feet of main 'rope,' and tied to that was another sixty feet of 'leader'; a finer 'string' made by braiding very thin strips of cloth together. This formed a very light line that I could attach to the iron hoop, to try and snag the grate. The shoe-laces I had tied together with a wad of strong cloth at the end for a handle. I'd had plenty of time to plan my escape attempt, and I had an idea where they might be useful.

Content with my work but feeling exhausted, I needed a rest before I made my attempt.

I made one last effort to get something to drink. I tried to lick moisture directly off the wall with my swelling tongue, but all I received was a tongue-full of grit.

I leaned against the wall and closed my eyes.

Sleep.

I jerked awake. I thought I heard something. I only half remembered where I was, and for a moment I thought I was still asleep. But then I could see the faint light from the grate and remembered my predicament. I started shaking with the cold.

"Help!" I shouted hoarsely. Silence.

"Help!" Nothing.

I had to run on the spot for twenty minutes or so to warm myself up. If I didn't escape soon, I would die.

Standing as nearly underneath the grate as I could, I swung the light cord with the hoop on the end. Swinging it round and round in vertical circles I released it at the right moment and waited. I heard it hit stone and stepped out of the way as the hoop clattered onto the stone in front of me.

Again and again, I tried, for what seemed hours. I tried varying my launch position, but only rarely did the hoop hit the iron grate with a faint 'ting.'

Despair again pulled at the edges of my mind as I imagined the hoop being too big to fit between the mesh of the grate. However, there was nothing else I could do.

The Devil has really got me this time!

The thought made me angry, momentarily, but then a sense of hopelessness and despair, greater than I had every suffered, broke over me, and I sat against the wall. I drew my knees up and buried my face in my hands, searching for something that would give me strength to go on.

Images flashed through my mind, all of them dark, but suddenly a pin-prick of light expanded into an almost lost memory of my wife, when I had only known her as the resistance fighter, codenamed 'Dora,' in Bulgaria during the War. On the run from the NKVD, we had holed up in a farmhouse with a big agent called 'Bear' and she had taken a bath:

After a few moments I heard water running and glanced at the door. My heart leaped.

It's slightly open!

Standing up with my vodka, I walked casually around the table, telling myself I just needed stretch my legs, but the temptation to look became irresistible.

As I passed the door I glanced through it and saw the shape of her body through misted glass. I moved closer to the door and peered into the bathroom. The 'shower' consisted of a simple shower head like a down-turned sunflower, at the top of a pipe on the right side of the room, over a large square of ceramic tiles, in a depression in the stone floor. I saw a simple neck-high screen of glass, but she had left it only half pulled out from the wall. I saw the long elegant curve of her legs topped by the most exquisite rear I could imagine. This led gracefully into the curves of her back which rippled as she washed her upper body. She took care to keep the water from her hair. The hot water streamed over her lovely body – slightly red with the heat, making her shape look smooth, like a beautiful sea-creature. I longed for her to turn around, and she did so several times, but without exposing herself to my awed gaze. Then, again she turned, this time to wash her lower back, and as she did she stepped slightly away from the wall, and I saw what I had longed to see. Her breasts were lovely – elegant with a smooth and well-defined shape. Then, I longed to touch them – to hold them. My heart thumped in my chest, not wanting this moment to end, and sure that she would see me, but she didn't seem to notice. She faced the wall to turn off the flow of water, and I retreated. Not wishing to make a noise scraping a chair, I stood there, looking at the wall, holding my almost-empty glass of vodka.

She padded out, wearing only a white cotton towel, wrapped around her, and tucked in on one side.

"Mm. That's nice."

"I'll have one in a minute," I said.

My face turned red, but I covered it by offering to make her another drink. I hoped she wouldn't see the bulge in my trousers.

I made small talk and told her about my parent's house in Highgate, but I could see she was tired.

"It's getting late, and we should rest," she said.

I took a shower, and, when I came out, I found her asleep on the bench, a pile of cushions underneath her – the towel half slipped. I took a blanket from the pile the host had left and laid it over her glowing body gently, but she woke.

"Oh. It's cold. Here. Come lie next to me, and we will keep each other warm."

"Okay honey" I said. My term of affection embarrassed me, but I knew this woman seemed like nobody I had ever met before, more beautiful and more soft and gentle. I felt completely captivated by her. I had become lost in a magic world.

I picked up another two blankets and threw them over her before getting onto the bench and lying next to her. I took her hand, leaned forward and, ever-so-gently, placed my lips on hers. I felt electricity when we touched. Her lips were like no others. I felt intensely happy. I felt I knew her like a part of me, and I felt I possessed her but not in a possessive way. She gave freely.

She shuddered slightly.

"You are the first to touch me in this way," she whispered. The towel around her slipped, revealing her breasts. I felt deeply touched and a little shaky too. I drew her to me and felt her soft warm breasts pressing against my chest. For a moment I dared not look at them, as if, in the presence of a real Helen of Troy I might be overpowered.

I pulled the towel completely away from her and explored her naked body. She moved under me, as my hands explored, and I knew she wanted me.

Suddenly, I heard a bang on the door. I jumped up, uncaring about my nakedness, my erect nakedness. I rushed to the door to listen.

She laughed. "It's okay. It's only a bear! They come around here when we cook. They used to come to look in the bins, but now they often bang on the door. If we were away, they would probably try and break in!"

As I lay on the bench and pulled the blankets over us again our host came into the room in a dressing-gown, holding a rifle. "Alright? Yes?" He said something to her, and she answered him quickly and matter-of-factly. Then he turned without replying, and we could hear him climbing the creaky stairs.

I lay looking at her – how lovely she was, and yet, for a moment, the spell had been broken. We gently kissed again.

"My real name is Rose," she said.

"Rose," I repeated. "It's lovely." I opened my mouth to tell her mine, but she stopped me.

"You are a Michael or a Dan, I think, but I don't need to know yet. You will tell me when you are ready."

Now I remember! God how I love her!

The anger returned again, this time burning incandescent deep inside me. It gave me the determination to keep trying.

Standing up, I felt surprisingly fit. For a seventy-year-old man I did not feel particularly out of breath. In France, I often jogged through the forests around Nevers, and I worked out with weights when I could. An agent always tries to stay prepared, even when retired. But now I felt like a man in his forties. Either I had been training hard since the last of my memories or I was going mad. Or else … . But no, I stifled the thought. It couldn't be!

I kept on throwing.

Once, the iron hoop did not come back down. An animal, "Yes!" sounded in my parched throat. I tried letting out some cord, but the slack wasn't taken up.

Of all the luck! It must be balanced on a bar or strip, or where they cross. Damn!

There was nothing I could do except pull the cord. It snaked down around my hands, and a moment later the hoop came tumbling down and clattered on the stone flags.

A thought penetrated my numbed and fuzzy thoughts. If it had balanced on one of the bars or strips, then it could go over and come down, which was what I wanted.

This is possible!

The thought gave me renewed hope, and I threw again and again, eagerly. Still it failed to catch.

Out of breath now, decided to try ten more throws before taking a rest. I put everything I had into the last throw. It caught.

My heart skipped a beat.

I stood in the dark, listening for a moment to the faint echo of the 'ting' and then my own hoarse breathing. Tentatively, I let out some of the cord in my hand. The weight of the hoop took up the slack as it came down through a hole other than the one it had gone up through. After a few feet it snagged, and I had to gently tug it to release it. I was expecting this, and it happened several times, during the long descent of the hoop. But eventually I held it again in my hands. I kissed it.

Now, there is a chance!

Checking again that the thicker rope was looped neatly beside me, I started to haul gently on the leader, to pull the rope up, through the grate and back down again. Soon I held both ends of the rope in my hands.

Maybe I am going to get out!

I tried to control my emotions as the thought crashed around and around my head like the sound of a demented trumpet-player.

I took off my socks which would only get in the way. I tied my shoes to my waist with a piece of rag I had left over. The belt I looped over my shoulder and under one arm. I looped the thin cord around my waist and tied it to the hoop, still on the end. I didn't know whether the hoop would be useful or not.

I was ready for the long climb. It would be too risky to pull the descending rope to haul myself up. The action of the rope running over the grate would almost certainly break it. I had tied knots, about three feet apart, for the last twenty feet of the rope, and clasping the two lengths together, I climbed up the rope slowly. Grabbing both lengths at the same time would make my ascent safer. I had made the knots thick. I had some small hope that, if the last length broke somewhere, a knot would catch in the grate and check my fall, as long as I was still holding the other length in my hands.

Exhausted, I finally reach the grate. Adrenaline pumped through me like rushing fire, and my hopes were raised further as I saw detail of the dungeon above for the first time. As I had suspected, it was empty of people. It was empty of everything except some iron hoops on the walls, benches and a large door. I wouldn't normally have been able to see the hoops, but my eyes had become super-sensitive to light in the absolute dark below.

Gripping a knot in the rope with my feet, I explored the grate with my hands and eyes.

The grate was roughly circular, with the hinged section being rectangular and consisted of five strips on each side, crossing each other to form the mesh. Each strip was about 1 1/2 inches wide, and the gaps were about 4 inches wide. No wonder it had taken so many attempts to get the hoop through it. This was about three inches in diameter. The corners of the square hatch were about four inches from the edge of the circular opening. The whole iron assembly seemed to sit on top of a ledge cut into the great stone forming the floor of the cell above at this point. A large, sliding bolt-lock held the hatch securely closed. This would be a problem but not one I had completely overlooked.

I took my time and carefully tied the two lengths of rope together, sometimes having to grip the grate with one hand to support my weight. Then, wrapping my legs firmly around the rope with my feet on a knot, I let go and tied the length of shoe-lace rope around a strip of the grate outside the hatch. I tied the cloth end to the belt. Then I let the belt down over my other shoulder until it formed a loop which I could sit in. Unfortunately, my feet gripped a knot which was too low, so I had to shin up the rope to be able to sit in the hoop. I let the assembly take my weight with my heart in my mouth. It held. At last I could relax a little.

Now I just had to pick the lock. Shaking with nerves, I couldn't steady my hands. I forced myself to breathe evenly and again found myself humming 'The Ballad of

Bonnie and Clyde.' This time I had the accompanying thought of 'good looking' which seemed irrelevant. I tried to calm down. Too low to see it from where I was swinging in space, I studied the lock with my fingers. There seemed only one possible way of getting the hatch open.

When I had almost stopped shaking I untied the iron hoop from my waist, and keeping it attached to its thin cord, I passed it through the grate. On the end of the hoop were two small tongues, which had been set into the two layers of the belt with stitching, to hold it in place. It had taken me a lot of effort to separate it from the belt. The tongues might now be my way out of here.

The iron lock was attached to the outer part of the grate by three rivets, crudely fashioned from iron. The edge of the lock didn't quite sit flush with the strip of iron to which it was riveted, so I slipped the tongue into the gap between them. I started wriggling it around to see if the rivets could be loosened.

The rivet at the right-hand end seemed looser than the others, so I worked on that.

As I worked on the rivet it occurred to me that whoever had jailed me had probably not figured on the ingenuity of a 21st Century secret services agent. The thought was a strange one but one of only many in my head. There too was the burning question of how I had ended up in an oubliette? And why was I so groggy when I first woke up? Had I been drugged?

I was working at the rivet, becoming more frustrated when a jolt dropped me six inches and nearly tipped me out of the loop, to the floor, far below. The sickening wrench of descent ended with a second jolt!

The rope is about to break!

I waited while the loop swung round in space. It still held my weight, so I held my breath and continued.

After a lot of effort and swearing, the rivet became
looser, and I could start work on the one next to it. At
first, I progressed only slowly, but as each rivet became
looser, I found I could get the tongue further into the
gap between the lock and the strip, and so get more
leverage. I frequently had to stop for breaks as, working
high overhead, my arms ached, and I became very short
of breath. It became painful. I watched blood stream
down my arms from cut fingers. Suddenly, there was a
metallic bang as the lock came right away from the
strip. I took a deep breath and took hold of the
underside of the hatch. With my weight suspended from
the grate surrounding the hatch, I opened it, pushing it
up and over until it swung over and hit the top of stone
floor with a clang.

My strength almost left me as I stood up in the hoop
and put my arms over the edge of the open hatch. With
a deep gulp of air and a grunt of determination I
launched myself up and started to pull myself over the
edge of the grate. I wriggled and struggled for all I was
worth before I finally laid on top of it, panting and
exhausted.

I felt free, but, of course, I wasn't.

When I had found my breath again. I hauled myself
to my feet and stumbled over to a wooden door; banded
with iron. The only light entering the room were pale
shafts through a grill in this door.

I examined the door at length but could find no
weakness. Constructed of an iron frame, with three
horizontal strips and ten vertical strips, the gaps were
filled with solid beams of oak. Even if I managed to dig
through one of these beams, the gap would only be
about four inches wide, too small for me to get through.
The door-hinges and lock were on the other side. I
could see no hatch for food, only the grill, but this

seemed rigidly fixed and too small for me to get through.

Defeat stared me in the face. I wondered if I could force the edge of the broken lock into the thin gap around the edge of the door. Even if I could, I wasn't sure what good it would do, but it was worth a try.

While trying this and making too much noise, I happened to pause to listen. I thought I heard the echo of a footstep somewhere outside. My stomach did a flip. I held my breath. The steps came closer and closer until they passed right outside the door. I had pulled back behind the grill, but as the footsteps receded I peered through it. What I saw took my breath away. A guard in a chain-mail tunic and iron helmet. The armour astonished me, but the state of it, more so. The glint of newly exposed deep dents and scratches showed that it had recently suffered battle damage and needed polishing. Locks of unwashed hair lay against the metal rings around his neck. This wasn't somebody who took time over his appearance. But then, would he, if … . The thought insisted on being framed clearly in my mind: perhaps I really was in the Medieval. Judging by his armour, I would have said this must be the 13th Century. But then who was I? I looked again at my underpants; Y-fronts from the 20th Century!

This is confusing.

As the guard's footsteps faded to silence, a new but desperate plan unfolded in my mind.

I looked around the door for a hiding place. The only possibility; a narrow ledge, about four inches wide, on top of the door-lintel. A distance of about four feet, above this, reached to the ceiling, but I could see there would be handholds in the poorly-mortared stone. It would be an easy matter to climb the door, using the grill ledge as a foothold. I hoped the guard would pass at constant intervals.

I detached the belt and hauled my sling-assembly up through the grate in the floor. I pulled up the rope too and quietly closed the grate, placing the damaged lock back in place to make it look as though nothing had moved.

My shoes were something I had thought I would need once I escaped, but now I had a better use for them.

I decided to count until the next time the guard passed. That would mean I wouldn't have to wait on top of the lintel for a long time before ambushing the guard.

Twenty minutes. Plus one kangaroo, two kangaroo ... .

When I reach thirty-five minutes he passed again.

Not too bad.

Waiting until he had gone, I threw both my shoes through the grill, onto the floor outside.

Then I waited. I had all my various ropes and pieces of make-shift equipment tied around me, more to conceal them than, because I thought they would be useful.

I counted and reached almost thirty minutes when I heard those familiar slow, lazy footsteps echo far away. I climbed onto the lintel and waited.

The steps reached almost to the door and then stopped.

Silence.

I heard the guard mumble something. Another long silence. I heard a scuffing sound and guessed the guard had picked up the shoes. I heard him drop them and then the sound of metal on metal when he drew his sword. Another long silence and then the rattle of a large bunch of keys.

This is it!

The guard put a key in the great lock and struggled to open it. I tensed on the shelf above. I took a deep breath and held it.

I heard the sound of the bolt releasing, followed by a slight pause, before he pushed the dungeon door open. The guard held back for a moment and then stepped inside. I could see the top of his helmet, with its battle-plume holder empty, right beneath me. The edge of his sword glinted slightly, reflecting the weak light from the corridor. He looked around the room, swung the door right back against the wall and walked in to its edge. He walked over to the grate, the door to my tomb. For a moment he seemed like a statue, and then he stooped and moved the displaced lock. He stood bolt upright.

"*Le Sorcier! Le Sorcier! Il 's'est échappé!*" he shouted at the top of his lungs. I tensed, and then I jumped. I ran through the door and closed it before he could move. The keys were still in the lock.

The fool!

I twisted the large key in the lock. Then I ran down the corridor and took the right turn, toward the light source.

"*Aide!*" the guard shouted from the dungeon. "*Aide!*"

I reached an iron grill, in the ceiling, which admitted the light.

I must find stairs and keep going up. They won't expect that.

I became aware of shouts echoing all around me, from every corridor. I ran on, around a curved corridor.

Probably at the base of a tower. A good sign. There should be stairs here soon ... . There!

On my right, a stair-well appeared, and I lunged up the anti-clockwise stairs. Being almost naked helped a lot. I reached the next level. Bright, harsh daylight hurt my eyes. They began streaming while I desperately tried to see the castle's surrounding by peering through an arrow-slit. For just an instant, I caught sight of tree tops, just above the slit.

I tried to force myself through the slit, but it was too narrow. A bell started clanging somewhere above me.

God! I hope there is a moat! Hide somewhere? Wait until things calm down? Ridiculous! Up!

My eyes were quickly adjusting to the daylight, and on each level, I peered through an opening to see the surroundings. My tower, at least, did have a moat below it; a big relief. Not all 13th Century castles had moats. But I couldn't find anywhere, from where to jump. As I ascended higher, it occurred to me that the moat would probably silted up and might only be three of four feet deep, this close to the walls.

I'm too high already! I'll kill myself!

I saw several guards and a serving-woman in the passageways. The guards both saw me and started in clanging pursuit of me, hollering at the top of their lungs. By now, the sound of shouting, clanging armour, swords on shields and the bell had risen to a cacophony.

I ran into something hard metallic. I was face to face with an ugly, dirty and astonished face, a face from the 13th Century. He didn't look clever, but he looked like he meant business. I pushed his arms away, trying to go around him. With cat-like reflexes, he brought his axe from its position, the head cradled in his other hand, up toward my head with a great grunt and grimace. I had to jump back to avoid losing my head.

I could be no match for a brawny, determined knight, at my age and naked, apart from my Y-fronts. I slowly removed my belt from around my shoulder and undid the buckle while he watched me suspiciously.

He froze, as if expecting a surprise. Then I remembered what they had all been shouting.

"Le Sorcier! Le Sorcier! Il 's'est échappé!"

"The Sorcerer! The sorcerer! He's escaped!"

So he thinks I am a sorcerer.

Holding the other end, I aimed the buckle-end of the belt at his head and lashed his helmet. It impacted with a satisfying, 'dunk' and left a dent in his shiny helmet. Angry at this insulting weapon, he charged me, forgetting to block the stair-well he had been guarding. I darted past him, getting a nick in my soft arm from his swinging axe for my troubles, and ran on up the stairs.

Shit! That was close!

With all the action behind and below me now, I emerged out onto the roof of the turret. Crenelated walls framed the French countryside below me. I was greeted by a bright and glorious afternoon, and if I hadn't been in such a tight spot, I would have cried out with delight. I ran from wall to wall looking for a way out. Sure enough, *there* was the muddy moat, far below me. I estimated I was about five floors up; perhaps one hundred feet. Beyond the moat, I could see a bank and, further on, an open space with some woodpiles and a small hut. Beyond this, I could see a track, leading into a wood. In the far distance, I could see a river, a bright ribbon of silver, curving away to the horizon. The country looked very fertile and green; good enough to eat. The sky looked its usual serene, majestic self. And yet there was something different about the air.

I had no time to study it. Peering down through a gap in the crenellation, I saw what I wanted. Two long, stone spouts, emerging from a buttress three floors below me, right over the brown water in the moat. Memorising their position, I ran back down two flights of steps but had to halt at the sound of metallic feet on stone, coming up the stairs. The footsteps were accompanied by much shouting and the sound of steel on steel.

I took a turn to my right, into a long straight stone passageway lit by the sun in stripes from arrow-slits.

I must be just below the highest level of the main castle walls.

I tried each door on my left until, thankfully, one opened. Between gasps for air, I heard two metaled feet approaching. Looking around the room, I saw a broken spear shaft and rammed it between the door-latch and the door, bracing the splintered end against the floor.

The latch rocked in its cradle as somebody tried the door. I held my breath. The footsteps moved on. They seemed to go to the end of the corridor, and then the sound petered out. I waited for just a moment and then unlatched the door.

Back at the stairs I descended to the floor below and ran around the circular landing.

There!

I saw the short corridor to the garderobes; medieval toilets. The chutes I had seen below the parapet were their discharge chutes.

The only way out!

I clambered up onto one of the two bowls and pushed myself feet-first down the tube, toward the spout. If I found a grill, which there sometimes was, I would be finished. But there were usually only grills on garderobes, at ground level. Suddenly my feet were in empty space. I hesitated.

No, there is nothing else for it!

With one big shove on the sides of the tube, I was slipping and then falling though space.

All my emotions merged into one blinding adrenaline-rush.

I had enough time for one gulp of air, and then I splashed into brown, murky water. My feet sank into the silky, silted bottom and touched stone. I kicked off for the surface. Emerging into the cool air I felt the exultation of survival against the odds. I told myself not to drink in the murky water, but the impulse became too much, and I took several long gulps of it while I swam to the bank.

Hauling myself on to the bank, a welter of arrows assailed me from the castle parapet. Villagers, no doubt loyal to the Lord, were pointing at me, and the soldiers were shouting.

"Le Sorcier! Le Sorcier! Il 's'est échappé!" came from little voices far away.

At any moment I expected to be hit! I ran past the woodpiles on wobbly legs, past the hut, over the space and into the trees.

Free! I am free! While there is light I must keep moving!

I stumbled through the trees, feeling, for the first time, the effect of the life-giving water on my brain. The thick-headed, thumping, fuzzy thoughts, started slowly to fade, and the pain receded slightly. I ran and then jogged, and finally, after perhaps an hour, I slowed to a walk.

I descended a long, wooded slope into a valley, having avoided the track-ways that I had spotted. The leaves on the trees were just turning autumn-russet, and the early evening sun stippled a dance between the waving branches.

Just as the sun touched the far horizon, I reached the top of the bank of a stream. Next to my feet, under the roots of a fallen tree, I saw the entrance to a small tunnel.

Probably the old home of a badger or fox.

It looked disused.

This is an opportunity. Think! You can't run forever.

I stood stock-still, not knowing quite why. I wanted the cool of the water so badly.

They might have dogs!

The thought terrified me. I had to try and put them off the scent. I thought carefully and formed a plan. I walked down to the stream, taking equal-length, short steps and noting their position. At last I plunged into the cold water. I drank deeply, threw some water over my head and drank again. Within a few minutes I drank all I could. Quickly wading downstream for a few yards, I climbed out onto the bank. I made sure to break a few twigs and disturb the soil enough for any reasonably good hunter to spot. Then I waded back upstream to a point opposite the tunnel. My heart thumped harder with each blare of the horns, which were coming closer.

I walked carefully, backwards, from the bank to the tunnel, placing each foot in my previous footsteps. I crawled into the tunnel backwards, using a branch to spread any signs of my entrance. Of course, the dogs would want to explore the hole, but the soldiers would think the dogs were just distracted by the smell of a fox.

I pushed and scrambled to force myself deeper into the dark, earthy tunnel and then started to bring down the tunnel roof ahead, between myself and the entrance. When I had finished, I could finally lie down to rest in complete darkness.

It will be a long sleep in my new tomb. What will be, will be!

I heard the barking of dogs, though the musty sweetness of the soil in front of my face, and then silence. I waited, I don't know how long. Eventually, I became convinced the danger had passed, for now. Exhaustion took me, and I fell into dreams of freedom and happiness for a moment.

***

I awoke, cold and clammy; sealed up in earth. For a moment, I thought I was dead and buried. Then I remembered the dogs. I started digging with my bare hands and soon found myself looking up into a clear, black night-sky. Everything around me seemed grey shadow. I crossed the stream and started walking, heading south, slowly and painfully. I reached the top of the hills on the other side of the valley before dawn and then stopped for a moment.

Funny. Of all the things I have seen, only the stars seem to be as I remembered them.

***

Chapter Two

*Have you ever had an out-of-body-experience? Have
you felt your spirit, freed from your body, flying through
the night air toward somebody you love or hate, or
perhaps some unknown destination? Then you have
been in the animal state. It's God's way. But the Devil
uses it to tempt spirits. People who commit evils while
in the animal state are lost forever. God will not forgive
them. They have taken the first step on a journey to
Hell. If you have been in the animal state, you have
glimpsed what is like to be a werewolf.*

Just after copying those words from my journal dear
reader, I put down my quill and stopped writing for a
moment. I looked out of my garret window and
watched the sickly winter moon, broken by waving
black branches in the night. In the next room my patient
moaned. I listened attentively, but soon the moans
stopped, and I could return to my contemplation. I
wondered if I, if we, will ever get back to our own time,
the 20th Century. I made a decision.

With grim concentration, I poured a glass of the red
liquid from the large vial into a clean wine-glass and re-
corked the vial. I stared intently at the glass of red
liquid, willing it to change into red wine, but *that* would
not happen.

Taking a very deep breath, feeling my pulse quicken,
I lifted the glass to my lips and drained it in one gulp.
Placing the glass again on the oak writing-table I saw,
out of the corner of my eye, the red residue holding to
the inside of the glass. But I could not look at it.
Pushing my tongue gently against my hard palate, I
noted with indifference that blood doesn't taste that bad
after all, slightly metallic but not unpleasant.

Putting another log in the fire-grate, I picked up my quill again. I found myself thinking about half-lost memories from childhood, things I have not thought of for many years.

I remembered a small, cheap musical box, barely more than a tin-can, with gaudy pictures of soldiers and kings and queens painted around its sides. It was a child's toy and had a crank sticking out of the top that a tiny hand could turn. When it turned, little metal tongues were flicked by pins somewhere inside to play a crude, metallic tune which I still remember the words to:

Soldier, soldier will you marry me,
With your musket, fife and drum?

I never thought of myself as conventional; even as a kid I knew there was something different about me. But somehow, from the distance of a few centuries, it didn't seem as if my childhood was any different from any other. It seemed to be all primary colours, reds, blues and greens; so simple then. Suddenly, that England, where a little boy had once seen the changing of the guard at Buckingham Palace and where he had turned the handle on that cheap child's musical box, seemed so very precious.

Soon you will learn my name for the first time, but before that, let me tell you what I remembered next when I awoke the morning after my escape.

***

Half awake, I smelled something awful and alcoholic. I wondered for a moment if I had been waylaid again. But the bed was too soft, so my eyes stayed closed.

Complete and clearly, into my mind, came more of the events which must have led to me being there.

Happily, after only one year of marriage, Edward's new wife, Diane, gave birth to a son, to be named Michael. While Rose and I were over the moon, I felt some disquiet. Michael would no doubt grow up with similar powers to myself and be 'called' to join Ordo Lupus, just as I had. But I had many unanswered questions if I was to pass on any knowledge to him, as was surely my duty. It seemed to me that my grandfather had not had the chance to pass on this knowledge to me, which had almost led to disaster.

This happy birth was overshadowed though when Rose suffered a stroke while gardening. Luckily it was fairly mild; her left hand could no longer hold anything very firmly, she found even walking difficult and tired easily. She improved considerably over a long course of physiotherapy, but her health would always to be fragile from then on. Used to being so independent, she fell back on me for support, more and more.

Michael's birth renewed my interest in the arcane arts, but Rose's stroke curtailed my research somewhat. Besides, I had already promised Rose I would leave that life behind forever in pursuit of teaching career.

The parchment in the British Museum represented one way I could further my knowledge as a teacher and help little Michael at the same time. This is, because I knew there was a strong tie between Ordo Lupus and the Knights Templar. My grandfather had said as much. However, I did not understand the roots of this connection. Bernard of Clairvaux was instrumental in strengthening the Knights Templar. I was interested in any document which might relate to this, especially one which purported to list descendants of Dagobert II, a King believed by history to have left no heirs. I had to see that parchment. But when the day finally arrived for me to visit the museum and gain access to the document, I found a message on my answer machine.

"This is Susan Lawrence from the Manuscripts Department at the British Museum. I understand you have an appointment to view documents BC 10 to 21 today at 2 pm? I am sorry to have to inform you that the documents are no longer available. Please resubmit your request in the usual way, in perhaps in a few weeks' time. Once again, I am sorry for any inconvenience caused. Good bye."

Rose was finishing her coffee in the kitchen.

"Well! *Really*!" I said to Rose. "Did you hear that?"

"No? What is it darling?"

"Bloody BM is canceling my appointment. I've waited almost a year to see this document and now they say I can't! Huh!"

"Did they give a reason?"

"No! That's just it! They didn't bother. I'm going to call them!"

I hastily found the number and called the Manuscripts Department. A familiar voice answered.

"Hello? Manuscripts Department."

"Ah! Is that Susan Lawrence?"

"Ye-es. How can I help you?"

"I had an appointment for 2 pm today, but you left a message on my answer-phone saying that it had been cancelled. But you gave no reason."

"Yes. Hang on a moment … . Sorry! Things are pretty hectic here. The *reason* you cannot see the documents is because they're not with us anymore. We have the police here right now. You see the documents went missing, apparently last night. I can't *tell* you any more than that."

"*Oh*! That's quite alright. I didn't realise … . So sorry. I do hope you find them, or the culprit, soon."

"Thank you. I have to go. Good bye."

"Good bye." She had already hung up.

I was very disappointed. My Latin wasn't the best, but what I had learned at school I had developed over recent years, and I relished the opportunity of being the first to translate these manuscripts.

However, that wasn't the end of the story.

Shortly afterwards, I had another recorded message on my answer phone, this time from the Holborn police station. They wanted to see me about the investigation into the missing documents. My expenses would be reimbursed by the Museum. When I arrived, they played me a short section of video tape and pointed to a blurry image of a man in a black suit, walking directly behind a British Museum security guard. For just an instant, the man in the black suit looked up at the camera. The police also had a blow-up of that frame and had enhanced it to sharpen his features. I was in no doubt who it was.

The officer sitting opposite me swiveled the screen away from me and pointed to the colour photograph under my fingers:

"Sir, the reason we have asked you here is because this man, whoever he is, left something unusual behind when he persuaded the guard to give him the documents which you were investigating."

I smiled at the use of the word 'investigating.'

"Oh? What was that?"

"He left this."

From a drawer in his desk he took out a plastic sleeve containing something white and placed it next to the photograph. Through the plastic sleeve I could see a white, business-card sized piece of paper with a hand-written message.

"We have analysed the, er… ink and it's human blood."

"Yes."

"Oh? You don't sound surprised?"

"No."

"The message says that we should ask you who has taken the documents."

"Yes. I can see that. I know the man: he escaped from a French high-security prison nearly two months ago."

"Yes?"

"His name is Michel Georges. Um, I know him as Pastor Michel, but the French police told me, when he escaped, that his family name is Georges. I can give you the name and number of the officer who contacted me."

The officer was already writing down the name on a form in neat script, sounding out the name as he wrote. "Mich-el Ge-org-es. Thank you sir."

He leaned back in his old leather seat and rocked it gently backwards and forwards. He stared intently at me for a moment.

"Any idea why he would want you to identify him? What was he in prison for?"

"Murder, several murders. He is a religious freak."

"I see. But why would he allow himself to be identified. This, to me, is lunacy. Is he … a looney?"

"Well, he has tried to kill me." I lied. "Yes. I would say he is *mad*."

I began to feel a cold and very dark thrill which had begun somewhere near the base of my spine and working its way up my back.

The officer rocked the chair back and forth a bit more and then suddenly picked up all three documents, slapped them together and slung them in the drawer. He closed it with a punctuating bang. He smiled at me, disingenuously.

"Right. That's it for now. If you do hear anything more, you will let us know." He wasn't expecting an answer.

"Of course."

With that, he showed me to reception and left me. I had expected more questions once I knew who we were talking about. The officer must have been quite sly. He guessed that Pastor Michel's freedom made me nervous and counted on breaking my reserve over time.

He *hadn't* counted on the illicit thrill I had felt once I recognised Pastor Michel's challenge. The call back to Ordo Lupus was intense, dark and irresistible.

***

The image of a closing car door somewhere in France replaced the police station door in my mind. I recognised my old grey Saab and the road as the one near Nevers where Rose and I lived. It had been dusk, and I was doing over one hundred kilometres per hour. Visibility was poor. Coming up to a hump-back bridge, I suddenly saw, *through* the road, as if it were a negative photograph, the white shape of a woman pushing a pram. It might only have been a premonition or my imagination, but I had learned not to ignore these things, and my instinct cut in. I swerved to go around the image crossing the road, slamming on the brakes an instant later. Saabs are very good cars with excellent suspension and can handle most types of abuse without difficulty, but this was too much. I found myself careening toward the low brick parapet of the bridge with the rear of the car sliding out to meet the wall first. I steered into the skid but too late. Instinctively I put my hands over my face a moment before the seat belts jerked. I was thrown toward the windscreen. After that, all was a blur. I was vaguely aware of having hit the wall and of the car rolling. Every so often there was a loud bang and the sound of rending metal. As if in a daze, I found myself wondering if Rose would be watching her favourite TV programme. I felt quite calm; all was as it was meant to be. Then there was silence. And then the screaming.

"Aah! Aah! Mon Dieu!" A hand was reaching for me, tugging at my jacket-sleeve, and I realised that it wasn't me who was screaming. I tried opening my eyes but saw nothing except a red blur. I *could* move my hands though, and I clutched at the small hand clawing at me. I tried to speak:

"Ahh frink am oki."

A voice answered in French, "Okay! Okay! Don't move. There is a house one hundred metres from here. I will call an ambulance. Everything will be okay! I have to get my baby!"

I heard the sound of high-heeled feet trotting back toward the bridge and returning, now accompanied by the sound of slightly squeaky wheels which passed and went on, away from the bridge.

I must have passed out, because the next thing I knew, I woke up in Nevers Hospital. I ached all over, but to my relief, when I wiggled my toes, the bed-sheets moved where I expected them to. I could raise my hands and look at them. All my fingers were there, and I found I could see, hear and smell just as before. A stern nurse made me drink something foul-tasting and pointed to a newspaper on the cream, steel table, next to my bed. With some difficulty I pulled it on to my lap and looked in disbelief at the frontpage news of the local newspaper. A mangled knot of grey and silver lay in a road. Two gendarmes looked out of the photo seriously while two other men operated a bulldozer. The knot of mangled metal, I quickly understood, was all that was left of my car.

"Beauvais Hero is Hero Again!" ran the title of the article. It went on to detail the story of my adventure with the Beast in Beauvais Cathedral five years before; of how eye-witnesses had seen a snake fall to the altar and dissolve into a putrid mess, just as it seemed as if the cathedral would collapse under some calamitous curse. The journalist related how the gendarmes had down-played the whole incident, saying that the rotting corpse of a sacrificed sheep had actually been what had fallen from the trap-door in the vault and that the swirling vortex of cloud above Beauvais had been caused by natural summer winds. I could imagine how an underpaid journalist in Nevers would jump at the chance to write a big story, and they certainly milked this one for all it was worth. They had reiterated the supernatural aspects of the 'Battle of Beauvais' with the 'demon-snake' and pointed out similarities with the car crash. They called me a 'priest warrior of the occult,' a suspected Freemason and saviour of those in dire need.

The young woman with the baby had only recently moved to Nevers, so she didn't know that the bridge was an accident black-spot. Funneled in by the thick forest either side of the road, the sound of oncoming cars was concealed by the hump of the bridge, and many pedestrians had escaped with their life by the skin of their teeth. Two had been killed in the last twenty years. It had nearly been four. I don't know why I swerved; call it a premonition, or perhaps I really had 'seen' a shadow image in the spirit world, of the woman and baby. I thought about it afterwards and wondered if my special 'sight' had not grown stronger.

In any case, the town of Nevers had made a collection to buy me a new car, and The Mayor himself awarded me the freedom of the town, although the symbolic key and a wreath were actually bestowed upon me by the young woman, whom I had saved. She gave me a little kiss. Her young eyes were moist with gratitude.

Later, at home, after a prolonged silence while Rose made some coffee, and I looked for somewhere to put the key, I opened my mouth to speak:

"You know … ."

"Don't say anything." Rose gave me a little kiss of her own. I saw the glint of something new in her eyes. She believed me. She finally believed in me. Oh yes, she had believed that something strange really had happened in Beauvais Cathedral, but the car accident was something more real, more useful.

"Don't think I am going to let you go off chasing demons though," she added. She followed this with a girlish giggle.

***

Even though I was now fully awake, those images of the past were still clear in my mind. I had an itch near my hip which I had to scratch

And what's that smell?

I tried to separate out the elements of the strange odour, like nothing I had experienced before; bread, piss, grass or hay, sawdust and damp, mossy wood. My eyes opened, and I looked at the room around me. It was fully light already, and the sun's rays highlighted specks of dust, making them look like a myriad of tiny angels as they streamed through the open windows of my sanctuary.

I reached behind me, and my arm ached, just as it did after the car crash. I found the itch and found it's cause; a stem of straw sticking though the rough mattress.

Strange!

I felt the contours of the mattress surface which faithfully reproduced the jagged shape of many more straw stems underneath.

I looked at the rough structure of the building; heavy, crudely carved wooden beams and wattle-and-daub walls. I remembered that I was in a mill, but how did I know…?

"Ah! Mon patient est éveillé!" A large hand wrapped around the door frame and a woolly, silhouetted head appeared next to it.

"Bonjour," I answered, feeling clueless.

"You are rested?" he said in French. I waited until I could see his face before answering. It appeared; large, friendly with a beard and moustache and a great tussle of sun-bleached brown hair.

"Yes. Thanks."

"Here, have something to eat." He had to stoop as he moved off into the other room. I clambered out of the straw bed, aching and followed him into the parlour or front room, because it seemed more a like a factory floor than living quarters. A large table stood to the left, with shelves beyond, from which he took a half loaf of bread and a large chunk of cheese, half wrapped in paper, and placed them on a plate. He poured something into a wooden cup from a metal jug and placed the mug next to the plate, on the table. I sat down on a bench and started to break the bread while he busied himself around the room. He wore many layers of clothes, topped with a knee-length linen tunic, crudely embroidered across the chest and down a ridge of the arms. He wore two scarves; one red and one a faded, pasty blue. His legs were bound in linen.

"This bread tastes fantastic! It's delicious."

"Oui."

I grinned to myself. No attempt at polite conversation here. His hard pronunciation of every consonant told me he spoke Old French or Oïl, spoken until the 14th Century.

I broke off a large flake of cheese and tried it. It tasted rancid, but I felt grateful for anything to eat. I scoffed it down, along with more of the delicious bread. I washed the whole lot down with the cup of lovely, fresh water.

"You were very weary last night Monsieur. And you were very dirty. Until you spoke I thought you were a thief or vagabond."

Ah yes. I remember.

Not long after I had stopped to look at the stars, I had begun to feel safer. The adrenaline wore off, to be replaced by extreme weariness. I had to find shelter, so I banged on the door of a hut next to a river.

"You were almost naked and covered in filth. I cleaned you up, gave you some food and put you to bed in clean clothes. At first, you spoke in a foreign language, somewhat like the English. Fortunately for you, I recognised it. Around here people are suspicious of any travelers. Unless they come from Vezelay?" He looked at me inquiringly, and then his face broke out into a broad grin, revealing a set of blackened and mouldy teeth.

I thought quickly. Vezelay was a French Monastery in the 13th and 14th Century, famous for its relics of the Blessed Mary Magdalen, popular, because it was on the route to the Cathedral of St James of Compostela, Santiago de Compostela, itself on the pilgrim route to the Jerusalem. Vezelay also acted as the rallying point for some of the Crusades. Clearly this man thought I was an English pilgrim, and it seemed a safe enough cover until I knew more about this place and more importantly when I was.

"Yes. I'm a pilgrim," I told him. "Please could you tell me what month this is?"

"It's October, of course."

"And the year?"

He laughed. "You try to make a fool of me!"

"No. I cannot remember anything. I may have been robbed."

"Ah! Well it is 1213."

"1213?"

"Yes."

1213. 1213

I repeated the words to myself, but they made no sense. They made less sense the more I said them. I must have gone white as a sheet, because the big man gripped my arm. I shook and gripped the edge of the table grimly.

"You are alright monsieur? Let me get you something stronger to drink."

He stepped outside the building and returned moments later with a ladle of dark liquid. He emptied my cup of water onto the floor and filled it with dark liquid.

"Drink this, Monsieur."

Unsteadily, I picked up the cup and tried the liquid, sweet and very powerfully alcoholic; some kind of mead or cider. I gratefully gulped down the whole lot and looked into his blue eyes. They were compassionate, slightly sad but honest. It had to be true.

Time travel, as I had just discovered, carried with it, its own particular fear; that you might never return to your own time. I felt icy cold, but soon the shaking started to subside.

"You know sir, if you take my advice, you will not speak in your mother tongue too much."

"Why is that?"

"Ha! You speak strangely, even in French. Because we are at war with the English, at least in this part of France."

"Where is this place?"

"You mean here? It has no name. It's my house."

"The nearest town?"

"Ah! That is Lyot, perhaps one lieue away."

"Ah! A league."

That is about five miles.

"And the next big town?" I asked

"Ah that is Donzy!"

"Donzy!"

"Oui."

"I know it." Donzy is a sleepy little town, about 50 km north of the town where Rose and I lived, Nevers. Donzy looked very different when I last saw it though. I had a thought:

"Which way is Donzy?"

He pointed north, back up the river.

"A castle?"

"Yes. There is a big castle. Hervé IV of Donzy holds it now."

He pronounced 'Hervé' strangely, and I had to ask him to repeat the name. I still didn't recognise it.

I wish I had studied my local history more. Who is Hervé IV of Donzy, and why did he imprison me?

Between mouthfuls of bread and rancid cheese, washed down with more of the home-brew, I questioned him more about the area. When I had finished he suggested I lie down again while he worked. Gratefully I complied and fell asleep before I had time to dwell on my circumstances.

When I awoke, the fear, icy, still lurked somewhere deep in my soul. However, with knowledge of where I had ended up and when, had come a steely resolve; to somehow gain control again of my life and eventually get back to my own time. For the first time since the oubliette, the pain in my head had eased slightly.

I heard a deep voice humming a strange hypnotic song outside, so I walked to the front door.

Clouds of pale dust wafted across the courtyard, toward me and in its centre, sat my host, on a revolving wheel, turned by an old, decrepit horse. He fed grain into a hole in the centre of the wheel from a sack balanced on his lap. Every turn of the wheel, he would lean out, as if balancing a ship, and then return to a comfortable position again. He sang in time with the turning of the wheel.

"Vous êtes un meunier!" I called

"Yes. I am a miller, among other things," he replied. He broke into a toothy grin.

"What's your name?"

"Landric. People here call me Landric the Bergier."

"Ah – the farmer!"

He didn't answer. "And yours?"

"My name? John. John Rezor."

"Ah. Jean. Rezor is a place?"

"I'm not sure."

"You have a name and you're not sure what it means?"

"Many people where I come from don't know the meaning of their names."

"It's a strange place… where you come from."

The old brown and black horse, dusted white with flour, looked at me hopefully each time it passed a few feet away. It looked starved. When it looked away again, it hung its head almost to the ground.

About one hundred metres away, I could see the bank of the river.

"You live here alone?"

"Yes. No."

I laughed.

"I am with a woman but not at this time of the year. Her name is Marie. You will see her tomorrow."

"Children?"

"Two, thank God. They are only small, but I thank God for them every day. I need hands to help me before I grow too old!"

I tried to guess his age, but I couldn't determine it. If we were in the 20th Century, I would have said he was forty. He had an air of melancholy about him, but although very brawny and probably very tall for this period, he seemed kind and honest.

To my surprise, he carried on speaking. His sentences were broken into short statements, each time he passed.

"We had no children until last year … Now we have a child and a baby … .Three more we had … They all died … . Because we had them in winter I think … . Now my wife won't let me … . screw her until June … . And only then until September … . That is when she comes to stay here … . That way the babies are born in springtime … . The rest of the year … she stays with her sister in Lyot."

Again, he pronounced the town's name with a very hard 'T.'

"I don't mind," he continued. "I know her sister's husband … is no good in bed!" He laughed raucously at his own bawdy joke. I laughed too at his good humour.

"Why do you lean over on the wheel?"

"Ah like this?" He demonstrated and grinned.

"Yes."

"I bought the mill stones, second-hand from a monastery, and the top stone is worn in one place. The stones cost me everything I had. Apart from old Mignon here."

The horse didn't react to the sound of its name.

"When my wife comes, you must not speak in English. She doesn't like the English. She is a local girl.

Your French sounds like that of people from Bruxelles so say you come from there."

Ah. Brussels.

"It is a good idea Landric. Thank you."

"It will be well, Jean." He grinned at me. "Help yourself to some cidre. I make it myself but … . But not just from apples! Hah!" He thought this incredibly funny.

I went around the side of the ramshackle mill and found a great vat of liquid, slightly frothy and nearly completely covered by a canvas sheet. Behind it, I saw another of equal size and at the back, a smaller one. Each had a wooden ladle hanging from a hook on the side. The aroma of barley and apples wafted from the vats to my nostrils. I ladled a sample from the first vat; some kind of ale. I went to the second which also held ale, so I went to the third and smallest vat. Unlike the other vat's contents, this one's surface was covered with a flotsam of twigs, leaves and dead insects. I scooped a ladle-full of the cool liquid out and drank it down. It tasted just like apple juice, but soon after, I felt a wallop somewhere in my brain that spoke of its hidden power. After that, I didn't think much at all.

Clearly a man of talents, this Landric.

Still tired, I retired to the straw bed for a while. Landric woke me with a nudge, just after sundown.

"We will have fish tonight for supper! You have brought me luck. I haven't caught a *thing* in *that* river for over a week!"

I opened my eyes and found myself looking at a brace of fat, brown trout, hanging by their gills from his fingers, each a hearty feast.

Landric's, as well as a miller, was a fine cook.

"I used to be a fournier," he said. I had to ask him to describe what a fournier was.

"Someone who operates the communal ovens. They are usually owned by the local Seigneur or monastery."

"Ah. Oui."

Served, again with bread, this time hot from the oven and soft as a baby's skin, the fish tasted better than any I had ever tasted. I had watched Landric lightly douse the fish with oil and then sprinkle on some parsley and a salt. Then he had skewered them, and laid them on a hot grill. He turned them regularly for about fifteen minutes before serving. Mine must have weighed five pounds when it had swum in the river that morning, but I ate every last scrap of flesh from its bones.

"I could be happy living like this Landric!" I said, sitting up and burping.

"Ah. It's not too bad. I can work harder without Marie and earn enough money so that we can get through the winter. I miss the children though."

"Does she bring them?"

"Oh yes. They will be here tomorrow. She will bring me things from the market, and I will give her money to keep her until next time. She is a good woman."

"But not as well travelled as you?"

He laughed at my cheeky prompt.

"No. I am not from these parts. With hair like this did you think so?"

I glanced at his mass of wavy, bleached brown hair. His was lighter than most at this time but not exceptionally so. His blue eyes were even less typical.

For a moment I thought he was not in the mood for conversation, but he poured himself a large flagon of cider and sat down again, spreading his great hands on the table.

"My name is not really Landric Bergier. I just call myself that for the locals. My real name is Landric sur pont Loire."

"Ah. The Loire River?"

"Oui. Once I was a monk, you see. I was a Cistercian monk in Bourras monastery. I grew up, first as a serf, working in the kitchens, practically owned by them, and then later I became a cleric and still later, a fournier, operating their ovens. It was a good life. Good food!" He nodded to himself.

"What happened? Why did you leave?"

"I didn't. I was thrown out!"

"Why?"

"I was caught with a woman, during vespers."

"Ah."

"Any other canonical hour of prayer, and I might have been alright, but this was the worst. I was given some money and offered the chance to start my own mill on some land which they owned, this land. You see, they do not like to advertise the weaknesses of their own monks. They would lose face, not only with the community but with other monasteries. I was offered the mill stones too but for an exorbitant amount. I pay them twenty denier each year in rent and supply them with eight sacks of flour. In times of need, they would have the exclusive use of my services. It is a good arrangement considering what else I gained from the whole affair."

"What was that?"

"Marie was the girl I was caught with!" He laughed raucously at this, and I had to join in.

"Of course, it has not all gone my way," he added. "I always knew that the name the monks had given me concealed some truth. I was named Landric sur pont Loire because that was where my parents had come from. They had effectively sold me to a monastery when I was only three, probably, because they were having financial difficulties. I am told they were a noble family once. I entered the service of another monastery before Bourras, but it was *there* that they had given me my new name. It was probably some kind of perverse joke. I had hoped, one day, I would find out which monastery I was originally from and perhaps discover who my parents really were. That will never happen now."

"You could still find out."

"In these times?"

For a moment, I was surprised.

He went on, "I am lucky just to be able to feed my family. There is no money or time for anything else."

After a pause, during which we both drained our flagons, I tried to change the subject.

"How about news?"

"All everyone talks about these days is The Crusades."

He lit a candle against the darkness in the room, and we talked on. I found him to be very knowledgeable about local affairs, a cultured man, and yet very little interested in the world outside his own neighbourhood. As the cider began to douse my curiosity he caught me off guard with a question.

"I thought I heard dogs last night, hunting dogs."

"Oh. Really?"

"Yes. And when I found you covered in human excrement I had to wonder where you came from."

"Oh." I was embarrassed, imagining the state I must have been in. In the oubliette, the stench of decay had been so bad that I had hardly noticed the filth I picked up in the garderobes. I had washed myself in the river after emerging from the tunnel, but without soap, I had not been able to completely get rid of the smell or dirt.

"I don't know about the dogs. Perhaps it was poachers. As I said, I was robbed after leaving Vezelay." I felt bad lying, but would he believe me if I told the truth?

"I see." He slowly rotated his flagon on the rough table with his fingers and peered at me curiously from under his shadowy brow.

***

I don't remember going to bed. I think he must have carried me, because I could not have stood after all that cider.

I awoke to the sound of whistling and Mignon grumbling at his hard labour. When I poked my head around the door, there they were, Mignon circling endlessly around Landric, almost ethereal in a cloud of air-born flour and wheat chaff.

"Bonjour!" Landric called, waving. "Today my wife comes to visit, so it's a good day! She'll be here before noon. There is a… *razor* for you by the trough and a towel if you want to shave." He grinned at his little pun on my name. "I recommend you do. She is a very fussy woman."

The formidable woman arrived, children in tow, seated upon an ox-drawn cart just before midday, judging by the position of the sun. Even clean-shaven, I didn't meet with her approval, but after a whisper from Landric, she smiled politely enough.

Landric helped her get her considerable bulk down from the cart. She held her baby pressed close to her chest, and her one-year old lay serenely sleeping in a bassinet on the cart-seat.

With her safely installed at the large table, Landric and I started to unload sheaves of wheat and barley from the cart. There were also some food supplies and sharpened tools for Landric.

"She doesn't seem to like me Landric?"

"I told you, she's suspicious of strangers. Just look busy and be nice to her Monsieur."

After unloading the cart, we piled it up with sacks of grain. Then Landric led me into the house. He poured three glasses of cider and scooped up the older child. Both children were already wailing with boredom and frustration.

"Give them something to play with Landric dear," Marie said, gently stroking her husband's cheek, as if to emphasise, by their closeness, how unfamiliar I was.

Landric fetched a half-carved toy horse he had been making for his oldest, Hervé. The sullen boy's expression didn't lift at all, but he whacked the wooden toy violently against the table-top enthusiastically.

"Monsieur. You're from Bruxelles?" asked Marie.

"Ah. Yes." I nodded to affirm the lie more completely.

"And you are on a pilgrimage?"

"I was. Yes."

"And your trade, sir?"

"Hm. I am a teacher."

"Ah! Bon! Then you have money at home?"

"Yes. But I'm penniless, I mean I have no money. I was robbed."

"Ah yes. My husband has explained." Suddenly she smiled at me. "But you can work?"

"Yes. Of course. I will help Landric for my keep."

"Ah. That is good."

With that she pulled up a hem on her blue linen dress under her armpit and turned away to breast-feed her baby. It seemed that my interview was over. I looked at Landric, but he just smiled back indifferently.

Marie stayed until about a few hours before dark. I fussed nervously about, hardly being able to get Landric alone, so I could quiz him on her opinion.

"It is not safe," he said as soon as the cart had rumbled out of site. "I asked her the news in Lyot, and she told me the only real news was of an escaped sorcerer from the Castle. She thinks that it is you. She will not keep quiet. Word will get around that you are here. Tomorrow you will have to leave. I am sorry Jean, but that is the best – for you. Marie is a good woman but as I said, she is nervous about strangers. I have been thinking … . Last year, in July, I met another miller at the Feast of Saint Mary. It is the main feast around here and everybody goes. He lives the other side of Lyot. I think he will help us. Tomorrow I will visit him, and when I return, you must leave. I will give you some money and instructions to get there. Marie does not know about him, so you will be safe."

I had to grab his hand and shake it. I was so grateful for the 'us' in his comment. At least he wasn't *abandoning* me.

"Now, let us drink more of this cider! You know, your eyes … " he said, gesturing toward my face while he tore a chunk from a loaf of bread. "One blue and one brown. We call them angel-eyes."

"Oh? Why?"

"It is because of stained-glass windows. Have you ever seen one? Most people around here have never even been in a cathedral or abbey, but still, it is a saying … ."

"Yes. I have seen cathedrals." I was itching to tell him about Beauvais, but, of course, it hadn't yet been built.

"I have been in the great Church of Saint Denis in Paris. Have you seen it?"

"Not for a long time. But once, yes."

"Ah. It is very beautiful. And in England you have Canterbury … ."

"Yes."

"Ah. I see that you do not want to speak much of this. But you know, I do not think you are a sorcerer. No, whatever you've done, I do not think you are a bad man. If you survive, remember me. My friend – he will be more useful to you. He does not have a wife and children to take care of."

***

I awoke with yet another sore head the following morning. Landric had already left, no doubt riding Mignon.

I sat by the stream for an hour or two, wondering about my future. I was there when he returned.

Landric packed a lunch for me, gave me ten denier, descendent of the Roman denarius and later to be called the penny, and took me to the cross-roads, only a mile outside Lyot, riding bare-back on Mignon behind him.

"Here we must part my friend. Don't forget me, and if you should happen to be at the Feast of Saint Mary next summer, I will see you there. It is noon now. Do not waste time in Lyot and do not speak to anybody – your accent gives you away. Go straight to the mill of my friend, and get there before dark. Good luck!"

He took my hand and shook it firmly. I grasped his shoulder with gratitude.

"Good bye Landric. I won't forget this. If I have a chance I will repay you."

"Do not worry my friend. Just stay alive. These are troubled times."

With that, he turned Mignon and rode away. I turned for Lyot. It didn't take long to get there.

Lyot was not much more than a village; a small cluster of ramshackle, oak-beamed houses huddled around a market square. These houses were those of the wealthy; the merchants and the money-changers. The rest of the hovels were really just a collection of lean-tos and hastily-raised huts, which were not much more than wattle-and-daub. Only the large houses had any

kind of finish, white stucco. One of them displayed a
board with a crudely painted castle on it.

A hostel!

Most of the busy people around me were dressed
like Landric and Maria; the women wearing practical-
looking linen dresses, some coloured brightly, with bare
calves and boots on their feet. The men wore knee-
length tunics over various layers which showed at the
knee-hems, cuffs and collars. Both men and women
wore heavy leather belts with large, bright buckles. All
of this, I knew, was typical for this period, but they
were distinguished by the various ornately decorated
buckles, clearly a local tradition. Most had a look of
indifference on their faces, along with an air of dogged
determination, while they went about their business.
There seemed to be a hushed calm in Lyot.

*I am looking at a real piece of history! Not too
different from the text books but more squalid.*

As I walked up the street toward the hostel, the
stench of decay and human-waste assailed my
unaccustomed nose. I dared not look in the wide gutters
in front of each house, but a few mangy dogs and one
cat explored their contents with their noses and tongues.

In a small courtyard, next to the hostel, three horses
were tied up; a small brown mare barely more than a
pit-pony, a taller grey and a large brown mare.

I half expected somebody to walk up to me and ask
if I needed help, but I was ignored. I pulled my collar
up to my nose. It was possible that Lord Hervé IV of
Donzy might have posted a few agents around the
towns, men who saw me that day in the Castle. If I were
him, that is what I would do.

I knew I should pass straight through the town, but
the hostel drew me. It had the attraction any meeting-
place would have for a historian and an intelligence-
agent. If there was news or information to be had, it

would be here. I walked up to the open doorway and stepped inside. Perhaps fifty voices filled the large room with the music of murmuring conversation. A hearth fire sent a lullaby of flickering orange light up which made shadows dance on the ceiling. I stepped up to the bar.

"Ale please."

"Monsieur!" The large, swarthy man behind the bar, swung around and scooped a large leather tankard of ale from a vat behind him.

Faster than pulling one.

"Quarter obole," the man said, holding out his hand.

I was at a loss. I took out the four denier and other assorted bits of coins Landric had given me and held them out in the palm of my hand. The man took a quarter fragment of a silver coin and shook his head.

"Merde! Here!" He scooped up another tankard of ale and banged it down on the bar-top, splashing ale all over himself and me.

"Oh! Okay."

Each tankard was about the size of two English ones so now I had four pints of ale for a tiny fragment of a coin. It seemed like a bargain.

I glanced over to the other customers at the bar, to make sure I hadn't stirred up too much attention. Then I hastily retired from the bar with my double-pints to an empty table. I sat down and tried a taste of the warm, frothy liquid. It was definitely watered-down but tasted good enough. As I watched the different faces in the bar, trying to read their thoughts, profession and in some case, lips, something nagged at my subconscious. A well-dressed man at the bar, paid and left.

He looks quite rich. Must be a merchant or craftsman.

Some of the faces *were* now watching me. I closed my eyes to avoid their gazes, and an image floated into my mind. It was of a pair of steel-rimmed glasses.

Strange!

The image wouldn't go away.

Glasses? Glasses? Do I wear glasses? Surely, I would remember that. Anyway, I can see okay.

I ran the image through my mind to see it more closely.

Steel rimmed, yes, and modern. And ... sitting on a bar! I must have seen them on the bar! That man!

It's a strange phenomenon that when in a different time, something belonging to your own time can seem not out-of-place at all. Until you think about it.

My heart beat fast, and I swallowed hard to control my emotions.

Somebody else is here, from my century. No, wait. Perhaps they are my glasses after all.

I had to find out. But I didn't want to attract attention. I gulped down the rest of my first tankard of ale, a feat born of desperation, and headed for the bar. I slid the tankard over the counter.

"Good ale! Do you do vitals?"

"Yes. Bread and cheese. Or meat if you have the money."

I looked up and down the bar, to check that the glasses weren't still there.

"That man. He's a teacher or something? I saw his glasses."

"His what?"

"Those little eye-pieces he wears, to see clearly?"

"I don't know what you mean. He's not a teacher. He's a scribe. Comes here regularly. Do you need something written?"

"Yes. Actually, I do. He comes in here regularly?"

"Yes. About once each week. He'll be back next week."

"Next week! Oh no! Where did he go?" I couldn't control my own fury at the missed opportunity.

The hostel-keeper shrugged. "Who knows? All I know is that he goes from town to town on that beautiful mare of his. Don't worry, he'll be back."

I walked briskly out of the hostel and looked to where I had seen the three horses earlier. The large, brown mare was gone. I walked to the middle of the square and looked down each road as far as I could see.

He's gone! Damn! No point going back inside now.

I set off east, out of the town, following the directions Landric had given me.

As I trudged along the muddy track, west of Lyot, I tried to understand what I thought I had seen.

If there are others here from my century, is there also a way to get back? Perhaps. Now I have to think of a way to contact this man when he comes back. Leaving a message with the hostel-keeper is an option, but I need to think it through. It could be dangerous.

Black clouds started to form ominously above me. When there was no shelter to be found apart from a few straggly tree branches, the rains came down.

Since my escape from the castle, my experience had been mainly positive. Although not like the idealised images in history text books, which I remembered from school, the bright sun and easy climate had lent the area a beauty which had started to seduce me. Now, the full horror of medieval life hit me. The clothes Landric had given me quickly became water-logged. Worst of all were the shoes. They became so heavy, it was hard to lift my feet, and they chaffed. The lane became a quagmire with each step being more difficult than the last. Mud came up above my knees when my feet sunk in. I tried traversing among the trees, but my face was whipped by stinging branches, and the mud was, if anything, stickier.

As darkness descended, two knights on mud-spattered horses passed me. I called to them for help, but a menacing look from one deterred me from calling again.

The few remaining miles, which should have taken me less than an hour to cover, seemed to stretch away forever. I was at the end of my tether and exhausted when I finally saw a pale, yellow light from a window on a bend in the lane, just where Landric said it would be.

Thank God!

I waded toward the light like a fish swimming toward a fisherman's lantern. *This* mill was situated next to a small, fast flowing stream. Crossing a slippery wooden bridge over the race, which was dug deep beside the stream to give power to the great mill-wheel, I banged hard, twice on the heavy oak door.

The rain streamed into my eyes while I waited.

"Come on! Come on!"

I stamped my foot hard, to keep warm, just as the door opened, so I had to smile to disarm the man facing me.

"Monsieur Guillaume?" I asked.

"Oui?"

"Jean!" I held out my hand, but he didn't take it. "Landric sent me."

He looked into my eyes, trying to penetrate my soul, but the rain and my pitiful state defeated him.

"Come." He turned his back and led me into the darkened interior of his mill. Its resinous smell spoke of new timber. Much more austere than Landric's mill, there was only a little furniture and even fewer ornaments. He led me to a raging log-fire in the main room and indicated that I should strip off my wet clothes. Hurriedly, with fumbling fingers, I complied and warmed my naked body in front of the flicking flames.

Guillaume returned with dry clothes and threw another couple of logs on the hearth. He sat down to rest in a wooden chair, furnished with a large, green cushion and uttered not a word as I dressed. I was too grateful to care about his reserve.

Without speaking, after about a half hour, and when I had finally stopped shaking, he placed a wooden bowl of some kind of gruel in front of me. Next to it, he placed a wooden tumbler of water. His face was stern and impassive. Clearly, I wasn't going to find a largesse of conversation here, *or* a well-provisioned table.

"Landric! Is he well?" The first word came like a shot from a gun and pierced the near-silence. I jumped, and it was some moments before I could compose an answer.

"Yes. He's very well. And his wife and two children."

"Ah yes. He has two now."

If there had only been a question mark on the end of that … . Then, a conversation would have been possible! But it was delivered as a dry statement of fact. Guillaume was dressed in several layers of cotton tunics, like Landric, but these were without any decoration. He stood up and fetched a tumbler of water for himself. Then he sat in his chair opposite, without a cushion under his considerable bottom, and stared past me at something invisible on the wall. I wondered if he was grieving or in some other way unhappy. Unlike Landric, his hair was short, and he had no beard or moustache. His nose wasn't the usual ruddy red of the other villagers, but instead his whole face and hands were quite pale, almost white. Since it was only October, this seemed odd for a man that spent much of his life outside. For just an instant I was suspicious, but then Landric's assurances quelled my dark thoughts.

I glanced briefly around the room. For furniture, apart from a roughly cut shelf which served as a mantle-piece about three feet above the fire, there was only a large, wooden table and a third chair. On the table was a three-spigot candle-stick; a large bowl of apples and brown, bruised pears; and an open, leather-bound book. My heart fluttered slightly at the sight of the book, which I hadn't seen, at first.

A learned man. And with books! Good.

I made my mind up quickly to take care wooing this man's affection. If he had books, knowledge of the wider world and more importantly, was bold enough to display the fact, perhaps he really could help me.

The gruel, although course and thick, was hot and tasted good. I soon finished it.

"Ah!" I exclaimed. I licked my lips and patted my stomach, in an obvious display of pleasure. Guillaume laughed, a short dismissive laugh like a swordsman's cry when he thrusts. He took my bowl away and brought it back full.

"You're from Angleterre, but say you are from Bruxelles?" His English was not good, and he reverted to French words wherever possible.

"Yes. Landric told me to say that."

"Oui. It is good. But you are not working for King John?"

I looked into his eyes at the mention of that familiar name. The stare from his dark eyes, whose iris-colour I could not yet see, was penetrating and steady. The whites of his eyes, coloured orange by the firelight, gave him a slightly satanic air. I could see he was challenging me. Perhaps the sudden question was designed to shock me into making a mistake if I was a spy.

"No." I chewed slowly on the gruel. "My story is more complicated than that."

Guillaume liked the answer. Again, there was that swordsman's cry laugh, and he slapped his knee.

"Ah. This will be an interesting partnership!" he observed.

This time, he surprised *me*. I smiled.

"Wine?" he asked.

"Yes. Indeed, if you have some?"

"I don't drink it myself, but for guests … ."

When it arrived in a stone jar held by his ham-fist, the wine was a rich, dark, red. I gratefully sampled its luxuriant perfume and pungent taste.

"Good?" he asked.

"Yes."

"They say the wines here are the best."

I had to smile ironically at the truth in what he said. One day they would be known the world-over as the best.

"Un pomme?" he asked, pointing to the bowl of fruit.

"An apple please."

He threw over a rosy red specimen and took one himself. He rubbed his on his tunic hem to polish it and then took a knife from his pocket. He proceeded to skin the apple precisely, until there was just the naked off-white flesh left, each facet a slightly different shade from the reflected, ever-changing firelight. He threw the skin into the fire. This seemed an oddly extravagant gesture to me for a poor man.

"You don't like the skin?"

He shrugged.

I took a large bite out of mine, hearing the tough skin yield with a snap as I bit through it. A drop of the sweet juice ran down my chin when I chewed the flesh.

"What of King John?" I asked boldly.

"You haven't heard? He is planning war, along with Otto, Emperor of Allemagne. Many here are sympathetic to John … . Mainly, because he opposes King Phillip. Many young men are afraid that they will be forced to fight, either for France or the Emperor. He has many spies and sympathetic knights here. It is said that Hervé is himself sympathetic. People see spies everywhere."

"And you think … ?"

"Yes. I believe there will be war but not until after the rains in the spring. No king likes to fight in the mud of winter."

I hunted my memory for a war in history that might match this one. Unfortunately, my memories of such regional conflicts, many and various down the ages, was sketchy at best.

"They will think you are *one*." he said.

"What?"

"A spy. Or sorcerer."

"Sorcerer?" That was the second time I had heard such a term applied to me recently.

"Your eyes."

"Ah."

"It's a sign. They say a man with different eyes can be in two places at once. Some say he serves God and Satan at the same time." He looked like he believed it. "I have *never* seen such eyes before."

"It's nothing. It's just a defect … caused by a punch when I was a child."

He nodded but seemed unconvinced.

"You must cover one eye with a patch. I will make you one. Tomorrow you'll begin work."

He upended his tumbler to drain the last of his water, lifting its base higher than before. I noticed, highlighted by the firelight, a strange symbol carved into the base of the tumbler. It was a rough circle divided in two, with the left half carved deeper than the right and angled at the top where the two halves met. It looked rather ornate for a maker's mark, especially on a wooden tumbler. I dismissed it and looked at my pile of wet clothes on the floor. A pool of water had spread out from them, almost reaching my feet.

Guillaume swung a fire-jack, an iron rail with hooks on it, out from under the lintel of the hearth and indicated I should hang my clothes on there.

"When the fire is low," he said walking toward the doorway in the opposite side of the room from which I had entered. "Don't stoke the fire or put on more wood."

"Where do I sleep?" I asked, hopefully.

"There," the disappearing back said.

***

I was woken by a violent dream. I had been on horseback in battle, wearing heavy armour, and interminably charging an enemy in black armour, whose face was covered by a visor. Each time I charged, I was assailed by a hidden fear. When I woke, I found myself wondering what the fear was.

Some weakness in my armour? Yes, something like that. A crack or weak plate.

I remembered what Guillaume had said about the coming war. I knew one thing for certain; I didn't want to be anywhere near it when it happened.

I had slept surprisingly well on the floor. I had used the cushion and two pieces of sacking, which I found in the main milling room, as a mattress, and I must have fallen asleep immediately, because I couldn't remember thinking anything at all after I laid down. The last thing I did remember was the orchestra of rain drops, clattering on the newly built wooden surfaces of the mill.

As I lay there in the morning, I could hear murmuring from the next room. Immediately I feared the worst.

Guillaume is shopping me to the authorities!

But the murmur continued in an unvarying tone. It was just one voice. I relaxed.

He must be praying.

Guillaume was already a mystery to me; a man living alone in a very austere mill. What did he spend his money on? If he was poor, why did he offer me wine and yet drink none himself?

I struggled to my aching feet and padded around the room to stretch my legs. I looked sadly at my inadequate clothes hanging on the fire-jack.

I supposed it was only polite to change back into them.

That hat is worse than useless. It's like wearing a soggy bath-towel in the rain!

"Ah! Awake," my host, entering said. "Good. Some food. And then work!"

Wow! Three words in one sentence! Yeah. Like, after some heavy conversation, then the fun bit!

The breakfast he gave me was a stiff chunk of black bread, accompanied by some berries and dry cheese, washed down with water. Then he took me to the main mill room and pointed to the piles of sacking.

"Landric told me you're a good worker. We shall see. It's too wet outside now. Hang those empty sacks up on that beam and thrash the old chaff and grain out of them with this!" He handed me a baker's paddle, shaped like a boat paddle, and left me to figure out the rest myself. At first, it seemed an easy job. I dragged a barrel underneath the low beam and pinned the sacks to the beam on nails that were already driven in there. Then I began to thrash. Within moments, the large room was filled with flying chaff, so dense that I could hardly see or breathe. I opened the large oak doors on the side of the building, used for loading wagons, to let the material escape. This helped a bit, but it revealed to me two more piles of empty sacking, each of the three pressed-down piles being four feet thick. I swore to myself. My usual headache seemed to worsen for a while. I noted to myself that only substantial meals seemed to dull it since the oubliette.

By judicious use of frequent breaks to drink water, I managed to survive until Guillaume called a break for 'midday repast,' as he called it.

"Hm," he said looking at my work. "Let's go along the river. I want to catch some fish for supper." He handed me a willow-rod with a silk line and hook attached to the end. He carried another rod.

"Ah. Fish!" I offered tentatively. "Yes, Landric has lovely trout from his river too! Very good!"

He didn't answer but strode off, out of the front door, around to the back of the building and along the river bank. I dutifully followed. We walked nearly a mile before he stopped, facing a line of trees ahead which ran down to the river's edge.

"Do you fish here often?" I ventured.

"Sometimes I make more money from fish than from bread," he said, not quite answering my question.

He started forward again and picked his way carefully though the dense undergrowth of a copse. Wet stinging-nettles, ferns and brambles slapped and tore at my leggings, bare knees and thighs. I noted that Guillaume's legs were better protected.

Thanks for warning me!

After only a minute or so, I was surprised to find that we had emerged into a very large open space of a few acres, dotted with raw tree stumps. The soil appeared to have been recently tilled, though very roughly, and strands of dead, dried nettles and brambles lay along the grooves like some strange warp in a brown cloth.

Only one tree remained, an old oak in the centre of the clearing. Guillaume made straight for it.

"I thought we were going to fish?" I said.

"Eat first."

"This is a strange place!" I said, as we nestled ourselves in the thick roots of the oak.

"It's an assart," he answered, somewhat cryptically.

"Assart? Assart … assart … . Assart! Ah yes. I have heard of assarting. Ancient med- … . I mean, a way of clearing trees?" I hadn't heard the word used as a noun before and hearing an ancient word used intrigued me.

He opened a small bag he had around his shoulder, took out an apple and handed it to me.

He looked at me strangely. "Yes. That's right. This is a small one, only a few mansus. We have cleared much bigger ones, some as large as a hundred mansus in the Morvan Forest."

Half way through my first bite of the apple, my mouth stopped with the juices oozing through my teeth.

Assarting was highly illegal, punishable by death in these parts most probably, and yet he said 'we.'

He went on, "That is where the wood for my mill came from."

"Ah."

"We leave it like this for a year or two, to see if the Seigneur notices, and if not, we sow crops. We always leave a tree wall around it so that it remains hidden. These we leave for a while," he said, pointing to the tree stumps. "Later the stumpers will remove them. Of course, it will be found out eventually, but by then we will have made quite a good living from it. We are poor and have to fend for ourselves."

"Why did you leave this tree?"

"It's old. And you never remove all the trees. That's just common-sense. Besides, the livestock will need shelter in the rain."

Some crows, high in the branches of the tree above, cawed as if to emphasise the dark nature of his story.

He turned to gaze at me and for the first time I could see clearly the colour of his eyes, lit by the strong, late-morning sun. They were a deep brown, almost black, like the loamy soil beneath our feet. His age was clearer now. I estimated he was a man in his prime of about thirty years.

"Do you have a wife?" I asked him. His shoulders settled as if he were relaxing. Possibly he had been testing me with his trust.

"I have no need of a woman. At least not in the way you mean. I like the company of women, but there are higher goals to pursue."

An ascetic.

"Your mill has no ornamentation of any kind. You are an ascetic? A holy man of some kind?"

He let out his short shot-laugh. "Ha! No, not a holy man. But … perhaps one day … ."

I didn't press him further for now.

"And you? Wife? Children?" he asked.

"Yes," I answered. "I have a wife and a son. I had a daughter once … ."

"Where?"

"My wife? Angleterre. And the boy too."

"Your daughter died?"

"Yes." I felt, rather than saw, him looking at me, and so I stared back. His penetrating eyes caught more from mine than I meant to reveal. "Look!" I pointed to a large-winged bird flying away from the river, about four hundred feet from us. It flew straight toward our oak and lowered its gangly legs to land on its branches. "A heron. And a big one!"

"It's good luck!" he said.

"I will tell you my sorry and bitter tale," I began.

I didn't know what I was going to say, but my host deserved a story, even one with some truth in it.

I bit into the juicy apple again and noticed a movement in the white flesh.

"Ugh! A maggot!" I put the apple on the ground but noticed that unmistakable feeling of malevolence sweeping over me. It was as strong as I had ever felt it before. The sky looked the same, but, somehow, I knew that doom was in the air. It seemed to be above us.

"Move away from the tree Guillaume!"

"What? Why?"

"Just do as I ask. Now."

He shrugged and lazily got to his feet. I had already stood and moved about ten feet from the tree's trunk. I heard a great crack above us and lunged for Guillaume, grabbing his arm. I yanked him away from the tree, and we fell in a heap, he on top of me.

Behind him the ground erupted as one of the oak's giant limbs hit the ground, sending mud, stones, branches and leaves flying in all directions. A twisted section of the long branch lay right over our heads and further out, the branch lay flat on the ground.

"Phew! Lucky!" I gasped.

"Mon Dieu! Mon Dieu! How can I thank you enough! You saved my life Monsieur!" Guillaume hugged me and kissed me twice, once on each cheek. He was filled with passion, something I had not expected in him.

His eyes were wide with fear and wonder, as we struggled out of the green prison. Guillaume wandered over to the base of the tree to look for his bag. It had vanished under the root of the branch which was at least three feet in diameter. At its base, it was quite rotten, the fleshy part a dark brown colour showing how long it had been peeling away from the trunk.

Guillaume slapped his thighs in disbelief.

"Look! The rods are still intact!" I said, picking them up and handing one to my host. "Now we will have to catch our lunch."

"Oui! That was my plan anyway," he replied.

I set off for the river, and he followed meekly.

There were no more questions from Guillaume that afternoon. We caught a brace of trout and a large tench, olive green with beady red eyes. All would be good for the pot that night.

***

"It's true what they say then?" he asked me. "You are a sorcerer!"

Returning to the mill, I had set to work with the sacking again, but Guillaume no longer gave me disapproving looks when he saw me. In fact, he seemed to care little how hard I worked now. Nevertheless, so as not to exploit the good nature of my host, I put in a good afternoon's work for him. By supper time, I was ravenously hungry and thirsty for that wine.

He had just set the table before me when he asked his question.

"What do you mean?" I replied.

"The tree!"

"Ah. Just luck!"

"Non! I am not a fool."

He stared intently at me. I shifted uncomfortably on my chair.

"I am not a sorcerer. But it's true that I have some kind of special sight, a sixth sense if you will."

"Ah!" He pointed at me.

"Second sight. Yes, you practice magic then?"

"No … ." He looked disappointed. "I can see Evil. Clearly. Sometimes I can see it before it can see me or at least before it can do any harm to me. It's a strange talent to have… and bitter in some ways."

"Ah! The Earthly God." He startled me with this term. I had heard it several times before, though only in the most exalted academic circles. He served the grilled fish; to each of us half of the tench and a trout. The tench must have weighed three pounds or more, so it was a princely plateful. Some brown bread, a pile of something sweet-smelling and white and some radishes filled the rest of the plate. I smelled the white substance.

"Turnip?" He didn't recognise the name, so I tasted it and confirmed it. I took a sip of the red liquid in a tumbler next to my plate and concluded that it was the strong-tasting wine of the evening before.

I began to eat, but questions about my host tugged at my thoughts. I started with something simple.

"I suppose you don't always eat fish? Do you keep any livestock?"

"Non. I don't eat any meat. Only fish."

"I see." I glanced up and could see in his restless eyes that he too had many questions. I was determined to get a question of mine in first.

Must ask him about the lack of decoration. That is interesting.

"The design on the bottom of your tumbler," I said, with a mouth full of trout and lightly boiled turnip. I pointed with the back of my fork-hand to his tumbler in front of me.

He dropped his wooden fork on to his plate and took a sip of water. Slowly, he chewed his mouthful of food while watching me.

"What do you think it means?" he asked.

I put down my fork and slowly finished my mouthful. The food was delicious.

"I've seen such a sign before, but, at first, I couldn't place it. Now I remember. It's like what we call a 'yin and yang' sign, but I know this particular sign is a local one. This, along with your asceticism, leads me to one conclusion."

"Which is?"

"You're a Cathar?"

He looked perplexed.

"Sorry. I forgot that this is a term you may not actually use yourself. Erm … . You're a religious man but not a Catholic?"

He bellowed with laughter, making him seem very young for a moment.

"I call myself a 'Good Man.'"

"Ah yes, I've heard that term. Yes, you're what we call a Cathar."

He's a heretic!

I narrowed my eyes, probing him for fear. I found it there.

"Who's 'we'?" he asked.

It was my turn to burst out laughing. "Ah!"

We both laughed together.

"You don't speak like any other man from Angleterre that I've ever met. In fact, you speak like *nobody* I've ever met. There's much about you that's strange Monsieur."

"Yes. Probably. I want to tell you, but I don't think you'd believe me … . But do you really believe that the Earthly God is the Devil?"

"Diabolus? Well, the Bible itself in Matthew 12:24 says Satan is 'the ruler of the demons,' 'the ruler of the world' and Second Corinthians 4:4 says he is 'the god of this world.'"

"Really? You know your subject. I'll have to check."

"I *should* know what I'm talking about. I've spent most of my life on the run; from priests, wanting to burn me at the nearest available stake!"

"You're a perfecti?"

"Un parfait? Non!" He laughed. "But maybe one day. For now, I'm just a credentes."

"I see. It must have been hard."

"Hard! Yes, you could say that," he added sadly. "Both my parents lost to the great Inquisition, my oldest brother exiled and the two others forced into monasteries against their will. In the last seven years I've lived in five different towns!"

We continued eating, both lost in thought. I reflected that we weren't so different, both set apart from those around us, both exiled from mainstream religion.

I yearned to talk of Ordo Lupus and the sword in the Temple, which had once belonged to the Cathars. Most of all I longed to warn him about what would happen in Monségur Castle in thirty years, the massacre of the last Cathars. It was an irrational wish, since Guillaume would probably be long dead before then. Nevertheless, the wish was there; to let him warn others. I held my silence.

"That was delicious," I declared, pushing away my plate. There was still some fish left there, but I couldn't eat another mouthful. I drained the last of the red wine, and he took my glass to refill it.

I was wrong about my host. A generous man!

I thought he seemed relaxed enough to try him on a new subject.

"I saw a man in the hostel, on the way here."

He swung around to face me. "You shouldn't have gone to the hostel! Looking like that, you will have been recognised! That was foolish."

"It was dark. I don't think anybody could have seen my eye colours."

"Hm! Maybe not … . Still … ."

"Anyway, there was a man there, with a horse. The hostel-keeper said he was a scribe. He had some small eye-pieces that interest me." I paused to let all this information sink in. Guillaume looked slightly perplexed for a moment.

"Ah! *The* Scribe, not *a* scribe," he said. "I think he's the only itinerant scribe around here. And he's a most learned one too. But what of these *eye-pieces*. What do you mean?"

"Ah, well that's a good question … ."

Guillaume pushed away his plate and leaned back in his chair. He folded his arms and readied himself for a full answer.

"Where I come from…" I started cautiously, "…we make eye-pieces which allow us to see better. He had some, but they were very well made. They were not from around here. I want to meet him and find out more. Where he comes from, for instance."

"I see." Guillaume rocked gently, back and forth on the rear wooden legs of his chair. "Don't go and meet this man."

"Why not?"

"It's just my advice. He knows a lot of people. How do you know he won't talk? Perhaps he might guess something about you, and news might reach Donzy Castle? He knows Hervé. The Seigneur." A swallow caught in my throat. I stared at his face in the gloomy firelight, searching for the truth. Guillaume was impassive, but he must have recognised the look in my eye. "Ah! You have met the Seigneur yourself!"

"Not exactly. I have been his… *guest*."

"So you will know he's not to be taken lightly."

"Yes. I know *that*, but this is very important to me. More than you can know."

"I see. In that case I can only warn you. Landric told me you would soon move on. I guess we all have a mission. But let me tell you this; The Scribe is different to most men. I have met him. Some say he *too* is a heretic. In any case he's not known for his orthodoxy. But just because he is a heretic of some kind, doesn't make him my friend. I don't trust him."

"Is there any particular reason why?"

"Just a feeling. I think he serves his pockets more than any god. But who can tell what drives a man in these troubled times?"

"I will take your advice to heart, but nevertheless I shall meet him next week."

"Be very careful then."

On that troubled note, Guillaume made his excuses and retired.

***

Chapter Three

Almost a week later, on the Wednesday, I found myself trudging through the mud on my way back to Lyot. Guillaume had told me that everyone knew The Scribe visited the hostel on Wednesday and Fridays.

During that week, I had remembered more from my past. Waking up at the sound of my host's voice one morning and weary from the previous day's work, I had not been able to raise myself from the makeshift bed I had installed in the parlour. I had drifted on the edge of consciousness for a while. It was then that I began to remember.

***

I remembered waking up, my head swimming, in a cold, dark stone-lined vault. I beat on the walls with my fists and shouted for help, but nobody came. Then I had an image of me in the roof space above the vault in Beauvais Cathedral. At first, they both seemed unrelated, but then the sequence of events fell into place.

After the accident near Nevers, which had left me in hospital, I had started to think again about the secret temple in Beauvais Cathedral. It plagued my mind. I had the nagging feeling that I'd missed something, something very significant. I needed to see it again.

That was going to be difficult, however, because the temple was off-limits to the public and barely mentioned in any academic papers let alone in the Cathedral's own literature. The Head Verger had changed since I had last been there so when I parked near the Cathedral and walked up that wide flight of stairs to the main doors, I knew I would be unrecognised.

"Uh hm. I'm sorry. I cannot help you," was the hesitant reply from the new Head Verger when I asked if it would be possible to visit the secret temple in the roof space above the vault. I had come armed against this response.

"I know exactly where it is and how to get to it!" I said in my best French.

His eyes widened at my affrontary.

"I have been up there you see. I was there at the time of that battle with the demon!" His eyes widened even more, but he didn't guess that I was there at exactly that time. "It doesn't matter. I'm a well-known historian, and I can get the Minister of Culture to grant me access if I am pushy and go over your head!" I deliberately tried to sound arrogant and impatient. "The problem is that I was just passing and wanted to take a look … . On the other hand, it could well be worth your while to let me see it for a few minutes now … ."

The verger, a tall, elegant man with plucked eyebrows and skin like Chinese porcelain, waved his hands in front of me. "Absolutely not!"

"It would save a lot of trouble for your superiors … ." I said cryptically. I unzipped the bag hung from a shoulder strap and indicated with my eyes that he should look inside. For a moment, he hesitated, and my heart skipped a beat. Unable to resist, he peered inside the bag and gasped. He cleared his throat and quickly regained his composure.

"Monsieur, come this way, please." I followed him to his little office and emptied the entire contents of the bag onto a table. I had calculated that five-thousand francs would not only get me in to the temple but would make sure he would keep quiet about it for the rest of his life.

"Mon Dieu!" He almost seemed to want to stop the cascade of notes from the bag, but when the small table was overflowing with notes, he opened a drawer beneath it and quickly shoveled the cash into it.

Within a few short minutes, he had taken me behind a blue curtain, unlocked the small door to the secret staircase, now lit by cobweb-covered bulbs, and left me alone in the magnificent temple.

Now known in academic papers as 'Le Temple de Ordo Lupus,' nothing in the space had been touched since my last visit except the hoist, which had been repaired. Yellow and black tape had been left hanging between some of the coffers, as if it were a crime-scene. That made me laugh.

Knowing this might be the last time I ever saw the temple, I went over it with a fine-toothed comb. Starting furthest from my intended target I started at the back of the room and inspected each coffer, one at a time. It wasn't long before I reached the altar cloth and this is where I suspected something important might have slipped my eye. Everything was uncared for. The green altar-cloth had patches eaten away by moths. In the centre, where the chalice had been, there was a large brown stain. I glanced again at the procession scene of succubi and that of the Garden of Eden, which had made such an impression on me.

However, my attention was caught by the border of the cloth. Two rows of rectangles, one inside the other and divided by embroidered decoration in blue and white, ran around the border. I had to lift the hem from behind the altar to confirm that the pattern did, indeed, run the whole way around. In the outer row, Roman numerals, in black on a yellow background, seemed to divide the cloth into months. I quickly worked this out, because the sequence of numerals ran up to twenty-eight, thirty or thirty-one before continuing from one again. Thus, I guessed there were, in total, three hundred and sixty-five sections. While most were yellow, at the front of the cloth, one month, May, had partitions coloured red. The four partitions in this month were coloured white.

4th May must be significant!

Turning my attention to the inner row of yellow partitions, I immediately saw that each rectangle, the same size as each outer partition, was divided into twenty-four squares, four rows of six. The rectangle adjacent to the white partition in the outer row, was also coloured white, but the third mini rectangle on the third row was coloured red. This colour choice was confusing, but it did indicate that 3 pm was a significant time if you assumed that the mini-rectangles represented hours. The Roman numeral for twenty-seven, embroidered in the red rectangle, could also indicate the twenty-seventh minute of the hour. I noted all this down in a pocket notepad. Then I wandered up and down the length of the altar a few more times, looking for any more significant details. I couldn't find anything new. It occurred to me that the silver chalice was the one item missing, but even looking under the hem of the alter-cloth, I could not find it.

I looked once again at the sad state of the little temple and then retraced my steps back to the stairs.

"4th May. Same arrangement?" I said bluntly, to the Head Verger when I found him. He had been nervously hovering near the curtain concealing the secret door, so it hadn't taken me long.

"Mais non! It's impossible! We're always closed on the 4th May!"

"Closed? Why?"

He shrugged his shoulders. "It is a day of special prayer for this Cathedral. It's said that we are visited by the spirit of Guilllaume de Grez on this day, one of the builders of the Cathedral ... ."

"Yes, yes. I know who he is ... . What sights?"

He leaned close to me. "I have seen strange sights near the altar … ."

"Like … ."

"I cannot say … . It's forbidden to speak of it outside our own grou … ." He bit his lip at his indiscretion.

"So it will be hard to get in?"

"Impossible. I'm sorry!"

I noted his weakening conviction.

"If the rewards were more this time, say fifty percent more, it might be possible?"

"Fifty? You mean in all respects?" His eyebrows raised to their highest extremity, and his eyes widened, at the possibility of such an extreme reward.

This is going to bankrupt me!

"Yes. In *all* respects. How can I contact you?"

He shook his head. "Non! I cannot." He grabbed my arms and tried to turn me around. "You must leave. Now!"

I resisted his pressure, and he fell slightly against me. He looked angrily down into my face and suddenly seemed transfixed. His mouth fell open.

He mastered himself, leaned close and whispered a telephone number into my ear.

"Call me soon," he whispered. "Now you must go!"

I turn and left, without looking at him again.

Luckily, 4th May was not far off, and I returned with my notebook and another bag full or bank notes. This time I had been given instructions telling me exactly when to arrive, where to go and that I should wear a monk's habit with the hood pulled over my face. I had some trouble locating one but turned up suitably attired, wearing the habit over my own clothes. Quickly, the Head Verger ushered me behind the curtain. I was about to unlock the secret door when he thrust a leather bag at me. I took it and opened it. It was full of bank notes. It looked like all the money I had given him before.

"Monsieur … ." he said quietly. "You are Jean Rezor?"

"Err … . Yes! How did you know?"

"Your eyes … . I am most deeply sorry. Please take the money."

"But … ."

"I don't want it. You, of all people have a right to visit the Temple."

This confirmed what I had suspected. "You are a member of Ordo Lupus?"

He nodded. "It's very dangerous for you to be here. There are only three of us now, and I, alone, believe that you are one of us. The others have not been convinced. They will not allow you to be here. I have studied the history of the Order most deeply; I believe I have seen evidence that you are one of us. I've been expecting you." He put his hand gently, almost reverently, on my sleeve for a moment and smiled benignly.

"But won't they go to the Temple today? Surely I cannot go up there?"

"They are not true believers. We are a dissolute Order now, attempting to carry out the traditions of the Helpers, but the others do not understand The Power or The Light. In fact, they *fear* it! They will try to protect it from outsiders, that much of their duty they understand, but they won't go there themselves. *Not* today. If they do, I will attempt to stop them. If I cannot, I will explain who you are. It may cost me my life and you, yours. But those are the risks we must take. Now go."

He gently pushed me to the door, turned and vanished through the curtain.

Astonished, I had little time to think. I grinned while I climbed the narrow staircase.

At last, I have met someone in Ordo Lupus! They exist! I knew it!

I soon found myself staring again at the dusty altar-cloth. It was 2 pm and getting hot under the lead roof of the Cathedral. I had to admit that underlying my curiosity about the altar and the Roman numerals was a feeling I had known since Annie had been taken from us; that somewhere her spirit still existed and that I had to find her. It was probably irrational, but even the notion that she might, in some way, still be conscious and thinking that I had given up on her, was unbearable to me. This was the real reason I found myself back in Beauvais Cathedral. I silently munched on some peanut butter and apple sandwiches, a recently acquired taste, and swigged from a can of 7 Up.

What's going to happen? If anything. Probably nothing!

I had pondered the meaning of the numerals and patterns many times at home but each time had come to the same conclusion; somewhere, on 4th May, something must happen or once did happen. I guessed it was every 4th May because there had been no hint that any particular year was significant.

As 3 pm passed, still nothing happened. But about fifteen minutes past the hour, something caught my eye as my gaze wandered around the temple. A red glow emanated from a space between the two rows of coffers, only about ten feet from me. I watched as the small patch of light became an intense column of light, stretching to the roof beams far above my head. Fascinated, I walked around the beam at a safe distance wondering what it could be. I had never seen anything like it. With my hands stretched toward it, I could feel warmth from the beam. This was not intense. The beam seemed to beckon, but common-sense told me to be very wary. I watched and waited and after about five minutes, the colour changed to orange. I could hear a vague humming, almost subsonic, coming from somewhere indeterminable, and I could feel a gentle pulsation of the air. It was almost like the sound one felt, rather than heard, at some very loud rock concerts.

Curious, I drained my can of 7 Up and tossed it gently into the orange beam. It disappeared.

A portal of some kind! I knew it! It's a gate! That explains, perhaps, how the serpent came to be here.

I put the tip of my right index finger cautiously into the beam. Although it was warmed, nothing else happened.

I scratched my head and wondered what to do next. Then, unexpectedly, the beam turned white, hurting my eyes somewhat, and the sound increased. The throbbing started to shake my insides so that I felt a bit queasy.

My better judgement told me I should retire to safety and report this to the authorities.

But I am the authority on the Serpent. And who will listen to me anyway? This may be the last chance I get to find Annie!

I resolved to try the beam. I hastily scribbled a note for Rose, telling her what had happened, left it on the altar, and then I stepped into the white beam.

I remember feeling as if I had been hit over the head by a ten-ton block of concrete, and then I knew no more until I came to in a stone lined vault.

At first, I felt too sick to move. My head swam, and I vomited several times. I then tried to stand but found I had to hunch over, because the roof of the chamber hung too low. Shouting for help and banging the walls with my fists seemed to achieve nothing, so I slumped against a great stone slab to consider my fate.

Remembering the white beam in Beauvais Cathedral, I speculated that I had probably 'beamed' myself into some subterranean cave. A horror that I would never get out swept over me.

"Annie!" I said weakly to myself, as if blaming her. As my eyes slowly became accustomed to the dark, I began to perceive the faintest glimmer of light from somewhere about ten feet in front of me and above me. I could only see it, however, through some separate space in the chamber and there seemed no way I could reach the chink of light. Great stones, balanced on top of one another, blocked my way. I could still see daylight, however, and this reassured me.

Then, the light fade.

Perhaps somebody might pass?

I shouted for all I was worth and thought I heard an answer. I shouted again. "Hey! Hey! In here! Help!" and a dog's bark answered. I shouted louder. "In here! Get help!" I laughed at myself.

As if the dog will understand!

However, the barking receded and returned a few minutes later, accompanied by a man's voice. I couldn't make out what he said to the dog.

"Hey! Help! I'm in here!" I shouted again.

"Mon Dieu! Allo?"

"Hey. I'm here. How do I get out? I've been in here for hours! Thank God you've come!"

"How did you get in there, Monsieur?"

"I'm not sure. Can you get me out?"

"Oui! Wait." The dog barked as if possessed, but slowly the barking receded. I waited, cramped and tired.

Shortly after this I felt the thud of a pick-axe cutting up earth outside and then the grate of metal on stone. I could hear the man grunting with the effort and the occasional, "Merde!" before finally, a chink of light appeared in front of my face, and then a face appeared, backlit by a powerful torch beam.

I crawled toward the face, and incongruously but most politely, he extended a hand. I shook it before emerging.

I found myself in the back garden of a well-to-do country cottage, and he fussed about me until he had me in his parlour, feet up in front of a fire, drinking a hot mug of coffee.

Through the French-window I could see my prison, a large green tumulus on the edge of his lawn.

"What is it?" I asked.

"Who knows? It's been there for thousands of years, I've been told. Part of the condition for owning this property is that I will maintain it and give access to archeologists, should they wish to explore it. None ever has though."

"And your name?"

"I think I should know your name first since you are an uninvited guest!"

"John."

"You can call me Miguel."

"Hm. You don't seem at all shocked to have found me in there, not really."

I glanced again at the scene in the garden; a black maw in the side of the tumulus; a slab of grey stone lying flat on the grass and a pick-axe lying beside it. It told a strange story.

"Non! I have been expecting something like this for years!"

"You're a member of Ordo Lupus?"

He looked down at his hands and refused to reply.

I attempted to quiz him further, but he wouldn't answer.

"Monsieur – John, we both know what has happened here is … unusual and I, for one, don't see the need for the authorities to know. If you keep silent about this, I too will keep silent."

I nodded slowly in agreement.

"Now, it being Sunday, the next train will leave for Paris in two hours. Where will you be going?"

"Wait! Sunday? That means I have been in that hole for four days. But that cannot be! I would be dead."

"Obviously you're not. What date did you leave?"

"4th May."

"Well it's now only the 3rd May. What year?"

"What do you mean? What year is *this*?"

"1996."

"But that's a year later than I left! Impossible!"

"I assure you it's true. May I suggest you spend the night here and then return to Nevers tomorrow? I doubt your car will still be in Beauvais."

"No, I guess not!"

***

Could I have travelled back to 1213 using the same device? The question filled my mind as I entered the hostel in Lyot, looking for The Scribe.

The hostel-keeper recognised me, even wearing the new eye-patch, which Guillaume had fashioned from leather. It covered my left eye, the brown, damaged one. I spoke my best French to everyone in the hostel.

"Bonjour Monsieur! Have you returned with work for The Scribe?"

"Oui. Is he here?"

"Not yet, but he will be." He returned to wiping spilled beer from the counter.

I took a seat behind a table near a wall, placing myself in the shadows away from the fire. I couldn't completely escape attention, however. A thick-set man with red curls leaned toward me from his perch on a barrel at the corner of my table and said, "Le Guerre!"

"Ah, the War! Yes, I've heard it's coming!"

"Will you fight Monsieur? If it comes?"

"No. I don't think so."

"But there will be great wealth and glory to be had!" He sounded less convinced by the virtues of the second.

I smiled and took a long draft of beer from the pewter tankard. He tired of me and returned to the conversation with his companions, which I could hear. People seemed to be thinking of nothing but war.

I noticed that some referred to Hervé as Compte and yet others, usually those less supportive, called him Seigneur, a lesser title more akin to the English 'Lord.' Some even referred to him with contempt as Chevalier, a title little more than 'Knight.' None seemed to take Phillip, King of France, seriously. In general, people seemed much like poor people the world over in all times; dissatisfied with their lot, angry with the ruling classes but utterly determined to make the most of any pleasure they could squeeze from each day. I had arrived mid-afternoon and by early evening, the dark mutterings had given way to raucous laughter and song. I myself, after four pints of the heady brew, found myself tapping my feet to the roughly rendered folk tunes. Finishing my latest pint, I staggered to the bar for a refill.

"Another, my good man!" Eager to make conversation with the hostel-keeper, I hazarded a crude question. "Are you a supporter of the King of France?"

It was a joke, and I expected no serious answer, but his eyes narrowed, and he leaned close to me.

"None around here support the King. And you'd do well to remember *that*! He's not the worst, it's true, but all these lands once belonged to Henry II of Angleterre and times were good under his reign. We had food aplenty and there were less petit chevaliers riding around, imposing petty laws on us. Anyway, Charles is still a despot. He has launched war against the Flemish. Even recently, he obtained a ransom of 30,000 marks for hostages, they say, but do we see a single mark? *Non*! And the war will bring trouble! The only good thing that can come of it is invasion by King John of Angleterre! *That*, all around here are hoping for!"

With that, he dismissed me and returned to wiping down his counter.

"Wait! Do you still expect The Scribe? He seems late."

"He won't come now."

"Oh."

Very disappointed but with nothing I could do about it, I returned to my seat by the wall to finish the last pint. Once again, the red-haired man turned and smiled at me. I smiled back trying to mask any emotion, but he saw through this.

I listened in to his friend's conversation and noticed they were talking about buying and selling something. As I listened I became more curious. It seemed they were bargaining for items they didn't recognise. Curious, I peered between them, to see items randomly strewn on their table. Instantly my heart stopped. Unmistakable, a set of car keys lay next to what looked like a 20th Century wallet. Unlike the moment I saw the glasses, this time I knew the significance of what I could see. Furthermore, I had the distinct impression I had seen the keys before. The green BP fob looked very familiar.

Swallowing quickly, I tapped the red-haired man on the shoulder.

"How much?" I said, pointing at the green fob. He picked it up and held it up for me to see.

"Four obole," he said shrewdly assessing my wealth from my clothes.

I drew a circle in the air around all the items. "How much?"

He looked at his friends. They grew silent. The red-haired man turned to me. "Twenty obole!"

Without hesitation, I reached into a little leather pouch, which I had tied around my neck, and took out the four bits of silver coin that I estimated equaled his price. I put them in his outstretched hand. He checked them and scooped up the items from the table. There was: a small, folded AA pocket road map of France for the Languedoc-Roussillon Region; another torn-out page of map, folded tightly; a few francs and centimes; a compass and a pocket handkerchief. Placing them in my hands, he leaned close to me.

"There's more." he said.

"More?"

"Oui. Clothes. Are you interested?"

"Maybe. Where did you get these things?"

"Friends of mine found them."

"Where?"

He looked like he wasn't going to answer. I put my hand back in my pouch and took out the two silver denier which Guillaume had given me. The equivalent of two months wages at least, it was the rental value of a modest house for a year. Much more than I had *earned*, Guillaume had generously called it a 'loan,' guessing I would need hard currency to deal with The Scribe.

The red-haired man's eyes widened.

"Could you take me to where you found these things?"

He grabbed for the coins, but my fist closed around them. He wiped his mouth with his sleeve. One of the other men said something to him, with a sly glance.

"Oui. Tonight if you like," he replied

"Oui. Now?"

"No. The one who knows the way isn't here, and we need some things, lanterns and some weapons for defense. Do you have anything?"

"No."

"Don't worry. We'll look after you. Meet us here at ten bells."

I immediately set about buying a dagger for myself with the obole bits that I had spare. I would be outnumbered by at least four to one, so I wouldn't follow them into the woods unarmed. I couldn't find anywhere to buy a dagger at night, but I bargained with an old drunk, slouched against the post of an empty market stall in the village square. Now I was the proud owner of a cheap iron blade with a wooden handle, notched three times and pitted with rust. However, I would only need it for jabbing.

Soon after ten bells, I followed the red-haired man and his friends into a copse. We left by the road to Landric's mill and then turned left into the trees.

The darkness of the cold night drew down closer under the trees, so I felt relieved when we soon emerged into a rough meadow. We followed this north and crossed several more fields before entering more trees. Now, we were in a proper forest, and I kept one hand on the dagger hilt, fastened to my waist by my belt.

Suddenly, the leading man, silhouetted by the swaying yellowish light of a lantern, stopped. We all stopped behind him. Somebody spoke, and then the red-haired man spoke to me.

"No further without payment," he said, holding out a hand.

"One now, one when I get back safely," I said, placing one silver denier in his hand.

He scowled and muttered, but soon we were on our way again. Wet weeds whipped my legs as we moved quickly in the dark. Occasionally I caught glimpses of the pale moon through half-dressed trees above us.

We emerged suddenly onto a rough, narrow track, which ran north-east. We followed it. The going grew much easier now, but we kept on for another three hours.

"Almost there," my guide said, finally. I guessed we were about half way back to the castle from which I had escaped.

Suddenly my legs wobbled when I found myself crossing a shaky wooden bridge across a stream. I slipped and almost lost my footing.

"*Shit!*"

"*Shh!*" my guide whispered.

"Monsieur!" A broad hand pressed against my chest, stopping me in my tracks. "We're here."

I looked around me.

"Shh!" he whispered again. I listened. I heard only the faint hoot of an owl and the rustle of dry autumn leaves in the cold breeze.

"All clear," a voice said from the front of the line. Once again, I turned my attention to my surroundings. We had emerged from trees into a small open space, perhaps sixty feet in diameter, with a tiny brook running between four large boulders in the middle. Each stone stood about four or five feet high, and they formed a rough ring around an open space. The grass grew thick here but trampled in a line from our feet to the circle. The mud between the rocks was impressed with boot marks. A similar path to our own led west from the circle and our own path continued on around a kink, to the north-east.

"This is where we found the articles," my guide said, pointing to the circle. "Some say that the Compte gathers his men here for one night each year for a magic ritual. I've met a man who said that he saw the ritual, and a man appeared from the air!"

I stood stock still, trying not to reveal my emotions.

"The Compte's men were here and caught a man a few weeks ago. They took him to the Castle. They say the man is a sorcerer!"

"These were his clothes," the leader said, returning from clump of trees carrying a bundle. He untied it and threw the clothes at my feet. I knew they were mine. Among some less recognisable clothes, I saw my familiar blue parka. My heart banged in my chest. "Have them all if you want," he said. "Now we must go. Quick. It's not safe here."

I had to admit that being so close to the Castle gave me an extra chill. I glanced suspiciously at the path that led on to the north-east and turned away. Picking up the bundle of clothes, I tied them together again and then followed the men as they left the clearing.

We had not gone far before we halted again. All the men confronted me.

Here we go! I was expecting this.

But it *wasn't* what I had expected.

"Take off your eye-patch!" ordered the leader, brandishing a sword. The other men pointed pikes and swords at me.

"Why?"

"We want to see. Compte Hervé is looking for the Sorcerer, a man with differently coloured eyes."

"Well, it's not me. My left eye is missing!"

"Show us!" the red-haired man said. Another broad-shouldered man jabbed me with the tip of his spike.

I drew the dagger, and the leader laughed. "Oo! He's going to prick us with that! Ha! Ha! I won't ask you again. Show us your eye!"

"No!"

The leader threshed the air, just in front of my nose, with the tip of his sword. I didn't have time to swear. The darkness had made him misjudge the distance by only a fraction. I jumped back and felt my footing give way.

The brook!

I turned on the heel of my foot and leaped over the water, reveling at my new level of fitness. Something whizzed by my ear and stuck in a tree trunk behind me.

A pike! A stroke of luck.

"Idiot!" shouted the leader. "Now he's armed!" He growled and took a few steps toward me until he stood on the far side of the brook, swaying in the gloom. Clearly, he underestimated me. I withdrew the pike and thrust it toward him. With skill learned as an agent during the war I held on to the rear of it with my right hand, the shaft with my left and jabbed toward his face. The tip went straight through his neck and withdrew in a fraction of a second. He fell to the floor, gurgling red blood from his mouth and waving his arms in protest.

Angered by the loss of their leader, the remaining men had just enough courage left for one charge. In a line three-abreast, they crossed the brook and aimed two pikes and a sword at me. I pretended to look afraid and half-stepped back, before lunging forwards and launching the pike at one of the men similarly armed. He dipped his shoulders, and the point passed him harmlessly before I could pull it back. The pike was growing heavy, and my arms ached. I jabbed at him again but at the last moment swung the pike to the right and hit the other man squarely in the chest. The pike disappeared into his flesh and almost wrenched from my arms as he fell into the water.

I tried to retrieve the pike, but his weight trapped it.

The last two men howled with a mixture of fear and rage and took aim at me. Forcing the wooden shaft of the pike down, I snapped it with my foot and jabbed the splintered end at them.

I howled at them as fiercely as I could. It was too much. They turned and ran. I ran across the brook after them. But in the gloom, I didn't see one of them twist on his heels and launch his weapon at me in self-defense. I felt it hit my temple. Like a mighty iron fist, it spun me round, and I fell to the ground with blood pouring from an open wound. Feeling dizzy, I tried to stand, but then the world spun, and I felt no more.

***

My head swam, and then clear images came rushing into my mind. Now I could see clearly what had happened! After my adventure in the 'time-gate' in Beauvais Cathedral, I had returned home to a distraught Rose.

"I thought you were dead! The Gendarmes have looked everywhere for you!" she said, grasping me tightly and crying her eyes out.

"But the note!"

"Oh, the *note*! I didn't believe that. Some kind of portal! Ha! Science-fiction or fantasy, I don't know which."

"But it happened. That's where I went. To the future!"

I explained what had happened, how I had discovered that Ordo Lupus actually existed and why I had gone to Beauvais.

"Annie! Annie! Always Annie. I thought we agreed that you would settle down now! *No* more adventures! She's *gone*," she replied.

It took a long time to calm Rose down; weeks. One day she confessed that she had handed my cassette tapes of my adventures in Beauvais to some writer.

"What do you mean, you *gave* them to him! They're *mine*! They're *private*!"

"But you were gone for a *year*! I didn't think you were coming back!"

"So? Were you just after the *money*?"

"No! *No*! I just thought it might lead to some information about you. Actually, it was the idea of the Gendarmes!"

At this, we both broke into laughter; I, because it seemed so ludicrous, and I didn't really care if the whole world knew about Beauvais and Rose, she, because her tension suddenly released, and, of course, it seemed all so ludicrous.

I actually have a ghost-written novel published about myself! Ha!

I began to puzzle out what had happened in Beauvais more recently. Clearly the man with the tumulus time-portal had some connection with Ordo Lupus in some way. But there seemed little point pursuing that line. I asked him again several times what he knew of the Order in the morning, but he refused to answer.

All he would say was, "I expected you. Or I expected someone anyway. I'm just a guardian. There are many of us. And clearly you didn't expect to go forward in time. It's best left like this. There are others who will help you, but we will probably not meet again."

Although bleak, his answer did give me some hope. He had hinted that it should be possible to go back in time. I resolved to work out where I had gone wrong and try again. Getting Rose's support would be harder. We had to tell the press that I had suffered amnesia while traveling. The police were less easily convinced and kept a case-file open for me.

While reluctantly conceding to Rose that I would not pursue knowledge of the time portals further, secretly I reviewed my notes and planned another visit. Needing more information, I called the Head Verger once more and arranged to visit. This time I took a compact colour camera and four rolls of film. I captured every possible view of the altar-cloth. I took a few of the coffers, including the one with the lid still split from the blow of the Serpent, and some of the armour for good measure.

I had these photographs blown up as large as possible and pored over them for many hours in my study, away from Rose.

What I saw, unnoticed before, were names of places, woven in fine thread, over the sleeves of the Helpers in the processional scene on the altar-cloth. Unfortunately, only two of the old names could I identify; Beluacci, the Latin name for Beauvais and Pas de Lupe, a mountain pass in the Languedoc-Roussillon Region. There were other strange names, but I could not identify them using the index of my AA Atlas of France.

I further noticed that from each Helper's arm, with the place name embroidered on it, a hand, and its index finger extended. In some cases, this finger pointed behind them, in others ahead of them. Over the other arm were draped different coloured cloths. The Beluacci Helper's cloth was red, the Pas de Lupe one, green. The Beauvais helper pointed ahead of himself, and the Pas de Lupe helper pointed behind herself.

Could this be an indication of the direction one would travel in time using a portal at that location?

The thought intrigued me. I took Pas de Lupe to be a corruption of 'Wolf Pass.' A check on an ordnance survey map of the area revealed it, indeed, to be a mountain-pass. The word 'wolf' particularly intrigued me about this location. But that wasn't all. It was close by Monségur Castle, last stronghold of the Cathars, and also Rennes-le-Château. Given the myths of treasures and conspiracies surrounding this place, it amused me to think that there might also be a time portal there.

One last thing I discovered from the photographs; there were other coloured rectangles around the hem of the Alter Cloth. At first, I'd missed them, partly because of the prominence given to that for Beluacci. A green-coloured rectangle for the same hour as for Beauvais but on the 10th October could have been for Pas de Lupe.

I made the mistake of telling Rose this last fact, hoping that it might raise her interest. It did the opposite.

Rose curtailed any further research. After the original Beauvais incident, I'd promised her to settle down and not go off on any more, wild adventures. That had been the cornerstone of our rebuilt marriage, and if I wanted to keep Rose, I had to forget the adventures.

She finally capped this prohibition by arranging a skiing holiday in the Pyrenees, dates arranged by her to include 10th October.

That was how I found myself skiing near Gourette on the 7th October the following year. An Anglo-French couple, Nick and Marie, whom we had met years before in London, accompanied us as chaperones for good measure. Nick, a very accomplished skier, guided Marie, who, like me, was an amateur. Rose was, of course, an expert, having grown up in the mountains around Sofia, but the stroke reduced her mobility.

All went well until one particularly crisp morning. A fresh fall of snow the night before left the landscape looking virgin-clean. Like the first people ever, we left our tracks and prints as we explored the unblemished snow-fields around the resort. Crossing a wide slope of new snow, Nick suddenly started waving at us from ahead. Rose and I had been following the younger couple because Rose couldn't ski as fast as she used to. I waved back at Nick, thinking him just friendly. He pointed energetically behind me in response. I turned to see a vast wall of snow careening down the mountainside, far above us. At first, it seemed ghostly quiet, but then, as we surged off down the mountain as fast as we could, I could feel the mountain rumbling beneath our skis.

We reached a wide, shallow valley and started up the other side. I thought the avalanche would stop well short of us and that we were safe. However, Nick, waved us on and surged ahead with Marie. I followed, now very out of breath, with Rose just behind me. I remembered shouting, "Come on Rose!" pointlessly just as a cloud of dusty snow enveloped us from the slowing snow-tsunami to our right.

Something slammed into my back and pinned me to the ground.

I came-to, half covered with snow but feeling quite calm, until I remembered Rose. I crawled over the rough piles of snow-boulders behind me toward where I thought she might be. In the distance I could hear Nick's voice shouting my name.

Seeing something dark on the snow, I picked it up; a leather wallet, covered with a Rosary necklace. I shuddered at the site of the familiar Concilium Putus Visum calling-card. Opening the wallet, I found a neatly folded piece of white paper. I unfolded it and stared at the single line of words, written in that ink of human blood: 'Rose has gone into the past.'

Not again! You bastards! Rose!

"God! Why did you allow this to happen? Not Rose!"

Though we searched for hours, we found no more trace of her. Marie had sent word back to the resort for help.

"John, we have to wait for the emergency services," Nick said to me.

He sat down, defeated.

"She's not here, I'm telling you!" I shouted angrily.

"But she must be! Where else could she be!" he replied.

I couldn't explain to him what I meant. I hadn't shown either of them the wallet and beads. I just knew Rose had been taken from me. It seemed almost as brutal as Annie' abduction, but I hoped that at least Rose might still be alive.

I knew why she had been taken from me; it was a trap, and they wanted me to follow. I also knew that I would follow. As soon as I had given a statement, and the authorities let me leave, I caught the first flight from Pau Airport to Lyon. I drove home at illegal speeds all the way, fetched my notes and went back to Lyon to get a connecting flight to Toulouse Airport. On the morning of 10th October, I wound up the side of the Pas de Lupe in my thickest blue parka jacket, pockets stuffed with notes, maps and a compass. In a backpack, I had a thermos and sandwiches. Between cursing myself and moments when I could barely hold back the tears, I forced myself to concentrate on working out the correct way to use the portal.

"I'm too old for this," I told myself between gasping breaths.

I neared the site of an ancient cairn, now gone, which had marked the summit of the Pas de Lupe. According to a local guidebook, there should be a smallish cave near the cairn, where I could shelter from the biting wind. A storm was brewing.

I reached the cave and settled down with a cup of steaming hot coffee to wait. It was 2.55 pm. At the lip of a ledge, in front of the cave, I could see the cairn ruin, consisting of just a few roughly piled stone.

Beyond that, a steep scree slope, led down to the road, nearly six hundred feet below.

Taking out my crumpled notes, I considered again my theory about the timing for the portal. I had stepped into the beam when it glowed orange in Beauvais. I hadn't stayed long enough to see whether other colours were possible. But now, I hazarded a guess that they were. If I had studied the altar-cloth more closely before, I might have understood that the red background to the small rectangle for the hour of 3-4 pm was misleading. Furthermore, in the tree of the Garden of Eden scene, there were fruits coloured red, orange, white, yellow and blue. The wolf behind Adam seemed to be pointing to a white fruit with a raised paw, and the white fruits were bigger than the rest. I guessed that the white beam was the correct one to enter and this seemed confirmed by the pattern displayed on the cloth in the order of the coloured fruit in the tree. In each of four lines, the order from left to right was red, orange, white, yellow and blue, not dissimilar to the colours of the light spectrum.

Once more I agreed with myself that I would step into the white beam if it appeared. I waited. 3.15. I stood up and paced up and down outside the cave, looking for signs of a beam. Sure enough, under the lip of the cave, just behind the cairn stones, I saw a faint, red light. I could only hear the whistle of the wind, but I could feel a faint vibration. After five minutes the vibration increased, and the beam turned orange. I packed my thermos away and thrust my notes back into my pockets. I stamped my feet and watched as the beam turned white. I would wait two and a half more minutes, until half way through the white phase, before stepping forward. Perhaps in this way I might travel the furthest. I had speculated that the reason I only went forward one year in Beauvais might be, because I had stepped into the beam so shortly after it even turned orange.

Big, soft, white snowflakes began to swirl around the beam.

I counted off the seconds, but as I reached thirty, I saw a movement from the corner of my left eye. I thought about jumping forwards then but hesitated. It wasn't the right time. Something hit me from the side, and I heard a yell:

"Argh! Now my friend! A little journey for you!"

I knew the voice.

"You! Where's Rose? What are you do- … ?"

I had no time to remonstrate. The man seemed much younger than me and as strong as an ox. For such a slight and sickly-looking man, his strength was incredible. He had hold of me from behind and pushed me toward the beam. I tried to get purchase on the cairn stones with my feet, but he lifted my weight clear of the ground and pushed me into the beam.

I had just enough time to shout, "Not now!" and then that familiar blow-to-the-head feeling knocked me out.

I just barely remembered a voice speaking over my body in the forest at Lyot when I came-to, before I passed out, and they carried me to the castle. The voice had sounded smooth and cultured.

"We do not treat servants of the dark one lightly. We do not burn them either, for fire is their natural state. No, we put them in a dark place and forget them."

****

All this, I had remembered by the time I awoke, on my back, in the forest near Lyot after being attacked. The sun had not risen far above the eastern horizon, and I was freezing cold.

Well at least the blow to the head did me some good! I remember it all now!

I felt a dry crust of blood on my temple, and my throat felt even dryer. I tried to stand, but, at first, my head throbbed too much. Eventually, I managed to stagger back to the village and then on to Guillaume's mill.

"*Mon Dieu!*" he exclaimed, grabbing me and pulling me into the parlour next to the warm fire. "What happened?"

"Well, I didn't meet The Scribe, but it didn't work out too bad!" I noted wryly.

He rushed off to get hot water and a clean cloth to wipe my head-wound and by the time he had returned I had laid out the contents of my pockets and the bundle of clothes on the floor of the parlour. The bundle included the spare clothes from the backpack, but the pack itself and the thermos flask were gone, no doubt kept by one of the Compte's men.

I couldn't think how to explain the whole of my story to Guillaume, but I could give him half an answer. He returned and stood staring at the jetsam before starting to dress my wound.

"These are strange things Jean. What are they for?"

I pushed him away and picked up the compass and some coins.

"This is called a compass and these are … well, these coins are from very far away." I placed one in his hand, and he turned over and over the neatly pressed franc in his hand.

"It's … . *So* well made? Who could make such a thing?"

"Ah. I think it would take too long to explain to you Guillaume, but I'm from the future, and it seems I'm here searching for my wife, Rose."

He shook his head. "Future?" Then he laughed. "I think the bump on the head has affected you Monsieur!"

Nevertheless, I could see a look of uncertainty in his eyes.

"You still haven't told me exactly what happened?" he asked.

"Well I met this red-haired man in the hostel and saw him selling these things. I recognised them as my own and paid him, with your loan, to take me to the place I must have been found. I couldn't remember exactly how I got here, but now I know."

"You remember?"

"Yes. Then, they tried to mug me."

"'Mug'?"

"They attacked me."

"Ah. It's very common here."

He grew thoughtful while finishing dressing my wound. He wiped his hands on the cloth and threw it into the fire.

"Has anybody … seen you … on the road between here and the town?"

I had to think. "Yes. I think so … several times I have seen travelers."

"Mon Dieu! It's not safe for you here anymore. You must leave. Stay the night, but first thing in the morning you must go! Did these men see your eye?"

"No."

"Good. But still, if any survived, they will tell the Compte. He will pay more than a year's wages for you."

"Yes. Some did get away. You're right."

"His men will search every house until they find you."

"But I *need* to find The Scribe."

He thought for a moment. "He'll come tomorrow. Along this road. I'll go with you as far as the road and we'll wait for him."

"But you don't … ."

He held up his hand. "It's not generosity that makes me accompany you but self-preservation. I don't want you getting into more trouble and anyway, it's safer to be out of the mill tomorrow."

I reluctantly agreed and ate some gruel and dried fish before sleeping as best I could. I had a restless night.

On the move again!

I had come to quite like Lyot. The hostel, with its raucous crowd of drunk complainants, all sporting bad hair and teeth and concerned only with their own restricted lives, had begun to feel quite homely to me. At least I now knew why I was here; I was searching for Rose.

But why on Earth did Pastor Michel push me?

I guess the Concilium Putus Visum's motives has always been obscure to me. Their allegiance seems to shift this way and that, and although they have never explicitly served the Serpent, or Evil, as I see it, they have never sought to protect or ally themselves with Ordo Lupus either. They seem to pursue a pure vision of Catholicism which means siding with whoever serves the CPV's purpose at the time. In the past that seems to be a search for the one surviving ceremonial sword, which provided the only way to kill a Serpent. This had led to them pursuing me to the Temple, where, they correctly guessed, the sword was kept. Now, they seemed to be allied with the Compte, probably a pragmatic man. Though always religious, in the 13th Century, most of the nobility were largely self-serving. He probably served somebody else, but who that was, I couldn't see. Perhaps he held Rose in the Castle. Well, he *did*, I would need some powerful support to get her out alive. I needed more information. Maybe The Scribe had it. Maybe he too, with his modern-made glasses, used the portals.

Just after dawn, Guillaume and I were waiting near a place where a road to the south joined with the road from his mill to Lyot. We were only half a mile from the village, so we stayed hidden in a clump of bushes next to the road.

I was standing under a blue sky, for a change, so I took off my over-tunic to let the heat from the sun warm my bones. Its warmth felt good on my closed eyelids.

"Here!" Guillaume said, handing me an apple and some bread after a couple of hours.

"How long do you think it will be?"

"Who knows? He keeps no regular time. Nobody knows where he goes."

We ate a very satisfying lunch, washed down with some more of the wine by myself, a parting gift from Guillaume.

"I will miss you Guillaume!"

"Me too Jean. Though we're from different worlds, we're not so different. I think we have similar aims. No matter what people say of you, I don't think you're a bad man."

I pondered his words in silence.

He went on, "You have opened my eyes to strange things. I'm getting old, and I would like a quiet life, as far as my beliefs will allow. I don't want any adventures. But remember me well. I may not be able to stay here much longer, but if I move on it, will be eastwards or northwards, and Landric will have word of me."

I nodded.

The soft, rhythmic thudding of a heavy, shod horse coming along the track, alerted us.

"Is it him?" Guillaume asked.

"I think so," I said peering through the branches of the bush.

"Go! I will wait here."

I stepped casually onto the road, as if I had just been resting, and watched the approaching rider. When he drew close, I knew it must be The Scribe. I held up my hand, and he pulled his large brown mare up.

"Ho!" I said.

He looked around himself warily, and the mare tossed her head. He looked nervous for a moment but then rested his elbows on the pommel, leaned over and studied me.

"Oui. Good day to you Monsieur. You're a traveler?"

I smiled. "Yes, you could say that. I was looking for you at the hostel two days ago … . Oh well, never mind that. Are you The Scribe?"

"Well, that's my profession. I am Robertus, but you can call me Robert, the modern corruption. And you are?"

"Jean. Call me Jean."

"What can I do for you my friend? I don't have much time." The mare fidgeted.

The strange man was tall, in proportion with the large mare and wore heavy leggings and velvet trimmings on his tunic of a well-to-do merchant. As the horse shifted its weight from leg to leg, I heard the faintest clink of something metallic, and I guessed he wore chain mail under his clothes. This would be appropriate for one who spent much of his time travelling alone. He also bore a long sword and, strapped to his saddle-bag, he wore a bow. No doubt he used it to shoot game on his long journeys. A brace of rabbits, slung across his pommel and tied together by their hind legs, seemed to confirm this. He wore a wide-brimmed brown hat with a domed top. This gave him the appearance of some kind of religious cleric. As he lifted his head, the sun revealed his face for a moment; intelligent blue-grey eyes, a well-cropped salt-and-pepper beard and grey hair. His age was difficult to determine, anywhere between thirty and fifty, but I saw an awareness in *his* yes which I hadn't seen those of others within Lyot. He didn't seem of the 13th Century. His face became obscured again, a moment later. Most distinctive of all about him was the long peacock's feather stuck in the band around his hat, no doubt to signify his profession.

As I had rehearsed to myself, I took out the compass and held it up, watching the little needle move to point north, behind me. I watched him for a reaction but saw none.

"You're going east," I said. "To Lyot. From there, a road runs north to Donzy and from there on to Vezelay. Do you ever go there?"

He lifted his head again to study me more closely, and I stared hard into his eyes. I could perceive no curiosity about my compass, an item not familiar in the 13th Century.

"Sometimes. *Usually* around the time of the festival."

"Ah. I thought I've seen you there, but on the other hand, the man didn't look quite like you."

"Oh?"

Having aroused his curiosity, I thought it time to pose my question:

"But you both had something in common; small, well-made eye pieces. I saw you with them the other night in Lyot."

He said nothing and didn't move.

"I am interested in buying such a pair of eye-pieces."

He seemed to think hard for a moment. Then he raised his arm from the pommel and pointed lazily at my face.

"You have problems with your eyes?"

"Ah. The patch? Yes."

Again, he seemed to be thinking for a long while.

"They were a gift to me from the one I serve."

"And who's that? Hervé of Donzy?"

I heard a rustle in the bushed behind me, followed by a thump, and Robertus glanced warily in that direction, before resettling himself in the saddle.

He laughed. "You're very curious, stranger. I have not met your like for a long time." He paused. "*That information* I would only give to one man in *this* area at *this* time."

This was a lot to take in. Clearly very intelligent, The Scribe had out-manoeuvred me at every turn. I felt the ground slipping from beneath my feet.

"What can you offer me for the glasses?"

He used the word 'glasses'!

To my surprise, he dismounted and stood right in front of me, his hand on his sword-hilt. I felt a strong urge to step away but resisted. I took the three, silver denier, which Guillaume had given me as a parting gift that morning, from my pouch.

For a second, he appeared to study them, but then, quick as a flash, he raised the eye-patch from my face. I had not time to look away before he saw what he sought.

"Sorry friend. I had to be sure. Now I know who you are."

Now I'm really in trouble!

"I don't want your money," he said. "But I don't think you want my glasses. I serve one called Herleva, far from here." With that, he mounted his horse and started his horse toward Lyot.

"Wait!" I shouted, but he didn't stop.

After a few moments, Guillaume emerged, brushing twigs from his hair and tunic.

"What was all that about?" he asked.

"I'm not entirely sure … . But I do know that I need to find this Herleva, whoever she might be."

"Hm … ."

"What? You know her?"

"Well, I knew of a Herleva. *Once*. Far from here."

"Well? Who *is* she?"

"A sorceress! She lives near Falaise, in Normandy."

"That could be *her*! How do you know of her?"

"Ten years ago, or thereabouts, when the Inquisition was at its worst in the Languedoc, I escaped as far north as I could and lived in Falaise, as a potter. There, I heard about her. But she's a dangerous woman! You don't want to meet her. I've heard that she boils the flesh of men alive, to make her spells. And she can come to you through the air at night and take your soul!"

"Ha! Ha! Old-wives' tales Guillaume!" I slapped his chest. "But anyway, I think she's my woman. How do I get there?"

My companion looked sad for a moment. "Follow the road west to the nearest town and then head north. Keep going until you reach the mouth of the Seine. They say Herleva can be found around the Abbey of Grestain."

"The Seine? But that's the other side of the country!"

"Yes. Its many days ride from here."

"Ride? Thanks Guillaume! Well, I guess this is it."

"Yes." He held out his right hand meekly. I took it and turned to face west.

"Don't forget this, Jean!" he said holding out the corked flask of wine in his left hand.

"I won't forget you Guillaume!" I said, taking it.

"Your sight is a very special gift Jean. It speaks of powers you perhaps haven't talked about openly, but I can see they're very great."

A pang of guilt overcame me. I wanted to explain a little more to him. "Guillaume, I am actually one of an order called Ordo Lupus."

"Ordus Lupus? I think I've heard of it."

"You have?" His poor Latin amused me.

"Yes. We Good Men consider them allies!" He beamed with approval. For the first time he seemed completely at ease with me.

"You do?"

"Yes. Your order is small and obscure. They are a Catholic Sect, are they not?"

"Yes."

"Normally we would not be allies, but we have a belief in common … ."

"What's that?"

"Neither of us believe that our life here on earth is the only reality. Am I right?"

"Ah. I see what you mean. But to be honest I am only beginning to find out what it means to be in my Order. I am not really clear yet what we believe in. But it's true I believe there are many things happening that are outside our normal view of reality."

"Exactly. That's a belief the Holy Roman Church does not condone."

We suddenly grinned at each other, and I clasped him around the shoulders. He turned and walked away.

"Look for me at the Feast in Vezelay next year!" he shouted, just before passing out of ear-shot.

***

Chapter Four

There is not much I need to tell you about the journey to Grestain. It took me nearly a month to walk the 240 miles from Donzy to there. I didn't have enough money for a horse. At first, the going was good, but the poor shoes were my undoing. Blisters plagued me from the chafing of wet feet on wet leather and after a week, I barely covered ten miles each day. Some days, the pain grew too great to walk.

Only two incidents of note happened.

On the eighth day from Donzy, thieves took all my money. This left me with little choice but to sleep in hedgerows and barns when I could find them.

The second incident would not have happened without the first.

Waking one morning in a hedgerow to the sound of barking dogs, I peered between the tall grass stems just as a startled hare shot past me.

I had been sleeping on the edge of a large area of cultivated land. I guessed it belonged to some local lord, and the dogs were his hunting dogs. They looked sleek and well-cared for, unlike the mutts I usually saw on country lanes. I looked warily around for horsemen, or at least hawkers, but I could see nobody. The dogs seemed to have been let loose. Too sleepy to react, at first, I watched the hare doubled back on itself in the field of stubble and passed close to me again. Its eyes bulged from their sockets as if trying to take in all the light for what might be its last image of this century, branded with white-hot fear. Almost exhausted, it swerved unsteadily across the track, and I perceived an opportunity.

Close to starving, having not been able to buy any food for over a week, I existed on scraps I could find outside houses, or vegetables from the fields. A freshly-dead hare would be a relief from the cramps in my stomach. I trailed the madly barking dogs across a lane and into a second field and then saw by their frenzy that they had caught the hare. I ran up to them, brandishing an improvised walking stick and shouted at the top of my lungs. Startled, the dogs jumped back from the hare but then closed in around me. I smashed the stick into the head of the first dog to attack me, knocking it to once side, where it got to its feet and trotted away, yelping. The second dog saw an opportunity and lunged for my thigh. I brought the stick round and into the dog's ribs. I cracked one or two, judging by the sound, and that dog too, shuffled to lick its side. I saw blood coming from his mouth. The other dogs seemed less certain and backed away. I was prepared to fight dirty, desperate as I was, and they knew it. While they were confused, I leaped forwards and grabbed the bloody mass of limp fur. The dogs snarled at me, but I wielded the stick and after a few whimpers, they trailed off.

I didn't hang around. It would be a crime, punishable by death, to be caught eating the game of a lord, so I walked on for an hour before sitting down to eat.

Worried about the risk of smoke from a fire, I ate the hare raw. The slowly congealing blood oozed between my teeth as I tore apart the tender meat. I found the sensation strangely calming and deeply satisfying. My headache left me completely for the first time since going through the portal. Never having felt this way before, I cast my mind back to search for other occasions when I might have drunk fresh blood. Perhaps in my youth I had, but I never felt like this.

When I had eaten all I could, I packed the rest in a cloth and went on.

I finally arrived in Grestain, near Le Havre, on a very blustery day in late November. Starving, cold and wet, I had one other thing bothering me. I had drawn closer to the war that I would have liked.

Close to the estuary of the Seine, where a small tributary met with a larger one, the Abbey itself nestled among trees, near the village of Berville. The village was a loose conglomeration of long, low, thatched barns and sturdy stucco houses with the only real concentration of stores being along the waterfront. It didn't take me long to locate Herleva. A few not-so-subtle enquiries pointed me toward a manor house just outside the village. Part of the endowment of the Abbey, the manor looked surprisingly run-down. Set into a low hillside, the thatched stone building, not much more than a barn, swarmed with chickens, pigs, various peasants and children going about innocuous daily tasks. A few glanced at the ragged stranger, but none barred my way or even spoke to me.

"Please can you tell me where to find Herleva?"

"Arlette?" said a little, blonde, curly haired girl, her smiling face covered in mud. "The lady is up there!" She pointed to some rough stone stairs, half way along one of the long walls of the manor. I stepped carefully between the large puddles and tried to wipe my shoes clean on the tufts of dirty grass which struggled for life against the foot of the stone wall.

Dusk cast its mysterious shadow over the scene. The few lanterns were casting long black shadows around the activity in the courtyard, making it look like a shadow-play.

A titan of a man with dark brown hair and a long beard, stepping on to the top of the stairs from the open doorway, shouted:

"Stop! Speak your name!"

"I'm a traveler. From Donzy. I wish to speak with Herleva."

He looked me up and down disapprovingly.

"I'm very hungry," I said grinning.

"I can see that. I don't think she'll want to see you. Where are you from?"

"Donzy."

"Never heard of it. You'll have to wait. She still has some business before I can ask her. But you're wasting your time."

"I'll wait."

He shrugged his shoulders before disappearing inside again. Occasionally I would glance inside. I could see a fire warming his feet, and he had a large flagon of ale to drink from. I smiled at him, hoping I might solicit some beneficence, but this only brought further insult:

"Stay out there!"

It started to rain and, before long, I was the only one left in the courtyard. I stamped my feet to keep warm. If I hadn't been so hungry and without any means whatsoever, I wouldn't have gone straight there.

When despair had brought me close to leaving, two well-dressed merchants bustled out of the door and passed me. The guard tapped his feet and looked at me a few times before deciding a polite interval of time had elapsed.

"Wait there!" he growled and slowly climbed a short flight of stairs. I strained my ears, but I couldn't hear anything.

He emerged again and clumped slowly down the steps toward me.

"You can go up. But stop at the door and answer Her Lady's questions."

His closing smile beamed radiantly.

I did my best to stand up straight and look dignified in the doorway at the top of the stairs while the water dripped from my cloth hat onto my nose and then to the dry-stone floor.

"Your name?" a deep, but soft, feminine voice asked from the room beyond, only very dimly lit by a candle so that I couldn't see her features.

"Jean."

"And you're from Donzy?"

"Yes."

"You're English, are you not?"

I hesitated for a fraction of a second. "Yes."

"Why are you here?"

"I met somebody who said he knew you. I … I need advice. I think you could help me."

"Who … did you meet?"

The voice was velvety, almost hypnotic. The 'who' was accentuated, as if a line in a song.

"Robertus. At least he called himself that. The locals call him The Scribe."

"Um. Robertus. Yes, he would know. Did he send you here?"

"Err. No. My host, Guillaume, knew that you were here. Robertus simply said he served you."

"Hm. You are John Rezor?"

My shock silenced me for a moment. I had no choice but to admit it. I nodded.

"Good."

The voice, so melodious and hypnotic, made me want to close my eyes and sleep. I have never heard a voice like it.

"Go now. Gerard, the guard, will find you accommodation. Recover, and we will speak again. But do not tell anybody else your name. If they ask, simply tell them you are my guest. Stay inside as much as you are able, for now. There are prying eyes everywhere these days."

I fell asleep the very instant I laid down, after being led to my room by the tall guard.

***

The bed was only of straw and in a leaky outhouse at that, but when I woke it seemed like I had slept for a week. I was always brought my food by one of the small girls, sometimes the one with blonde hair who had smiled at me. Once I could hobble around, I spent a good deal of time playing a version of boules with Gerard and the other men in the courtyard. One thing struck me immediately; how much happier people were here than in Lyot. Clearly, if Herleva was their mistress, she had to be a benevolent one.

On the third day, the little blonde-haired girl told me that Arlette was waiting for me in the orchard behind the courtyard.

"Can you show me the way?" I asked

"Oui."

"What is your name?"

"Elayne," she said as if it were itself a question.

I found The Lady walking under apple trees which had been planted long ago in neat rows. Bereft of fruit and leaves in late autumn, they looked somewhat mournful, but the long grass and wild flowers lent the orchard a more cheerful air.

The Lady was wearing a green, velvet, long-sleeved dress which reached the grass, covering her feet. Under its arms, through double rows of eye-lets, gold-coloured braid laced the dress right up to the armpits. The braid continued down both sides to the hem. On a young woman one would have said it was sexy.

Herleva was elegant and only slightly shorter than myself. As I walked beside her I looked at her hair. It was long, grey and plaited into one long ponytail. In the brittle November sunlight, I could not be sure that it was truly grey. Sometimes it seemed almost blue and at others, almost blonde.

When she finally turned to smile at me, I was instantly bewitched by her clear green eyes. They seemed to hold nothing back. Though lines scored her face and she looked old enough to be my mother, still she was beautiful.

"So what did … your Guillaume say about me?" she asked with that deep, sonorous voice.

"He said you were a sorceress."

She laughed, quite raucously for such a refined face.

"He told me you eat men's flesh and steal their souls."

"Ah! The first is a lie."

"And the second?"

"That may be true." She flashed a smile at me that had just a hint of wickedness at the corners of her mouth.

"You are well now?"

"Yes thanks."

"You had a long walk … to see me."

I didn't know what to say.

"I have been looking for you," she added, almost coyly.

"Really?" I laughed. "That comes as quite a surprise as I've felt very alone since I arrived here."

"From?"

"Oh, you wouldn't believe me … ."

We walked in silence to the end of the orchard, and then I turned, as she turned to retrace her steps. A blue-sheened beetle briefly settled on her sleeve to catch the heat of the sun before taking off again.

"Robertus is one of my spies, you know." She smiled as if only half-serious.

"Oh?"

"I sent him to find you when you were supposed to arrive … in the forest on the 10th October. But you didn't arrive."

Can she possibly know?

I felt stunned.

"In fact, you arrived a few days earlier. I would like to know why. I have a feeling somebody knew we would be waiting, and so arranged for you to come a few days earlier. We only found out you were coming a day before so the plans must have been changed at the last moment."

"I would like to answer your question … . But there's so much I don't understand. I hope you will see that I'm not sure who to trust."

"Of course. Does it have anything to do with Hervé?"

"You know him?"

"Of … him. Robertus *knows* him."

"Ah. You see that's what makes me nervous. Why, or how … does Robertus know him?"

"Robertus is a merchant. It's his business to know Hervé. But, also, Hervé is my enemy. He serves a greater power, for bad. That is why Robertus spies for me … on Hervé."

"Ah." I pondered this for a moment. "But what I don't understand is why you even know that Donzy exists. Most people on my travels here hadn't even heard of it. How do you know of Hervé?"

"Simply because one of the main Gates is in the forest at Donzy; the Gate where travelers from the future come back. It is not the only one."

So she does know about the portal, or Gate, as she calls it!

"I *came* through the Gate."

"Um hm. I said it was so."

"But I was pushed before I was ready."

"Ah. That is why. It makes sense. They didn't want you falling in to our hands."

"Yes. But why did you want me?"

"I didn't … particularly. I just knew you were coming. I foresaw it. It is my duty to protect those who travel through the Gates for *good* reasons."

"Do you know my reason?"

"Actually, no."

"I've lost my wife. Some bad people called the Concilium Putus Visum have taken her into the past. At least that's what a message told me."

"Hm. I have not heard of these people. Who are they?"

"They are a Catholic cult, zealots who assassinate people. They're *very* unpleasant."

She puzzled over this for a moment and then seemed to brush it aside. "Your *wife*?"

"Yes?"

"When was she taken?"

"A few days before I came."

"Yes, yes … ." She seemed to be speaking to someone, or possibly herself. "I have seen her, I think. At least a woman came though shortly before you and went on, far into the past. Another woman led her. I lost track of them after that."

"Really!" I felt like grabbing her arm but propriety prevailed. "Do you know how far back they went? Where from?"

"I don't know any of these things. But I will attempt to find out."

"Yes. Thanks. Er … . Thank you very much."

"You have been a very good conversationalist. You are very charming. We will speak again soon."

I left her reluctantly. I felt that many more questions had been raised than answered. In particular, I felt that she had some role intended for me but was reluctant to reveal it.

***

Two days later, during the afternoon, Elayne came to me while I walked in the orchard. I had been bored and was glad of some company.

"The Lady wants to see you tonight. Come at nine bells."

"Thank you little lady." Seeing some wild foxglove and poppies, I stooped to pick some. Elayne bent down to help me. "For Arlette," I said. "Why do you call her Arlette?" I asked.

"She has lots of names," Elayne replied knowingly. "Arlette, Herleva … ."

As we walked back to the courtyard with two bunches of flowers, Elayne extended her little hand, and I took it.

At the sound of eight bells, tolled from the nearby Abbey bell, I made my way back to Herleva's room. Gerard smiled enigmatically when he stood aside on the small landing beneath her stairs.

The door was open, so I walked confidently in, holding out the bunch of wild flowers. The room was still only dimly lit. Though I could see her outline clearly by candlelight, Herleva's face was still hidden.

"Close the door," she said softly.

As the door shut softly, and I let down the latch, I heard a little laugh from behind me.

"Flowers! You are such a charming man! Here, put them in this vase." She poured water from a tall, pewter jug into a stone vase on a small table, and I stepped forward.

A large chandelier, directly above her, cast bright light and harsh shadows around her body, but a veil of drapes and strange nets shrouded the light from the front of the room. Like fishing nets, these held all sorts of curiosities; animal skulls and especially bird skulls, sea anemones, starfish, shells, branches from trees and dried flowers of all descriptions. On my side of this curious veil there were two tall candles. Behind were several more. Each cast a warm, flickering light that danced among the harsh shadows cast by the chandelier.

On shelves around the room, stacked loosely on both small tables and on the floor, were many leather-bound books. She stood behind a high-backed chair and behind her, two more heavy and richly decorated tapestries hung, drawn together in the middle.

It was an extremely sensual room, a boudoir.

Her face suddenly emerged from the darkness as she looked up, and what a face! I had to suck in my breath. Gone were the wrinkles and soft parchment skin. Yes, the eyes were the same, but now they were ringed by kohl, and her lips were ruby red. Her hair shone now the deepest brown. Or was it black? She looked not a day over twenty-five and was absolutely gorgeous. My senses were overwhelmed. She wore a blue gown, similar to the one worn in the orchard but with less fussy-decoration and with clasps up the chest to her neck. Two of these were undone revealing the ends of her collar bones, the most female flesh I had seen on display since I arrived in this ancient and religious century.

She smiled at me, and I felt myself stiffen.

Remembering, at last, what I was doing, I put the flowers in the vase. As she reached forward to guide the stems, our fingers touched. I almost recoiled at the intimacy. She seemed calm, assured.

"You read a lot," I ventured, trying to make sense of the situation.

How could I have guessed her age so badly? Perhaps she really is a sorceress.

"Yes. So do all who wish great knowledge. That has been my aim though out my long life, that and to do Good with it."

"You are some kind of mystic then?"

"Mystic? No. A sorceress would be more accurate. Isn't *that* what they call me?"

"Ha! Ha! Yes. Do you mind if I look?" I asked, pointing to the rows of books.

"No."

Running my index finger through the air just shy of the soft leather book spines, I tried to read the Latin titles. As I struggled, she came up behind me. I thought she would assist me, but instead she placed her elegant hand gently on the nape of my neck. I breathed out and closed my eyes.

"Come, let me show you my greatest treasure," she breathed. Drawing aside the tapestries, she revealed another room. Lit only by candlelight, the room had, at its centre, a large bed; dressed with black silk covers that seemed to shimmer in the candlelight.

On the bed a large, bound book lay open and on the open page were two large, colour illustrations of amazing complexity.

She lay on the bed, on her side, and the dress's clinging shape revealed to me the generous curves of her supple body.

My groin already ached with a need for her, and I could feel the blood pulsing through the arteries of my neck. I swallowed and sat down on the opposite side of the book.

"What's it about?" I asked.

"See here?" she said. "These are The Serpents of Satan. One inhabits your century now. They were once wolf-spirits who have become corrupted by murder or deeds worse."

I looked at the red serpents, their scales like faces of lost people, and I recognised the Serpent. "I've seen it. But it is no more."

"Ha! Ha! You cannot destroy them so easily, but it is perhaps possible that he will no more trouble in your time. You're a brave man if you fought with him. I have long been curious about them." She peered closely at his image and seemed for a moment like a little girl. "What was he like?" she asked innocently.

"Terrible. It's hard to talk about. He took my daughter from me."

"Oh. I'm sorry. I didn't know."

Below the two entwined serpents in the illustration were lower levels of Hell and beasts yet more terrible and distorted. At the bottom of the page, I saw the upturned face of Satan, his tongue extended to form the floor of Hell upon which the beasts stood.

We cast our eyes to the righthand page.

At the top angels looked down upon white wolves, who were entwined around a tall, green tree.

"What does the tree represent?" I asked, pointing at the illustration.

Herleva rolled onto her back. Her dark brown hair fell back from her flushed face. The mounds of her breasts were inviting my fingers to touch her as they strained the clasps down the centre of her chest. She entwined my extended hand in her own and kissed it softy.

Before I could think of it I found myself moving over her and kissing her open lips. She closed her eyes and returned the kiss passionately.

"I want you," I said under my breath.

She smiled serenely and put a hand behind her head, all the opportunity I needed. I unfastened two clasps on the front of her dress to reveal the curve of her breasts, but her other hand gripped mine suddenly, and her eyes flashed a warning. They read, "Not too fast".

You mustn't do this John! You're married! Look where it got you last time. Stay loyal to Rose.

I felt helpless, powerless, against the bewitchment of this woman.

"I don't want to get too close to you…" I murmured.

"Why?"

"Because I know somebody close to me will die. It might be *you*!"

"Ha! It will take a lot to kill *me*. Don't worry."

With that, my last wall against her charms fell.

"It's been so long," she said. "So long … . Jean, you're the first man I could admire for a long, long time. You cannot know how long."

Continuing to unfasten her dress, I pulled the velvet cloth aside to reveal her rosy nipples and the complete curves of her breasts. I began to pull the dress from her shoulders, and she raised herself to help me. Soon, she was naked to the waist and, with her eyes closed, she unfastened the belt of my tunic. We were both beginning to breathe hard.

Her flesh blanched where I kissed it, so that after, it seemed to bruise for a moment in little orange blooms. The candlelight made her flesh seem to undulate and ripple.

Suddenly she sat up.

"Wait" she said. She wriggled out of the rest of the dress, and I saw that she had been completely naked under it. Her gorgeous, white body against the black satin sheets seemed to me like the vision of an angel exploding in my head. I heard the music of a thousand beasts and birds screaming raucously somewhere around us or in the depths of my soul, I could not tell which.

Then she let the back of her hand rest lightly on her lips, as if hiding her shame at her nakedness. For a moment she opened her eyes and looked into mine. She seemed so young, so vulnerable.

And then the spell was broken.

"I can't do this!" I said. "I'm sorry Herleva. You have bewitched me, but I can't do this!"

Standing and pulling down my tunic, I grabbed my belt and left the room.

***

I agonised over my decision the following day; here was the most powerful ally I had found, and yet I had insulted her, possibly even hurt her.

Was it the right decision? I love Rose, but if being faithful means not getting her back, abandoning her to whatever fate awaits her, then I could not live with that. Given another chance I would do it this time. God, I hope Herleva doesn't hold this against me!

When I caught Herleva's eye early the following evening, she smiled coyly at me. Little creases of delight at the corner of her mouth suggested she wasn't angry with me at all, and yet I couldn't be sure. When she summoned me again to her boudoir, I still roiled an agony of indecision.

The room seemed the same, but Herleva sat formally on the edge of the bed this time.

"Sit down Jean," she said, her melodious deep voice oozing kindness and patience. "I have found out a little about your wife."

For a moment, I felt stunned.

Why should she help me?

"Really? What have you found?"

"A woman, called Georgiana, brought her back," she replied, pronouncing the first 'G' softly as if it were a 'Y.'

"Georgina? If it's the same woman, I know her. Young, dark-haired and a servant of The Serpent?"

"Yes, that's her. You do *know* her."

"How do you know?"

"She was once your lover."

Oh shit! Now I am really in trouble. Insult definitely added to injury.

I nodded slowly. "If it's the same woman, then yes, that's true."

"Worse, you still love her."

This emphatic statement needed no answer.

"Don't worry, Jean. It's nothing to be ashamed of. Servants of the Serpents are endowed with the greatest allure. The worst of them are succubi. You had a fortunate escape, and you cannot be blamed for … succumbing." Her wordplay delighted her and made me smile. "Anyway, Georgiana took … . Rose back through one of the least used Gates. It's another powerful one and takes you back centuries, like the one that brought you here. It goes back to the 7th Century. That is almost all that I can tell you. It took a great deal of effort to locate them in the mists of energy that flow through the Gates. You have not much time Jean. This Georgiana intends to sacrifice Rose. The sacrifice will take place at midnight, but I don't know when."

I opened my mouth to shout in protest, but Herleva cut me off with a raised hand.

"It's a common ritual for servants of Satan. But most preferred of all are human sacrifices, these they save for generating the most powerful energies. I don't know what Georgiana or Satan has in mind, but they are scheming *something*."

"Well then, I must *go*! How do I … ?"

She laughed. Her laugh again seemed like that of a delighted girl. "You cannot just rush into a journey through such a Gate. There's much you need to learn about these practices. For example, did you know that the reason you lost your memory for a while was because you did not drink blood before using the Gate?"

That hare I ate. And how it felt to drink the blood. It did seem to quell some kind of discomfort inside me and those headaches!

"It will be very dangerous for you to use that Gate, Jean. Few would be prepared to follow you."

"But if I don't go soon, how will I get there in *time*! My wife might already be dead!" My voice rose in anger.

Herleva seemed to be listening for something for a moment, her head slightly cocked to one side. "No. No, your wife *is* still alive on the night the Gate opens. I can feel it."

Suddenly, in my mind a switch clicked. I knew I would make love to this woman, because I feared that she might hold something back from me, and I had to save Rose.

"You are being so good to me … ." I stepped closer and sat on the bed. I took her small, white hand in mine and kissed it softly.

"Jean … . You don't … ."

But I leaned toward her and, wrapping my arm around her, kissed her red lips. Her mouth yielded and she breathed deeply. She seemed to try to speak but could not form the words, and I kissed her again.

This time, when I turned her to unfasten the dark blue dress, similar to the first, she asked softly, "Are you sure?"

"Yes."

When she lay completely naked, her eyes closed, I kissed her slowly from head to foot, taking a lot of time to arouse her by kissing her nipples. I knew she was ready by her deep breathing, so I slid inside her, gently moving up and down over her gorgeous, white body.

She wrapped her arms around me as we moved faster and faster, in that timeless melody of movement, until we finally climaxed. I felt as if my insides were being drained of the very last energy I had. It felt as if she were sucking something out of me, and then I fell, exhausted, on top of her, breathing hard into her silky, dark hair. She kissed my ear, but then I knew no more.

I slept very deeply.

My thoughts were filled with the howling of wolves. I found myself running with a pack under a full moon, and I ran on all-fours. We ran and ran, until dawn when I howled at the fading moon in the pale blue sky of early day.

I woke with a start in the darkness of Herleva's boudoir. There was only the sound of her breathing to break the silence. The candles were not much further burned down. It could only have been a few hours since I fell asleep. I turned over and looked at the sensual beauty lying next to me. I wanted her again. My loins were on fire as I leaned over, pulled the hair from her cheek and kissed it.

"Um," she moaned.

I hauled her over on to her back, pinning her hands above her head on the pillow. Her eyes opened wide, and I saw that they burned red. The green colour of before had turned a deep red, flecked with amber and orange, like the flames of a fire.

She panted while I kissed her roughly, all the way down her body and then hauled her off the bed. Lowering her to a bear-skin run beside the bed, I made her kneel, and then I took her from behind. I took her as if she were nothing, as if I owned her and she was worth nothing. As she climaxed she seemed almost to growl. It seemed as if she were resisting an intensifying urge to release a pain inside her. Just after I climaxed she moaned loudly. She panted for some minutes before I released her and threw myself on the bed. I hardly noticed when she lay down beside me and pressed herself against me.

When I woke, Herleva playfully teased my hair around her fingers and looking into my eyes.

I remembered how I last made love to her.

I can't believe I did that to her. It's so unlike me! I won't say anything. Let's just see how she acts.

"Hello," she said before raising herself and kissing my lips.

"Hi."

"Hi? What does that mean? Is it good?"

"It's something we say in the 20th Century. It's a good thing."

"Hm. I have seen your 20th Century, but I didn't care much for it. Everything happens too fast."

"Yes. I suppose so." I didn't say any more, but I had the uncanny feeling Herleva could read my thoughts.

"You didn't need to make love to me, Jean. I would have done all I could to help you anyway."

I blushed. She touched the end of my nose delicately with her forefinger. I wanted to change the subject.

"I've only heard your name once before, the name of William the Conqueror's mother."

"But how did you … ? No, you couldn't have. Jean, I think perhaps you are psychic too!" She laughed, that little girl's laugh, clear and bright like a sparkle of daylight. "Anyway, they call him William the Bastard around here."

"I don't know much about Herleva; only that she was the daughter of a tanner and had something to do with the founding of an abbey."

"That's not true actually. Her father was a burgher. And yes, she did found an abbey, this one. Actually, Jean, darling I have something to tell you which is going to shock you."

"Unlikely, but go ahead."

"You were closer than you knew when you said that you had heard my name only once before."

"Oh?"

"You *have* heard my name before. Jean, you know I said I was old? Well I am much older than you think. I am over two hundred years old. I *am* the Herleva you refer to. I was William's *mother*. I am not the same woman I was then, so foolish, so young … ."

"But I don't understand? How could … ."

"I have The Power. A power you only dimly perceive. It's been possible to extend my life with spells and potions. Sometimes though, I don't think it's been worth it. I've seen so many terrible things and wonderful things. Losing the second is worse than seeing the first. I've lost all that I loved."

I looked into her eyes, and I believed her. I had seen many strange things in my lifetime and this seemed no stranger.

"So can you help me?" I asked her.

She laughed. "Of course. But you must do something for me too."

"Ah. I thought there would be a catch!" I joked, not meaning it at all.

She kissed me quickly on the lips.

"It's about Hervé. I want you to make him an ally. I want you to bring him over to our side. Robertus has tried, has been trying for years but cannot do it. I think you could be more persuasive. Robertus is clever and resourceful but one thing he certainly isn't, is a soldier. Perhaps that's why he hasn't been able to befriend Hervé … "

"Hm. And what is 'our side'?"

"The good side, of course! Ha! Ha! You will need to gain his trust anyway."

"Why?"

"Because the Gate to 7th Century is in one of his strongholds, the Aunay Tower. Peasants call it the Labyrinthe Tower. He keeps everything most valuable to him there. I believe the Gate to the 7th Century, Ireland, is right inside the tower, but I have never been there. Unluckily for you, the Gate in the tower opens one day before the full moon in September. Perhaps that's significant. You never know with these things. You cannot be sure Georgiana won't make the sacrifice, somewhere in the 7th Century, the next night. I can feel that your wife is still alive on the night of the 11th. Let's hope she is still when you reach her. The tower is in Aunay, near Nevers. You will never get into it without his help … . Unless you have an army and a big one at that. He is Compte de Nevers now and acts as if he is King. Indeed, he *is* to most intents and purposes. His power is *absolute* in that area. The King's power and influence do not reach so far."

"Labyrinthe Tower? Why do they call it that?"

"Probably because of the Gate but maybe something else. There are lots of rumours about it; treasure and something dark and secret to catch the unwary."

"Phew! You don't ask much! So how am I going to accomplish all this?"

"That's up to you, but I will get you some basic training so that you can pass as a Knight, and then I will give you a squire to accompany you back to Donzy. I am thinking of Gerard."

"Me? Trained as a Knight. At my age. You have got to be joking!"

"You're not as old as you think, Jean. Have you looked in a mirror lately?"

"No. I haven't seen a mirror since I came to this century."

"Over there! On the table. Take a look."

"I stood up from the bed and took the hand-mirror which lay face-down on the dressing table. Holding it to my face at such an angle that it would catch the flickering candlelight, I looked at my features. My hair no longer looked grey but dark brown again! I looked like a man of forty, not one of seventy!"

"It's a bloody miracle! But how … .?"

"It's another thing you don't understand about the Gates. I don't understand myself how it works but when you travel back in time, if you stay for any length of time, you start to get younger. The further back you go, the faster you become younger. It's the opposite if you go forward; you get older. If you stay too long in either place, it is fatal. I don't know what happens then, but I know that some have never returned. It's not something I want to try."

"Strange. What's the furthest you have gone back?"

"You ask too many questions. Let's just say that there is a limit to how far you can go. Now, Jean, I have many things I must do. We will speak again soon. Gerard will know what to do."

Suddenly an involuntary laugh escaped me. "I just realised," I said. "You're the oldest woman I ever made love to. Over two hundred years old! Ha! Ha!"

***

I didn't like the sound of the Labyrinthe Tower. Labyrinthe translates into English as Maze, but either way, I didn't like the sound of it. I didn't have much time to worry about it though. Gerard did know exactly what to do. He began to train me intensively in the art of combat. Once a soldier, he seemed to know all there was to know about being a knight. I had the best teacher for swordplay, archery horsemanship and combat on horseback that I could wish for. Nevertheless, after as long as a month, I felt I still would not persuade even the youngest child that I was a knight!

"So … you … are … to be … my Squire!" I said between sword strikes, during a practice fight with Gerard in the courtyard.

"Well … perhaps … ."

"Argh!" Though the blades were blunt, a swinging blow from his sword caught me on the neck and brought me to my knees, in pain. The chain mail shirt I wore had cut through the heavy wool under-tunic and bruised my skin, leaving a purple tattoo of chain links impressed on my skin.

" … you should be my squire, and *I* should be the knight," quipped Gerard.

"Look what you've done!" I complained

"Ha! It's a scratch. Get up! It's early yet."

Gerard was a good-natured mountain of a man, once you came to know him. Wary, at first, once Herleva had told him of her plans, he quickly adopted me as if I were his son, albeit one a lot older than him.

Christmastide, as Gerard called the twelve days of Christmas from 23rd December to 5th January, came and went. Christmas Day itself, was a sombre affair with many visiting the Abbey for a service and then partaking of a feast back at the Manor.

In the chapel, several local lords with their families, sitting in separate pews near the front, amused me. They reminded me of Mafia families, and the impression was reinforced when we emerged from the chapel. The lords' retinues, in the shape of burly knights and sergeants, were standing around in full armour, observing the other factions with caution.

***

"*Jean*! Come! I've something to show you!" Gerard called shortly after breakfast, one frosty morning. I joined him in the yard, and he led me through a door into the stables. A large, white mare stood panting there, and, arrayed before me on a cart and on the straw, lay a full set of mail, a choice of helmets and all kinds of weapons. A tall but obsequious man stepped up to me, lank, dark, hair crawling out from under his cloth cap of dubious quality.

"It's been a long, cold journey Monsieur, and I have many customers today. Please may we get started?" He wrung his hands and then gestured expansively to his wares.

Gerard bellowed with laughter and hollered for somebody to bring a pot of mulled wine for the guest. "Don't mind Abellard, Jean. He will make enough money from his rounds today to warm his feet for one hundred years!"

Abellard ignored this impertinence and proceeded to take out a length of thread, knotted at equal intervals.

"Raise your arms Monsieur!" he instructed, and I complied. He proceeded to measure every aspect of my body, from my arm length to the circumference of both feet. Each time he wrote down the measurement on a piece of parchment with a fine quill pen, dipped in an ink pot resting on a straw bale.

He seemed very content with his measurements when one of the young boys returned with his steaming mulled wine. While he sipped and watched, Gerard began to heft some of the weapons. "Try the mail on, Jean!" he shouted, swinging a great sword around his head.

I struggled to lift the mail shirt and lowered it over my head. It hung down to my calves and weighed as much as a teenager. I felt its weight cramping my breathing.

"Now this!" shouted Gerard. I looked up just in time to catch the great sword by the hilt as it sailed toward my head. It weighs almost as much as the mail!

I swung it cautiously around my head. After ten or eleven revolutions, sweat poured off me.

"Choose," Gerard said, indicating the array of weapons. From them I chose: a long-sword, not as long as the great sword and, indeed, the shortest of the long-sword; a finely made dagger with an ivory hilt; a cross-bow, long-bow and a mace. Then I tried on three helmets: an open-faced one; one with a half visor and one heavy helmet with a full visor, the classic Crusader helmet. Shaped like an upturned bucket, it had the slanted eye slots and brass fittings. It was clearly second hand.

"Genuine Crusades helmet that. Used at Acre I believe," Abellard said, noting my interest.

It had a fine collection of dents and scratches, and I quite took a fancy to it. "This one," I said.

Apart from anything else it will hide my eyes completely. Looks pretty intimidating too.

Lastly, I chose some mail boots, and then Abellard exclaimed. "Right! We have it all!"

"Two weeks mind! Make sure they are ready … . Or you won't get paid!" Gerard said.

"They will be ready," the armourer said, as he began to pack up his wares.

"How much will that lot cost?" I asked Gerard as we walked back out into the morning sun.

"Not as much as the horse! But don't worry. The Lady will be paying."

***

Those two weeks passed quickly for me, learning as much as I could. I became exhausted at the end of each day. I quickly learned that there was a lot more to Gerard than I had first guessed.

"How on earth did you learn all this Gerard? It's far more than the average squire would know."

"In the Crusades."

"You *went there*?"

"Yes." His short answer, delivered grimly, seemed to offer no more by way of explanation.

"In service of a knight, I guess?" I could just imagine Gerard standing by the stirrups of some great knight.

"I *was* a knight once, Jean," he replied sadly. "More than that."

He raised his arm and showed me a tattoo; a red Templar's Cross.

"You … are a Templar?"

He shook his head slowly. "*Was.*"

"What happened?"

"It's a long story … ."

"Give me the short version. We'll have plenty of time for the long one on our journey."

"Jean. It's not something I like to talk about. Only The Lady knows the story."

"I wondered why you weren't married … ."

Only when we were relaxing with a jar of strong mead, days later, did Gerard finally tell me more of his story.

His tone became, at first, sad, but as he recounted the earlier parts of his life, he seemed filled again with the vision that had once fired him.

"As the second oldest son of a lord, I was destined for the church, but I had some talent with a sword. A Templar taking shelter in our Abbey saw me shadow-sparring with a stave and offered me a position as his squire. After some persuading, the Abbott agreed, and that's how I eventually became a Templar and went to the Crusades. Unfortunately, I was captured by the Saracens and imprisoned for many years. All who knew me thought I were dead. Indeed, sometimes I thought I *was* dead. It was *Hell*, but a strange stroke of luck saved me. The man who wounded me in combat, by some strange twist of fate, became my gaoler. I believe the war had not gone well for him, and he was demoted. Anyway – Ibrahim was his name – he took pity on me and taught me chess. We quickly became friends, and so life became bearable for me. He even petitioned for my release. I'm not sure, but I think I am one of the very few, if not the only, Templar to be released from a Saracen gaol… and without even so much as a ransom."

"Yes. I know normally Saracens hated, I mean, hate Templars."

He continued, "When I was released, I had to hide my face and hands; the whiteness, especially since I had been kept away from the sun, would have attracted attention in a Saracen city. After a long journey overland and a voyage across the sea, I found my way back to France, but I was in for a surprise. My Order would not accept me. They called me an apostate and stripped me of my post."

"But why?"

"They say so much time with the Saracens could only have corrupted my mind. They said, too, that I would no longer be able to kill a Saracen. In this there may be some truth … ."

"Gerard … ." I wanted to touch his shoulder. "What did you do?"

"I wandered around for a while, offering myself as a mercenary to local lords and comptes. There is plenty of such work if you don't mind the mindless thuggery."

"And then?"

"And then I ended up here. I was just lucky. There are *many* who aren't."

I sat silently for a moment, reflecting on how holding back my own story had denied me a deeper friendship with Guillaume.

"Gerard, there's something I can tell *you*, too."

He looked at me and smiled.

"Have you heard of Ordo Lupus?"

"Yes. Yes, I think I have. They are one of many obscure mystical cults which are not quite outside the Church but not inside it either. Shape-changers, aren't they? At first, when told of them I was led to believe our Order only tolerated them. But my teacher later told me that in time of need and in the fight against Satan, they were our allies."

I had hardly heard anything after the term 'shape-changers.'

Could I be a shape-changer? Surely not.

"I met one once," he continued.

"Really? Where?"

"In The Holy Land. He was in the retinue of Hervé, in fact. His first name was Guillaume. I can't remember his family name, if he ever gave it."

"Was he a shape-changer?"

"Well. I'm not *sure*, but some nights, his bed would be empty, and we never found out where he went to. I don't know much about it. My Lady will be able to tell you more about that. Why do you mention them?"

"Well, I would have said I was a member of the Order until what you just told me. I'm not sure I'm a shape-shifter … "

He raised his eyebrows for a moment but said nothing.

***

We were to collect my armour and weapons on the way to Donzy. The night before we left, Herleva once again summoned me to her chamber. I had been waiting to speak with her for some time.

"So you are to leave in the morning?" she asked.

"Apparently," I said, slightly peevishly. I felt that she had not yet shared all her plans with me.

"Don't be like that darling." It was amusing to hear the term of endearment which I had taught her. "Don't you know how to leave a woman? Shouldn't there always be an uncertainty in her mind that you will come back – that you will think of her?"

I laughed. "Anyway, what do you expect me to do with all this training and the facade of a knight?"

"Befriend Hervé and in time … " She walked up to me and ran her index finger under my chin. The end of an expansive sleeve of her dress was attached to her finger by a tiny loop of silken thread. Almost regal, the blue dress was far more formal than the previous ones I had seen her in. She looked set for a ceremony. I guessed she would be in the mood more for talking than love-making.

"There's something I have to tell you Jean. It won't be easy and perhaps you had better sit down. A drink?"

She offered me something in a golden goblet. The drink was dark and red. I eyed it suspiciously. It was the first time she had personally offered me a drink.

"It's only wine," she said.

I sipped the spicy drink and sat on the edge of the bed.

"Gerard told me there might be something you wanted to ask me."

"There are many things I would like to ask you … . But one thing in particular … about Ordo Lupus. You know of them?"

"Of course. All we who deal in the occult know of them and other groups. There are many."

I thought for a moment. "So Gerard is your spy then?"

"No." Her direct gaze reassured me.

"Yes. I am curious about something he said."

"I think I know what that is. Was it about shape-changing?"

"Go on." I prompted.

For a moment she seemed irritated, but then a kind smile spread across her face.

"Jean. You want to know … if you are a shape-shifter. The answer is not so simple. I can tell you that shape-shifting is in your blood, as it were, but you haven't yet learned it."

"You're being kind. Just tell me the truth."

"Alright. Yes, you *are* a shape-shifter, you can change shape into a wolf." Suddenly she seemed embarrassed. "It's not as rare as you might think. Even I … ."

"You're a werewolf too?"

"Werewolf? I'm not familiar with the term."

"It's a term used in my time. It's largely derogatory." I laughed nervously. "Sorry. It's a bit of a shock. Are you of my Order then?"

"No … .No, but shape-shifting is a common enough … attribute among the Worthy."

"Worthy?"

"Sorry, that is a term of *my* Order. I mean; among the peoples who are not confined to this world."

"Ah!" I nodded slowly, feeling like I had taken a body-blow.

"The blood-drinking is a part of it, Jean. Shape-shifters were the first to use the Gates, to escape. Drinking blood simply numbs the pain. But there are other times you can drink blood."

"Wait! The Gates? What are they, and who made them?"

"I don't know exactly. Nobody knows. It's said they have been here forever."

"And *why* are they where they *are*, and how do they *work*?"

"I will tell you more, later Jean. You'll need knowledge of them."

This quelled my raging curiosity.

She stroked her forehead for a moment, as if not sure how to go on. "Drinking blood just before a full moon is how you can learn to access the animal world."

"What sort of blood?"

"Oh, any kind will do in my opinion. They say the higher the species, the purer the effect, but I haven't found much difference."

"That's a relief. I don't want to go drinking a person's blood."

She laughed. "No Jean. There are others that do that, and we do not speak lightly of them. That's not your way."

"So what else do I need to do; at the full moon, I mean."

"That's *it*. It's best you find your own way. It will be a lot to learn for you, but it is much like learning about life. It's not the same for any two people."

"I see. But one thing I don't understand; if my Order are shape-shifters, why did I not learn of this in my century. My grandfather, too, was a prominent member of Ordo Lupus, and I don't think *he* ever changed shape?"

"Yes. I don't understand this myself. Perhaps it is a quality that lessened over the years. Or perhaps it is no longer needed. Isn't it said that the Great Ceremonial Sword of the Cathars fell into the hands of Ordo Lupus, and this became their greatest weapon in their fight against the Serpents?"

"Yes, that's true!" Her knowledge astonished me.

"But I have a warning for you Jean."

"Oh? What's that?"

"When you explore the animal world, that's when you will be most vulnerable. That is when Satan will try to tempt you, set a trap for you. When we're in that state, we are subject to base emotions and instincts only. You will not be able to apply rational thought to your actions. Beware!"

I looked at her cool expression, her calm, clear green eyes and felt that a thousand miles of hidden space drew me in. For a moment, I felt as if I were falling, and then I shut my eyes.

"I'll be careful."

"Good. There is not much more to say Jean, for now, except our farewells. I trust the horse and armour suit your *purpose*?"

"Yes. Very generous of you. The horse is a little skittish, but Gerard tells me that is a good thing in a young horse destined for battle!"

I swallowed at the thought of battle. I had no intention of being in one, but somehow it seemed more likely now than before.

"Oh, I nearly forgot!" She giggled. "The Gate!"

"Yes. I need to know how to use it."

"It's normally very simple Jean, but you will need to use it in a special way."

"Wait! First, I need to know *what* they are. How *many of them* there are and *where* they are?"

"Well, they're all over the place. There are few Kingdoms which don't have one. Even in the Far East they exist, I believe."

"I know there's one in Beauvais, and here, and one other near Monségur. So how will I get back if I need to follow Georgina through the Gate in the Aunay Tower?"

I have written it all down on this parchment, all you need to know.

"Oka-… I mean alright. And now tell me how to use Hervé's Gate. And if I need to gain time on Georgina? I can catch up? You told me I could."

"Yes, that's right. Most spirits who use the gates use them in the conventional way; waiting for the white light before crossing over. They ignore the other colours; red, orange, yellow and green. These can also be used but are usually more dangerous. You need a greater knowledge of the gates to use them." She seemed to consider for a moment. "You will need to use the orange light."

"As I understand it that will make me arrive early?"

"Yes, up to a year early, well almost… to within a few hours. But since you are too late for the white light now, you will have to wait until next year and then use the orange ligh-…"

"Next year! Next year! 1214! Are you sure that will work!"

"Trust me Jean. It will work! It's the only way."

1214! 1214! There is something significant about that date, but I can't remember…

"As I was saying, the red light will make you arrive one-hundred and forty-nine years early, but it's very dangerous to use this. Your body can be torn apart by the violent forces in the ether. Sometimes men have arrived with an arm missing or a leg. The yellow light will make you arrive up to one year late and the green, light up to one-hundred and forty-nine years late."

"So you always travel the same distance in time?"

"Yes. Provided you use the same colour and moment."

"But they are only open once per year?"

"Yes, this is generally so although I think there are exceptions."

"Well I need to *know about them*! What if Georgina uses one of these exceptions?"

"I cannot tell you everything, Jean. I told you I think there are exceptions, but I have never seen one or used it."

"Okay, so if I use the orange light, I can arrive on the same day that Georgina did?"

"Yes. You will be a few hours behind them, but it will have to do. You will just have to make time on her. I don't know where she is, but obviously she will be close to the Gate."

"Okay. I mean alright. So what moment do I step into the orange light?"

"Just a few seconds after it changes. Not too soon or you may be lost forever but not too late. Count slowly to three and then step forward. Like this – One, two, three." Her counts were about two seconds apart.

"So do all the gates arrive at more or less the same date of the calendar but somewhere else entirely?"

"Yes. I believe so."

This seemed strange to me. I didn't pursue this any further with Herleva.

"So when I come back, should I use the white beam and right in the middle of it?"

"Yes."

"And that will bring me back to this year?"

"It will bring you back to the same year you use it immediately, but if you wait a year, you will come back a year later."

"One last question; what date do I use Hervé's Gate?"

She looked perplexed for a moment. "Didn't I say? On the 10th September. The Gate opens on the same day. The full moon is on the 11th September!"

I took a deep breath. "Well I think that's it then."

She put down the scroll and came up to me, holding out her hands very slightly. I took them eagerly. This evening she seemed much older than twenty-five, and I felt that she was more like an old friend. I leaned forward and kissed the soft skin of her cheek. "Thank you."

"Be careful, Jean!"

"You too. I know you say you are safe, but I will worry about you. Bad luck follows me wherever I go."

"Nonsense. You are one of the chosen. *Fate, doom,* if you like, surrounds you, just as it must always do for those souls that have lived *so* long and hold great power in their hands. It is not *bad* luck."

"Nevertheless, be careful."

With that, I turned and left her.

***

Gerard and I rode south and stopped on the second day to collect my armour and weapons. The large white mare had been broken long ago but seemed to forget this at times.

"What's she called?" I asked Gerard when I first saw her.

"That doesn't matter. You must think of a new name."

"Annabel!" I said impulsively, remembering my daughter, taken by The Serpent.

"Ah! In French it is Amabel. That would be better. It would attract less attention."

"Amabel it is then!"

We collected the armour, loaded it onto the grey mule we had taken with us for the purpose and continued on our way, just as the first winter snow began to fall.

"The snow has been late coming!" I said to Gerard. "In Angleterre it would have snowed nearly two months ago."

The landscape seemed eerily quiet, once blanketed with the cleansing snow. Its virgin whiteness made the view look even more like a crude woodcut from my school text books; black ink on white paper.

The soft crunching, tearing sound of the horses' hooves soothed me to the point of sleep on the second day. I forced my mind to focus in order to stay awake.

Just as Gerard and I mounted our horses to leave the Manor, Herleva had come bustling up to me and whispered in my ear. What she had said, I had not had time to fully digest until now:

"Jean! I have been awake all night trying to find out more for you. I've had some success, but it doesn't comfort me. In any case none of this may be true, but I thought it best to tell you!"

Her face almost seemed to frame a question when I looked at her, so I nodded.

"I think that a man accompanied Georgiana, one of Hervé's men. A military man I think."

"Alright. Thanks."

"Wait. There is one more thing. Georgiana will sacrifice … your wife, Rose, in a tower. Yes, I think it's a tower, a strange tower."

"Where is that? The Labyrinthe Tower?"

"I cannot tell. She is blocking me. She is gaining strength fast as a sorceress, this Georgiana."

"Oh God! Rose!"

She handed me a leather pouch. I weighed it and shook it slightly.

Coins!

"It's not gold. The mere sight of gold would bring every rogue chevalier and his men down on you. But it should be enough! God's speed Jean!"

Gerard moved off on his horse, and I spurred mine to follow.

Now I turned over the information in my head again. Most of it made sense but questions remained. Who was the man accompanying Georgina? Where was she taking Rose?

***

I wish I could say the journey back to Donzy passed as uneventfully as the journey from it, but only a few

days later, I learned just how loyal Gerard was to
Herleva:

Gerard had proved pretty handy with snares.

"My father's estate was run by a sergeant who had a
nice little business on the side," he told me. "When he
caught poachers, he would offer them their freedom for
a price and then keep the snares and bounty. It made
him feel good and provided extra food for his family.
But he also set the snares himself, and if he was
discovered he would blame a poacher or any other man
that he didn't like. Of course, there would be no proof
so no prosecution would normally take place. He taught
me to snare when lessons were finished, and my father
wasn't watching. I became pretty good!"

"Yes, I can see!"

Gerard had just caught a nice brace of fat rabbits. He
commenced skinning them next to a stream outside
some other town we had just passed through.

He lit a fire and, with vegetables we had rooted-up,
we cooked a fine meal. As night descended, he kicked
out the fire and served up the rabbit stew.

"Here Jean!" he said when the nearly full moon rose
above our heads. "One last toast before we sleep!"

I was almost blind-drunk, but it seemed impolite not
to acquiesce. "What shall we toast to?"

"Whatever you like!"

"To The Fair Lady then!"

"Fair Lady," he echoed, lifting his leather mug to his
lips.

I held the neck of the stoneware bottle to my lips and
tasted the rich nectar of locally made red wine. It tasted
a little richer than usual, but I hardly noticed. I only had
a mouthful before stretching out under the heavy
blankets to sleep. It was a clear night still and cold. But
the wine and food had numbed me.

"Good night Gerard."

"Good night, knight."

Not sure if I dreamed or not, I suddenly found myself running with a pack of wolves. Aoooow! Somebody, no something, howled, and it was me. I was a wolf too, running at the limit of endurance, the soft pads of my paws making a slight scrunching sound in the fresh, soft snow. How long had I been running? Where were we? Who were all these other wolves? Who was I? I didn't know. I just ran and gasped for air to fill my hot lungs. Then, the leader, a she-wolf, swerved to the left across another field. Her pace quickened. She had smelled blood. She drew close to her prey.

We halted by a stand of evergreen trees. The she-wolf walked among us, snarling instructions, so I listened. When she reached me, she pierced my gaze with her icy, blue eyes, and I knew her. I blinked once, to acknowledge her and licked my lips. She continued to the end of the line, and then we spread out.

We set off across the snowy expanse of field, gradually closing in on a flock of sheep. The ram circled behind his flock, trying to cut us off. But we were many and he, only one. The she-wolf, largest of us all, charged at him and growled. That was the signal!

Keeping an equal distance from the two wolves either side of me, I closed in on the herd and picked out a plump ewe to take down. I felt something hot coursing through my veins, and I couldn't stop growling to myself. It was a feeling of power and lust, longing for the drip of hot, fresh blood.

Suddenly the flock broke and spread out, aiming for the nearest trees, but we were too fast. I sprang on the back of the ewe and dug my claws into her haunches. I smelled the hot blood which had called to us and directed the she-wolf earlier. It was my destiny to drink it and, heaving the bleating ewe under me, I launched myself at her neck and bit hard into the soft flesh of her throat. She twisted to escape but only fell clumsily on top of me. I continued to grip with my jaws, and when I found purchase, with my claws too. I knew it was all over. She was mine. Her hot blood drained from her into my mouth, taking her life with it. Then she struggled no more.

We ate heartily, dividing the spoils of the small flock among us and ripping apart the curious, white bodies until there nothing but bone, blood and red-smudged wool lay strewn across the soiled snow. Some dragged off the carcasses to sleep on and feast upon in the morning, but I howled at the moon and turned away.

The she-wolf howled once. I glanced at her. I saw recognition and a farewell in her eyes. I turned and ran into the night. I ran and ran until, near dawn, I reached my destination.

"What the fu- … !" I jerked away, sitting upright and swore out of impulse. "Jeez! What a dream! That was *really* disturbing!"

Gerard, turned over, grunted once and continued to snore.

I found that I was shaking, not from cold, but from fear and exhaustion.

Was it that bad a dream?

As I often did when stressed, I began to hum Tom's Theme from the classic Hollywood film Tom Thumb. Eventually I felt calm enough to lie down. Now, cold beads of sweat dripped from my forehead into my eyes and onto my ears. The first rays of dawn's light were probing the pallid sky, but it would be too early to travel. After a while I managed to doze for a bit and then woke, feeling more tired than ever.

Gerard busied himself, preparing something hot to eat.

"Is all well?" he asked, humming to himself.

Funny! Gerard never hums.

I tried dozing again for a few minutes, but I felt restless.

Suppose I better get up.

I pulled the heavy blankets off of me and sat up again. I rubbed behind my ears and pulled my increasingly long fringe from my eyes.

Something tickled the underside of my nose, and when I felt for it, it tugged at my lips. I opened my mouth to pull it out. Holding it up to look at, I nearly jumped out of my skin.

I saw a little piece of whitish wool! Looking closer, I could see it was stained red! I felt the blood draining from my face, and I wanted to urinate immediately.

"What the … !" I stood up and began to pace up and down. I noticed one of my woolen inner-boots was missing. I knew I had been wearing it when I went to bed, because I had last put it on well before I had become drunk. A cold shiver ran down my spine. Then I felt a growing anger rising in me. I continued to pace up and down, trying to retrace my movements of the night before.

Despite my outburst, Gerard continued to hum as he boiled the stew on a small fire. I saw no snow around us, but this seemed a minor discrepancy compared with other facts which were beginning, in a horrifying logical way, to add up to something.

Gerard knows something!

After a few more lengths of pacing, I could contain my anger no longer.

"Gerard! You know something! Something happened to me last night, and I want to know what!"

"Me, Jean? I don't know what you're talking about. I was asleep all the time!"

"I bet you *were*, but that doesn't excuse you … ." I felt exasperated, because I couldn't even begin to explain what I thought. Only the memory of what Herleva had said to me offered a glimmer of hope for my sanity:

"When you explore the animal world, that's when you will be most vulnerable. That's when Satan will try to tempt you, set a trap for you."

A tiny bead of ice-cold sweat formed again on my right brow and grew slowly to a drop, big enough that it would presently run down into my eyebrow. Into my thoughts came the hazy memory of the last glass of wine during the previous evening.

"Gerard! That last glass of wine? It wasn't wine, was it? I thought it tasted a bit *strange*!"

"Jean." His eyes were calming and looked innocent enough, but I wasn't going to be denied.

"Gerard. We are traveling together. We're both soldiers, and it's more than likely we will face death together, possibly even die together. But we won't take another step together unless you tell me the truth! Now!"

"Merde! Jean! It wasn't my idea. I didn't want to do it, but My Lady told me to … . I'm sorry!"

"Shit! Shit! *Shit*! Herleva! Of all people. She's betrayed me!"

"No, Jean. She wouldn't! She would only be trying to help you. I don't understand these things, but I know she can be trusted. Complex she is, but a traitor she isn't!"

This made me even angrier, and I stamped my foot, before beginning pacing again. I could bare it no more. "You made me into some kind of *werewolf*!"

Gerard grew silent. He had stood up too now, but he looked down at his leather-clad feet and didn't make a sound. I could hear the wind rustling the bare branches of some beech trees nearby, and one of the horses snorted.

As quickly as it has come, the anger left me, and I felt only curiosity. "How long was I gone for?"

"I don't know Jean!"

"Well, *guess*!"

"A few hours. No, more, perhaps five! I don't know!"

"What time did I go?"

"Not long after you lay down. You made a hell of a rack … !"

"I don't care if I made a hell of a racket! What time did I come back?"

"About an hour ago. Maybe less … ."

"Jesus. I could have gone miles, many miles. I could have gone almost *anywhere*!"

"What was it like?" Gerard, with the look of a child, seemed suddenly very curious.

"Sh … ! Weird! If you want to know! *Weird*!"

"Oh."

"Does The Lady ever do this?" I asked

"I don't know. Some say she does. I've seen her go out late sometimes, usually near the full moon, and she doesn't come back until dawn … ."

"Hmm. Well, it's done now. I guess I'll survive. It's a big thing to take on though. It's like my life is suddenly not what I thought it was. This is going to take some getting used to!"

"I suppose so."

"What's for breakfast?"

"Rabbit stew."

"You know, I'm not hungry!"

***

It wasn't until we had harnessed the horses, mounted them and moved off that another bout of anger burst over me.

"Gerard! Let's get one thing straight. I need you to be loyal to me from now on, not The Lady. You cannot be loyal to her and to *me*. If we're to go on together, you must forget loyalty to her. It has to be to *me*, or I don't need you. *Understand*?"

"Yes, Jean," he said, sheepishly.

"If I even *suspect* you have done something without my knowledge of consent, betrayed me, that will be it!"

The word 'betrayed' made him wince. He nodded slowly.

"Understand?"

"Yes."

"Alright then."

I began thinking later about the she-wolf. That *something* I had recognised in her eyes reminded me of Herleva.

Could it be?

Though I thought around the problem for some time, I could come to no conclusion.

We moved south through the morning and passed among fields laden with newly fallen snow.

So this is where I went to last night?

The thought disquieted me even more.

New Year, 1214. Why does that date ring inside my head? 1214. Oh well, at least I'm traveling away from the war. That, at least, is something. It's about the only good thing at the moment.

The horses' hooves, slipped and bit, making that familiar tearing sound on the new snow. I started to plan how I would befriend Hervé. Herleva had first suggested I should remove the patch.

"Around here, that will cause more suspicion than the colour of your eyes!" she said.

I still had it with me, but I felt reluctant to put it on again. I could easily imagine Hervé asking me to remove it early on, and that would be likely to increase his suspicion. After some thought, I presented my plan to Gerard.

"It seems to me that an early display of my prowess with a sword would be best. He's looking for a sorcerer, and where I come from, a sorcerer is a guy with no fighting skills – all brains and no brawn. A quick demonstration of my skills before he sees my eyes, and he will at least have doubts when he *does* see them. From there it's just a matter of working on him until he trusts me!"

"You make it sound so simple!"

Da! Nah! Yeah, I know what you mean.

"Well, do you have any better ideas?"

"No."

"Right then, we just have to arrange a joust or something!"

"What's a joust?"

"Ah, I was forgetting … . You probably haven't invented the word yet!"

"I?"

"No, I mean the French!"

"Ah. You talk in riddles sometimes, Jean." He seemed lost in thought for a moment. Then he turned to me. "Where do you come from, Jean?"

"The future!" I said, flippantly and slightly vindictively. I was after revenge for his manoeuvre with the bloody drink.

Instead of shock, Gerard displayed a studied silence, which surprised me.

"Has Herleva spoken of it?" I asked.

"A little, but I don't understand such things. I'm not sure I *want* to understand them!"

We stopped for a break. Gerard had become very quiet and short of conversation, I suddenly remembered the parchment Herleva's had given me before we left. I took it out and unrolled it.

Jean

I used all my powers of perception to probe
the time you will find yourself in, when you
pass through the Gate at Aunay. I only
managed to sense a name, Abbot Cathal. It
might be useful to you.
There is a Gate I know in Angleterre. It is
near Salesberie. Next to a wide river? I am
sure you will find it. The Gate back to our
Century is on a hill nearby, but I cannot
remember exactly where. Ask in the hostel
for one called Henri le Tanner. He will help
you.
You will arrive on a plain near Paris. If the
Serpent's enemies are expecting you, this is
where they will wait too. But they will
expect you on 17th September. Don't come
back on that day. When you have
committed these things to memory, destroy
this parchment. Do not let it get into the
wrong hands.
Your Herleva

I memorised the facts and later destroyed the
parchment.

***

As we moved south, my lessons continued daily.
Usually we would break for an hour in the morning and
one in the afternoon. Then, Gerard would help me into
the full suit of armour, and we would spar. I'd used a
bow before, in an archery club as a youth, and I soon
mastered the light bow I'd chosen. The crossbow was
much more like a rifle, and I became an expert with this

very quickly. Gerard wasn't comfortable with the weapon and marveled at my quick mastery. The sword, I steadily improved with, but the mace was a different matter. I simply hadn't the muscle strength to wield it effectively, at first.

Once he had shown me the correct way to fight, Gerard began to demonstrate how to break the rules and even use dirty tactics. It reminded me of my days training with M.I.6. I quickly decided I would find a way to turn the tables on Gerard but for now I had to bide my time.

The rest of the journey passed quite uneventfully. Rumours of war on the Flemish border with France abounded wherever we stopped to speak with strangers, and I thanked God that we were heading south. Twice I thought we would be ambushed by outlaws. Both times we were followed by dark looks from men lurking in shadows, but they seemed too wary to try it. From the start of our journey I had packed my armour under the blankets, but when I hid the helmet Gerard stopped me.

"Keep the helmet on top of the blankets. It's an old trick of knights everywhere. Once they know you're a knight, few robbers will dare to attack you."

He had been proved right.

"Another variation is leaving the horse's head-armour on, although we only did that when passing through villages; too uncomfortable for the horses," he told me

"And why didn't Herleva give us enough money to arm the horse too?"

"You cannot expect her to provide everything! No doubt she expects you to buy it yourself. How much do you have?"

I hadn't counted the money until then, so we stopped. I poured out the silver denier coins onto some grass.

"Two hundred and fifty!"

Gerard whistled though his teeth.

"Is that enough to equip the horse?"

"Probably. But don't worry. There are few these days who armour their horses. I doubt that even Hervé does that."

"Still it would be nice to get some head armour. That would impress him!"

***

Chapter Five

Spring often comes very early in France near Nevers, and so it was that we reached the outskirts of Lyot on a bright, crisp afternoon in late January. Approaching on the road that passed Guillaume's mill, I keenly anticipated the sight of smoke rising from his roof. When we reached the building, however, I saw no sign of life at all. We entered the courtyard next to the mill-race, just before the sun dipped below the horizon, and what I saw shocked me. Nothing looked like it had been used for some time, and a few brave shoots of weeds struggled from between the fibres of hessian, grain sacks lying scattered around.

I quickly dismounted and went to the door, which had been left ajar. Taking a deep breath, I pushed it open and stepped into the gloom.

"Light!" I shouted out to Gerard, who used his flints to light a small piece of sacking, which he tied to a discarded broom handle.

"What's happened Jean? I don't like it!"

"Neither do I. But I think whoever did this has gone. I pointed to broken furniture and the few tools and other belongings of Guillaume's which lay on the wooden floorboards."

The place stunk of human waste. A rat suddenly broke cover, startled by the torch.

The large table, on which I had last eaten a hearty meal with my friend, seemed to be the only item still intact. I peered at one corner of its wooden surface.

"What do you make of this?" I asked Gerard. He looked at the dark stain next to my pointing finger.

"Blood."

"Yes."

"Your friend's?"

"I guess so. I … I don't know. I hope not. Christ, if it's because of me … ."

Gerard put his large hand on my shoulder. "Who do you think did this?"

"Hervé's men … probably."

I set one of the chairs, now missing an upright of the backrest, right-side up and sat on it to take stock.

Gerard started to rearrange things to something representing normality.

"That book goes on here, not on the mantelpiece," I said tetchily.

He closed the damaged book, picking up a few loose leaves that had fallen from it and placing them on top, put the book down on the table.

"There's been a fight, but I can't see enough blood for death," Gerard said, encouragingly.

"Yeah. We can stay here tonight, but it's not safe. Tomorrow we better go into Lyot and put our plans into action."

We rolled out our blankets next to the fire, which I lit, and settled down for an uneasy night.

I lay awake thinking about Guillaume, wondering what might have happened and what I might do about it. A loud bang made me jump.

Door!

I quietly picked up my sword and stood to one side of the doorway. I could hear something, or somebody, shuffling about in the large front room. I couldn't be sure if they would have seen the horses or not, tied up as they were in the small shed that served as a stable. The firelight would have alerted them though.

I stepped briskly through the doorway and held up the sword so that the red light danced along its silver length. "Who goes there?"

"No. Don't kill us! Please. I beg you. Monsieur! We've only come to fetch our things!" said a muffled, male voice

I could only just make out two human-sized bundles of rags, holding hands near the door onto the courtyard.

I could see they were holding something else, and I dimly remembered seeing a pile of unfamiliar blankets when Gerard and I had come in. For a moment, I felt unsure what to do. I took a step closer. The man revealed his face, still half covered with cloth, to me. It was an old, frightened and malnourished face.

They mustn't see us together.

"You can go. Be quick. Come back tomorrow when I will be gone."

Without an answer, the bundles of rags shuffled out into the cold night and slipped into the shadows.

When I returned to the parlour, Gerard was still snoring.

* * *

"You remember everything we've talked about?" I asked Gerard when we neared the junction where I had met Roberto, the following morning. Gerard nodded. "Let's go over it one more time."

"No Jean. I know it."

"Alright. I tell you, if Hervé has killed Guillaume or tortured him … ."

Gerard said nothing.

"I may have to kill this Hervé, you know."

"No Jean. Herleva wouldn't like that."

"Gerard? Are you with me?"

"Yes Jean. At least … I will not betray you."

"Hm. Good enough for now."

As he rode ahead of me at the junction, I called after him, "Tomorrow at the twelfth bell! In the village square!"

He turned in his saddle, nodded once and continued on until he disappeared around a corner.

I turned off the track and took a leisurely early lunch. The sun's warmth warmed me, making it pleasant, lying back on the grass munching on some slightly stale bread and a few apples I had rescued from Guillaume's pantry. Early in the afternoon, I continued, on Amabel's gently undulating back, into Lyot.

As planned, I took the best room available at the second hostel, one I had not visited before. Staying out of sight as much as possible, I nevertheless broadcast my arrival as widely as I could. Ordering the most expensive food on the limited menu, I made sure to include the price of a round for every patron in the bar. I also engaged a few idle young serfs to advertise the presence of the World's Greatest Knight.

I set one of the serfs to conspicuously polish my armour and brush down my horse outside the hostel, in plain view of Lyot's public. The other, furnished like the first with fifty obol's worth of silver coin, went from house to house, stable to stable and shop to shop, announcing in a small but strident voice the presence of the eminent Knight. Both, when asked for more information, replied that there would be a demonstration at noon the following day in Lyot's square.

Gerard, meanwhile, had taken a room at the hostel I had first visited in Lyot and made it known he was a soldier for hire from Nevers, on his way north to the War. He substantiated this by bribing, with a whole silver denier, some scoundrel into backing up his story when asked.

I retired for the night with the pleasure, not entirely without apprehension, of knowing that tomorrow I might actually be able to start moving events in my favour.

***

"Come and see the Greatest, Most Dangerous and Most Completely Skilled Knight in the World!" shouted the little voice from under a mop of blonde hair, a few minutes before noon on the following day.

I winced at the enormity of the exaggeration. I didn't think for one moment I could convince a seasoned fighter like this Hervé that I was a real knight; being a Compte, he would no doubt be a seasoned fighting man himself. All I could hope for would be an introduction and thus, just possibly, a way into his castle. From there I would have to inveigle my way into his affections by some means not yet apparent to me. In short, I would have to wing it.

The little blonde-haired serf, really no more than a child, ran up to me grinning.

"You have a good crowd Monsieur! Can I watch? I've never seen a knight fight before."

"Of course. Here's something extra for you. You've done an excellent job. Get yourself and your friends something nice to eat."

I handed a snippet of silver, cut from one of the coins. His eyes lit up, but he bit the silver to check it, nonetheless. Satisfied with its content, he held it up.

"Thank you, Monsieur, very much!"

A crowd filled the centre of the square, huddled around an area I'd had roped off to create a clear space large enough for two men to fight in. A long table with a chair had been placed along one side of the rectangle.

The man I had employed only in the last hour, walked behind me nervously and pulled his scarf across the lower half of his face and his hat down over his ears.

"Monsieur! He whispered hoarsely. I'm not sure I can go through with it. If the Compte finds out, he'll have my head!"

"Nonsense! If you succeed in making me some money, there will be two more silver denier for you."

He said nothing, all the way to the table. I, dressed in full armour including the heavy helmet, struggled to stoop under the rope and then stood facing my audience.

This is a bad idea!

Before resting the heavy helmet over the velvet cap on my head, I had taken a last look at the sky; bright blue. But ominous dark clouds were scudding in from the south west indicating rain later. Now, the beard and moustache, which I had been growing since Herleva told me to remove the eye-patch, itched inside the helmet. Sweat began to drip down my cheeks and nose.

Just don't rain during my demonstration.

The crowd jostled each other good-naturedly, but they were definitely getting impatient. I nodded once, slowly, and my man at the table cleared his throat.

"Good day to you faithful brethren! To you all, thank you for coming! What you are about to witness will astonish you! Sir Guillaume the Invincible will defy the laws of combat to prove to you that he is the Greatest Knight in the World!"

I nodded at the sound of 'Sir Guillaume,' to assert my false name. The audience, at first, shifted their feet uncertainly, but then one clapped and shouted, getting into the mood of the event, followed by a few more.

Through the narrow eye-slits, I could only see a row of three faces at a time, more if I stared at the back rows of the crowd. I tried to keep still so that I could hear what my accomplice said.

"First of all, Sir Guillaume will demonstrate his crossbow and archery skills, *all* while fully armoured!

Later I will require a fighting man from the audience to
spar with Sir Guillaume."

The audience sighed.

"Worry not, dear friends! The volunteer will not be
harmed, and he will earn two silver denier!"

Now, I heard a loud howl of excitement.

"Yes! And there will be another benefit to you all!
But more of that later! Witness now the amazing talents
of Sir Guillaume!"

I proceeded to hit bulls eye after bullseye with the
red-flighted arrows from my bow, creating a little
rosette of arrow shafts in the centre of the straw target.
Some of the audience nodded in approval, but so far,
they were not impressed.

Then I took up the crossbow. First, from thirty feet I
placed six bolts inside the rosette, two of the bolts
clanging against bolts already embedded in the straw.

I knew I had talent with any weapon that had a sight,
and the audience clapped and wolf-whistled
enthusiastically.

Then I walked off to sixty feet, well outside the
roped off area. When I turned, the audience parted like
a wake, leaving a clear corridor of air to the target. The
crowd seemed to hold their breath as I took aim. I held
my breath too as I squeezed the well-oiled trigger, and
the bolt flew straight to the centre of clustered bolts.

"Oh!" The audience collectively shouted. Now they
were impressed.

I nodded once, turned and walked on, counting my
paces until I reached roughly ninety feet from the
target. I had actually part way down one of the streets
that led out of the square.

Some of the audience laughed. Others talked
excitedly.

I turned, drew back the yew lath, or bow, of the
weapon by the string and loaded another bolt from the

small quiver around my waist. I took careful aim and then paused. A slight breeze shifted the top of some trees I had been watching to the right of the target. I waited until the branches settled again.

I took aim again, allowed for deflection and gently squeezed the trigger. The bolt flew away, and I heard a loud cheer from the audience. I could only assume I had hit the bull's eye again.

I bowed briefly, turned and walked even further away. I stopped opposite the doorway, which I knew, from an earlier check, stood exactly one hundred and twenty feet from the target.

The crowd were all shouting, but I couldn't hear their words any more. An old man, stooping in a doorway near me, shouted, "Impossible!"

I waited for a minute. The audience hushed. I could just make out the strident voice of my accomplice. I knew he would be telling them that such a shot had never been achieved before, and so he hoped they would allow that three attempts would be necessary. I could see the audience nodding enthusiastically.

He gestured for the space behind the target to be well cleared.

Right then John! This is where you earn your money!

I tried to remember all my rifle shooting training in the Air Defense Cadet Corps and my subsequent experience working with M.I.6.

Breathe evenly, watch for any breeze, aim at the top of the target … .

A little girl broke from her mother right at the front of the crowd and ran toward the target. Her mother screamed, and my accomplice raised his arm to halt the attempt. Soon the little girl stood safely back within her mother's arms, and I planted my feet firmly apart once more. I shouldered the beautifully made crossbow and took aim. I had to wait for another breeze to pass before loosing the first bolt. It sped toward the target on what looked like a good trajectory, but then the audience sighed.

Missed!

I took aim again, and this time I must have grazed the target because there were a few muted claps.

Damn. One last try. Better get this!

I breathed in deeply and thought of Rose. I said a quick prayer, took aim and gently squeezed the trigger. Just before I released the bolt, a drop of sweat fell into my eye and blinded me. But it was too late. The bolt was away! I cursed my luck, but then a huge cheer went up from the crowd and hats flew into the air.

Done it! I guess ... .

I walked uncertainly back to the arena and straight up to the target. Sure enough, the last bolt must have struck exactly in the centre, because I could see no bolt anywhere else in the straw target.

I raised my hand once to receive the accolade.

"Now friends! I need a volunteer! Do we have one?" asked the disguised man.

As prearranged, Gerard stepped forward. Two other men also stood up uncertainly, but the man at the table beckoned Gerard forward.

"Your name, Monsieur?"

"Gerard!"

"And you're a fighting man?"

"I was once a knight. I have fought in the crusades."

The crowd collectively seemed to suck in their breath.

"Good. Good. That's good. Now friends. I want to offer you a little wager. What odds do you think we should give for this man beating Sir Guillaume?"

The crowd murmured in confusion. Gambling so publicly was strictly forbidden in devoutly religious provinces. This was no exception.

"Two to one!" a single voice said.

"Evens!" another voice said

"Five to one!" said another, hopefully.

"Two to one, it is!" said the disguised man, now my betting officer.

Suddenly, the crowd rushed for the table. My betting officer disappeared under a sea of bobbing heads. Gerard walked up to me. One of the other lads I had employed brought forth my horse and the mule. From the mule Gerard took a cheap mail shirt we had bought a few days previously and put it on over his tunic. He tightened a belt, holding a sheathed dagger, around the mail. Then he hefted a choice of two long swords ostentatiously, before choosing one and then putting on mail gloves and an open-faced helmet. I put on mail gloves, took my sword and a large shield.

"You're mad!" Gerard said, leaning close to me. "Nice shooting though! I didn't think you could do it!"

"Just remember to let me win! But don't make it obvious!"

"And *you* just remember all the tricks I taught you, and then perhaps I won't have to let you win."

We went and stood facing each other in front of the table while the crowd, having placed their bets, fell back.

My first parry jarred my arm badly.

Jesus! What was that!

"Gerard! Not so serious!" I said.

"We want to make it look good?"

We skirted around each other, exchanging blows and pretending to size each other up. Of course, we had rehearsed this many times, and we executed almost every move as planned. Then Gerard suddenly threw a move on me which wasn't rehearsed.

Okay, wanna play rough, do you?

The tempo picked up dramatically, but somehow, Gerard's intense tuition all came together, and I moved up a few gears so that the fight began to look real. A few of his blows actually nicked my skin through the mail shirt, drawing blood which seeped through the links and ran down my arms.

I didn't notice, but Gerard had worked me out from the shadow of a large cottage. Suddenly, the reflected light from his shield completely blinded me. He had turned to focus the light through my helmet slits.

With one swift leap, he passed behind me and brought the flat of the sword down squarely on my back. I fell to the ground, stunned and slightly winded.

All I wanted to do was lie there and catch my breath, but this was no game. I forced the weight of my body, in full mail armour, to roll to the left. I swung the sword in a great arc blindly behind me.

"Argh!" I heard.

I dragged myself to my knees and peered through the eye slits as my breath began to return. Gerard crouched on his knees, some way, off clutching his chin. Blood seeped from between his mail glove-fingers.

With a great deal of effort, using the sword as a prop, I managed to stand up, too short of breath to speak. I waited for him to say or do something.

"Bâtard!" came from under the brim of Gerard's helmet, but he didn't sound truly angry. He raised his head, and I could at last see that the wound didn't seem too bad. I had just nicked him.

For a few moments more, we stood facing each other, getting back our breath. Then Gerard launched another ferocious attack on me. But this time I had other ideas. Remembering my combat training from M.I.6, I swung on my heels, using the sword's weight to counterbalance my own and swung out of his way as he passed under my sword arm. I continued to spin around on my heels. Faster than Gerard could react, I had completed the turn and launched myself at his back, my sword's tip aimed at his backbone.

At the very last moment, I remembered to angle the blade so that it didn't penetrate his mail. I knew then that my blood was up. Then I heard a howl echo around the square. It was mine.

Gerard went sprawling in the dirt. His long sword clattered away on the muddy grit.

"One all!" I shouted.

Much to my surprise and delight, the audience yelled and clapped.

I'm winning them over!

Gerard, though fitter, was still much older than I and becoming very tired. If he had any tricks left, he would try them now. We launched into a long exchange of flashing, clashing blows. My shield became so dented and buckled, I had to discard it. His sword, longer and more unwieldy than mine, was nonetheless wielded with great expertise, making its strikes painful and debilitating. The long sword is an impressive weapon. I began to feel that he was winning back the audience.

His blows came quicker and quicker, until the moment I had expected when he used the weight of his sword, twisting mine around and around, to try and force mine from my hands. Many times, we had practiced this, but its effectiveness still astonished me. I very nearly lost my grip on the hilt of the sword, so great was the pain in my wrists and fingers. But I held on and managed to flick his sword away at just the right moment.

With a howl of rage, I stepped toward him, under his guard. Then I astonished him by grabbing his own dagger with my left hand and holding it to his exposed neck.

"That's not fair!" he said under his breath. "It's just not done!"

"Well, I just did it!" It's a move I had thought about often over the last few days, and at last I'd had the audacity, and need, to use it.

The crowd became silent for a few moments, stunned and perhaps a little confused by the move. A roar of approval suddenly burst from a large section of the audience, only slightly marred by the 'boos' of others, who had lost money. Both were mostly men. Women and children surged toward me when I turned to accept their congratulations.

"The winner!" announced the man at the table. He began to pay out the won wagers.

"He won't like it!" Gerard said, as he took off his armour. "No Compte that I ever heard of will allow gambling within his domain. At least not without a cut for himself! Ha! Ha!"

"That's what I am counting on! Tomorrow, same time?"

"Hah! Alright Jean, but tomorrow, not so fierce please. I think you really were enjoying that!"

"No, not enjoying it. But we must be more careful next time. Sleep well Gerard!"

"I will! I have spied a nice blonde wench in the bar!"

"Ha!"

***

I, myself, did not indulge in any blonde wenches that night. I was too exhausted, even if I had felt free to indulge so. After a very large and, I must say, gastronomically adequate meal of roast lamb and thick, crusty bread, washed down with a dense, fortified red wine, I crawled onto the large straw-stuffed double bed and fell asleep instantly. I woke, sprawled across the covers, full-dressed and rather cold. Since I had no real reason to get up, I undressed to my underwear, crawled under the sheets and dosed fitfully for another two hours. The sound of howling wolves, sometimes distant and sometimes around me, seemed to inhabit most of my dreams these days. But today, the thought of the fight ahead also disturbed me. Gerard and I had been lucky the day before. Why neither of had been badly wounded or killed, I wasn't sure. It had to be down to luck.

Must be more careful this time. I can't control that violence in me once it's unlocked.

The tenth bell tolled in a small church at the end of one of the streets near the square. I rose and ordered something to break my fast. At eleven, as planned, my two assistants joined me again in my small lobby. When they signaled that the coast was clear, I walked quickly to the stable where they had already saddled my horse and laid out the armour they had brought earlier from the hostel.

"Don't worry Monsieur. Nobody has seen you," the blonde-haired boy said to me. Although they were respectfully silent while they helped me into the armour, I could tell they were both bursting to ask questions. Finally, the older boy could hold back no longer.

"Did you really fight in The Holy Lands, Monsieur? Where did you learn to fight?"

"Of course," I send ambiguously. "I learned in England." I kept one eye-half closed at all times to conceal its colour until I had my head in the great crusader helmet.

It wasn't long before I faced Gerard again in the square.

This time we were on horseback.

We were armed as on the previous day, except with maces instead of swords. On the drop of a white scarf from the betting officer we clumsily approached each other, swinging our maces wildly.

"This will never do!" Gerard had said when we had rehearsed this. "Knights don't fight with maces from horse back!"

"But the crowd will love it. It looks good!"

"Hmph!" Gerard had not agreed, but he went along with my plan, nevertheless.

My dented helmet, straightened crudely by the local blacksmith that morning, took the first of Gerard's powerful blows. A moment later, another smashing blow numbed my arm. We made several passes like this, each time one of us landing a careful aimed blow at some well-defended part of the other. Of course, we had choreographed all this but not what happened next.

Approaching each other once more, my mare Amabel suddenly became distracted by something and veered to the left, away from Gerard's horse.

"Come on Amabel! This way!" I shouted hauling the rein across her flanks with my shield hand. But she wanted none of it. My swinging mace head sailed past Gerard's mail-covered shoulder and caught in the chain of his mace. Both were entangled, and the horses were still moving at a steady pace. In the blink of an eye, and before either of us could think of letting go the maces, we were yanked from our saddles and fell with two great metallic crashes to the dirt.

"Jesu- … !" I shouted, before running out of breath.

"Merde!" came from somewhere nearby.

I wasn't sure if I had broken anything or not, but, once again, I had been winded.

A few moments later a heavy blow came down on my back.

"Wait!" I gasped, in a whisper.

"Come on. Get up. We have company!"

Through my eye-slits, all I could see was a large grey stone and some smaller one, pressed into the oozing mud. I twisted my head this way and that, but apart from some spectators' feet and flashes of grey sky, I could make little out. I pushed myself to my knees just as another blow hit the top of my helmet, almost making me bite through my tongue.

"*Gerard*!"

"It was your idea! I told you it wasn't a good one!"

At that moment, I felt so tired, I thought if I never put that helmet on again, it would be too soon. With a deep groan, I stood up and swung at Gerard's voice. I missed him.

Another blow slammed into my back and out of pure anger, I swung my mace in a long arc to my left, pivoting on my heels. I caught my opponent a glancing blow on his helmet and sent him tumbling.

Now John, you mustn't get too angry. This is just a demonstration.

"That's better" Gerard said, from under his helmet, as he slowly stood up. I could see even he was tiring.

"One last chance, Gerard!" I shouted. I waited until he straightened up and then charged him with my shield arm. The shield too can be an offensive weapon. The crusader's standard shield has a sharp point at the base and two, less sharp, at each upper corner. Shaped like a curved 'V' there were many ways you could use the shield to inflict damage on your opponent. At the last moment, I flicked the shield up, aiming the base-point at Gerard's face. He saw my move and leaned back to avoid it, but distracted, he did not see my mace come around behind him in a wide arc and crash into the back of his shoulders. He yelled with pain as the chain links bit into his flesh. I wasn't to be deflected from my goal now, though. I shoved him with the shield and a moment later, brought the mace down on his shoulder.

He fell away from me and crashed onto his back. I stood over him for one last blow. I swung back the mace and then felt it get caught by something.

"Stop!" I heard from behind me.

I tried to release my mace, but something held it firmly. I turned around and came face to face with a very large knight and to the right, the face of a large war-horse. The knight gripped my mace head in two mail gloves, while on top of the horse, sat a man in a nobleman's red and green robes.

The knight grinned at me.

A voice different from the first, spoke to me from above the horse's head.

"You are from a foreign land, are you not, knight?"

I nodded.

"I guessed so, for only such a one would not know that fighting for wagers is strictly forbidden, at least in this part of Christendom."

I said nothing.

"And I, for one, am not a Lord to allow others to make money on my land without my permission, even if it were sanctioned by the Holy Roman Church."

The voice sounded silky-smooth, and he spoke impeccable French laced with Latin words that showed his noble birth. I recognised the voice as the one that had spoken while I had been led away in the forest, after arriving through the Gate.

We stared at each other for a full minute before he spoke again. His wore his jet-black hair, cropped very short, and he had a moustache and beard, both very short, black and neat.

"Remove your helmet, Monsieur." His voice souned calm, measured, and he spoke without haste.

"Alas. I cannot!"

For just the slightest instant, anger flickered across his face, like a shadow cast by a passing storm cloud, and then he smiled.

"As you wish. As you are knight, it is your privilege to do as you wish with your armour. No doubt you have no liege-lord?"

"No."

"And yet you fight … skillfully." I didn't think 'skillfully' was the word he wished to use.

He nodded in the direction of the betting officer. "The wagers will be donated to La Bourras monastery. You have no prejudice against Cistercians, I presume?"

I could see two of his men, one of whom I thought I recognised from the day before, restraining the struggling, unmasked betting officer while a third shoveled silver coins into a leather saddle-bag.

Though he could not see my eyes, or perhaps, because he could not see them, I stared hard into the face of the man who must surely be Hervé of Donzy. It wasn't a cruel face, nor one filled with malice. In fact, it seemed quite a cultured one. I thought perhaps I could like this man.

I shook my head. "I have nothing against Cistercians."

He laughed. "You are bold, Monsieur. Good day to you." He turned his horse away.

"Wait! I am looking for the employment of a … liege-lord." My flattering choice of words seemed to halt him. He turned his horse back to face me.

"Really?"

"Yes." I wanted to convince him, but I could think of nothing more to say.

"I am not sure … ." Then he seemed to make up his mind. "But perhaps I could use you." Again, he turned his horse away. "Make yourself known at my castle when you next have a free day!" he called over his shoulder as he moved off, accompanied by his entourage.

The knight holding my mace-head released it and mounted a heavy grey, before racing after his master.

"That seemed to go well," Gerard whispered, standing next to me.

"Yes. Although I nearly killed you again."

"You really must watch that temper!"

"It's not temper."

***

I had an excuse to visit the castle three days later; I simply couldn't wait any longer. I went alone.

Approaching Donzy castle on Amabel, this time I could take in its detail at leisure.

The castle had actually been built into the side of a rocky outcrop, which I estimated rose to about the third floor at the rear of the castle. The whole thing reminded me of a man, sat for a moment to think on a convenient hillock.

I wore full armour, including the great helmet. As Amabel's iron-shot feet clattered across a wooden bridge over the moat, I shuddered at the close proximity of my former jail. And yet I found the castle keep quite impressive. Its grey stones were roughly cut at the base of the walls and only dressed further up.

A serf led my horse away and after establishing my name, a soldier led me up the wooded stairs to the keep entrance on the first floor.

There I had to wait in a large reception hall for the Compte to receive me. Since I had arrived in the late morning, this could take all day. But after being generously provided with a leg of rabbit and a glass of wine, Hervé arrived, dressed much as in the village square but wearing instead soft leather slippers on his feet.

"Ah! Sir Guillaume the Magnificent!"

I took off my mail glove and extended my hand, but he didn't take it. A soldier behind him looked nervously at me. I wasn't going to kneel.

"Still wearing that ridiculous helmet, I see? You will have to take it off if you are to feast with me."

Relenting, I removed the helmet, revealing the eye-patch, which I had put on again despite Gerard's opposition. I hoped to conceal my eye for just a little longer.

"You don't look so deformed to me!"

"Did I say I was?"

"No, but … "

He showed just a moment's awkwardness before he recovered his poise.

"Come with me to my feasting hall. We are just about to take the midday meal before hunting. I trust you will join us for the meal?"

"Err. Yes!"

Over the meal in a great chamber, which stretched nearly all of the keep's eighty feet from front to back on the second floor, he questioned me.

"I said you fought skillfully in the village just for the ears of others. Actually, I found your technique most … unique! I am certain of one thing; you have not fought in the Holy Lands."

"But … "

"Please!" he said raising his grease-soaked hand. "I have spent my whole life as a soldier. I have fought in many battles and recently in the Crusade against the Heretics in the South. I know a battle-hardened soldier when I see one. Raul here, is such a soldier."

The huge, burly, red-haired soldier, who had held my mace head in Lyot, grinned from his seat at the table opposite me. His face had many scars and many of his teeth were chipped or broken off.

"You have not a single scar."

Ah!

"So why did you invite me here then?" I asked.

Hervé sat back, made a church and steeple with his hands pressed together and studied me like a seasoned politician.

"I have use for many different types of men here, not just fighters. There are many things moving in France at the moment, political things and a man with your particular skills might be of use to me."

"What skills?" I had the almost irresistible urge to swallow.

"Self-agrandisement, showmanship, timing and a little, shall we say, theatrical creativity?"

He means deception!

"You will stay with me for a while and train with my men. Later, I will decide if I have use for you. Of course, your stay will be at my expense. Is that agreeable to you?"

I nodded. He glanced at my eye-patch for just an instant, stood, bowed out of politeness and then left for the hunt with his men. A servant led me to my quarters, a cramped turret room on the floor above, and left me. Through the arrow loops, which gave the only light into the room, I could just make out the river to the south and the patch of dirty green below me on the other side of the ditch that I had called a moat while escaping.

There is little of interest to tell regarding the next few months in Donzy Castle keep.

After some days I suggested to Hervé that the man I had fought in Lyot might also be a useful addition to his small army. I mentioned, of course, that Gerard had truly fought in the Holy Wars and had the mark of the Templars on his arm to prove it. Hervé's curiosity overcame him, and he sent a man to find Gerard. After he arrived, ensconced, as he was, in the main barracks room with the poorest of soldiers, I found few chances to meet with Gerard, but occasionally we would make whispered observations on the activities in the keep. On one such occasion, Gerard corrected a misconception of mine.

"I must say, Hervé doesn't seem as powerful as Herleva made me believe," I commented. "He has only a small retinue of men!" I said.

"Ha! This isn't his main castle! That's at Nevers. Didn't you know? He has become Compte de Nevers!"

"Oh!"

"This is the family home town, so I guess that's why he spends so much time here. Make no mistake though. He is very powerful and I've heard that he has ambitions to be King of France!"

"Ah! That doesn't surprise me. He seems very politically astute. I have to go. Have you heard anything at all about Guillaume?"

"Your friend in the dungeon?"

"Yes. If he wasn't thrown in the oubliette, there is a chance he's still alive."

"I've been able to find out nothing."

"Me neither."

The arrival of Gerard seemed to be the trigger for Hervé to test me. He organised an armed contest between myself and Raul in the courtyard.

It would be fought with swords and shields only, a classic knight's combat.

I swapped my crusader helmet for an open-faced one with a nose guard; Raul was a big man, but he moved fast, and I needed to see everything.

"He's just a clumsy oaf," Gerard suggested. "Remember all I taught you and some of those dirty tricks you think up yourself. Then you can beat him."

"Come on, Gerard! This man is a seasoned warrior and a giant!"

"You told me you'd fought in a war?"

"True."

"And then there is that temper of yours. Use it!"

"I keep telling you, it's not temper!"

"Well, whatever it is, use it."

Raul and I squared off against each other in a rectangle marked off by four poles. Hervé sat on a chair raised on a dais at one end of the rectangle. His master-of-arms, an old, bald man with a salt and pepper beard and brawny, tattooed arms, stood by his side.

This really is not going to be pretty!

I had no doubt at all that Raul had the better technique. Hervé probably thought the same, but he had hinted several times that he was most interested in my intellect and wit.

Raul grinned at me. "Ah!" he yelled, lunging forward with his sword aimed straight at my neck. I parried the blow just in time, his great sword clanging off the metal of my shield and sending sparks flying.

I circled him, beginning my strategy of trying to tire him. If he didn't tire, he would grow frustrated and angry, and then he might make a mistake. I sprang forward, aiming the point of my shield at his chest, but at the last moment I spun round on my heels, bringing the sword round in a wide arc to make contact with his helmet. It met with empty air, and I almost fell over. There were hoots of laughter from the audience.

"English fool!" said one voice.

"All flash and no fight!" another said.

"Told you!" a third said.

When I looked for Raul, he stood about two paces further away than I had expected. I pulled off my helmet and threw it away.

There was a hushed silence from the audience. My gesture would be considered most dangerous. It could only mean one thing; that I meant to fight to the death.

Their respectful silence acknowledged this. Raul no longer grinned. We circled each other again, and then he swung a blow with terrific force against my shield, forcing it against my chest and almost knocking me over. Before I could recover my balance, he had swung from the other direction and caught me under my arm. I felt the bite of the chain rings in my flesh and yelled in agony.

Through blurred vision I saw his arm raise for another blow, but I charged into his knees, knocking him over. Surprised, he lay struggling for a moment while I tried to catch my breath and regain my sight. Feigning incapacity, I continued to stoop, breathing in great gulps of air until I heard Raul's steel shod toes on the flag stones.

"Aaaah!" he yelled, his voice close to my ears, but I jumped to my right, away from him. He passed by me, off balance. I turned about and saw my opportunity.

Raul will expect this now and will either jump to the right, keep moving, or if he is really clever, jump to the left, under my guard. To the left, I think.

Gripping my sword rather like a dagger, I held it at right angles to my fully outstretched arm and hooked it around his body, just after he had stepped to the left. I pulled the sword back toward me and drew the blade across the face of his helmet.

"Aaaah!" There was a great yell, rising to a crescendo from Raul. He clutched at his face.

"Raul!" shouted the weapons master. "Do you want to concede?"

The great head of red hair shook slowly from side to side, and then he turned to face me.

A great gash, oozing dark blood, ran straight across the bridge of his nose and his left cheek. It looked to be down to the bone of his cheek. I shook my head to indicate that he should stop, but again he grinned, showing his set of poorly kept teeth.

"Fight, Angleterre! It's just a scratch."

"Alright, you big bastard! If that's what you want. But I don't want to kill you!" I was bluffing.

Enraged, he took off his shield slowly and with both hands raised his great sword above his head. He walked toward me raining arm-numbing blow after blows down on my shield until it had been completely beaten out of shape and become useless. I didn't even manage to land one blow. I felt a growing anger, and then that cold, killer instinct cut in.

I will kill him!

Another voice cut in.

No. Remember to control it!

With one last bellow of animal lust for victory, Raul swung a blow that would have removed my head cleanly if I hadn't ducked in time. The blow caught my shoulder sending me spinning around so that I ended up swaying, both feet far apart, facing away from my assailant.

I heard gasps from the audience but knew not what for.

Then I felt it. As I had many times before. I sensed the presence of evil, and I knew exactly what Raul thought.

I felt as if a voice inside me instructed me; right leg lift, jump to the left, stay on your left leg, sword behind me to the right and lunge!

"Uh!" This time, Raul sounded resigned and in great pain.

Immediately after my lunge, I had spun around on the ball of my left foot and planted my right foot, ready for another strike, but I had no need. Blood dropped on the grey flag stones from Raul's right leg. The thrust had gone up under the lower hem of his knee-length mail coat and sliced his thigh along the bone.

There were cries of astonishment and glee from the men watching us. Moments later, they all started clapping o banging their shields with their swords.

"Guillaume! Guillaume!" they shouted, but I noticed they left off 'the Magnificent.'

The weapons master whispered something to Raul, but the Compte silenced him with a raised hand and stepped down from the dais.

He came up to me and said so loudly that all could hear, "My weapons master tells me, that move is not in any of the books he has read! No, that's not quite true; he says it's not within any rules he has read! Ha! But to me that matters not! In war, any move that disables the enemy is the right one. You are not a conventional fighter Guillaume, if that is your real name, but you have a rare and strange talent." He gave me a curious glance that no other could see. "This is a rare victory. You are the first to beat Raul in a straight contest since I have known him and that is since we were boys. The glory is all yours."

The crowd of men erupted with admiring applause. Even Raul stood up in pain and shook my hand. He nodded once, avoiding my glance, before moving away.

"How did you do that?" Hervé said into my ear. "Later, you must tell me. I have never seen anything like it!"

But when I looked into his eyes, I could see more than the curiosity of a soldier there.

The Compte leaned in close and, with one quick, unexpected movement, pulled off my eye-patch.

He wasn't pleased to see my brown eye, which didn't match my blue eye, and left the courtyard without saying a word.

For a while after this I did not see him so much. I heard suspicious whispers behind my back although the hospitality of the keep still extended fully to me.

As spring bloomed into a warm early summer, life continued agreeably enough in the castle. When I wasn't invited to banquets, more often than not as time went on, meals were brought to me in my room. There, even on the coldest nights in late winter, a small fire kept me warm enough. I often reflected that I was lucky to live in such luxurious accommodation. And yet fear for Rose gnawed at my very soul, night and day. Finally, my patience wore out. I was on the verge of giving up on my plan and suggesting to Gerard that we should leave.

Then, one evening in June a serf collected me for my first banquet in weeks. I was able to purchase fine clothes with Herleva's silver. The clothes were all purchased for me or manufactured by castle staff. I must say I felt that I looked presentable as I entered the large hall on the second floor once more. I wore a red velvet tunic over yellow breaches and leather slippers over long white socks, laced to the knees with leather thongs in the currently fashionable style.

Minstrels played a light-hearted dance in the gallery suspended above one side of the banqueting hall, just under the rows of heavy oak roof beams.

For the first time since my arrival, brightly dressed women were to be seen dancing with men. Mathilde, Hervé's wife, dressed in a long green gown embroidered with gold thread, entered the room on the end of his arm. Quite a pretty woman, she had dark hair and looked to be in her mid-twenties. I knew immediately that this must be a very special banquet.

Hervé extended his hand warmly to greet me near one of the large stained-glass windows at the south end of the hall, furthest from his own table. He had left

Mathilde for a moment. A wolf-hound tugged impatiently on the leash, handed to him by the recovering Raul.

"Ah. Guillaume! I have good news for you!"

"You do?"

"Yes. The great tides of politics are moving Guillaume. And there is a possibility they might move in my favour. John Lackland of Angleterre is set to move against Phillip of France and in one month, King John will be at Paris. He will be joined by Emperor Otto of Allemagne."

He put his arm around my shoulder and wheeled me away from curious faces.

"I see."

"We will leave in two weeks to join John's army. We will draw Phillip south while Ferrand of Flanders will attack Paris from the North. Then I will take my army on to Paris! And you will join me! What do you think?"

I felt faint and wanted to sit down, but I swallowed and found an answer that sounded appropriate:

"It will be … a great honour, my liege-lord!"

"Good! Good!" He slapped me heartily on my back twice. "Now come and meet my good wife, Mathilde."

My face probably turned white as a sheet when he introduced me to his pretty wife, but she was good enough to smile and ignore my blanched look. She held forward a pretty, bejeweled hand, and I bowed to kiss it delicately.

"My Lady."

She said something in old English, but I couldn't pick out more than a few words. I must have looked confused because she switched to Latin.

"An English gentleman! I didn't think they crossed the water these days!"

Her Latin was flawless.

"We travel far and wide in pursuit of beauty My Lady!"

"Ha! Ha! Did you hear that, dearest? What a sweet-tongued man he is!"

"Yes, charm is one of his many talents dear." Hervé looked at me suspiciously.

A little girl of about ten peeped out from behind her mother's green dress. Her eyes were open wide as she stared intently at me.

"Ah! Meet my daughter. Agnès, this is Sir Guillaume. Sir Guiliaume, this is Agnès."

My mind reeled. His voice seemed very far away. Automatically, I knelt down, and the little girl extended her tiny hand, courteously. I kissed it. A green dress sleeve, exactly the miniature of her mother's, adorned her arm. Her mouth open, the little girl stepped out from behind her mother and stood boldly in front of me.

"Guillaume the Magnificent?" Her tiny voice sounded like ice in a crystal glass.

"The very same!" I answered before Hervé could say anything.

"Come and see my painting," she said, suddenly recovering her poise.

Only too glad to escape, I followed her meekly toward the other end of the hall.

War! War! No! And I tried so hard to avoid it!

From underneath a green bonnet, a miniature of her mother's, I could see a few wisps of baby-soft blonde hair. She instantly reminded of Elayne in Grestain, and I felt a pang of longing for Herleva.

The little girl led me deftly through the swirling skirts and burly arms holding flagons of ale or wine. Considerations of class forbid her from holding my hand, but occasionally she would reach out, as if grabbing the air in front of me might lead me the right way. At the end of the hall she stopped, facing the base of one of the walls.

"Look!" she said pointing.

Most of the white, plastered walls were covered in paintings of hunting scenes, but here, at a child's height, the nativity scene had been painted. Although the figures were quite crudely drawn, the choice of bright colours showed some talent in design.

"Very good!" I said honestly. I knelt so that our two heads were inches apart. I pointed to the different figures, asking Agnès to identify them; the Virgin Mary, Joseph and the Three Kings. But when I pointed to the figure in the manger, she lost patience.

"Silly man. You must know who that is!"

"Jesus!"

"Yes." She turned and smiled at me. She looked so innocent that I wanted to pick her up and cuddle her. She reminded me how alone I really was. She also reminded in some ways of Annie, and this brought a tear to my eye.

"I would normally be afraid of a man like you."

"You would? Why?"

"Your eye-patch! You could be a Barbary pirate! But my maidservant Joan said she had heard that you are the greatest knight in the World! Is it true?"

"Um! I might be. It's difficult to know, because I haven't fought all the other knights yet!"

She leaned close, conspiratorially, and her little hand brushed against mine. The touch seemed not to bother her. "And some say," she whispered. "That you have magic powers too."

"Ah. Now *that* isn't true."

"Oh." She sounded very disappointed. "But Joan said…?"

"Agnès dear. It's time for you to retire, I think," Mathilde said, from behind us. I didn't think she had been close enough to hear our conversation. Agnès straightened up and answered brightly, "Yes mother. Good bye Sir Guillaume. Good night mother."

A maid stepped forward, took Agnès' hand and led her out of the hall.

"She wanted so much to meet you," Mathilde said. "There is little enough to occupy a child's interest in these parts." There seemed a great sadness in this woman. Though she had an almost regal manner, she had warmth too. In her eyes, I saw just the hint of flirtation when our glances intersected for a moment.

As soon as I could get away, I went to my room to lay on my straw bed. I knew even a great deal of drink could not quell the terrible thoughts of war.

"I have to do this for Rose," I told myself, over and over again, but it was hard to be convinced.

***

The very next day, workmen began to dig foundations for an outer wall beyond the ditch. I watched them working from my narrow, arrow loop window. Wagons began to leave, carrying supplies ahead of the army.

Training immediately intensified in the courtyards of the castle. I persuaded the Compte that Gerard would make a good companion for myself in battle, so we began to spend more time together. Hervé was often away in Nevers, but he had left orders that we should start to join his men in their forays around his territory. These trips were usually for the purposes of collecting taxes or tithes, but sometimes they were simply to harass peasants. This duty even extended to the extreme of burning down cottages of disobedient tenants, a duty I endured for the sake of my main mission alone.

"You don't like it Monsieur Jean. But it's the way of these times!" Gerard shouted to me, while setting a burning torch among the thatch of a cottage. "I've done worse in the past!"

A few times we visited the border of the Compte's land to engage with knights of rival barons, but apart from one minor skirmish, these resulted in sabre rattling displays of arms.

Two days before we were due to leave for Flanders, I finally found a way to get information about Guillaume.

"Hey you, boy. Come here!"

Gerard and I had stepped out of one of the Compte's last feasts to discuss the journey north and the possible battle. As we talked, I noticed two or three boys dressed in rags, carrying sacks of vegetables up from the stairs that led to the undercroft; the ground floor where stores were kept. When the tallest boy passed me for the third time, I smiled at him. He looked away but on his fourth trip he glanced nervously at me. That's when I called out to him.

"Monsieur?" he replied.

I took a silver clipping, a quarter denier, from my pouch and held it between my finger and thumb. He eyed it eagerly.

"I would like some information for this."

"Monsieur?"

"Do you have access to the dungeon?"

He glanced nervously up and down the corridor. "We don't go there often, but I can if I wish."

"Good. What's your name?"

"I don't have a name, Monsieur."

"Well, what do the other boys call you?"

"Rathead."

"Rathead. I see. Hm. Well anyway, a woman came to me the other day in Donzy market." I thought fast and made it up. "She said her cousin had been taken away by the Compte's men, but she didn't know where they had taken him." I waited for his reaction.

He nodded that he understood so far.

"I wonder if you could find out for me whether he's here or in the dungeon of Nevers Castle."

"Why don't you ask the Compte?" he asked, suspiciously.

"I will … if I get the chance, but he's a busy man, and we are going away to the Flanders War in two days. All I want to know is whether this man is well."

He thought for a moment. Then he glanced at the silver in my hand. "Alright! What's his name?"

"Guillaume. He's an old man and not much danger to anyone. Just one thing though."

"Yes?"

"Do you know the oubliette, the cell underneath the main cell?"

"Oh yes!" He laughed. "How do you know about that?"

"Ah! Somebody told me."

"What about it?"

"Well, it's possible he's in there. Can you still find out about him?"

"It will be harder … ."

"Alright. Well, another half a denier if he is in there and you can tell me." I told him which rooms Gerard and I were staying in case he found himself unable to get to my room from the kitchens.

"You can come to me … or Gerard any time, day or night, with the information. We haven't much time though."

"Don't worry, Monsieur. It won't take me long."

I gave him the silver, and he sped off.

"Probably spend it on a whore … or gambling … ." whispered Gerard.

"What, at his age?"

"Yes. They live like rats, the servants' runts, in this castle. Most of them don't even know who their parents are. Life's hard for them, and they will take anything they can get … when they can get it."

"Well, it's the only chance we have."

***

We didn't hear from Rathead that first night and by the second, our last in Donzy, I believed my silver had gone for nothing.

A loud rap on my door in the middle of the nigh came as a welcome relief, because I couldn't sleep.

"Monsieur Je- … . I mean Guillaume! It's me, Gerard!"

"Wait!" I dragged my tunic around my waist and unlatched the door. Gerard waited until I had shut it before speaking.

"The boy, Rathead, came to me. He's located your friend. Good news. He's not in the oubliette after all!"

"Thank God. And he's alright?"

"Well he's alive! Don't be too greedy Jean. That's enough, surely."

"Yes! Gerard. I must see the boy again. I've something he can do while we are away."

"That will be difficult … . But we can try. Jean … . I need to talk to you."

"Go on … ."

"This war … ! Surely there's another way, Monsieur? Why do we have to get involved?"

"Yes, I know. I've racked my brains to think of another way! Have you even heard Hervé talking about a time portal, one of the Gates?"

"No."

"Exactly. We have to gain his trust. Or at least I do. There seems now to be only one way I can do that. I *have* to go to war with him. Believe me, it's the last thing I want to do! But it's the last thing an enemy would do, fight for him. To him, it will be proof of our loyalty. If it weren't for Rose … my wife, I wouldn't even contemplate such a thing! War! I have been in one myself Gerard. It is a terrible thing! In our war, millions died."

Gerard began to pace up and down. The timbre of his voice raised. "I don't understand such things Jean; all wars are bad. But I have heard news … news of the war. They say that John Lackland is in trouble and fleeing south!" Now I could see that Gerard was angry. "This could go very badly, very, very badly, and we will find ourselves on the losing side! We won't survive *that*! Think man. There must be another way!"

I stood up. "I can't think of it! I tried, but there seems to be nothing!" We stood facing each other, and the air seemed to burn and frizzle between us. Then, just as suddenly as it came, the anger left.

"Monsieur Jean. I'll go with you. Don't fear. We will go together," Gerard said calmly.

"If we had a small army, we could try and attack the castle with the Gate while Hervé's armies are away. It's in Aunay. Herleva told me. But we don't have an army, Gerard! Perhaps, if I didn't have … have these eyes! Then I could find a way in. But the moment I left here or any of Hervé's men found a man with blue and brown eyes trying to get near a Gate, there would be trouble. Hervé has powerful allies, Gerard, more powerful and more evil than you can know! They are watching for me! And his men are watching for a sorcerer. It's my fault!"

Gerard put his arm around me. "No Jean. It's not. Now let's go and find the boy, Rathead!"

"Anyway, I have to befriend Hervé, or else I'll be letting Herleva down. And she has helped so much … . Without her I wouldn't stand any chance at all of finding my wife again. Alive, anyway!"

We found one of the other boys, running errands from the kitchen, which rarely ceased activity completely.

"Can you fetch Rathead for us?" I asked. I gave him a few obols, and within minutes, Rathead stood in front of us, bleary eyed.

"Sorry to disturb your sleep sir!" I said humorously.

"That's alright!" he said, grinning.

"You did well, getting the information. Here's your payment. Now, would you like to earn three silver denier?"

His eyes nearly popped out of his head, and his mouth fell open. But he recovered his wits quickly.

"Yes!"

"We leave today, and we may not be back for two months. In fact, we may not be back at all, but for as long as you can, I want you to help Guillaume in his cell. Do you think you can find a way to get some proper food to him? Clean water? Or even a little wine, once in a while?"

"I don't know Monsieur. Perhaps. It will be dangerous."

"Yes, I know. Here's three denier for the food and wine and three for you. When that runs out, I want you to find a man near the river, this side of Lyot. His name is Landric, and he owns a mill. He'll be easy to find. Tell him where Guillaume is, and Landric will give you more money. Do you understand all that?"

"Yes Monsieur. Keep getting food to Guillaume … and wine and find Landric in Lyot, at the mill by the river when the money runs out!"

"Good. If you tell anybody else about this, and something bad happens to Guillaume, things will go badly for you when I return!"

"Don't worry Monsieur. That won't happen!"

"Good. Fare well then Rathead. See you when we return!" I ruffled his greasy hair.

"I wish I could come with you as your squire Monsieur. I can handle a horse, and I can rig him too!"

"Well, we'll see! If you do well while we're away, I might take you on as my squire, yes?"

"Do you mean it, *Monsieur*?"

"Yes."

"I won't fail you. Fare well, Monsieur Guillaume!" He saluted me, and I returned it.

"Probably a waste of money!" muttered Gerard, as Rathead disappeared.

That night, my last in Donzy Castle, would be a restless one. Only toward dawn did I manage to sleep a little, fitfully. Twice I awoke from dreams. The first continued a dream I had first had in Paris soon after I had met Georgina, in fact shortly after I *thought* she had died. There again, I saw the robed and hooded monk walking across an inner courtyard of a marble building. Again, I watched it all in slow motion; his sandaled feet making no sound on the marble. Again, he reached the step down to the path and raised his hands to his hood. He pulled back the hood slightly with his hand, upon which he wore that ring that shone so astonishingly brightly, and I saw the long, slightly hooked nose of an old man. This time I stayed in the dream just long enough for him to look at me directly before looking away. His eyes were hypnotically intense, and I felt myself losing my balance. I started to fall. But just before I jerked awake, clinging to the bed, I saw him drop a half sheaf of parchment, and I recognised it; that torn half of the parchment page I had wanted to see in the British Museum. At last I knew with certainty the identity of the monk. It wasn't my grandfather as I had so many times conjectured. It was Bernard of Clairvaux! As I lay awake I felt uplifted by this thought.

My second dream, however, was not so pleasant. I can't remember anything much other than an uneasy dread. I was wrenched awake by the fear of a voice I hadn't heard since getting trapped in the Highgate Cemetery tomb as a child. It was that voice whispering like a bear. It said, "I am waiting for you. I will be waiting in the Tower."

***

"If I could remember my history Gerard, I might know how this war ends. Then I might know whether you and I survive or not!"

"Huh?"

"Never mind!"

We were on horseback, traveling north in Hervé's retinue, late in the afternoon of the first day's march. Four hundred more men had swelled our ranks from the castle in Nevers so that we were now five hundred strong. Two-thirds of these were infantrymen. We rode near the head of the column, a few ranks back from Hervé.

"Full moon, Monsieur," whispered Gerard. Immediately after the contest in the courtyard, Gerard had called me Monsieur for the first time and now refused to call me anything else. "Be careful," he added.

It was the 23rd June.

"Don't worry, Gerard. So where are we going? You normally have a good ear to the ground."

"Northeast, Monsieur, to join the Emperor Otto. But rumour has it he is taking a wife and has stopped off for feasting and revelry!"

"You and your gossip Gerard!"

More bad news came to us that evening while I dined as a guest at Hervé's table in a large marquee.

Sitting to his immediate left, I heard the whispers of a man who came in and leaned close to Hervé's ear.

"Compte, I have news of the Chevalier Lamoinson. It's not good. I am sorry, but he has aligned himself with Phillip. He refuses to join your army although he will not ride north to join Phillip either, yet."

Hervé wasn't placated by the last bit of information and threw his knife so that it stuck, prong-first into the wood, shuddering with the impact.

"Mon Dieu! Must all go ill for us! I will kill the miserable … ." Then, remembering his present company, Hervé seemed to gather himself. "I will pray and seek the guidance of our Lord the Saviour! Thank you." The man left.

The Chevalier Lamoinson's small keep had been where we had planned to stop off the next day for supplies. His territory lay to the northeast of Hervé's. Raul, sitting opposite me, his face bandaged and still suffering pain in his leg, stared at my beard and moustache. He seemed to be trying very hard to remember something. I still wore the patch, if only to make me look even more different from when I first arrived in the woods near Donzy.

At the end of the meal, the guests handed round a great pewter jug. I noticed only about a dozen of the fifty or so men sitting at the table drank from the neck of the jug. I was curious.

Hervé drank first, and then the jug passed around anti-clockwise until it reached me, last. Now my position at the table made more sense to me.

I raised the jug with both hands and drained a little of the liquid. It tasted of iron; bitter.

Fresh Blood!

Raul had been one of those who drank. I glanced at him and then Hervé. Both looked at me with eager curiosity. I almost put the jug down but impulsively took a few gulps of the thick, warm liquid.

Why not? I am curious to try running with a pack but this time, with myself being more in control.

I did not admit to myself that the impulse had been born of a strange kind of desire, irresistible and profound.

Shortly after, I went to my bed in the tent, where I found Gerard snoring. His head lay in the entrance, to catch the occasional breeze. It was now very warm, even at night. I patted Amabel's muzzle and stepped over his head.

It suddenly occurred to me that I had become close to Gerard.

Perhaps he will be the one to die because of me? I really hope not, but what can I do now? He wouldn't leave me if I asked!

I dismissed the thought and turned to my horse.

"Soon, Amabel. You and I will see battle. It will be too soon, I fear!" The white flanks of my horse shivered, and she tossed her head once.

I remember lying awake late into the dark hours, waiting for some great change to take place in my body, but I must have fallen asleep.

My first sight in my wolf-state was of the lead wolf squeezing through a well-worn gap in the hawthorn entanglement of a hedgerow. I followed, along with others of my kind, and we sped across an open plain toward I knew not what.

One of those just behind the leader had a bad gash across his face and rear, right leg.

It could be Raul.

The thought was crude, half-formed and lasted only an instant.

We ran and ran for what seemed like hours. I felt like never before; like being part of a song, a symphony even. Everything seemed in tune; my body, my mind and the world around me. Almost, we seemed joined so that I could not tell where I ended and the world began. Panting for air and on the limit of my endurance, I could not have been happier.

The leader, a great black beast with shining yellow eyes, halted, so we drew around him. He cast a glance over his shoulder to a dim, yellowish glow in the distance.

A man pack!

"We attack!" the leader howled to the full moon.

We sped off toward the glowing, yellowish light, but I felt disquiet in *my* heart. *Murder* burned in the hearts of the others, and I felt doubt. I ran after them, but I wanted to stop. We reached the stone walls of the keep and through a gate that had been left ajar in the outer wall. Creeping low, on all fours, we passed across the courtyard to an inner portcullis.

A man challenged us, but the others brought him down, tearing out his throat. Still I held back, but I felt the bloodlust in me rising. I knew before long I would be unable to resist.

The leader tried to force his way under the portcullis. Two others simultaneously tried gaps to both sides, but the great weight would not lift.

Furious, the pack-leader leaped onto the first story roof of a stable and ran along its crest until he reached a gap of fifteen feet or so to the keep's own wall. With a mighty leap he reached the second storey roof of a building that ran out from the keep itself. We followed onto the first storey roof and then the second, where I could see, for the first time, a large shuttered window. The shutters were wide open.

How was this known?

The thought was vague in my mind, with no subject or object. Nevertheless, I was aware of my own thoughts and that my thoughts were not like theirs.

They are going to kill Lamoinson.

I still had a choice, but the bloodlust had almost overpowered me. I felt torn.

"Be careful," I heard a voice say inside me.

"Beware!" said another, feminine, voice of one I loved.

I turned aside and sped from the keep, crossing fields and not looking back. The pain of departure felt like that of leaving a lover. I felt as if part of me had been lost.

I woke sweating in the marquee, naked. Dawn had broken, and Gerard had gone to eat.

***

As we rode north, we were supplied by the wagons at intervals, but we took from the land and peasants when we had to. Hervé became increasingly agitated.

The general plan of battle, brokered by King John of England, was that John would draw Phillip's forces south from Paris by generally harassing his property while moving north and threatening war. As soon as Phillip went south, Ferrand, Duke of Flanders, aided by Otto and other allies including Hervé's, would attack from the north.

First, the news came that Otto was too far behind to meet up with us if we were to attack Paris from the north in the last week of July when John should have engaged Phillip.

Then, on the 5th July we learned that John, threatened by Phillip, had turned and fled to the south.

Hervé was enraged.

At supper that night, he paced up and down cursing John Lackland's cowardice and inconstancy.

"He had promised his daughter to John's son, you know," whispered a knight to my left called Jospin.

I thought of little Agnès and shuddered.

Well at least Hervé won't be murdering John Lackland!

Lamoinson had not been mentioned since that night at his keep. I had several times reflected that although I wasn't counting at the time, the number of animals in the wolf pack had seemed about the same as the number of Hervé's men who drank from the jug of blood. Looking around the marquee, I knew now who these men were and *what* they truly were.

The second thing that went wrong was that Phillip, having scared off John, returned north toward Paris. Nevertheless, Otto determined to press on and join up with Ferrand in Flanders.

Gerard told me that Otto's forces were so great that he felt he could take Paris and therefore France, by himself, if necessary

We passed east of Paris, and on 12th July we finally met up with the forces of the former Emperor Otto at a town called Nivelles in Flanders. There were many English mercenaries, led by William, Earl of Salisbury and John's half-brother. Altogether it constituted a huge army, and this cheered Hervé for a while. We enjoyed much feasting and mock-fighting, both very affective in raising morale, as we moved north.

Hervé himself, however, now had grave doubts about the whole campaign, but he felt indebted to the former Emperor and unable to withdraw.

"We're going to be slaughtered!" I shouted to Gerard, one day.

"Yes, Monsieur" he answered simply.

We both felt glum as we continued northwards.

The heat at midday grew almost unbearable, and many knights rode without armour – reckless, I thought.

***

Just before we reached Valenciennes on 25th July, a spy for Otto rode into the camp with news that Phillip had gone north, reaching Tournai, in a bid to confront the Flemish forces who he thought before him.

By now all thoughts of a coordinated attack against Paris were forgotten. Otto's single aim had been determined; to head for Tournai as fast as possible and engage Phillip's army. With twenty-five miles to cover, we left Valenciennes early on the morning of the 26th and marched until dusk. Otto and all his Generals, most of them Dukes or Counts, sent out spies in every direction to try and keep track of Phillip's army.

Seeing the small church at a village called Saint Amand in the early evening, Otto ordered a halt. In small groups, all the knights, some of the sergeants and some of the more religious foot soldiers filed through the church to pray.

"This will be your last chance, Jean," Gerard said, taking his place in the line. I joined him. With nearly 25,000 men including 3000 knights and 3000 sergeants, the queue would take all night to file through the church. As senior knights – Gerard by association with myself – we were lucky to visit before the evening meal.

There was a sombre mood in the marquee at supper. A very tall knight, whose niello armour he had covered with a black cape, stood silently near the flap of the tent. He had joined us only two days before. I had seen him speaking with Hervé several times but hadn't been introduced. As I left the tent, our eyes met for a moment. I saw something in his stare that I recognised and found disturbing at the same time.

As soon as men had visited the church and eaten, mostly in silence, they began purposefully polishing their armour and weapons.

"What's going on?" I asked Gerard. "Is there any point polishing armour for battle?"

He didn't answer me but ran a whetstone down the length of his long sword.

As dark descended, the clamour became incredibly loud. I could only guess that this must be some kind of mental state these soldiers liked to get into before battle. When I caught Gerard's eye, I saw a grimness there which told me battle was imminent.

Such a mood of intent focus wasn't mine though. My mind raced, thinking about the battle ahead and many other things which bothered me.

The date of 1214 still unsettled me. I grew certain that the date was significant in some way, but though I racked my memory, I couldn't recall what that significance was.

Something else, almost intangible, tugged at the corner of my mind. A collection of tiny details seemed out of place.

This thought had been growing for a while. Before that, it had been a feeling that I hadn't acknowledged. It started in the keep at Donzy. Several times, I had that feeling of a malevolent presence, but I put it down at the time to my growing dread of the battle.

I felt it again but much more strongly when I looked into the eyes of the leader during the attack on Lamoinson's keep. I had assumed Hervé was the human form of that great black beast with yellow eyes and from that moment, I was sure that from Hervé himself originated that feeling of malevolence.

But a little incident on the evening of the 23rd July had jarred this picture.

Sitting in the marquee at supper on that night of a full moon, I had fully expected the pewter jug to be handed around, and I wasn't disappointed. However, none sipped from it, not even Hervé. I, of course, forwent that indulgence too. Battle was too close, it seemed.

The knight with the dark cape had joined us that day and stood apart from the rest of us in the tent. He remained silent, but I hadn't yet caught his eye. As often happens when one's mind is busy, while the knight stooped to talk to Hervé, my thoughts turned to something distant and almost irrelevant. I wondered why the Gates were always open on the same day each year. Surely if they occurred naturally and had been around for many millennia, this shouldn't be so; the Gregorian calendar, an invention of man, has been shifted around several times. Dates should no longer coincide. Surely, somebody at some time had organised them. But who could do this? The thought puzzled me.

At that moment, I felt suddenly overwhelmed by the awareness of great evil close by. I knew this feeling well. I looked for its source and felt certain it came from the strange knight.

Now, as I sorted through all these strangely disparate thoughts, I became certain that the look in the eye of the strange knight was the same as that in the eye of the leader during the attack on Lamoinson's keep. Perhaps Hervé wasn't the leader of the wolves after all. But if that was the case, this other must surely be more senior than Hervé in some way. Who was he?

All my thoughts seemed turned on their heads. Something was going on here which I didn't understand.

"Gerard? Who is that knight in the niello armour, who talks to Hervé all the time," I asked just before we lay down that night.

"Ah! Him. Yes, I wondered the same thing. Won't talk to anyone you know, Monsieur!"

Suddenly, I realised that this had been the first time Gerard had spoken all evening. I wanted to laugh and tell him, but the air felt thick as lead.

***

When we rode off the following morning, I looked back down the columns; it was an astonishing sight. The morning sun glinted off armour and weapons so that they sparkled like thousands of stars following behind us. Shadows and highlights glanced off trees as the soldiers walked. The glints blinded me when they passed across my face.

I had been told I would serve with the cavalry. My horsemanship, under the keen but suspicious eye of the weapons master, had improved until I could steer Amabel in any situation and with any weapon, using just my knees.

The thought of being slightly safer on horseback brought me no comfort, however. I had an absolute dread of the battle. While I had lived through WWII, the thought of a bullet was, to me, far less chilling than the thought of a half hacked-off limb. The barbarity of these times was a horror I had never imagined I would face.

"We are to fight in Otto's cavalry, Gerard."

"Very good, Monsieur."

"God, Gerard! You sound so calm! Aren't you worried at all?"

"What's the point? I'm ready, Monsieur."

***

We were only nine miles from Tournai on the 27th when one of the spies returned, galloping in to the camp at a furious pace. A dust cloud went up where he braked his horse. Minutes later, word came down the line that Phillip's army had retreated east from Tournai.

"Probably so as not to be cut off by us," speculated Gerard, half to himself.

We immediately swung east and moved as fast as we could go. The wagons containing wives and lovers were sent south with many a tear and long kiss goodbye. Battle drew very close.

"It will be this day, Monsieur," Gerard muttered, sniffing the air.

More word came down the lines as other riders rode in; Phillip's army stretched for miles this side of a bridge over the river Marq.

Otto and Ferrand now sent riders out ahead of us and late that morning the first reports came back that they had engaged the rearguard of the French King's forces.

"This is it!" Gerard said.

"But it's Sunday!" I protested.

Gerard shook his head. "This is war."

All at once, everyone talked to everyone else. Orders were being issued and messages were being sent up and down the lines.

All the knights were summoned to a field where we formed a circle around Ferrand, William of Salisbury and Otto. An argument was in progress when I arrived. Renaud, formerly Compte of Boulogne and liaison between Otto and King John, was speaking. By his arm movements I could see he was clearly heated-up about something.

" … would not be very honourable to wage battle on such a solemn day and to sully this day with death and the spilling of blood!"

Otto replied, "Renauld is right. If we fight on such a day, I can never boast a joyous triumph!"

Hugh of Boves lost his temper at this. "You are a despicable traitor, Compte Renauld. Look at all the lands and large possessions you have received from King John's generosity! The postponement of the battle to another day will bring irreparable damage which will harm John, and one must always have cause to repent when one has not grasped a favourable opportunity!"

Hugh answered indignantly, "This day will prove that it is I who is loyal, and you who are a traitor; because on this Sunday I will, if need be, fight to the death for the King while you, as usual, on this same day … you will show to all by running away that you are the evil traitor."

With this, Hugh went to horse, mounted and taking all his knights with him, rode for the front line.

Otto, exasperated, issued a few brief orders to those closest to him, including Hervé, and then mounted, himself.

"We ride in the third battalion, Gerard!" I shouted.

Passing a large forest to our left, we joined a road heading due east. Some said Phillip had halted his army at a bridge a few miles further on; one of many confused pieced of news that passed our ears.

We formed short ranks across and either side of the road to give us some protection in case of ambush and moved in an orderly fashion at a pace the infantry could manage.

Then we emerged onto a wide plain which ran as far as the bridge. I heard a sergeant shouting its name as he rode rearwards.

"What did you say the bridge was called?" I shouted after him.

"Bouvines!"

Bouvines. Oh no! 1214! The Battle of Bouvines!

Now I remembered! My worst fears had been realised. The Battle of Bouvines was probably the single biggest and most bloody pitched battle of the 13th Century; a battle between the heads of state for three countries fighting to control France. And the worst thing was that Otto lost.

"We're doomed, Gerard!"

"It doesn't seem very likely. I just heard somebody say that they number only 14,000!" He grinned.

As we neared the battlefield, clouds of dust rose up from where Hugh of Boves had charged into the rearmost of Phillip's ranks. In the far distance, over the heads of the mounted knights and through dust cloud, we could still just make out the spire of the small Bouvines chapel. To the far right of the battlefield, stood a village and to the far left another. We had no time to learn their names.

As we crossed the plain, perhaps 5000 yards wide or more, Otto began to organise his troops into three lines at right angles to the road and each of those into two ranks. We were with Otto in the front rank of the middle line, Renaud and William of Salisbury, John's appointed Marshal for the campaign, were to the right and Ferrand's troops were to the left. Behind Otto, thousands of pole-armed infantry stood waiting.

For now, the French rearguard, which had turned to face him, was holding off Hugh's ferocious attack.

It was noon. Phillip had the river and the sun, behind him. The sight before my eyes was truly awesome and struck the fear of God into all those that saw it.

***

Chapter Six

Eventually, Hugh, realising he could not achieve much on his own, began to fall back with his knights. The French royalist forces did the same, falling back to their right flank where space had been left for them.

"Remarkably well organised!" Gerard observed.

We were stationary now, but the horses stamped their feet and tossed their heads, restless against the clamour of war.

"Jean! Your bow!"

I was awe-struck at the sight of our enemy's lines.

"Jean! Your bow!"

"But they're out of range!"

"You won't have time once we charge!"

I had a sharp urge to urinate at the sound of the word 'charge.'

Crossbow!

"I can use this!" I shouted.

I took the crossbow from its strap on my saddle, primed it, loaded a bolt and aimed high over the enemy's heads.

"Aha! Good idea Guillaume! You truly are the most versatile knight in our ranks!" shouted Hervé, seeing this. His black stallion, a highly-strung beast, reared up at the enthusiastic shout of his master. Hervé's burnished shield, three black diamonds on a white background with two fleur de lys either side of the base diamond, glittered in the sun. We who served in his ranks all had the same design on our shields.

Otto was to Hervé's right. The Emperor flew a standard; a golden eagle above a dragon. His shield, and all those of his knights, bore the emblem of a black eagle on a golden background. Five hundred yards in front of us, I could just make out the blue background of Phillip's banner.

I squeezed the trigger, and the bolt flew away. I let loose five of my twelve bolts in this way but couldn't hear or see whether they met any target.

Hervé, suddenly called to Otto's side, returned to speak with me.

"Aim for the horse under the Royal Standard, Guillaume. Bring down Phillip!"

I found myself suddenly sweating as I lifted the sight to my eyes.

How can I kill the King of France! I have no quarrel with him! It wouldn't be right!

"I have heard you have an aim of supernatural skill Guillaume," Hervé shouted.

I tried not to think about what I was doing, tested as I was by Hervé's trust. Though I released all seven remaining bolts as accurately as I could, only once did we see Phillip's horse shift away as if from something hitting the dirt in front of it.

Thank God!

Suddenly, Arnould, the Castellan of Rasse, charged with all his knights from my left, toward the French Royalist right flank. Their shields facing me, of those few left handed knights, were of a red, inverted 'V' on a golden background. They rode straight between two lines of the Royalist right flank, and we saw one Royalist knight brought down before Arnould returned, waving his sword. Knights from our lines banged their shields with their swords, and many of the infantry roared their approval.

I was transfixed.

Is this how it will go? Charge after charge?

Next, Ferrand, Compte de Flanders, led his men from the left toward the Royalist knights who were charging at him. The two met in the middle, but the

Royalists had to retreat after only a few minutes. Our knights pursued them toward the Royalist lines. Again, a roar of approval went up from our side.

Then a household of Royalist knights charged our knights who were harrying their retreating knights. They were led by one with a shield that bore five gold roundels on a blue background with a gold strip at the top. First another household, led by one with a shield emblazoned with a check pattern of blue on gold, joined him. Then other household of the Royalists joined them so that many hundreds of horses thundered toward the centre of the field.

"You had better put on your helm Monsieur," Gerard shouted. My heart thumped harder, faster.

Our knights slowly returned to our lines, one on foot. Some showed terrible injuries, but our men shouted their approval of their valour.

Next one of our knights, Baudouin de Praet, his shield emblazoned with a red oblique cross on a golden background, charged the Royalists with all his contingent. He engaged a knight, riding ahead of his household, whose shield we could not see. The two knights met each other with sword and Baudouin brought the Royalist to the ground.

Suddenly, I heard a great roar from the Royalist right flank, like the sound of a thundering sea. Their whole right flank, led by one bearing a shield with a white Maltese Cross on a black background, and whom I later learned was the Bishop of Guerin, moved off toward us.

"This is it!" shouted Gerard. I could hear Otto shouting orders, and my senses became overwhelmed.

Our left flank, led by Ferrand, moved to meet the Royalists, and then, to my surprise, Otto let forward the large part of his infantry. His knights, including us, had to move aside to let the sea of pikes and mail pass by.

Phillip did the same, and the two lines of infantry met in the centre of the field, flanked on our left by the knights and infantry of Ferrand and Guerin.

God, please let me survive this! I will never be unfaithful to Rose again ... . Or do anything else wrong!

Gerard could see the fear in my eyes and tried to calm me. "Your wife had better be worth this Monsieur!"

I laughed, though it rasped in my dry throat. "Too late for you to find me a little blonde in Lyot, I suppose?"

"I think so Monsieur. Put on your helmet!"

I did as he suggested. I had painted it white with a red cross, right down to the lower rim. I hoped that my enemy might think me a Templar and become awe-struck.

As I placed the helmet over my cloth and velvet cap and tightened the leather chinstrap, I could hear my own hard breathing. I had to swing the helmet up and down before I could see Phillip's banner again through the narrow eye slits.

It waved furiously.

"Our men are through their lines!" shouted Gerard. "They are at Phillip!"

On impulse, I sought out the niello-armoured knight.

There he is, right beside Hervé as usual. The ornate engraving on his armour makes it look black.

"The black knight," Gerard had jokingly called him. I thought he turned to look at me. He too wore a full helmet on, so I couldn't be sure.

Sure enough, suddenly the knights in Phillip's vicinity turned to gather around his standard. They made short work of Otto's more lightly armed infantry who began to retreat steadily toward our lines. The first of the wounded began to reach us.

"Phillip was unhorsed! But then his knights came to his rescue and beat us!" a man said, shaking his head, as he limped past us.

"Hold the line!" came the order, passed along from Otto.

"Why don't we charge?" I asked Gerard.

"I can't hear you!" he shouted.

A horn suddenly blared, and I heard a ripple of sound coming along the line toward us. It swelled to a roar:

"Charge!"

I looked at Gerard and saw him nod to me and spur his horse forward. I soiled myself as I spurred Amabel forward. I had, indeed, managed to find some head armour for Amabel, and I would soon be glad of it. She reared up once and then obediently moved to a steady trot.

Somebody shouted, "Fuck! Fuck! Fuck!" It must have been me.

I became vaguely aware of our right flank angling in toward the French centre, just before we reached the Phillip's line ourselves. I had wanted to use my bow but never had the time.

Our line of knights, including Hervé and the 'black' knight, formed a protective arc around Otto as he moved forward with his personal guard arranged around him. Gerard, as my guard, checked behind him several times to keep us the right distance from Otto. I found it too awkward to try and see behind me more than once. On a huge white stallion, quite tall, with dark hair and a heavy physique, Otto made an impressive sight.

I had no more time for thought. A knight, with a diamond yellow and red checkered shield, charged straight toward me and aimed a fierce blow with his sword at the base of Amabel's neck. I pulled her neck to that side with my shield hand. The flare at the base of her armour caught the edge of his sword and deflected it with a clanging sound.

Then I swung at him but missed, because he was on my shield side. I had so little movement in the armour, I knew I would have to get him on my right side to land any sort of useful blow. I turned Amabel to confront him again. Infantry and horses swirled around me like a sea and dust rose in clouds obscuring all but that closest to one. I became aware that since the first blow with the enemy knight, my fear had left me. Now, my only thought was death for him, which would result in my own survival for just a few seconds more.

He swung his horse around quicker than I and again brought his sword down over his horse's neck. We were still both to each other's left, the wrong side for a blow. I aimed another at his shoulder but switched from a swing to a stab at the last moment. This caught him off-guard so that he swung back in his saddle. For a moment I thought I had unseated him, but he used his knee to turn his horse away, this time to the right.

The press of bodies had grown so tight, I could barely make Amabel turn at all. Gambling he would again turn to his right, this time I turned to my right but in a wider arc. As I had guessed, he found himself to my right when he returned, and before he could recover his wits, I had sent my sword point toward his groin with all my might. I saw a few links fly off his suit and a thin gash of white and red flesh, but he still came on. With only an open face helmet on, his eyes were visible, and they burned with lust for death. At the last moment, I saw him raise his sword for a blow to the top of my head. I had no time to raise my shield.

Designed to stun me, his blow did just that, forcing the helmet down into my shoulder armour and making my head swim with the sound and vibration of the impact. So dizzy that I had begun to slip from the saddle, it took all my instinct to find my balance again.

We turned again and Amabel's head armour caught his horse a glancing blow to the brow, cutting a gash in the dapple's black fur. I spurred Amabel to leap forward and held my sword out toward the knight's chest, in the hope that her momentum might drive it through his mail. But he moved too fast. His sword parried mine, and again we passed. When I finally managed to turn, he was going flat out, cutting through the swath of men, toward Otto.

I had no time to reflect on this because first a sergeant rammed a spear into Amabel's flank, causing her to veer, and then a mace blow slammed into my back. My groin slammed into the saddle pommel, which stopped me from going over Amabel's neck, but only the firmest grip with my knees of her flanks stopped me going sideways as she veered. I had to turn in my saddle to see behind me as I could no longer find space to turn my horse.

I turned just in time to see the black knight deflect another blow from the mace-wielding knight and then thrust a fierce blow at the man's chest. The links parted and blood seeped from a wide wound. The man slumped in the saddle.

"Thanks!" I said impulsively, inside my helmet, but, of course, he couldn't hear me.

"Behind you, Monsieur!" I heard a familiar voice bellow.

What? Where?

I turned to my front and saw the sergeant, who had caught Amabel in the flank, aiming another blow at her soft belly. Gerard was moving slowly toward us on his grey horse, but he wouldn't get to us in time.

I reached right over and parried the spear thrust with my sword. I almost overbalanced but, gripping the reins tightly, I risked one more, quick stab to his neck. The blow went under his helmet and neatly sliced a deep gash just above the collar of his jerkin. Blood spouted from his severed artery, and he clutched at the wound. I wasted no more time on him.

I felt calmer now and time seemed to be slowing to an almost supernaturally slow pace. I looked around me and could see Otto wielding a great axe from side to side, just a few knights away from me. Behind me the black knight and Hervé protected Otto's right flank. I became aware that we were heavily outnumbered. While we were small islands of two or three knights and a few men on foot, the enemy were like an ocean current, swirling around us.

Nevertheless, a surprising order existed in what seemed like chaos: messages were passed from knight to knight.

"Renauld, on the right, is overcome," somebody shouted to me. I passed on the message.

"Hugh of Boves has left the field," remarked another impassively. With remarkable detachment, I thought that ironic.

"William Longsword still holds the right!" came another message as I urged Amabel toward another Royalist knight.

This one's shield had an emblem of a white and black diamond check. We urged our horses together. I quickly checked Amabel's white flank. Where the spear had struck, I could see no more than a trickle of blood, though the gash looked bad. The spear had hit bone and been stopped by it from doing further damage.

A piece of luck!

"Come on, Amabel, my girl!"

My sword arm's overworked muscles burned, so I approached on the knight's left side, hoping both to protect myself with my shield and reduce his opportunities to strike at all. Our shields clashed, making a metallic, grating sound as the surfaces slid across each other. I came within two feet of his eyes. I saw no fear in them.

With no room to pass, our horses stood side by side while we exchanged many blows. I had been considering switching to my mace when I saw a weakness; a rent in his mail, just above his waist. He kept it hidden behind his shield most of the time, but when he raised it high, I could see it for a moment. His flesh could be seen through the rent, and a thin red gash oozed a steady trickle of blood. It wasn't a bad wound, but it represented a gruesome opportunity. My pulse quickened as that awful sense of purpose took over.

I leaned in toward him, taking a shield parry under the chin strap so that he could see my eyes. I hid my intent from him. I wanted him to believe I had not seen the wound. Leaning away from him, I twisted the shield with my wrist in the straps until I had the base point aimed at his neck. I drove it into him with all my strength. Forced to parry with his shield, he exposed the rent, and I slid the sword surely and silently, deep into his body through his wound.

He let out a deep sigh just as my sword touched a rib on the far side of his chest. He slid slowly off his horse to his right.

I breathed a sigh of relief and straightened up, hoping for a rest. Something again slammed into my back. This 'something' must have had quite sharp, because I felt links of my mail pinging and others being forced into my flesh just to the right of my backbone. The blow pushed me right down onto Amabel's neck, and she lurched forwards and to the left, not knowing what my command meant. Unbalanced and unable to react anyway, I found myself sprawling on the ground, face down and winded. I had fallen half on an astonished Royalist infantryman, who rose to his feet quickly and moved away. The press of bodies threatened to submerge me. I *had* to stand.

I could feel Amabel's front right leg against my shoulder, so I gripped it, slowly drew myself to my knees and then, painfully, to my feet. I felt as if my back had been almost been broken in two. The pain nearly made me faint.

No sword!

I peered thought my eye slits at the tiny patches of mud that appeared between bodies and feet but could see no sign of it.

Mace!

I fumbled for the rear of my horse's saddle and the strap for the mace that I had packed there.

It's still there!

But before I could pull the shaft of the mace from the strap, another blow came down on my helmet. My teeth took off the front of my tongue, and everything went black for a moment. I clung to the pommel with my right glove, as my legs went from under me. I felt sick.

This is no good. Rose.

I could see nothing, anymore, but ducking under Amabel's belly as my legs became useful again, I came up on the other side.

"Bâtard!" I heard from somewhere.

I reached over Amabel's saddle, and fumbling, managed to pull the protruding mace handle from its strap. Gerard had taught me to place it high, like this. "Always make every weapon as easy to draw from any angle as possible!" I heard his steady voice say.

My vision still hadn't returned as I grabbed the weapon. I wielded the mace menacingly in the direction of the swearing voice, but still I couldn't see. The fatal blow could not be far off.

My time has come. At last. The fatal blow … .

"Monsieur! Duck!" I heard Gerard's deep voice, coming from the other side of Amabel. I did as instructed and felt something clang against the top rim of my helmet. "Jesu Christos! In the name of all … that's right … . There!"

In some nightmarish world of blurry images and crystal-clear sound, I heard the drama in all its gory detail as Gerard dealt the fatal blow to my assailant. His last word had sounded soothing, gentle. I wasn't sure if it he intended it for me, the enemy or himself.

Some blurry vision at last returned.

I heard a yell of glee as a sword swung toward me. It cut deeply into my shoulder somehow, making me gasp with pain and sending me reeling against Amabel. I leaned on her for just a fraction of a second, eyes closed, weary as I had ever been, and then I leaped to my left. My eyes were clear!

I had a clear shot at the knight, and I could see that he had an open face helmet; a weakness, because he would need to protect his face. I swung my mace and stepped in behind it. I aimed my second swing directly at his face, and he tried to take a step back, but the press of bodies behind stopped him.

"Monsieur Jean!" To my left, Gerard suddenly appeared, and while I stared at the Royalist knight, who glared back, my friend came to my side. He had a deep gash, oozing blood, on his right cheek and had lost a glove. One of his fingers looked broken. Together we faced the knight who didn't look so confident now. My breath came in great gulps as Gerard spoke.

"You're alive, Monsieur!" He spat and blood from his mouth spattered his sword and armour.

"Only … just! Without you I would be gone. I can't thank you enough, Gerard." The huge knight seemed not to hear my words. As if a tide, suddenly our remaining infantry around us, which were already few in number, began to back toward Otto. "What's going … on?" I asked Gerard.

"We have lost, Monsieur! Haven't you heard? Ferrand has been taken and William Longsword too! When our right … flank attacked Phillip they must have outflanked us."

The taking of John's Marshall had evidently defeated the morale of our forces.

"All remaining chivalry is to protect Otto!"

"I'm sorry about all this, Gerard. I am sorry I brought you into this!"

"Nonsense Monsieur. I feel alive! For the first time in many years I am really quite enjoying myself!"

As our infantry ebbed away, their places were taken by Royalist troops, but I had time to see the ground littered with dead corpses and fruit of a thousand hackings; piles of severed limbs. I felt almost nothing looking at them. While we gasped for breath, my opponent turned and walked back toward Otto. In only moments we were surrounded by enemy infantry. Lightly armed, they barely took any notice of us. Only one aimed a sword blow at my back and swore.

"Bâtard!"

At that moment there, I heard a horn blare, and the standard of Otto began to wave furiously.

"Come on, Monsieur! We must get to Otto!"

With that, we started to surge through the swarm of enemy infantry that were ahead of us. We really had no choice but to cut them down as we went. Following Gerard's example, I quickly fell into a rhythm, swinging my mace from left to right, sweeping men aside with howls of pain. They became no more significant to me that stalks of wheat.

Ahead of us I saw through the dust the backs of some Royalist knights, including the one I had fought

with the diamond red and yellow checkered shield.
Between a large ring of enemy knights and Otto's
personal guard of six knights were all that remained of
ours; perhaps sixty knights. We were among the few
remaining of our forces outside this ring. My shoulder
felt very stiff, and I could feel wet blood coursing down
my arm inside my mail shirt. I glanced at my shoulder
and saw where a weak link must have given way,
causing adjacent links to break and leaving a line of
broken links in the mail. Blood seeped out of the
wound.

We engaged a Royalist knight with his back to us,
who quickly turned to keep us away from his
vulnerable back. Gerard took a mighty swing with his
long sword at the man's neck, and the knight leaned
back to avoid the blow. It cut him slightly on the cheek,
but at the same time I swung my mace behind his knees
and took him down. Not stopping to finish him we
stepped over his sprawling body and joined our own
ranks again. We turned and took up our positions,
Gerard to my left. A few knights to my right and just
ahead of Otto's own guard, I could see the black knight
and Hervé. The Compte's right arm hung limp, and his
mail had become stained red with blood. He had
switched from using a sword in his right hand to
swinging a mace with his left. Now, more than ever, he
would need the protection of the mysterious knight
beside him.

Gerard and I exchanged blows continually with the
pressing enemy knights.

"I'm so tired, Gerard!" I shouted. My right arm
muscles burned, my left arm was numb from repeated
blows to the shield.

"Think of a … woman, Monsieur. I find that
normally helps. One of those little … hah! … whores
in Lyot!"

"But I don't want a little whore in Lyot."

"Well, your wife then! Is she still beautiful?"

"Yes! She is!"

Strangely, I did find that thinking of Rose helped, either because it numbed the pain, or because it released some adrenaline. I could only make out some red and yellow on the battered shield of my opponent; I couldn't make out the design. His eyes burned red with a fierce desire to kill and reach Otto. No doubt Phillip would have offered a great reward for any who killed the former Emperor, and, of course, there would be great glory.

A fierce shouting and screaming came from around the perimeter. That noise formed a more or less continuous background to the metallic clangs of weapon against weapon. However, there appeared to be something of great significance going on to Otto's right. I managed to steal a few glances in that direction and saw a huge Royalist knight break through to the side of Otto's white stallion. He threw down his sword and grabbed the reins of Otto's horse. With all his strength, he tried to pull the horse in the direction of the Royalist line, but the strong and loyal horse could not be moved. Another knight with no shield took out a knife and drove it into the chest of Otto.

I had to look away for a moment to parry a blow, but then when I glanced back, the second knight had aimed another blow at Otto, but it missed and passed deep into the brain of the rearing white horse. Pandemonium broke out as the terrified horse threw Otto and charged through the lines of knights. Many were killed or wounded as it left the field.

"To the Emperor!" went up a cry.

"Hold the line!" somebody hollered nearby; Hervé.

We continued to protect Otto's left flank. Gerard kept me updated.

"The knight with the … knife is down. Three knights on top … of him. I can't see the other. A black horse is being brought … to Otto. He's up! He's alright. He's back on the horse."

Another Royalist knight inserted himself between the two fighting Gerard and myself, and then I saw, on a fully covered horse, the figure of Phillip himself, perhaps twenty yards ahead of us. His blue standard flew steadily above him. Helmetless as he was, I could see the face of a handsome man with receding hair and a ruddy complexion. He looked on proudly as the fight continued.

The knight with the the diamond red and yellow checkered shield suddenly seemed to find an opening in our defensive line to my left. He struggled through foot militia right up to the side of Otto, who now rode the black horse.

Gerard peeled away from me to take down this knight, and my attacker almost overwhelmed me with heavy blows.

Again, the black knight parried a blow for me and with a mighty sweep of his long sword, took off the head of the knight in front of me.

We both faced a line of about ten knights; I felt sure this would be the end. But then I felt that sense of malevolence that I am so sensitive to. Remembering the moment in Hervé's marquee, I glanced at the black knight. He opened his mouth and howled; a sound such as I have never heard before or since. It seemed to come from the very pit of Hell. I heard a loud crack, and the air seemed to become like water around me.

Oh no! Not again!

A slit opened in the air right over the heads of the enemy knights, and the figure of the black knight seemed to become a shadow. He grew taller and joined with the liquid form of a giant serpent whose great head protruded from the slit in the air. Quicker than the eye could follow, the apparition seemed to kiss the top of each enemy knight's head. The whole thing took less than a second, but when over, they dropped to the ground, their helmets crushed in to half their original sizes. Bits of bone and brains spewed all around the shoulders of the fallen bodies.

With a howl of anger, the beast pulled back through the rent, and the black knight regained his solid form beside me.

I felt too grateful for life to stop and think about what had happened. Only later, did I wonder why the beast had protected me and not killed me.

I turned just in time to see the knight with the diamond red and yellow checkered shield reach the side of Otto's black horse.

He grabbed at its neck and tried to pull it down. The terrified horse pulled away, turned, and then Otto let it surge away toward the rear of our lines.

"It's over!" shouted Hervé. "Every man for himself!"

Where is Gerard?

I twisted to look behind me and to my right. A blow caught me on the back of the helmet, but I ignored it. I climbed over bodies to reach my friend and patted him on the back.

I had to shout to be heard over the desperate clanging of steel.

"Gerard! We must leave! We can go now!"

For a moment he seemed determined to fight on but then stepped back.

"Oui Monsieur. We can go!"

We had to fight through three lines of Royalist knights to escape, but they were weary of fighting, and now, with the victory won, they no longer cared to risk dying. Finally, we were through and running as best we could across a field of broken bodies. All around us were the last of Otto's knights. A few horses still stood still, loyally waiting for their masters. Each retreating knight grabbed the reins of one, mounted it and sped from the field.

A group of Hervé's knights were huddled around something to our left, and we instinctively made for these.

"What's happening?" I said, breathlessly, tapping a knight on the shoulder.

"Ah, Sir Jean!" he said, standing aside. Beyond him, I could see Hervé himself lying on the ground. A gaping wound in his chest oozed blood. He smiled up at me through a grimace of pain, and I knelt beside him.

"Sir Guillaume!" he said.

"My Lord!"

"You fought bravely. And I know why … ."

"You do?"

"Your wife … . Tower. I know … . Georgiana has her."

"You knew … *that*?"

"I know now that you are the one I sought in Lyot. You were in my oubliette and escaped!"

I said nothing.

"Well, you don't have to admit it. I know it! I have not much time, nor much breath. I want to spend time with my knights. But, actually, you don't have much time either!"

One of his most loyal knights held Hervé's steel-gloved hand tenderly.

"Go to Aunay as quick as you can. There may still be time. You know … ? Sacrifice?"

"*Yes* Hervé. I must save my wife. I love her *very* much. How do I get into the tower?"

"Heavily fortified … . Many men … . Ah, if we had won! They will be expecting treasure wagons. The password is Agnès. Tell them; it may get you throu- … ."

Suddenly the Compte's eyes grew very wide, and he stared into the heavens. I felt sure he no longer saw this world. But I had one question left to ask:

"The black knight? The one who saved me? Where is he?"

One of Hervé's men tried to silence me with an upheld hand.

"Knight? Gone … . Sorry Jean. I serve the same masters as the one you call the black knight. At first, they wanted you killed, but then they changed their *mind*! I don't know *why*! I was only a pawn after all … . Where is my horse … ?"

With that, he began to ramble men pushed me aside. Those closer to him than I would attend his last moments on Earth. I had to leave.

"Come on Gerard! We must go."

Stumbling on across the desolation of the battlefield, I saw a white horse to our left. On a whim I called a name.

"Amabel!" The horse raised its head and looked at me. I ran toward it, dropping my mace at last and easing the shattered shield from my left wrist.

Gerard followed me and took the reins of a large brown stallion.

We mounted and rode from the field, going eastwards away from the lowering sun.

***

Neither of us spoke as we rode. I felt too exhausted, I could barely stay in the saddle. Were it not for the shock, not just of what I had seen but that we were still alive, I don't think I could have kept going.

Only when we rested in a copse of trees, late that first night, did I discover the extent of my injuries.

Once the adrenaline had ceased coursing through my body, the pain in my back had returned with a vengeance. Gerard took a look at my wounds after carefully pulling off my mail.

"There's a bruise the size of your head, and a lot of blood is lost from that shoulder wound! You look pale!"

I couldn't straighten my shield hand either, and that began swelling up.

Maybe it's fractured.

We pressed on.

* * *

We went without food for three days but finally stopped at a farmhouse where we were given a full meal. On horseback, little had gone through my mind. I became practically delirious from blood loss and pain, but when conscious, I felt just grateful to be alive. I said little. Gerard, however, didn't stay so quiet once we were beyond danger.

"Monsieur. I have to thank you!"

"What for?"

"For restoring my dignity. I have not fought as a knight should since being cast out of the Templars. This, at least, is a battle worthy of a tale or two!"

"I am just surprised you're still alive! I thought you would be dead for sure. I would have missed you!"

"Hm!" He seemed much put out by my familiarity and stomped off.

But Gerard seemed much happier from then on and actually hummed to himself from time to time; a deep and unmelodious sound.

We rode night and day for next three days, changing horses when we could for the silver deniers, stamped with his head, which we had earned in Hervé's service. As we rode, my back became so stiff I that I couldn't move and several times nearly passed out from the pain.

Gerard had to make a corset from rags and tie me to the horse to stop me falling off. My shoulder became caked in dry blood; it had stopped bleeding. But the loss of blood had weakened me terribly.

"We'll have to stop for a few days, at least Jean. You cannot go on!"

We found an abandoned barn on a wild spread of land and Gerard lay me down on some hay in the cool shade inside.

That night I became delirious with fever. I lost all track of time. My mind wandered lost pathways as I drifted in and out of consciousness.

"I fear the worst for you, Jean!" I thought I heard Gerard whisper.

I'm going to die! I'm going to die!

I found myself drifting back to the time with Georgina in Paris. Georgina; that elemental force of nature! How I had loved her and then lost her! Her soul, strung out somewhere between good and bad. In my delirium I was still making love to her in Paris:

She had sat down next to me but this time pulled her legs up under her and leaned against me. She put a plate of expensive confectionery on my knee, and I politely took a chocolate. It tasted delicious. I felt that she wanted me to put my arm around her, but I couldn't do it. I had never been unfaithful to Rose, and I just didn't feel comfortable in this situation with a strange woman.

"You said I was in great danger?" I said.

"Yes. So am I."

"You said you had something to tell, some information you could give me?"

"All in good time. How is the champagne? Wait. I want to put on some music. Is Ravel alright with you?"

"Yes. Sure. I love Ravel."

"I have been scared the last few weeks."

"Really?" I said.

I put my arm instinctively around her shoulder as I opened my eyes. She leaned into me, and I could see deep into her cleavage, almost the entire shape of her breast. It surprised me, and I felt a pleasant hardness between my legs. She seemed to be looking directly at my groin, and this excited me more, as if it were an assignation.

"The Good Pastor and his cronies have been hunting me all over Paris," she continued. "One night they smashed the window of my car and stole some documents which I had been studying."

"Are you serious? If they are religious men, how could they do such a thing?"

"Religious! Yes, their kind of religion. Intolerant and extreme. They will kill anything that they feel violates the Catholic Church's beliefs."

"Kill?"

"Yes. Kill. I do not exaggerate. Do not underestimate them."

"But one thing I don't understand. Pastors are usually found in the Protestant Church."

"No. If you go far back enough in time, Pastors were prominent in the Catholic Church too, and in the fundamental strands of the Church there are still fundamentalist Orders, usually of monks, but sometimes priests, who defend the faith."

"You know a lot about these people."

"I know a lot more, and I will tell you, but I need protecting."

"And I want to protect you."

I stroked the nape of her neck with the back of my index finger, and she lifted her face to look into my eyes.

"Am I really beautiful?"

"Oh yes." We hung there in space for a moment, her lips moist and eyes wide with eager longing and submissive desire, and then I leaned forward slightly to kiss her. Her warm mouth opened. I tasted the sweetness of her lipstick and then explored the inside of her lips with my tongue.

"Ah!" she sighed. The music was building now, painting a sound picture of mounting waves in the sea around the enchanted island, and as the satyric flute ran up and down the register, I gently pushed her dress down to reveal a naked shoulder. She pulled her arms through their openings while I continued kissing her, and then the dark blue dress fell to her waist. She looked stunning; lovely full breasts and a slim waist with just the faintest downy line between her navel and the top of the folds of her dress, just above her legs.

"You are so beautiful."

"Oh. Show me." I started to stand, to take her to the door which I thought led to the bedroom, but she stopped me. "No, here."

She had already started unfastening the buttons on my shirt, and I helped her, pulling it off and then unfastening my trousers. Before long I was naked. I pulled her dress off her hips and looking at her completely naked as it fell to the floor. She climbed on top of me and, hard as I was, I just lay back while she took control. She lowered herself onto it, allowing me to see the whole of her beauty, her face, her long black hair cascading around her lovely breasts and the soft 'V' just above my own hips. We rocked gently as I felt her youth taking the hand of my many long lonely years and showing me the rhythm and dance she wanted to explore. Finally, we came together, just as the music subsided at the end of the storm.

I wanted to say "Excellent choice of music," but I knew we would both laugh, and the moment would be lost.

She lay on me, her sweating forehead resting under my chin, and I rubbed her shoulders affectionately.

"That was great," she said. "That felt really good. I don't want to move right now."

"Then don't."

We slept for a little while, her light body on top of mine, and when we became a little cold, we walked hand-in-hand to the bedroom and climbed under the soft white sheets of a large bed.

We slept, but it seemed, in the middle of the night, somebody called to me. I got up and walked to the window where a pale, white light shone; all I could see of Paris. A voice told me:

"Jean. It's Herleva. You have a great deal of love to give, and I think you want to go on, but unless you give in to your passions, you will not wake up. Now sleep!"

***

If I have to kill her, to save Rose, I'm not sure I can do it!

The thought jerked me awake.

"Gerard!"

He too jerked awake.

"You have been dreaming lad. Talking. About Georgina, as you call her. You were close to death, very close! I don't know what brought you back, but your breathing had become so weak, I thought you had gone. I sat a long time watching you before I knew you were alive."

"Oh. I am very tired." I closed my eyes again. I may have slept, but then I asked, "Talking? Have I? Oh. What did I talk about?"

"Never mind. I understand a lot more about that witch now… A tortured soul… She sounds like she has other virtues, though! Ha! Eh?"

The fever finally left me. The constant pain in my back had gone, but the stiffness remained. I asked Gerard how long we had been in the barn.

"Almost two days."

I nearly lost my mind with the fear that Rose would be dead before I could reach her. Before Gerard could stop me, I had saddled Amabel and rode off, demanding that we head south at once. Gerard caught up and rode alongside me, protesting. We never stopped for more than a few minutes during the day. We only slept a few hours each night. Often, we saw columns of soldiers ahead of us, either on the road or crossing fields. Not knowing whether they were the King's men or not, we were forced to make long detours, which delayed us further

"You mentioned your wife in your delirium too Monsieur. You met her in that great war you spoke of?"

"Yes. She was a soldier too, a very brave one. Last of her … brigade."

"Ah. I thought you had said something like that. That seems very strange to me. A woman? A soldier, do you say? Very strange!"

"She's very good with a gun!"

"A gun monsieur?"

"It's like a crossbow. But very powerful." He seemed bemused. "Never mind."

"Things must be very different in the 'future,'" he offered, nodding sagely. "If she is so … capable, how can this Georgina hold her?"

"She is ill, Gerard. Her body is not as fit as it was. But don't worry. She won't make it easy for Georgina."

After another six days of hard riding, sleeping rough and taking food anywhere we could get it, we arrived at a crossroads a few miles east of Hervé's castle. The heat of midday was drawn as autumn slipped in.

"Master! I knew you would come!"

***

A tussle-haired boy sprang from his perch on top of a dry-stone wall and rushed toward Amabel. She drew back.

"Rathead!" I yelled.

"I heard you were all dead!" he replied. "But I didn't believe them! Only two knights came back alive, two days ago. The King's men are everywhere. They have surrounded the castle. I was lucky to get away. I had to warn you!"

Gerard and I sat on our horses, which shook with the irritation of flies on their sweaty flanks, but we still faced south.

"Aren't you coming back to the castle?" Rathead asked, suddenly confused. He took a stalk of grass from his mouth.

"We – I … have to go south, to Aunay. We are going to a Tower – it's called the Maze Tower – and we don't have much time!" I answered.

"Well then, I'm coming too!"

"No! You can't come Rathead! It's too dangerous!"

The boy tossed the stalk of grass away. Gerard eased his horse close to mine and leaned over to whisper in my ear:

"He *wants* to come! How can you deny him a future? I thought *you wanted* to help him?"

"I can't! I can't explain why…"

"Even to me?"

"Listen! Somebody close to me is going to die! I have this ability. I can see evil! I don't want it to be *him* … or *you*. Worrying about you is bad enough!"

"Close to you? Could be anybody! Your wife!"

"Yes. I know."

"More likely, but you don't want to admit it. Anyway, he can be useful, and you are not exactly rich by your number of friends!"

He made some good points and Rathead looked very dejected.

"Okay Rathead. Come on!"

Gerard hauled Rathead up behind him on his horse, and we rode on. We hadn't gone far before we encountered King Phillip's men in a loose cordon around the region of Donzy, no doubt on the lookout for men trying to reach Aunay. It took two days to thread our way through a forest teeming with soldiers.

Keeping to the back lanes and forests, we arrived in a copse on top of a hill overlooking the Maze Tower on the morning of the day before the full moon; just in time. I felt completely exhausted, and while Gerard scouted the fortress's defenses, Rathead scouted food and wine for me.

"So are you ready to be my squire?" I said when Rathead returned.

He looked down at me in the cool September light. For the first time I could see that his eyes were a warm blue. He smiled at me, and as I smiled back, he grinned.

"Yes, Sir!"

"You know I had forgotten … . Did you look after my friend? How is he?"

"He's well Sir!"

"Good. We must think what to do about him. We need to get him out. Have you spoken with him?"

"Once, yes. Once, the guard left the door open, and I went inside. Sometimes we're sent inside to clean, so I risked it."

"Good lad. What did he say?"

"He asked if I had supplied the extra food. I said, 'Yes,' and then he asked why. I told him about you, and he laughed … before choking a little bit. I mean … he is tied up, see? But he's alright. I mean. He's not dying. Um. Then he asked where you were. I told him you had been upstairs, but now you had gone to the War and might not be back. He had a message for you … ."

"Yes?"

"Wait. I'm trying to remember. Yes … he thanked you for the food but asked that; if you could possibly *manage* it, please could you find a way to get him out! That's *it*!"

"Ah! I see. Yes, we have to find a way. Do you have any ideas?"

"Me Sir?" He looked bewildered. "No Sir."

"I can't go on calling you Rathead! I will give you a name. How about Edward?"

"Uduward?"

"If you like. Ha! Ha! Yes."

"Umh Uduward. Uduard. Uduardo! Well, it's better than Rathead I guess Sir."

"Good. That's settled then. Now go and find Gerard."

"Yes Monsieur. He saluted me, not altogether without humour in his eyes."

"Gerard! Meet Uduward! I have given my squire a new name" I said when the knight returned.

"Ah. Pleased to meet you Uduward!" He ruffled the boy's hair, light brown now it had been washed a few times.

"I wish I had my own horse!" added Uduward.

"Uduward! A horse would be too big for you!" I said.

"No. I can ride any size horse!" Then he, too, seemed to find the courage to air his thoughts! "My crotch is sore from riding without a saddle!"

"Uduward! Say a Hail Mary, immediately!" I said.

"Be gentle with the poor boy, Monsieur! He probably doesn't have any religion!"

"You *do* know your prayers, don't you?" I asked my new squire.

"A few, yes, but I didn't have much call for them in the castle. Everything seemed equally bad there, and I never dreamed I would have anywhere else to go!"

"Well now's the time to learn. I will teach you. Come with me lad. We have some time."

The old knight had snared a rabbit, and later I made Gerard and Uduward drink its blood with me in case we had to use the Gate that day. Surprisingly, neither scowled at the taste. When asked why, they both revealed it wasn't the first time they had drunk blood; Uduward in the kitchens of the castle and Gerard in the deserts of the Holy Land.

***

"Well, Monsieur, you have picked a challenge!" announced Gerard after we had finished. "That place is bristling with men and weapons. And the walls! Come and see!"

We crept forward to a brow of the hill covered in short, sturdy shrubs. I looked down at the object of our interest

A wall ran out from both sides of the round Maze Tower encompassing some ancient courtyard. But around the whole collection of buildings, at a distance of some one hundred and fifty yards or more, I saw an outer wall. A much more substantial construction, it looked about ten feet thick and fifteen high, the parapet perhaps five feet wide, complete with a wooden palisade for the guards and embrasures.

A wooden stairway led up to the Maze Tower entrance; a portcullis on the first floor. Below this there were no windows or arrow-slots.

"How do we get in?" asked Uduward.

"We walk in," Gerard replied. "Am I right?"

I nodded.

"Now's the time for you to start acting like a squire Uduward. You can carry my crossbow."

As I looked down on the Maze Tower, I recalled that terrible voice, rattling a cage somewhere deep in my soul. "I am waiting for you. I will be waiting in the Tower." I shivered.

***

"Here we go!" muttered Gerard, under his breath. We were approaching the main gate of the outer wall on foot. Already a few lookouts had eyed our armour suspiciously.

"My mouth's dry," whispered Uduward. He did his best to look like a dignified squire.

"Halt! What business have *you*?" shouted a burly sergeant, brandishing a spear, from the rampart.

"We fought with Hervé at Bouvines. He told us to come here. There are King's men everywhere, and we need shelter!"

"Indeed. So does every other vagabond in these parts."

"Don't you want the password?"

"Go on … "

"Agnès!"

The sergeant's face disappeared behind the wooden palisade, and he barked an order. A few moments later, the double wooden doors in the gate swung slowly open.

"Come on!" I whispered, and we entered the fortress.

"Wait here!" a new voice, rougher than the sergeant's, ordered. "The boss has gone to see if the castilian will see you. It would have been better for you if you had something valuable, some treasure. Have you?"

His eyes seemed to grow out of his face, as if on stalks, while he looked us over. Obviously my expensive armour whetted his avaricious appetite. I had the urge to drop my great helm over his head and pat it tight down with the flat of my sword. I didn't answer him.

"Wait over there then," he spat, disappointed.

We waited for over an hour.

"It's an impressive tower!" Uduward said, trying to break the tension.

"One day in the future there will be buildings ten times as high as this in every large town and cars that go ten times as fast as a horse!" I said. He had proved himself a curious student of everything. I had started teaching him to read and write, and he had a voracious appetite for learning.

Gerard grunted with satisfaction.

"'One day … in the future … ,'" Uduward quoted. "I would like to go there! Do you mean in 1215 or 16?"

I laughed. "1970 actually!"

Gerard's eyebrows lifted skyward. "That's *a long way* away."

"It's the future!" offered Uduward.

"Thanks Udu. Yes, the future."

"How do we get there? Why can't all these people go there?" asked Gerard.

"It's not a place, it's a time! That's why they can't all go there. This is their life!" answered Uduward impatiently.

"Tch! I don't know … ." Gerard protested. "Where, I mean when, did you say you came from Monsieur?"

"The 20th Century!"

"It's the future, and everything is different there, isn't it?" added Uduward. I noticed, again, the cool blue of his eyes, like the sky above us.

***

The sun was well past its noon position, and I could wait no longer.

"The Gate will open in about an hour Gerard! We have to get into that tower!"

"Patience Monsieur. We cannot break in, just the three of us. You *said* we will walk *in*."

"What is a Gate, anyway?" asked Uduward, trying tactfully to diffuse the situation.

While I paced up and down I mused over the ancient myth.

Georgina as my Ariadne… great!

I felt angry with Rose for a moment. Why hadn't she made some attempt to escape? But then I bit my lip. She was no longer the woman she had been, since her stroke.

"What's happening to the sky?" I heard Uduward ask. It brought me out of my reverie. I looked up. Above us, what had been a blue sky, blemished only by a few fluffy white clouds, began to look like a thunder storm. Blackened clouds seem to be drifting into a giant vortex which stretched to all horizons. I frowned.

"What is *it* Monsieur Jean?" asked Gerard, astonished.

"I've seen it once before. It's not good. Evil is lurking nearby. Evil things will be done."

I waited another thirty minutes or so and then gave into my emotions. "We have to go. I don't care about etiquette, or risk. If you want to stay here, Gerard, that's fine. Uduward, you are too young to risk your life for somebody's wife. You *must* stay here!"

"If you're going, so am I!" he said defiantly. Gerard stood up to follow me.

I opened my mouth to protest, but there wasn't time for an argument, and I needed any help I could get.

"Come on then!"

Ignoring the dark looks of soldiers around us, I strode toward a gate in the inner wall. Once through, I went on to the base of the Maze Tower's wooden stairs. Gerard and Uduward held back, looking from side to side nervously. Gerard had his hand on his sword hilt, as did I. Looking behind me, I saw that none of the soldiers had approached within fifty feet of the tower. Some glanced at it fearfully, while others scowled and sneered at us.

I took a deep breath and put my right foot on the first step, gripping the rail with my gloved left hand. Under my arm, I carried the great helm.

"Monsieur! I'm sorry to have kept you waiting!" A sweet voice drifted down from the top of the stairs. "I am the castilian, Pierre!"

He beckoned us to the top of the stairs, and Gerard and I politely took our hands from our swords. From under my brow, I could see the sky had darkened, shutting out the sunlight. The air had grown cool. All my senses screamed, 'Danger!'

At the top of the stairs, Pierre walked under a portcullis, into a stone tunnel perhaps thirty feet deep. Above the lintel, were a row of runes, which I couldn't decipher. Pierre, a portly man with a rippling neck, turned and beckoned us on with a fat, bejeweled hand and a fleeting smile. I stepped under the portcullis and heard Gerard's metaled feet on stone behind mine.

Tunnel extends to the centre of the tower. Would be a useful killing zone during an attack!

I turned and looked up to see arrow slits high in the walls and the ceiling of this dim and murderous corridor. Along the top and bottom edges of the tunnel, were curious channels. I speculated that these might be for drainage. At its far end, another portcullis hung down a few feet from the ceiling.

"Why do they call this Tower the … ?"

"Good lu- … !" The clattering of the second portcullis, coming down right in front of his face, cut off Pierre's last word. The portcullis rattled down in its slots until it clanged into the groove cut for it in the stone floor. The castilian's right hand had been extended to reach something behind a corner of the wall.

A lever!

At that moment, the portcullis behind us also came rattling down landed in its slot on the floor. Uduward, at the rear, almost had time to dive under it but pulled up short and gripped the iron bars with his hands!

"Bâtard!" he shouted.

I turned back. Pierre turned and walked out of sight.

Terror edged into my mind, but I pushed it away.

Is this a game?

"Monsieur!" shouted Gerard.

"Don't panic! This might just be a game! It's probably Georgi-… Georgiana's idea of a joke. Wait!"

Gerard and Uduward fidgeted nervously, shifting from one foot to the other.

Suddenly, the ominous scraping sound of iron on stone assaulted our senses.

Uduward, whose eyes were quicker than Gerard's or mine, shouted, "The gates! They are moving! Sliding together!"

Sure enough, inch by slow inch, the gates had lifted slightly to escape their ground slots and were now moving toward each other.

Trapped!

I looked up and back, searching for some kind of escape. The arrow slots weren't wide enough to admit more than an arm. Even Uduward could not escape that way. I had to back away from the inner portcullis when it pushed against me. Only then did I notice the bosses, at the intersections of the bars, were sharpened to a point. A thin man, such as my squire, might align himself to avoid their prongs, but, even then, he might be crushed. Gerard and I, in our heavy armour, would be impaled. For a moment, I considered which would be less painful, but I shook myself free of such thoughts

We have to escape! It must be possible!

"Monsieur!" shouted Gerard, desperately.

I looked up again and examined the top of the iron grilles more closely.

Yes, there, at the top. A possibility!

"Uduward!" I shouted. I pointed to the top of the inner portcullis. "Could you get through that gap at the top of the grille?"

"Maybe Sir!"

"Climb! Go on!"

He took hold of the iron bars and placed a foot on the first rung of his ladder to escape.

"It's greased!" he exclaimed as his foot slid off. He tried again and managed to make it up the first four bars.

"Keep going son!" shouted Gerard. He moved to stand underneath my squire with his hands outstretched to catch him if he fell.

By now the grilles were not more than ten feet apart. They were about twenty feet high and Uduward had only climbed a quarter of the way up.

We're not going to make it!

In my mind, confused with so many thoughts of treachery, I had only one idea, for Uduward to reach the lever that Pierre must have pulled. But now it looked like he wouldn't reach the top in time! He too would be crushed or impaled!

As Uduward climbed, Gerard and I prepared to brace ourselves against the grilles. Perhaps we could stop them closing. I dropped my helm and placed my heels against the outer grille's base. The two grilles were now only four feet apart.

My shield!

Suddenly I remembered my shield, still strapped to my back. I quickly took it off, and Gerard, seeing my intention, helped me brace its point against the outer grille. We wedged the top edge of the battered shield against two bosses of the inner grille, keeping it as close to horizontal as possible.

"Our swords as well! Quick, Gerard."

While I held the shield in place, the old knight withdrew both our swords from their sheaths. He struggled to move in the confined space. Awkwardly, cursing, he wedged the two swords against the grilles as best he could. The grilles continued their slow rumble toward each other, and the shield began to flex. Both swords flexed, Gerards's springing lose with a clang and spinning around its axis in mid-air. It came to rest harmlessly on the ground, half under one of the menacing grilles.

I glanced up and nearly shouted with delight. Uduward had climbed half over the inner portcullis now, his chest supporting his weight on the top bar.

Gerard and I both shouted at once.

"Yes!"

"Go on!"

With a huge effort, the youth levered himself over the grille and placed his feet tentatively on the second bar down.

At that moment the shield finally gave up its valiant effort to hold back the forces pushing the two gates together. My sword sprang loose as well, and then only our two bodies, braces against the grilles, were keeping us from being crushed.

A few seconds more!

Gerard and I both screamed with the effort, our bones threatening to break as the great force bore upon us. I felt the blood spurt from my ears and nose as the pressure intensified. I heard bones cracking somewhere. The pain so overwhelmed me that I couldn't tell if the bones were mine or not. I opened my mouth for one last death yell before the end. But the grilles stopped moving.

"Are you alright!" shouted Uduward. "I don't know how this thing works!"

"Get it off … us!" grunted Gerard, panting. Blood ran from his nose and ears.

Suddenly, the gates began to close again!

"No!" Gerard and I both screamed.

The grilles stopped moving and then moved apart. After separating enough for us both to collapse, they stopped again, and then Uduward found the correct lever to raise the grilles.

He rushed over to where we lay panting on the ground.

"Never … !" gasped Gerard.

"Never again … did you mean?" I said, coughing and laughing at the same time. "That was bloody close!" After recovering for a few minutes, I hauled myself to my feet. "Come on Gerard. Time's running out. We have to go on!" The old knight struggled to his feet. He lurched after me.

The Gate would open in not much over twenty minutes. We had to find it before then.

Staggering under the inner portcullis, I saw what I had expected, on the back of the left wall; two levers. They were above a narrow ledge and beyond this, a steep staircase ran at right angles to the entrance tunnel. It had no windows, and so we couldn't see either end. Peering to the right, I could see up about twenty feet or more, but after that I could see only blackness. It was the same if I looked down to the left.

"Now what?" Gerard asked. He looked very pale

"Up, I would think!" I said. "I don't like it though! Look at that gap." On either side of the narrow stairwell, a small gap could be seen between the stairs and the wall. "Another trick of this maze, I bet!"

After a moment to catch our breaths, I returned and picked up my helmet and sword. The shield was useless. Gerard picked up his sword, and then we started up the steps to the right, Uduward leading.

"Careful!" I cautioned him.

We had climbed about twenty feet when, without warning, the steps disappeared to be replaced by a smooth stone slope.

"What the … !"

"Merde!" Gerard and Uduward both said, together.

I instinctively reached for the walls and tried to brace myself against slipping I couldn't. I slid back into Gerard, himself sliding, and then somehow, accidentally, he became stuck. Supported by his weight, we were both wedged precariously across the width of the oblique tunnel. Gerard's armour took most of the strain, but his sword clanged down into the dark depths, beyond the inner portcullis. My helmet followed.

I glanced upwards, wondering why my squire's weight hadn't fallen on me. Uduward grinned down at me. He looked almost comfortable, wedged with his back against one wall, his feet against the other. His blue eyes shone in the torchlight.

"I used to clean the flues in the castle for some extra food when I was younger," he said. "Our castle had the first chimneys in these parts!" he said proudly.

"Can you … get further up?" I gasped.

"I think so … . Let me try!" With some effort he began to inch his way up the sloping tunnel until I could no longer see him in the gloom.

"Can you hear anything? How much longer … ? Monsieur Jean?" Gerard asked, short of breath. "You have been eating far too well, lately!"

"Uduward!" I shouted. "Can you see anything?"

"Yes. A wall at the top. I'm almost there! There seem to be gaps around it. Maybe it's a door!"

We waited, sweating. I did my best to support my weight by using opposing force against both walls of the tunnel to alleviate the load on Gerard's armour and legs.

"I don't think it's a door!" Uduward shouted. "I can't feel a draft through the cracks. It's a trick! I'm coming down!"

He took less time to descend.

"Is there anything at all; a lever, a sign or something?" I asked.

"Somebody has written something there, but I can't read! And there's the sign of the cross too."

Some poor soul!

"Down!" I announced.

I left it to Gerard to make a suggestion.

"Shall we fall? Or climb?" he gasped.

"Climb, preferably. I will try to lift my weight off you. Can you climb?"

"I'm not sure Monsieur. I'm getting too old for this. My arms are very tired!"

"Try!" I shifted position, gingerly. Forcing my back against one wall and my booted feet against the other, I lifted my weight from him.

For the first few inches of his descent, things went well, but then Gerard exclaimed, "Er! Oh … no!" and then he fell. There was no time to even call his name before he clattered out of sight. I heard a loud cry from him and the clang of an impact, followed by silence.

"Gerard! Are you *there?*" I yelled. I heard no reply. Hesitatingly, I began my own descent. Sharp pain screamed up and down my arms as I tried to descend slowly.

Like a spider caught in a spider's web! Where is Ariadne, anyw- ... !

My thought remained suspended in its silken metaphor, as my own grip gave way, and I began to fall. I tried to stop myself but only succeeded in hitting my arm against something. Then something hit my head, and I blacked out.

"Sir! Sir! Are you alright?" I opened my eyes and dimly saw Uduward peering down at me. He peering over something. I remembered where we were and felt relieved to be alive. I could feel something solid underneath me. My whole body ached, and I feared I had broken something. Then, the something underneath me groaned and shifted. "Very, very lucky, Sir! Look!"

Uduward put his finger on the point of a long spike, which ended inches from my face. The spike protruded from the floor, and both Gerard and I were wrapped around it. A chill ran down my spine.

We should both be dead!

"This is crazy," came from the gloom below. "Let's go back!"

"Gerard! You're alive!" I answered.

"No thanks to you! Your wife has a lot to answer for!"

"We can't go back. Neither of us, even if we wanted to! There's no way up!"

The smooth, steep slope of the stone corridor stretched away above us. Far above, I saw a square of bright, yellowish light from the entrance passage. I though it incredible that we had both survived the fall. Only Uduward could get out now.

"Why didn't you escape?" I asked him.

"I could have … ." He grinned. "But I always wanted to find treasure. Don't they call this the Maze Tower? And I bet, if there is any, it's down here!"

Painfully, I hauled myself to my feet and stumbled against my great helm. I picked it up. It still seemed in good shape.

Testament to its good build!

In the dimness, I could just see a narrow ledge, about four feet above my feet. I hauled a protesting, groaning Gerard to his feet and then climbed onto it. Uduward sat beside me, swinging his legs nonchalantly.

"Designed to kill!" I said, needlessly pointing out the spike to Gerard who stood with his head just below our own.

"Monsieur!" announced Gerard. "I've had plenty of time to consider that spike and its purpose while my face has been inches from its base. In the darkness, you wouldn't know this, but it is itself a device, a trap, I believe."

"Why do you say that?" I asked.

Hoisting himself up beside us, he drew his sword and placed the flat of the tip on top of the long spike.

"May I?" he asked us both.

Not knowing what he meant, Uduward and I looked at each other and nodded, uncertainly. Gerard tapped the spike with his blade, and I then I heard a loud commotion. The spike disappeared through a hole in the vertical end of the corridor, and the bottom four feet of the corridor fell away. A large gaping, rectangular hole remained, only slightly blacker than the inky darkness around us. A slight draft wafted through the hole.

"Treasure!" shouted Uduward.

"Doubt it!" I said, dubiously. "More like skeletons."
I stood up and studied the dank space around me.

"We're underground," I said. "It's damp." I took off
my glove and ran my hand over the cool stone blocks of
the wall in front of me. At my furthest reach, to my left
I felt a thin crack in the wall. Through it a delicate
breath of air whispered over my fingers. "A doorway!" I
inched along the ledge until my left foot hit the sloping
floor of the corridor. I could go no further. In front of
me, I saw the left edge of the door. Reaching up and
running my hands over the wall to the left of this I felt
something curious and unexpected. I put my glove back
on to investigate. Not knowing what it could be, but
given recent events in the Tower, I suspected another
instrument of painful torture.

"Look here Uduward. There's something on the
wall! Can't make it out with my glove on properly. Can
you see it?"

We swapped places, and I held onto him as he leaned
out to the left, peering at the device. "Hm. Not sure
what it is. I can *describe* it to you … . There is a
squared hole in the wall … . It's about as long as my
arm and about as high as my outstretched hand … . And
in it, there's a long … erm … what do you call it? A
tube shape … ?"

"Cylinder?" I suggested.

"Oui! That's it. A cylinder. The cylinder is divided
into about … one, two, three … erm … ten parts. Lucky
I can count to ten! Each part looks like it
moves … turns. There are patterns or shapes on each
part. I think they're numbers. I can't see. Maybe later
when my eyes get used to the dark … . That's it, I
think … . Wait! No, one more thing. Above the hole, on
the wall, there is some writing. I don't know what it
says. I can't see it anyway. Erm … . That's all I can
see! What do you want me to do?"

"Erm. I don't know! God, time's running out. We have to get out of here soon! You'd better come back for now. Let me think about it."

I suddenly knew what the device was. "A tumbler of some sort, I think! I've seen them in books. Some locks work like that. We have to find out what the numbers are and understand the message on the wall. If we understand that, maybe we can crack it!"

I quickly explained the tumbler's purpose and how we might get it open. After some discussion, Uduward declared he could see more clearly. I looked around, and knew I could too.

"Let's try again," I suggested.

I stood on the ledge. This time, both Uduward and Gerard held onto me while I leaned out as far to the left as I could. My face drew level with the tumbler, and I could read most of the numbers without straining too hard. With my glove on, I gingerly turned one of the sections. I could see it had nine numbers on it; one to nine of the Roman numerical notation; not surprising, given the apparent age of the Tower. I had more difficulty reading the Latin text above the device.

"I can't read the first word." Slowly, screwing up my eyes painfully, I read out:

> "' … vos es prime intelligence,
> you ero suscipio of thesaurus.'"

I translated it:

> "' … you are the prime intelligence, you
> will be the receiver of treasure.'"

"The first word is probably 'if.'"
"Well, that's good. That means we must be close to the treasure!" Uduward said.

"No, I think it's more than that, Uduward. I think it's a clue. It's a riddle."

"Oh, I love riddles," he replied.

"I just want to get out of here!" added Gerard.

"Let me think. Ten sections … that's ten numbers. Ten words? No, more than that. Um. Tricky!" I found myself already sweating profusely from the earlier climbing and the fall. Sweat was pouring off me even though the air must have been cool, judging by the damp on the walls; I couldn't rid myself of the thought that we were running out of time. We had to find the Gate before 3 pm or risk losing Georgina and therefore, Rose. I thought harder, but that only made my thoughts muddy.

"I'm stuck!" I said, frustrated.

"Here, have this!" Uduward said. "I saved it for you." He pressed something against my mouth. I could smell smoked ham. I opened my mouth and bit into the succulent meat. Chewing it calmed me, and I sat down.

"The trouble is, thesaurus has many meanings. It could mean treasure or horde, or any collection of valuable things. In fact, it could mean anything valuable! Maybe there is an anagram in there!" I spent several useless minutes, trying to think of an anagram that would reveal what to do with the tumbler. Finally, I became so angry that I hit the wall with my gloved hand. It stung, so I took off my gloves.

Damn. I can't get stuck on this!

"What does it mean, 'prime intelligence'?" asked Uduward. "Does it mean that only one of us can find the treasure? That seems odd. Do the keepers only expect one of us to survive?"

"No," I replied. "I think it just means that if, together, we are clever enough to solve this riddle, then we can all be rich. That's what it means by 'prime' – if we are first among thinkers … . Wait though. Prime … .

Prime has another meaning! Yes. *Prime* numbers! Could be … ." Fired with a new idea, I quickly ran over my basic maths lessons at school. My only recollections of prime numbers were that they were only divisible by themselves and one. "The first prime numbers are three, seven, eleven, seventeen … . Oh wait! This isn't going to work. The tumbler sections only have single numbers!"

"Oh." Uduward said.

Uduward and I discussed possibilities while Gerard sat quietly. As the minutes went by, I grew more and more tense and frustrated. "We're going to be too late! I know it. If we don't get through soon, it's all over! There has to be a solution. But prime numbers is all I can think of! It has to be something to do with that. Just that the sections … of the tumbler … . Oh, I don't know!"

"But couldn't you use two sections for these numbers?" Gerard suggested.

"What?" I said, not quite hearing him, deep in my own thoughts.

"Oh nothing. I am not good with my numbers."

"No, go on!" I said, desperate for anything we could try.

"It's nothing. A silly idea. Bound to be wrong!"

"No. Please, Gerard. Anything is worth trying … ."

"Well, can't you use two of the sections for the … um … big numbers?"

I would have laughed at his childlike numeracy had I not been overcome with excitement at the obvious solution. "Yes! Yes! It has to be that. It's so simple, but it could work!"

Just as we were about to put my idea into action, the dim light in the shaft well became a blackness. Glancing up we all saw that the square of light by the entrance corridor had almost been erased.

"What's happened?" muttered Uduward. "It can't be night, yet?"

"No, but a darkness has fallen in the sky. It's a sky you don't even want to see. I have seen it once. It's a sign that great evil is here!" I replied.

Gerard crossed himself. "Sweet Go- … !" he began to mutter under his breath. But even this short prayer was cut short. The stone we stood on began to vibrate slightly, and I felt, rather than heard, a distant hum.

Uduward reached out and grabbed my arm. "Sir!"

"The Gate!" I shouted. "It's opened. We must hurry! There's only minutes left!"

I put my gloves back on. Remembering my history lessons and the vinegar that Leonardo DaVinci put in his tumbler design to protect secret documents, I feared the possibility of something like sulphuric acid in this one. But looking for the tumbler, I realised I could no longer see it. No light lit the shaft at all.

"I need light! Gerard, do you have your flints?"

"No, I lost them! But wait, I have a spare in my pouch, somewhere." From a small leather pouch around his waist he took items out, one at a time, identifying them by touch. He passed each to Uduward, who held them tenderly.

"Come on! Come on!" I shouted, beside myself.

"Be patient Monsieur. I don't want to drop it!" But he did. Just as he exclaimed in victory, "I have it!" it slipped from his fingers and fell onto the stone floor, making a tinkling sound. "No!" he shouted in anguish.

Quick as a flash, Uduward jumped down after it. He almost disappeared over the edge of the trap-door hole before shouting, "I have it!" How he saw it in the gloom, I will never know. I could barely see my hand. Perhaps his feral life in the castle had attuned his eyes to see things in dim light. Perhaps he just sensed it. However, further anguish followed our sense of relief.

"It's slipping!" Uduward whispered.

Gerard and I jumped down and grabbed his legs. We pulled as hard as we could.

"It's gone!" Uduward said when he finally turned to face us. "But I think I can see the floor. It's not too far down. I think I can still get it."

I had the sickening feeling that the Devil was playing his part in this story. I had a strong urge to give up. I took a deep breath and told Gerard to take off his sword belt. Tying them both together, I lowered Uduward down the dripping wall, into the hole. With only my legs held by Gerard outside the hole, and at the very end of my reach, Uduward let go. The belt in my hand went slack.

"Are you alright?" I shouted. My voice echoed back at me.

"Yes," came his echoing reply. "Monsieur, there are dead bodies down here! It stinks. I don't know … ."

We listened to his muttering as he searched for the flint. My heart pounded, threatening to break my rib cage apart. Barely able to contain myself, I held my breath.

When I was about to say, "Forget it, I'll do it by touch," Uduward cried out:

"Haul me up. I have it!"

I leaned over the edge of the hole, holding the belts and Gerard held on to my legs. Even then, jumping up, Uduward couldn't reach the belt buckle above him

"Lower!" I shouted to Gerard. He took hold of my feet and lowered me as far as he could. "Now!" I shouted, and I felt Uduward's weight suddenly pull the belt taught. "Up! Pull" I shouted. Gerard grunted with the effort, and I feebly pushed on the rock with my free hand in a vain attempt to help. Then I found myself on my knees, so I pulled Uduward out of the hole. Quickly we climbed back on the ledge. While Gerard held on to me so that I could lean out to reach the tumbler, Uduward struck the flint against Gerard's dagger. In little flashes, I caught glimpses of the numbers.

Staring furthest left, I turned the section of the tumbler to 'three,' 'five,' 'seven,' 'eleven,' 'thirteen' and 'seventeen.' There I stopped. There was only one section left, and yet the next prime number would be double-digit. "This can't be right *either*!"

"Why not?" asked Gerard, crestfallen.

"Because there is one number left *over*!"

"Are you *sure* you have them right?"

I went back to the first.

"Wait. I do remember that in my lessons, 'one' wasn't considered a prime, but one of the other students complained that this wasn't logical." I thought out loud. "The master explained that our conception of prime numbers had evolved and that in medieval times, 'one' *had* been considered a prime."

"*Well* then!" Gerard said. I began to wonder how good the old knight's education had been. He grasped mathematics better than I had expected.

I leaned out and made the adjustment. Sure enough, starting with 'one,' all ten sections were used up neatly. As I turned the last section into position, I heard a loud crack, followed by a rumble, as of a beam being drawn over rollers. The door didn't move. Hesitatingly, I pushed it. Still it didn't move. Leaning against it, I pushed with all my might. Uduward and Gerard helped me, and together we inched the door open.

Yes!

The moment the door opened, the humming became much louder, and we heard voices inside the room beyond the door. With one last heave, the door opened. The voices stopped.

"Wait!" I whispered. "Gerard! Your sword. We must be ready for a fight!" We both picked up our weapons, and I retrieved my helm. Then we were through the door. We ran down a short flight of stairs into a room awash with bright orange light. "The Gate."

Three guards turned to face us. Pierre stood to one side, looking slightly bewildered and not a little frightened.

"The guards!" I yelled as I rushed the closest. Gerard kept close behind me, and together we struck down the two unsuspecting and poorly armoured guards. The third managed to draw his sword and strike at my back.

"Kill him! Pierre screamed!"

I heard the clash of swords and rolled to the side, just as the guard's sword, deflected by Gerard's, clanged against the stone flags.

I considered what to do about the guards and Pierre, but at that moment the beam turned orange.

No time!

"Into the beam!" I yelled

"With you … Monsieur."

"Coming!" shouted Uduward.

All three of us stepped forward together.

* * *

Chapter Seven

The first time I had used a Gate after drinking blood went better. A second later, I felt a great pain in my head and heard a rushing sound, which drowned out all my other senses. Suddenly, the noise of the beam stopped, and I fell to something like wet grass in a large field. The others were strewn all around me. Apart from the spinning in my head, the pain in my shoulder was the only side-effect I felt. The perfumed of grass and earth filled the air, just as it does after rain.

"Where are we?" whispered Uduward weakly beside me.

"How do you feel?"

"Alright … I guess. My head and stomach hurt badly. But apart from that … ."

"What's your name?"

"Rathea- … . Uduward!"

"Good. You're alright."

I crawled over to Gerard and tapped him on the shoulder. "What's your name?"

"Err. Vwhhher!" Gerard vomited twice before finishing his sentence, "Gerard, Monsieur!"

"You're alright too then." I slapped him playfully on the shoulder again. After a few moments more, I found that I could stand.

"Where are we?" Uduward asked.

"Ireland, 7th Century!"

I stood up and looked around us. We were at the edge of a loosely planted corn field at the base of a shallow hill. Near the top of the hill, I could see a tall, stone tower above a thick stand of trees. A village lay near us and a track wound through the houses, around the skirt of the hill and up toward the tower.

"That could be the Abbey!" I declared, pointing to

the tower.

"I think this is a wild goose-chase anyway!" muttered Gerard. "She definitely won't be in this abbey, this witch."

I had to admit, it was a long-shot, but we didn't have anything else to go on.

For the first time in weeks, I had time to think. The late afternoon sun beat down on swishing stalks of corn and nobody attacked us!

"Let's go to the village," I suggested and set off. While I waded through the corn, I thought of the two women forcing my every move at the moment.

Georgina; that elemental force of nature from Paris! How I had loved her and then lost her.

With Rose, you could have a rational conversation about anything. She thought deeply but kept her deepest thoughts to herself. In conversation she usually seemed practical, but you were always certain that her views were based on deep consideration, not superficial values. That's why she so often surprised me. Sometimes her ideas were simply unexpected and unconventional, but at other times her sensitivity and perception simply took my breath away.

With Georgina, one felt in the presence of a storm whose very moods were dictated by the most elemental forces of nature. She seemed as much a victim of these as one felt oneself, so I found it hard blame her for her actions. I never felt comfortable judging her. Perhaps that was my weakness and one that had been exploited. But not by her. Others had used her to get to me. Though still filled with a bilious anger toward Georgina, I was beginning to suspect that she wasn't the puppet-master but the puppet, perhaps even a victim herself. Somebody else pulled the strings. The thought made me shake my head with sorrow.

I'm not sure I can kill Georgina!

Then something occurred to me for the first time.

What if Georgina is the one to die!

Despite what she had done to Rose and I, the thought made me angry. It made me want to kill someone, and I was just about to impulsively say that out loud when I was interrupted by a voice from the edge of the field. At the same time, the first drop of heavy rain fell on my hand.

A man with a straw hat was waving wildly at us.

"What's he saying Monsieur?" Gerard asked.

"I don't know."

We reached the man and saw that behind him, were four armed soldiers. They stepped forward to take us in hand. I heard the 'rhing' as Gerard drew his sword, but I motioned for him to stop.

"Let them take us. They might take us to the Abbey. Besides, we can't fight a whole village of people who don't understand what we say."

We were led to a sort of block house at the upper end of the village and, as I expected, presented to a well-dressed man who asked us in Latin:

"Who are you who dress so strangely? And what were you doing in Ainmire's field?"

"First of all, who are you?" I replied in my best Latin.

"I am the Magistrate of Slane Township. You have committed the crime of trespass. Answer for yourselves."

I considered carefully before answering:

"Well, we are dressed strangely, because we come from afar. We seek an Abbot, Cathal. We became lost. Our intention wasn't to trespass, but when we finally saw the road, we had to cross the field to reach it."

I saw Gerard flinch at the mention of the Abbott's name, but I ignored him.

The Magistrate, dressed in a finely embroidered tunic down to his knees, and with a bear fur thrown over his shoulders, nodded.

"Nevertheless. There will be a fine. Can you pay it?"

"I believe we can."

"Even then, I will have more questions before I can release you."

"Very well. How much is the fine?"

I heard him say fifty, followed by a denomination I did not recognize. From my soaking wet pouch, being careful not to disturb the other coins to give away our relative wealth, I withdrew one silver coin and held it up.

"Is this adequate?" I enquired.

He nodded and dipped his chin toward a less well-dressed man to his right. The man stepped forward and took my coin. From his pouch he took some copper coins and placed them in my hand.

After the exchange, suddenly the Magistrate smiled at us and said:

"You must forgive our formality. This is Slane. At the top of the hill is Slane College. Within its walls rests the Abbey and the Castle. The rich send, from all over Europe, their sons to be educated there. It is heavily guarded and any strangers who approach are bound to arouse our interest. But you said you sought Abbott…"

"Cathal."

"His name is not Cathal. There *is* no Abbot of that name that I know of in the Kingdom."

"But there *is* an abbot?"

"Yes. You want to have an audience with him?"

I glanced at Gerard and Uduward. Gerard nodded, but Uduward stared at his feet.

"Yes, if it pleases you Magistrate."

"It would please me if you would be my guests tonight. I always like to hear news from afar."

I didn't altogether trust this man, but we needed to get out of our present detainment.

"We would be glad to," I replied.

"Then you will find rooms available at the hostelry a short distance down the road."

He made it sound as if we could only find rooms, because we were going to be his guest. I agreed, and we left, accompanied by about a dozen curious locals.

After we had paid for two rooms we took some ale at the bar, fully intending to escape as soon as the attention died down.

"That was quite funny; when you asked for Abbot Cathal…" a man said to me from the next seat at the bar. His clothes were covered in soil; he smelled of that and cow manure.

"Why?" I asked.

"They wouldn't want to admit it, even if there was an Abbot Cathal. I had a brother who was a monk, once. He knew everybody in the College…"

"I see. Would you like a drink?"

"If you are buying. Times are hard."

"Here! I am tired. You buy it."

I took out a silver coin and slid it across the counter. He placed his hand over it and pocketed the coin.

"The only *religious* Cathal around here is *Friar* Cathal. My brother never was under him at the Monastery, but he told me this about him; the Abbot was a very deep thinker and wrote books. Popular too."

"Is he still alive?"

"Apparently, although he will be very old now."

"Where can I find him?"

"They say he lives in the old Hermitage in the woods, just up the road to the College, and turn left along a side path. It's by a stream. I haven't seen him for years though. Somebody sends into town for provisions. Could be him…"

"Was he pushed out of the Abbey then?"

"Apparently not."

"Thank you very much. There will be another silver piece for you if you keep quiet about this."

"Will do. Good evening."

I told Gerard and Uduward the good news.

"Let's just stay for a few drinks?" Gerard suggested. "There is a nice little blonde over there. And I think I can afford her."

"We have no time Gerard. Sorry!"

As soon as most of our clothes had dried on jacks next to the fire, and the patrons were too drunk to notice, we left the hostel. It was still raining.

We had to skirt a long way round the block house to get back to the track above the Abbey's outer defenses. We traipsed up the path, feeling quite hungry and tired. But we had to keep moving.

Time is running out!

I began peering into the trees to my right. Nearer the river in the bottom of the valley, my search became more intense.

"What are you looking for?" asked Gerard, irritably.

I didn't answer, not sure at all of my information.

"There!" I shouted. I stepped onto the barest of paths between the trees, and the other two followed. Tall grass and ferns brushed our waist, and several times we had to stoop under low willow and alder branches. A few dripping leaves still clung to the willows. "Udu, you scout up the track for a bit; see how far from trouble we are. Don't get seen."

"Does it *always* rain in the 7th Century?" Gerard asked. He got no reply. "Is this some kind of mad plan to double back to the Abbey Monsieur?"

"No."

"Only I think there will be a thunderstorm soon," Gerard continued. "I just wanted to know."

Gerard was right. The sky had become dark with thick, black cumulus clouds which I could see between the spidery branches of trees. Soon the path entered a gully, very steep sided on the hill side to its right and north side. Here, only ferns and tough grass covered the heathery floor. Mushy mud squelched under our boots.

"This had better be worth it!" Gerard muttered.

Aha! Here we are!

I stopped and surveyed the rough wooden building ahead, set into the hill. I saw a two-storey tower on top of what, I assumed, must be the Hermitage. The bank on the right rose level with its pointed roof. To our left, on the south side, I saw a single-storey construction and directly ahead of us a single, heavy oak door with an iron ring.

I walked straight up to the door and swung the hinged ring against the door.

I heard no reply, so I tried once again.

"Nobody here," suggested Gerard. "Come on. Let's go. I can't see anything for us here!"

I twisted the iron ring and pushed on the door. It creaked open.

I saw very little light within. The placed seemed to drip with damp, and much of the woodwork had a green sheen to it where lichen or mould had taken hold.

"Come on," I said, stepping inside. I put my hand on the hilt of my sword. Inside I could dimly see, beyond the tower, a nave with a single candle for light. The dim light made strange shadows dance on the walls.

To the left, and just beyond the oak door, a few steps led up to another door and just beyond those, more steps led down to a stone archway. The floor and walls, to the height of a single course, were of stone.

I couldn't see anybody in the tower; completely hollow, save for a single rope hanging from a single bell high overhead. A smell of horse dung came from the stone archway to the left, and I thought I heard the snort of a horse or donkey from beyond.

Only one option remained. I climbed the few steps to the other door and lifted the latch. This seemed so intrusive that I almost turned and left. With a deep intake of breath, I pushed the door gently. I watched as it slowly swung open, making two creaking sounds in quick succession.

"Ha! Who are you? An Angel!" a deep, booming voice rang out from the darkness.

On a pallet bed, lit by a single, tiny candle, I saw a man. Reclining against the far wall, he was leaning on his elbows. He appeared to be in a state of shock; hardly surprising.

"Don't fear!" I said quickly. "We are not robbers. I'd just like to talk with you. We're travellers, and I've heard so much about Abbot Cathal!"

"Eh? Are you *mad*! Anyway, it's just Friar Cathal now. But please tell me; who are you, for you have the light of an angel around you. I was dreaming a dark and strange dream just now, and then I awake, and you are at the foot of my bed. Pray, tell who you are!"

"I'm no angel. At least not in the biblical sense. But I do think we might have a lot to talk about. Are you the Cathal that writes books?"

"The same. Yes."

He still seemed frozen to the spot.

"Can I fetch you some water or something?" I offered.

"No. No! No, it's me who has bad manners! Forgive me." He quickly threw aside some very dirty looking blankets and stood up. A big man, taller than Gerard, he wore only a light undergarment, which reached half way down his thighs. For a religious man, however, he seemed not the least bothered by his immodesty. His grey hair hung in little strands from a bald head. I couldn't tell if he had been tonsured, because I saw no hair anywhere on his head but for the very outermost fringes. He had a strongly-featured face and was well built. I noticed, when he passed me holding the candle up, so we could both see each other clearly, that his eyes were piercing and blue.

"I don't have much!" he shouted, disappearing down the steps and through the stone arch. He came back moments later, cradling a large round loaf of bread, a segment of cheese and a stoneware jar. Placing them on one of the stone steps, he went to the altar and returned carrying three, small gold, communion cups.

"I shouldn't use these, of course, but then that's why I always keep a few spares! Is it raining outside?"

Gerard, who had kept silent until now, answered quickly, "No, but it will shortly."

"Ah yes, it usually is raining here. You noticed! Ha!"

He seemed delighted with everything.

"Bring the other things outside. We may as well enjoy some fresh air!"

He led us around the south side of the tower to an overturned stone pillar, lying in the ferns a few yards north east of it. On it were carved ancient runes, of a type I couldn't decipher. Here we sat and ate the hard bread and cheese. Cathal uncorked the jar with a very full set of strong, healthy teeth and poured us each a glass of an amber liquid.

"Ah! Very good," Gerard said. "Like one of our strong wines but better!"

I tried it too. It tasted pungent, like ale, but sweet and had quite a kick to it.

A single drop of rain fell on my nose, and moments later Uduward appeared.

"I couldn't find you in that funny little church, but I heard voices!" he said, before seeing Cathal and turning sheepish.

"Well. Bless my soul! A youth. I don't see many of those these days. Come here boy and have a sip of this. Quick before we go inside."

"Sorry Udu! I forgot about you. Did you do what I asked?"

"Hm. Very strange. I don't recognise that language at all!" Cathal said.

"It's Frankish."

"Oui Monsieur," Uduward continued. "But there is something I have to tell you!"

I took Uduward aside, and he whispered in my ear:

"I went as far as the walls; there are great walls around the whole… fortress. We will never get through except using a gate, which is heavily guarded. I climbed a tree to look over. There is the monastery and the Abbey, of course, but also a huge, wooden tower. There are soldiers everywhere! If your wife is in there, Monsieur, we will never get her out on our own!"

"I see…"

"But I wanted to help, so I crawled close enough to overhear the guards."

"But *you* don't speak Latin and anyway, *they* probably don't either!"

"Well, we may have some luck there. First of all, I have picked up a few words of Latin over the years. I didn't tell you… And they were speaking Latin. Perhaps they are from different countries. I couldn't understand much, but they mentioned the Sorceress and said she lived in the tower with the Chieftain, Cairbre."

I patted Uduward on the shoulder. "You did very well Udu. Thank you very much. Although this changes things. We can't go on alone. We need help more than ever. Looks like we need an army!"

I addressed Cathal as soon as we returned:

"Can I please talk to you about something very important? I don't have much time."

"Of course. But I think we'll have to go inside. It looks like it *will* rain and heavily. It's the only thing that bothers me about this beautiful country!"

Gerard and I looked nervously at each other. Neither of us were sure we would be safe without leaving a guard, but neither wanted to stay out in the rain.

"Now, what is it you want to discuss?" asked Cathal, sitting with his back against the chapel wall opposite the steps to his small room. Gerard sat with his back against the door and Uduward, and I perched on the steps.

A single large candle lit the floor in the centre of us.

"We have come from afar seeking one who has abducted my wife," I began, boldly. "A few hours ago, I met a man in the hostel who praised your qualities as a thinker and as Abbot of the monastery, and so I want to ask for your help. Believe me, I wouldn't do this if I wasn't desperate. Short of raising an army, I cannot see how to continue the rescue anymore!"

"An army! Do you know my son that thought has been in *my* mind ever since I was forced out!"

"You were *forced* out? But I thought … ."

"Retired? No, that is the way it's *usually* done, but in my case, I wasn't *ready* to retire."

"So what happened?"

"Well, the Prior, Tadh, was my deputy in these days but not chosen by me. He had big ideas, and *unfortunately* … my fondness for a drop of the sacramental liquid proved the lever by which he was able to open *that* door!"

"Oh, I see."

"But that wasn't what made me angriest, and not what I want to raise an army for. No. That has more to do with the Cairbre, the Chieftain. He's a very bad sort and communes with Satan, his followers too, in my view. There is a young woman … ."

"Georgiana?"

"Ah. I see you have met her."

"She's a sorceress."

"Yes. She is!" Cathal seemed astonished by my candid statement. "I see you're not only some kind of holy man but a very experienced one and candid to boot. A most unusual combination!" He refilled my cup.

"She's the one who has kidnapped my wife, Rose. I don't know why, and most of all, I don't know why it has to be here, but I have been told that she will try to sacrifice my wife at the next full moon. That's tomorrow night. I gather it's some kind of magic ritual, but I intend to stop her! I just don't know how. I think they have Rose in a wooden tower on top of the hill."

"Ah," Cathal said.

Gerard and Uduward had visibly relaxed since hearing Cathal's woes, and the knight now grunted his endorsement of each statement of the facts.

The rain outside was, by now, hammering on the south walls and the roof of the tower.

"Where exactly did you say you were from?" Cathal asked, after being silent for a long while.

"Ah, well that might take a long time to explain."

"Well, I could possibly help you, but I would need to know a lot more about you. If I act now, it will be the boldest move of my life. But then again, my life so far seems to have amounted to very little so perhaps the Lord is ready for a little boldness on my part. Why don't you stay the night, and we can discuss it at length?"

Uduward, and Gerard nodded vigorously their approval of this suggestion.

***

"I was dreaming of an angel with wings, just before you arrived," Cathal began, a short time later. "But there was something strange about this angel. It was a wolf."

We had accompanied him in vespers, and we followed this with supper; much the same as the first meal but supplemented with some roast pork.

I shifted my feet uneasily on the stone floor at the base of the steps.

"There's a lot to tell you Cathal and a lot to ask. I have many questions, and so far, I've met nobody who can answer any of those questions. I hope to find some answers, and I hope you can help me."

I told him my story, from the murder of Annie right through until our arrival at Slane. He listened patiently and, for the most part, impassively, while Gerard and Uduward nodded.

I skipped over most of the detail involving serpents, apart from the battle in Beauvais Cathedral, blood drinking and running as a wolf for these were what I wished to discuss at length.

"I've thought about this much," I continued, "and I now believe the Serpent at Bouvines the same one I encountered in Beauvais, only much younger. I think his powers were further diminished, because he had used a Gate to reach that battle."

"I knew it! An Angel! You *are* an Angel."

"Well if I am one, I'm a very strange one. What kind of Angel runs with a pack of wolves at night and drinks blood? In our time we have a name for those, werewolves, and believe me they are about as far as you can get from Angels."

"But you can travel though time! You are from the future. Time is no barrier to you!"

"But the blood drinking Cathal?" I said, sadly. "I am torn."

"Yes, that *is* a bit unusual, but don't you know Satan spends more time trying to tempt angels than he ever does bothering the world of men?"

I felt deflated by Cathal's enthusiasm.

"Can we have a fire in here?" asked Uduward abruptly. He shook from the cold. "I don't like to ask, but surely there must be a fire of some sort?"

"Of course! I forgot. I don't feel the cold anymore," Cathal replied. "In the stable you'll find firewood, down there."

While Gerard and Uduward set about their task willingly, we continued our conversation.

"You haven't seen my book my son – what did you say your name was?"

"Ha! I didn't. Sorry, we haven't even introduced ourselves. I was so intent on my explanations, I forgot. My name is John Rezor, the Knight is Gerard, and obviously you know my Squire is Uduward."

"Ah good. Well, pleased to meet you John. As I was saying, you haven't read my bestiary. In it I go to great length on all kinds of lupine creatures, and your Ordo Lupus sounds just like an order of the winged-wolves that I discuss at length. I see nothing strange about the idea that they, you, are Angels. It's one of my hypotheses."

"Really? That's fascinating. This quality seems to run in my family though, I would remind you. That would mean many hundreds of Angels, and I didn't think there were that many? But anyway, I digress. What I really want to understand are the Winged Serpents. What are they?"

"Well, that's a very good question. It seems you have more practical experience of them than I. Why don't you tell me all you know, and then perhaps we can work it out together. Theology, dear boy. That's what it's all about."

"Well … ."

"Excuse me Abbot Cathal. Do you have something

to use as tinder?" asked Uduward.

"Use some straw."

"Well, where do I start?" I continued. "Alright, I know that the Serpents only usually appear once every sixty years and then for only a few months … ."

Within moments Gerard had used his flint to get a roaring fire going in the grate.

"It seems," I said "as if, for some reason, the fabric of time and space, which is held together by God's will I presume, is for some reason weaker, and creatures from without our world, or non-physical beings if you will, are able to break through. So I don't believe that the Serpents are real. They're not physical like you or me. In fact, I don't think many people can see them. I'm the only person I know who can see them."

"Go on."

Gerard and Uduward had seated themselves beside us and were listening intently.

"Gerard? At the battle in Bouvines, I saw a Serpent; it crushed the helmets and skulls of a line of knights in front of me, but you didn't see anything, did you?"

"I only saw something out of the corner of my eye. When I looked I could see the knights lying on the ground. I must have seen them fall in a line. I thought it just coincidence. But it's true that their helmets were crushed in. It was as if they had been hit on all sides at the same time by many maces."

"You see!" I exclaimed. "Though he was right next to me, Gerard saw nothing!"

"He's not tuned to see though young John!" exclaimed Cathal. "The spirit world is not for all to see. Even myself, I have difficulties."

"Well anyway, what else do I know? Um. They seem to have various ways of killing, which seems to be what they like to do most. Most seem to revolve around a strange kind of crushing; it's almost as if they suck the life out of people. The image makes me feel sick, because it happened to my daughter, but erm … er … er hm, the body looks like … a piece of fruit that's been dehydrated or crushed in some strange kind of way. I actually think it might be what a body would look like if crushed under enormous pressure. I've never seen a body like *this* though. I *do* wonder if it's the intrusion of the serpent from a world *without* that is causing it."

"What do you mean?"

"Well, if the world *without* is not like our own, imagine that it might be like a vacuum. Have you heard of such a thing?"

"Yes. I studied the classics when I was a boy. I know the theories of Archimedes and Pythagorus."

"Well a vacuum is the lack of pressure which, if it touched the inside of a physical object in this world, say a body, it would make that body implode as if it had been squashed."

"I see. Yes, it's a plausible theory."

"I have fought with a serpent, possibly the same one as at Bouvines, and I can tell you they are horrific to behold. But at the same time, not quite there."

"You talk in riddles!" Uduward said, laughing.

"Sh!" whispered Gerard.

"Where was I? Oh yes before I forget, one other thing. When I was about your age, Uduward, I became trapped in a tomb in a cemetery. I was visited by a strange voice in the dark which whispered strange things to me. I forgot it for a long time, but now I think it's significant. I recently found out that this particular cemetery, Highgate in London, has been visited by strange beasts for many, many years. People say they have red eyes and turn to smoke in a moment. This is a lot like the Serpent I saw. He had red eyes which were deeply disturbing to look into. His scales seemed to be made of the bodies of deformed or mutilated souls from

Hell, and his voice was like the myriad voices of the dying. It made one want to despair, seeing and hearing him… it!"

"Truly, the creations of Satan are abominable!" added Cathal. "We are dealing with the very filth of all creation. To encounter them can make the weak lose faith."

"Yes." I shuddered. "I have felt that. I nearly succumbed to the beast in Beauvais. He told me things which … ." I shuddered again.

"Go on with your story," Cathal said, touching my sleeve lightly.

"Yes. I was going to say that I think the Serpents usually operate through someone. I think murderers are initially 'inhabited' by the Serpent and fundamentally changed by it so that when it leaves them, they go on killing in the same way, though in poor imitation, by themselves. In fact, I think the Serpents cannot exist in our world without a susceptible soul as a conduit."

"What's a conduit?" asked Uduward.

"A pipe or ditch, idiot!" answered Gerard.

"Sort of," I said. "It's something that can allow something to pass through it. Your throat is a conduit, and so can your soul be." I said.

"I see."

"Very well put, John," Cathal said. "So who acted the conduit for the Serpent at that battle you keep talking about?"

"Well, that's the curious thing. I saw a knight in strange armour who spoke very little. Later, I believe he led the wolves that I ran with in the night, but most, including himself, had become corrupt. I think they no longer serve God."

"You haven't read my bestiary … . They've committed great sins, the more so because God had already given them such a great power. They were tempted, and so abandoned God. He will not forgive them easily, and their feet are taking them toward Hell!"

"I thought they were damned forever!"

"No," Cathal said, thoughtfully. "Nothing and nobody is damned forever. Even Satan is capable of redemption. Only God can see how it could be done though."

"So you think men that were once wolf-Angels, and now serve the Serpents can be redeemed?"

"Perhaps. They have lost sight of hope, but they haven't yet forgotten the light of hope."

"That makes me feel better, because I know such a one. Anyway, in some way, this knight at the battle was a conduit for the Serpent. At first, I thought he simply brought down the beast. A rent in the air appeared, like a ripple in water, and the Serpent came through, but also it seemed to expand from the knight's body."

Cathal nodded. "And in the Cathed-ral?"

"Yes, that is harder to understand. But there was another there; Georgiana, the woman who holds my Rose captive right now. I think she thought the Serpent served her, but she found that wasn't the case."

Gerard and Uduward shifted their feet uneasily.

"Do you think this … . Serpent is up at the Tower now?" asked Gerard.

"I don't think so. At least I haven't felt his presence yet. It's a feeling of great evil, like a black thunderhead in the spirit world when he appears. I haven't felt *that* yet."

Both Gerard and Uduward smiled with relief.

"But how about your daughter. When she was … taken?" asked Cathal, confused.

"Yes. Now we come to it. This is the deepest, and darkest mystery of all. But now I believe it was I who acted as the conduit."

"But it can't be!" exclaimed Uduward.

Cathal's blue eyes tried to pierce my own.

"It's hard for me to admit and even harder to understand, but when we're young, Udu, we don't always understand our spirits and how the spirit world works. Sometimes, those who mean good are led astray by dark forces. Indeed, I know for sure that I caused the deaths of many men in a great war, in a battle fought in the sky when I was young. It wasn't intended. Perhaps I simply didn't know my own power."

"That is, indeed, it John," Cathal said. "Your grandfather would have understood. There's always that danger with any great power. Learning how to use it, you will make mistakes. And in your case, you had no tutors!"

"Anyway, terrible though it is, it may have been me that caused my daughter's death."

Cathal and Gerard nodded slowly.

"Well, I certainly have enough here for a new book!" Cathal said brightly, getting up and stamping his feet, which had evidently gone to sleep. "Now who would like another drink?"

"But what I really don't understand," I added, " … is why on Earth Georgiana has brought me here. For most surely, she has. Her trail has been easy to follow."

"My dear fellow," Cathal said, pouring himself a drink. "That is easy to understand. You clearly are somebody of great substance in the spirit world. Satan would like nothing more than to take you into his sinful arms. This Georgiana clearly has some very great temptation prepared for you. That is why she has brought you here."

I contemplated this, but before I had thought much, Cathal stood up again.

"Would you like a game of fidchell?"

"What is that," I asked.

"Oh, just a game. But it's popular here. You had better learn."

After only three games, I beat Cathal. He seemed delighted.

"Continue practicing," he said. "For myself, I need to get some sleep. An old man tires quickly you know. I think I can help you John. Tomorrow, early I will go and find a friend of mine, another chieftain. He is a rash man and partial to conquest. He has long had his eye on the community of Slane. In fact, he and I have discussed it over many a barrel of ale, but it has always seemed too great a risk. Now, perhaps it's worth that risk. One thing though, the only way we can take Slane is by firing the tower. If your wife is in there, you are going to have to think hard about how to get her out in time. He has a good heart, but like I said, he's rash, and once his heart is set on attack, he will not be easily dissuaded from his plans, which are usually all too crude. I suggest you come up with something very good in the way of plans to offer him. He won't listen to you alone, but together we might persuade him. It might also help if you have something to offer him as a friendship gift."

"Silver? We have some silver? But if he is a Chieftain, he will probably have a lot more."

"I leave that up to you, but if you want his friendship, it should be something impressive. That would take a lot of silver. One other thing; you should stay here. It's safe enough for an old man to travel through these parts but not for a Squire and two Knights. Stay hidden. There's food enough in the pantry until I get back and straw and some blankets. Stay up if you wish, but have a mind to that fire. This whole place is built of wood."

With that, he retired to his little room, and we were left alone.

After discussing flying wolves, angels and serpents some more, we too made beds of straw and blankets and lay down to sleep.

***

When I awoke at dawn, Cathal had gone.

"I like him," Uduward said, over a breakfast of bread and cheese.

"Let's hope he's as good as his word. He may come back with soldiers to arrest us," I added

"I don't think so," Gerard said.

"That's the first positive thing I've heard you say for a long time!" I said.

Uduward listened, boggle-eyed, while Gerard and I talked. I felt an air of quiet optimism and anticipation in the Hermitage.

"So how about that tower Gerard. Any ideas how we get into it?"

"Uduward has told me all about it. There's only one way; up the causeway Monsieur. I *do* have an idea. I have been thinking about it all night. It really depends on how big this chieftain's army is that we're going to attack with. If we can take the gates from inside the enclosure, I think I can get you to the tower. The problem is going to be getting out again afterwards!"

"What's your idea then?"

"Well, while you were still sleeping, I had a close look at the whole fortification."

Gerard described in much detail the small moat around the tower and other features like a defensive ring of earth further out. Lastly, he came to the causeway parapets. "They are just wood. They will burn like torches if it ever stops raining here. That will make the men on the parapets run! Then I think, if you are quick, you could get a few men up the causeway before the fire completely burns out the corridor. What do you think?"

"Hm. It might work. If it were me, and I am betting it will be, I would like to be wearing a cape soaked in water first. The heat will be intense."

"I will be coming too."

"Maybe. And the tower itself?"

"I don't know Monsieur. There's another gate at the tower end. You'll have to get through that somehow. And then you'll have to get up the ramp and through the door!"

"You can fly, can't you? If you change into a wolf!" Uduward suggested.

"Ha! No. If I do have wings, I've yet to find them. No, I fight as a mortal man." We knocked ideas around for a while, but the more we tried to crack the nut of the tower the more impregnable it seemed.

"What are you going to offer for this friendship gift?" asked Uduward, scratching himself.

"Ah. I have an idea."

Around noon, Cathal returned on foot, accompanied by a tall, muscular man with many scars. He wore leg thongs and had a brown cape. At first, I thought he must be the Chieftain. Cathal spoke rapidly and with hushed tones as if he feared being overheard.

"John, this is Donoch. He's the deputy of the Chieftain I have told you about. He wants to talk with you, and then he will take any messages back to his leader."

Donoch held out a meaty hand, palm up, and I placed mine flat on his. We clasped fingers, and then he withdrew his hand.

"Maolmordha greets you. He is interested in your plan to attack Slane. For many years he has coveted the income from the College and Abbey. Also, he is the sworn enemy of Cairbre, who brought shame to Meolmordha's ancestors. We can have an army here today. But first I must know your plans?" He spoke Latin crudely, but I could understand him.

However, put on the spot like this, I still felt ill at ease. The only idea worth considering was Gerard's.

"How many men do you have?" I asked.

"Perhaps four hundred … if your plan is good. Most of them fight for loot only. They are brave men, and they will risk all if there is profit enough. A few of us fight for other reasons … ."

I told Donoch the plan Gerard and I had worked out. When I had finished, Donoch nodded to Gerard who nodded back in that silent greeting of warriors.

"All I need is a few minutes to get to the tower," I concluded. "Meanwhile your leader and perhaps half your man should close in on the embankment around the tower. There are thick stands of trees to the north, and south, which will give some cover. When I give the signal, you must fire lit arrows and set fire to the tower. But not before I come out with my wife."

"But how will you escape if all is on fire?"

"I haven't thought of that yet."

I was astonished at my own flow of ideas. I had thought of pulling down the main gates to the causeway only as I had said it. It seemed plausible enough.

Perhaps using horses?

I waited to see what Donoch would say.

He nodded slowly to himself. "For us, your plan seems good. But you know it's difficult to get close to the tower. Many men will die before we can fire it."

"I have an idea for that that concerns a gift I have for your Chieftain. It's a secret weapon that will make it easy to fire the tower."

Donoch laughed. "Excellent. That is very good! I must go now. I will be back with Meolmordha and an army before the end of day." We watched him vanish silently into the night from the Hermitage door and then shut out the night.

"Well, that went rather well, I thought!" Cathal said. "Now if you don't mind, I think I need to rest. I had a few close calls trying to slip between Cairbre's allies."

"Friar Cathal, don't you have any books to read?" I said before he could close the door to his room.

"Books? Good gracious, no. I've read all the books in the world. Now I must set myself to digest them, and that takes a very long time. Good night!"

***

When he woke, only about two hours later, Cathal took us outside. He paced up and down nervously until he raised his finger:

"Listen! Hear that?"

A rustle in the leaves of bushes in front of us announced the arrival of two big men, moments before their moon faces appeared in the gloom.

"Ah! At last!" Cathal said.

"That shortcut you showed me, almost did for us!" answered Donoch, pulling thorns and sticky creeper out of his arms, cape and hair.

"Ha! You look funny!" Cathal said, laughing as the man behind Donoch stepped closer to us. Taller than Donoch, he was even more muscular. He had tawny hair and wore a red cape clasped around his neck with a gold brooch. On his arms were gold bands, and around his neck, above the brooch he wore a gold torque.

"Ha! You look funnier too, the older you get old monk!" replied the man. "Aren't you going to introduce us then?"

"I taught him his Latin letters, and he taught Donoch. You must admit he learned well!" Cathal said to me. "Meolmordha, this is John, a warrior and man of many hidden depths, great wisdom and strange abilities. John, this is Chieftain Meolmordha, a very great warrior, Lord, Prince, and leader of the Four Tribes of Tara."

Donoch had brought even more food and ale, and we settled down under the tower of the Hermitage, next to a raging fire, to a veritable feast. Afterwards, over a game of fidchell, Meolmordha discussed tactics.

"You be King John. My army is camped in some woods a few miles south of here, over the river. There is a ford, we discovered some years ago. It's only passable at certain times of the day, and its location is secret. That's where my men will cross be crossing now. Donoch told me your plan, which sounded good apart from your escape strategy. I hope your wife is worth a fiery death, because I cannot see how you'll get out of the tower."

"I am still thinking about it. I'll think of something. How many men do you have?"

"About four hundred. Your move."

"It's enough I think. You have any cavalry? Your move."

"Um. You play well, for a beginner. Your move. Only myself, my five brothers and Donoch here, have horses. Why? You have an idea?"

"Perhaps. Your move. You know of the defensive wall?"

"Yes."

"Gerard tells me it's about 120 to 140 feet, or pied, from the wall to the tower. Assuming their archers can reach about 120 feet from the wall, that means normally you would need to take a shot from 240 to 260 feet away to fire the tower. An accurate shot at that range with your bows would be impossible. Your move."

"It's true. Do you have a solution?"

"I have a weapon that can enable a shot from the safety of the trees at about 300 feet. Of course, I need to take a closer look."

"What is a 'feet?'" asked Donoch, after Meolmordha nudged him.

"This is a foot," I said holding my hands the correct distance apart. "If I'm right, you won't need to worry about the defensive wall. It's made from wooden stakes so that can be fired too. The enemy won't be able to defend while they are burning. When it is burned through, you'll be able to get to the tower. I have a solution for that; ladders. Um."

"Your move. I am intrigued by what you tell of this weapon. When can I see it?"

"Your move. As soon as we finish this game. One other thing. I will need at least two of your riders to pull down the main gates to the causeway with grappling hooks."

"Your move. Two of my brothers will help you there."

"There. I think I've reached the tower!"

"What! You're right. Well I'll be damned. How long have you been playing?"

"I learned just before you arrived."

"Meolmordha is considered one of our finest players!" Cathal said.

"The game's name means 'wood sense,'" Meolmordha said. "We say that it often predicts how real battles will go. It's uncanny. I see that our battle at the tower has good portents. Let us see this weapon of yours."

Cathal led the way through the woods to a clearing on the north bank of a river. Peering out of the bushes, we looked for any sign of strangers. The Chieftain suddenly stood up and walked out to the bank. He gave a call, like an owl, and a face appeared on the opposite bank. He and the man exchanged words in Meolmordha's mother tongue, and then he turned to us.

"It's safe. My men have seen none of the enemy for

hours."

"Watch this Meolmordha," I said. "See that tree down the end there, with the single branch hanging down over the water?" It roughly equalled the three hundred feet range that we would need for the battle.

"That little one?"

"Yes."

"But that's too far!"

I drew back the bow of the weapon and locked the stretched gut in place with the trigger mechanism. Loading a bolt, I took careful aim and fired. The bolt sped straight to the little sapling and split its narrow trunk about four feet from the ground.

"Holy God! That's incredible!" Cathal said.

"Can you do it again?" Meolmordha asked. "Perhaps it was just luck."

I took aim once more and fired another bolt. It hit the trunk just above the first.

Donoch nodded to the Chieftain.

"Where did you get such a weapon?" his leader said. "I have not heard of such a thing!"

"It's from very far away. Its like will not be seen around these parts for a long while yet. You will be the only one to own one."

"Me?"

"Yes. After the battle is won, it will be my gift to you. In fact, it's yours now, but it will be needed to take the tower. I will not be able to use it."

A tear rolled down my cheek while we ate our supper that evening.

"What's wrong John?" asked Cathal.

"For so long I've been on my own. Now at last I have people on my side. I can't tell you what that means. I almost despaired so many times."

"Well, it's not over yet!" he replied.

***

By dusk, we were all in position. Thankfully, it hadn't rained since the early afternoon. The full moon looked ominous in the night sky, and I found it difficult not to look at it. Under the clouds of a gathering storm, Meolmordha and I studied the tower once more from a bank in front of the trees, cut back in a wide circle around the Tower. Arrayed all around Slane's embanked perimeter and concealed within the trees, were the four hundred men the Chieftain had brought with him. Donoch and three of his brothers, Ardgal, Conall, and Tuathal, would be coming with me, into the compound around the Abbey and College. From there we would storm the gates to the causeway.

"You must leave now, John. At the sound of Donoch's horn, the attack will begin. Good luck!"

I said my farewell to Cathal, Gerard and Uduward and slipped away with Donoch to join the two hundred men waiting to go in through the main gate.

I had finally had an idea how I might escape the tower. It involved an unconventional use of the crossbow, something I had seen in a movie, and I had no idea if it would work. I had talked it through with Gerard, the Chieftain and Uduward and plans had been made.

Uduward, posing as a pedlar, went to offer the gate guards cheap ale in return for entrance to the settlement. Fortunately, they hadn't recognised him. They had confiscated the ale but hadn't let him in. This was fine, as far as we were concerned. As we approached, I hoped they were drunk.

"Who goes there?" came the challenge after we had called out twice. A face appeared over the parapet, and I hid mine. Donoch told him we were an advanced guard of the army Georgiana had sent for. The guard seemed confused but asked for the password, which, of course, we didn't know.

"Wait a moment. Let me come and see you." Down from the parapet came the man and stood swaying on the mud just inside the gate.

Donoch peered at him from underneath his leather helmet.

"I still can't see you!" the man said, stepping closer to the latticed wooden poles of the gate. He leaned forward until his face was only inches from the wood.

With the speed of a whipped cat, Donoch reached through the gate and grabbed the man by the throat. He gargled something but too weakly for his companion to hear. Donoch put a knife to his throat and whispered, "Open the gate or you die now."

The man hurriedly nodded and reached out to withdraw the bolt from its concealed position behind the central posts of the gate.

We were in!

After a short skirmish, our men had secured the area around the entrance to the causeway.

Three horses were led toward the gate. Conall blew his horn three times, paused and then blew another four blasts. Three long blasts in the distance from Donoch answered him. Conall and his two brothers mounted their horses, and I climbed up behind Conall. Then we moved off.

I may have to kill Georgina!

The thought hit me like an express train. I wasn't really sure I could do it, but I told myself, if I had to, I would.

With my heart alternately pounding, and then missing beats or stopping altogether, a memory suddenly flooded my mind. That evening, before assembling for battle, Cathal had come to me.

"The nature of evil, John. You seem to have a much more complete knowledge of it than I. I only see of the evil that men do. Tell me, in what other ways does it manifest itself?"

"Well, most often, to me, one experiences a sense of foreboding. Everything you do turns to ill. All decisions are bad and bad luck pursues you. I have thought more about it. It is like a wind. It's something you feel physically and have to push against. It steers all adventures to misadventures. Or at least it tries to. You have to fight it."

"Ah yes, I see."

"Why do you ask?"

"Oh, nothing. It doesn't matter."

The memory of this conversation suddenly brought calm to me, and my heartbeat steadied. I knew what I had to do, and I would do it.

"I'm ready!"

The three brothers and I, accompanied by the other riders, approached the gate, and at the same time, our men on the walls drew their short bows and fired upon the men on the causeway parapet. The two guards at the base of the gate shouted in panic, seeing our horses and drew their swords.

A single drop of water splashed on my sword, held out in front of my face. It caught the glimmer of moonlight for a moment, but I hardly noticed.

With arrows raining down on the enemy, I shouted, "Now!" and the three brothers spurred our horses over the last one hundred feet to the gates. Warriors charged after us on foot. When we were within range, the brothers launched the grappling hooks toward the top of the gates. Two of them, Tuathal's and Ardgall's, caught, and the riders veered their horses away, pulling at the crossbar at the top of the barrier.

One gate came away instantly and, with the rending sound of wood, crashed to the ground. The right gate held on, although the top had buckled with the strain from the pulling grapple.

I had no time to wait. The gap seemed big enough, so I jumped from Conall's horse and ran into the causeway.

Come on Gerard! Don't let me down!

From both north and south sides of the ground around the causeway, open to the enemy, dim shapes appeared over tussocks and from behind bushes and torches sputtered into flame. While hundreds of enemy arrows clanged into my helmet and tunic and many others flew over my head toward the enemy, I continued running down the causeway. Already the wooden stakes, behind and in front of me, were alight. The smoke stung my eyes as I began the long walk to the tower. I had perhaps two hundred feet to cover. As I moved forwards, I could barely see a way through the flames that lit up the sky ahead of me. There would be nothing behind me now but fire. I could hear screams from the parapet, as enemy soldiers jumped for their lives or burned like torches. No more arrows hit me after this. The touch of the helmet on my head became hot and then began to scald me. I began to run as best I could. Always there seemed just enough of a gap between the two walls of flame.

Yes, Gerard! Yes!

Ahead of me now, I could make out the gates at the far end. If we had timed this correctly, there should be just enough time to climb one of the short ladders.

I neared the end and could see a soldier attempting to detach the ladder. His feet seemed to be on fire. My armour started to scald my skin, the smoke to choke me, and the heat almost made me faint. I only had seconds left in the fire of Hell before I would be finished.

I charged toward him and barged him out of the way. He fell into the flames burning the gates and screamed in agony, flailing his arms. I began to climb without a moment's hesitation. The flames were already taking hold of the woodwork around the ladder. But then, a curious thing happened. The heavens opened and rain came down like the Biblical Flood. For just long enough, it cooled the wood around the ladder, and I reached the top. I could see it had been fixed to the parapet by only a single knot of twine, which smoked in the heat.

I stood on the parapet and then faced a single guard defending the top of the gate. I growled and ran at him. The sight of my helmet and armour must have been too much; he jumped down to the tower ramp. With the weight of my armour, I had to climb slowly down, and when I reached the ramp, I turned, just in time to see him disappear inside the tower and close its iron door.

For the first time, I could hear the sound of blaring horns, and swinging my helmet around to take in the view through my eye-slits, I watched fires burning on the wall of the outer ring around the Tower.

I reached the door of the tower and, of course, it had been bolted. From the undercroft I could hear the cries of men; some of it rhythmic, like a working song.

Lightning suddenly split the black sky above me and rendered the battlefield like a bright day. But the tumult of battle almost drowned out the rumble of thunder, only a second later. Another flash, and I saw the most incredible sight.

From the lower corners of the tower, what looked like Archimedes' screws, protruded into the tiny moat around the Tower. They were turning, taking water up into the tower. Moments later, the first flushes of it cascaded down the outside of the tower from near the top.

Genius! It can only be the work of Georgina.

I now stood under the overhanging balcony of the Tower. I had seen arrow slits all around the Tower at the level above, but no arrows had sped toward me. Either the defenders weren't expecting me, or they welcomed me. I didn't care which it was. I needed to get up to the next level. I paced around the small landing at the end of the causeway. Then I saw an opportunity.

Somebody forgot to lock the barn door!

I turned and began hacking a section of railing from the side of the landing. Consisting of a rail and uprights, which were mortised together, I calculated if hacked off at the base, it might just hold my weight long enough to get me to the next floor.

Why is nobody firing at me?

The thought plagued me. It made every cut of the wood last forever. At any moment I expected the sting of an arrow entering the back of my neck.

When I had cut off the complete length of rail from one side, I stood it on end and wedged it against the rail at the front of the wooden platform. I began to climb, keeping my feet right up against the rail itself. Unsteady, its joints cracked with my weight when I climbed. But it held.

Then I clambered over the wooden wall above the projecting balcony. Finally, I stood on the balcony itself. The smoke intensified as the heavy rain quelled many of the fires along the causeway. If the rain had come earlier, I would never have reached the Tower. If later, I would have never made it up that ladder by the gate. Now, it looked like it would preserve the Tower against any burning arrows.

I looked out over the battlefield to the south and thought I could see several arms waving to me. But then I heard the creak of a door opening and twisted around.

The coarse voice of a mighty man with red hair, dressed from head to foot in animal furs growled something at me in ancient Gaelic.

Cairbre!

"I don't understand you," I replied in Latin.

He laughed, and as his head raised with apparent glee, I saw around his exposed neck a magnificent gold torque in the form of a serpent consuming a wolf.

The sign of a servant of the Serpents?

He lunged toward me, wielding an axe.

It seemed that if *somebody else* wanted me alive, *he* most definitely wanted me dead. If he was the lover of Georgina, I could understand his determination. Perhaps *she* had wanted me alive. That would make him even madder.

I stepped deftly backwards, and his axe-head embedded itself in the wooden rail-top. He roared with rage and lunged toward me again. I stepped under his guard and sliced up under his armpit. His almost severed arm released the axe, but he caught it with the other hand and hefted it expertly. Blood drenched his wolf-fur coat, but he grinned as if the pain were a pleasure.

He followed me around the circumference of the Tower, exchanging blows with my sword but each time, tiring himself more. A big man and old for this time, he much overweight from too much food and drink. His ruddy cheeks told me he wouldn't last long. Several times my sword pierced him. A deep wound to his gut looked fatal. With his dying breaths he charged me full-on. Using a technique I learned in M.I.6, I leaned over, into his stomach as his weight fell across my back. I stood at just the right moment and heard his bellow of surprise and dismay as he hurtled over the balcony to the water below.

"Nice work," said a deep, dark voice, behind me.

I turned and saw a knight. A purple plume, on a helmet much like mine, enhanced his great height. I saw a niello pattern on his armour, giving the metal a black sheen.

Could this be the black knight? A servant of the Serpents? Maybe even a Serpent himself?

His had a vertical slit running centrally down from the eye-slits forming a 'T.' Over a full-length chain mail tunic, he wore a black cape trimmed with black fur. He wore two gold wrist torques, like the previous attacker, in the shape of serpents consuming wolves. I could just make out the pair of fleshy, full lips inside the helmet as they formed words. I recognised the mouth; that of the black knight I had met traveling north to Bouvines.

"Now you have me to deal with. And I'm not Georgiana's lover!"

"But don't you want me alive? You saved my life at Bouvines!" He didn't speak. "It *was* you, wasn't it?"

"That wasn't your time to die."

"And this *is*."

"Yes!" he laughed; a terrible laugh, ruthless and cold. "You haven't understood what is happening to you at all, have you? See that gully?" He pointed with his sword to a length of lead half pipe, extending from a slot next to the door in the Tower. "It's a full moon. Georgina will sacrifice your Rose any moment now. When your *Rose*, dies, you will see her blood coursing down that channel. It will drip into the moat, to be diluted to nothing by the water down there. Then, you will go inside, because I will let you, and you will kill Georgina. You won't be able to stop yourself. You will hate her so much. And then you will be mine. I will kill you, and you too, will become like us; a Serpent."

I understood the truth of what he said. I *would* hate Georgina. And I would have to kill her. I wouldn't be able to stop myself. But surely God would understand? Surely Georgina *had* to die, as a sorceress? I wouldn't be damned. I drove my sword toward his belly, but he moved quickly for such a large man. His cape swirled around him as he stepped aside, almost as if he were really a shadow.

"I can hear what you're thinking," he continued. "You think you won't be damned … but you don't know who you really are, not yet. There is a document in there. We will show it to you; proof of who you really are."

"I feel sorry for you that you haven't slept with Georgina," I said desperately, looking for any chink in his armour, mental or physical. "She's really quite good!"

"Oh? It's not something I think about; to sample the wares of the Sorceress. She is just like you, a small pawn in a big game." His turn of phrase intrigued me. He seemed like one from centuries hence and well educated. I also felt the stab of hatred. I wanted to know his identity.

He's trying to goad you!

"I want my wife. I will kill you and Georgina to get her back. She's here, isn't she?" He laughed. "Rose! Rose!" I shouted at the top of my lungs. No reply that reached me over the din of battle around us.

I have to reach Rose before Georgina kills her!

"All I have to do now is keep you outside just a little bit longer," he said. "It should be easy!"

"But I killed you, in Beauvais … ."

"Ha! You may have, but my physical body is like a shield. I can no more remember it than you could if you lost your shield a thousand times. You cannot kill me in this world."

I intensified my attacks and forced him first to parry and then fully engage me. As we engaged with our first blows, I could find no weakness in him. My spirits began to sink. On and on we fought, and there seemed no limit to his strength. I felt I wasn't even exercising him. Becoming weary myself, I paused to get my breath. I looked up at the sky, and my worst dread seemed realised. The clouds were swirling around in the thunderhead vortex above, just like the one I had seen over Beauvais that day. It looked like a black hurricane, building in the night sky. Faint glimmers of moonlight, around its periphery, only highlighted its awesome grotesqueness.

This a serpent, I'm fighting! Surely, I can't beat him!

A smashing blow from his sword made my helmet ring, deafening me and rattling my teeth. Stunned for a moment, I instinctively jabbed with my sword in defense and heard a gasp as he leaped aside. Not quick enough though. He caught my blow on his right shoulder. The angle made the sword tip slide under the links and force them away. His soft flesh felt the bite of just the tip of my blade. As my vision cleared, I saw him glance at the small wound, pink and bleeding. He seemed surprised, and I tried a quick series of thrusts to force him backwards. Catching me off balance, he brought down another slashing blow across my shoulder. The mail links of the tunic broke. The blade bit into my flesh. Such a blow no normal man could deliver. But then I saw a flash in the sky and a crack of lightning. The knight stepped back. An increase in the intensity of the rain, that slicked the wooden planks on which we stood, followed the flash.

I became suddenly aware of myself, as if I were out of my body, fighting this huge knight. I could see the whole battlefield watching us fight on the Tower.

We were two knights fighting to the death under the stricken light of a thunderstorm on the evil Tower.

It could hardly be more surreal, hardly be more elemental. Fitting then that Georgina should have orchestrated it.

"Ah! No! No! You *fool*!" cried the knight in anguish. It seemed as if he sensed something, something that had happened. He seemed to be talking to somebody other than me. He fought on. He no longer tried to delay me, he tried to kill me.

The wet, slick woodwork made our booted feet slip as we fought. I came terrifying close to toppling over the railing as I ducked out of the way of a heavy blow, and his leg caught against the inside of mine. I slowly became aware that this big man was finding it harder to find grip on the slippery wooden planks than myself. But my concentration slipped for just a moment. He feinted a blow to my free left arm and then twisted his body to give him the angle to sweep the blow across my chest and cut into my sword arm. I leaned backwards and drove with my feet against a ridge in the planks, to force myself backwards. As I did so I felt his blade strike my upper left thigh and bite deep into my flesh. The cut had gone too deep for me to feel anything but the cold dread of death.

This is it!

I tried to stand up but fell against the rail.

Just in time, I pushed myself back from the rail. His sword bit into the wood where my neck had just been.

His sword blade stuck, and then, trying to pull it out, his boots slipped, and he began to fall backwards. His great size and weight worked against him, and though he fell against the sides of the Tower, the slick wood didn't break his descent. Seeing him prone, I drove the sword as hard as I could at a sliver of bare neck which I glimpsed for an instant below his helmet.

My blade went right through his neck and pinned him to the wooden balcony. I put all my weight on the sword to pin him there, but he tore off his helmet with an unearthly howl of rage. He gripped my sword blade with both gloved hands and with a strength I had not imagined, forced the blade out from first the wood and then his neck.

At the same time his head seemed to extend from his neck, and my world became monochrome. Black and white shapes filled my vision, the only object in the sky being a round, white moon. I felt my mouth open involuntarily, and I howled at the friendly shape in the black sky. Besides me, an enormous white, winged-serpent reared up, and its forked tongue, tipped with the two faces of those I loved most, Rose and Annie, flicked toward my face. I tried to hack it off with my sword, but instead of the sword I found my extended claws raking the tongue, drawing thick, black blood that dripped like hot pitch.

I understood that I could move incredibly fast. As soon as I willed it, I had manoeuvred behind the serpent, and I ripped its wings with my claws and fangs. I became aware of some kind of power in my fangs, a dripping poison which I could use if I could find the right place to bite. I had known this for millennia; this was what I had been born to do.

In a white-hot world, we writhed and struck at each other. The fangs of the serpent burned me where they gored. After a while I felt my blood thickening and sleep overtaking me.

"You will sleep for a thousand years!" a voice said, inside me. I wasn't sure if it was a warning or a temptation.

I don't want to sleep!

I had become, at once, both man and beast and something else besides. I could still think, and I thought I might be able to outwit the Serpent. Its actions were ordered by a master who knew not love; who hated and dominated. I felt free to act, think and feel as I pleased. The thought made a new fire surge in my spirit-veins. I scrambled on the Serpent's back. Aware of the wound in my leg, I couldn't let it slow me down. As his great neck whipped around to give his fangs a clear strike at my head, I snapped my jaws closed around his neck. He had not seen this coming. I drove my fangs ever deeper into his sickly flesh and heard the joy of a myriad anguished souls willing me to end its life. For Annie, Rose, for all those that had suffered at the hands of the Serpents, for all those that had suffered at the hands of the Devil himself, yes, even for all the angels and God, I held on. The poison seeped from my fangs; the deeper they went, the more poison flowed. I held on and felt the ice-cold blood of the Serpent dripping down my throat. I felt exalted as the last spasms of life racked his body. I felt no pity as the grotesque imitation of life finally left him. With one last shudder and hiss of anguish he had gone, his evil form vanished from under me.

I reared up, forelegs on his carcass, and howled at the heavens. My whole face became a rictus of primeval triumph, and every muscle in my body strained against the bonds of existence. The day was infinitely clear, and I could see forever. Somewhere above the clouds, I felt I could see God and the Devil, and I seemed not so far beneath them. I yearned to escape my body forever, scorn the Devil and take conversation with God, but my energy peaked, and then my spirit began to fall back, into my body.

Then I saw a vast sea of yellow flame, stretching from horizon to horizon, miles below me. I felt as if I were floating above it, or as if it were underground. Among the flames, I half fancied I could see a vast city of enormous antiquity. In the vast ocean of yellow, one small black circle appeared and became an eye. It looked at me. From somewhere came the anguished howl of defeat from a multitude of tormented voices, all melded into one grotesque scream of pain. Far below me, the eye looked up at me with infinite sadness. I heard the scream of an eternity's anguish roaring in my ears until it faded to a hushed whisper and had gone.

Then, I heard only silence. It seemed I had cheated Satan again. Above us, the sky became real again. The black vortex of cloud seemed to form into the coiled shape of a winged Serpent for a moment, and then the shape had gone. The clouds became again broiling, turbulent, angry.

I lay naked on the soaking wood of the Tower balcony and saw the two swords crossed in front of me. My clothes lay ripped and soaked, in a pile underneath me. I painfully walked on my hind legs to the door and forced it open with my dextrous paws.

Entering the room within, I saw flames from an iron fire-basket and heard the scream of a woman.

I felt my size shrinking, and whereas I had stooped to enter through the door, now I seemed no taller than the room's occupants.

"John! You've come at last!" a dark-haired woman said, looking at me.

I knew her name. I uttered it, but all she could have heard was an uncouth growl. The other woman continued to scream. The first continued, "I'm glad you have come. But you know, I couldn't do it. The full moon has passed, and I *just couldn't* do it!" She looked downcast for a moment.

My paws slowly became hands, and I sank to my knees, exhausted. "Georgina!" I said. "What are you doing?"

"John! Is that you! Oh God, what is happening?" the other woman cried.

"Rose. Darling. I have come for you. Didn't you know I would?"

"Oh God! But … ."

"She's terrified, poor woman," Georgina said. "I must say John, you have good taste in women. I mean, if I am presumptuous enough to include myself. She really has a lot of fighting spirit! Caused me quite a lot of difficulties!"

"Rose!" I said again, letting the yearning that had so long driven me be heard in my voice!

"Well, she's not *that* interesting!" declared Georgina!

"Shut up, Georgina. You've done enough damage. I'm taking her, and don't think you can stop me!"

I hadn't much time to take in my surroundings. To the left of the door, in the corner of the Tower, I saw what I sought; a staircase.

"I don't want to stop you John." Suddenly Georgina looked so sad and frail. Her hood had been cast off, and her raven hair captured the full beauty of her young face in the glowing firelight. "I tried to do it. I want the eternal life which your friend Herleva enjoys so much, but to take your wife would make you hate me forever. I just couldn't do it. You see, I still love you."

I stood up unsteadily and walked over to where Rose sat, wearing a blue gown. She had been strapped by her wrists, behind her back, to a wooden bench.

"She looks quite pretty like that, don't you think?" Georgina continued. "Perhaps we could come to an arrangement?"

I took a long knife, with a vicious crescent blade, from a table and cut the rope from my wife's wrists.

"Come on Rose. We're going. We have to get out now. Georgina has another army coming!"

Blood from the deep wound in my leg had formed a slippery pool around my feet.

Rose seemed too exhausted to resist when I drew her to her feet, though she also seemed repelled by my touch.

"I ... I cannot stand," she murmured.

I slung her over my back and turned for the staircase.

I could hear the mechanical sound of something in the walls. I knew it must be the Archimedes mechanism.

"Wait!" shouted Georgina! "I can't kill her, but I can stop you leav- ... ," I heard her cry, as she lunged toward me.

I twisted and easily caught the hand that held the crescent dagger toward me. I twisted her small wrist and put the dagger to her face. For a moment we looked into each other's eyes, and I remembered how much I loved her. Her eyes seemed to say, "Don't!" but it wasn't the fear of death that I saw in them.

With a cruel grimace, I turned her wrist and slashed her dress down from her neck to her waist. She was naked underneath. Her breasts looked as beautiful as ever. With her small fist still gripping it, I slowly drew the blade across her belly twice, cutting into it the sign of the Holy Cross. Blood poured from the wound and dripped on the floor. She fell to the crude boards, covering her own wound with both her hands.

"I thought you had more power than that," I said.

Just as I carried Rose up the stairs I heard the last of Georgina's words, petering out to a confused murmur.

"John. I wouldn't use it on ... . Take the parchment on the tabl- ... . There is something up stairs you should see too ... ."

Painfully, I struggled up two flights of steps and pushed open a wooden hatch over my head. We emerged into the torrential rain. Above, in the night sky, black clouds tumbled over each other in a chaotic pattern like a cauldron sea.

"Can you stand Rose? Please try?" I let go of her and she clung to the railing edge around the roof of the tower.

I waved my arms, but the night was still black, the moon having long been obscured, and I knew nobody could see us.

I clambered back down the steps and into the chamber where Georgina lay motionless on the floor. Remembering the sword belts which I'd slung over my shoulder, not having time to untie them in the Labyrinth Tower, I fetched them from the balcony and lit a brand from the fire in the chamber. I looked for some rope everywhere but could find none. I glanced at the table and saw a single leaf of parchment there. My curiosity overcame me, and I grabbed it before retracing my steps.

On the floor above, I stopped. Something had moved and made a muffled cry in the room.

I hesitated for a moment and then walked between the single large bed and wardrobe; the room's only furnishings.

"Don't kill us! Please!" pleaded a youth with blonde, tonsured, curly hair, protecting an even younger woman with fine features and brown hair.

"What are you doing here? You should get out. This tower will be fired any moment now."

"We have been kept here as prisoners for months now. We have a little baby, but he is kept in the Abbey. How can we get out?"

"Who are you?"

Suddenly, realising I wasn't going to hack him to death and no doubt less intimidated because of my nakedness than he might have been, he stood up. He had a handsome, if boyish, face and couldn't have been more than twenty years old. He wore a green and red tunic of something like velvet and silk. The woman wore a black dress, less well made.

"Take this!" he said. "It's all I have left. They've taken everything else, the Sorceress and the Knight!"

He held out a large gold signet ring, embossed with a face that looked distinctly like his, wearing a crown, and holding a sceptre.

"Wait, I guess I don't need this now," I said, remembering the spare belt and Rose's condition. "I don't know if it will work, but it's the only chance you have. Take this, and follow me!"

"Come on Mechthilde. We're getting out!" he said to the girl.

Her voice came so thin and weak, I barely heard the girl's answer:

"How about Hermine? Will we find her?"

"Yes, dearest," the young man answered.

I led them up the top flight of steps.

On top of the roof I brandished the torch for all I was worth and saw it answered by another some distance off. I could no longer tell north from south.

A few moments later, the bolt, which I had waited for, thudded into the woodwork below the railing. The bolt embedded itself in the tower, its point sticking out of the internal surface by an inch.

"Take this Rose!"

"What?"

"Just put it somewhere safe!"

She folded the sheet of parchment neatly and slid it inside her sleeve. I reached over and started pulling on the thin line attached to the bolt. I hauled for what seemed an age until my fists encountered a knot and then, beyond it, heavier hemp rope. I pulled the rope over the parapet and tied it around a plank of the parapet.

"Come on Rose. We're going. Hang on to me!"

I unfastened the belt and wrapped it around my fist.

"Come on. Hold on to me."

We climbed over the parapet and down to a ledge where I could pass the belt over the rope. Arrows from the enemy thudded into the woodwork, but they were becoming even fewer. Meolmordha and the others had breached the outer wall long before and were now pouring over the inner wall, using the ladders. As Rose held on around my neck with her hands and my waist with her legs, the first of the Chieftain's lit arrows hit the side of the Tower. It penetrated one of the animal hides which smoked but didn't burst into flame.

I passed the other end of the belt over the rope at waist height and, wrapping it as best I could around my other wrist, balanced with my feet on the flat surface of part of the wall construction.

"Don't wait Dagobert. Do exactly as we do, and hurry! It will hurt like hell, but don't let go. The enemy is right below us!"

I leaned forward and let the rope take our combined weight. For one sickening moment, I thought the rope would break. It flexed so much that we sank vertically for about twenty feet before the rope whipped us back up again, almost tearing the belt from my grip. I knew I had only to hang on to survive and save Rose, but my wrists were on fire as we slid down the rope, over the little moat, over the heads of a few astonished enemy soldiers and our own front line. We came to a tumbling halt on the wet grass, and I lay there, gasping. Moments later, Dagobert and Mechthilde landed in a heap just to our left. Whoever had anchored the other end of the line hadn't expected four arrivals but swung the rope at the last moment to avoid a collision.

"Monsieur Jean! You made it! You old rascal!" came the familiar voice of Gerard, rushing up to us. "Oo. I see you are a little less well formerly dressed than earlier! That's the effect of a beautiful woman, I guess!"

Rose turned onto her back and smiled up at him.

"And you are the Lady Rose, no doubt.

Pleased … and relieved to meet you. We've had a devil of a job finding you. But perhaps I shouldn't use his name!"

Rose and I laughed. My laugh came out as a gasping cough because of the grass against my lips.

"Gerard," I mumbled. "Good to see you. I'm exhausted!"

"And who are your guests?" asked Gerard.

"I don't know. They were prisoners in the Tower. Take care of them."

"That wound looks pretty nasty Monsieur."

Gerard beckoned some men who led the young couple off. I didn't see them again.

"Well, we must get you away from here," Gerard told us. "Meolmordha's men are firing the tower! Or trying to. It just won't burn. Actually, he wants to save it now, but I don't think he can control his men any more. They saw what happened earlier, and that Tower is a symbol of Evil for them now. They will not stop until it's destroyed."

I turned over and saw Uduward's smiling face, looking down on me. He had a bad cut above his right ear and held his arm but looked otherwise unscathed.

"Hello there, Monsieur!"

"Udu! Thank God you're alright. Nice shot, by the way! How is Cathal and the others?"

He looked at Gerard.

"Come on Monsieur John. We have to go." Gerard said.

He called a few men over, and they carried it toward the trees, south of the Tower. The dull ache in my leg, which I had felt since landing on the grass, had become a searing pain.

We found Meolmordha and his brothers. The Chieftain called over a girl to stitch my leg. She had to get a soldier to hold the wound together. Before she started I had her find some wine to pour into the wound. It stung like mad. She tut-tutted, not understanding why I had done it.

"John! You're safe," the Chieftain said, while she stitched. "What a great day! If I never live to see another like it, it will make me a legend for all time!"

"We must get away fast Meolmordha, but before we go, how is Cathal?"

"You must hurry John. He has not long." He waited for the girl to finish with my leg while I protested at the pain.

When she finished, the Chieftain said, "Come with me."

Somebody handed me a fur cape and a pair of leggings, both of which I pulled on hurriedly.

Held up by the Chieftain's own arms, I hobbled to a small crowd just under the trees. I saw Cathal, lying flat on his back and gasping for air. I stooped over him.

"Ah! John. You made it! I knew you would. Where's this wife of yours, we've all suffered so much for."

I beckoned to Rose and some men carried her to us. In the torch-light, she looked even more beautiful than ever. Her hair was brown once again and flowed like little waves around her face.

"Ah, the lovely Rose!" said Cathal.

"Rose," I said. "This is Abbot Cathal, who has made all this possible. Without him, I could not have saved you or at least not so quickly!"

"You young rascal!" Cathal said. "This is no time for jokes." He coughed twice and blood spattered his chin. "Took a nasty axe blow to the gut. Serves me right for wanting to learn first-hand about war. Friars should never meddle with war. That's another piece of wisdom I've added to my long list. Oh, and it's Friar Cathal, my lady, not Abbot. So, John, I have to ask you one of two questions before I go."

A tear rolled down my cheek, not just at Cathal's bravery, but his indomitable spirit.

"Go on. I'll answer if I can."

"What's the future like? Tell me a little of it?"

"Well, what can I say? People are no happier, perhaps, but there are amazing things to see. Man has landed on the moon, and people fly in craft called aeroplanes. In fact, it's quite normal to fly half way around the world on a holiday for two weeks, every year."

"Amazing! Flying you say? But what's a holiday?"

"It's a day when people don't do any work. They simply have fun. It's … oh well it doesn't matter."

"Amazing! I could do with a few of those myself. One last question; is the world Christian?"

"Well, it's about half Christian. There's another religion called Islam, which is also very popular … ."

Meolmordha tapped me on the shoulder, and I looked up at him. He shook his head, sadly. I looked at Cathal's face. It had relaxed into a smile, but there was no life left in it. I took his head in my arms and cradled it. Tears welled in my eyes for this man who had made everything possible; everything from nothing.

After a while, I stood up. We had to leave. I looked at the Chieftain, and he, too, was weeping silently. As I looked around me I could see that each, and every person present had been deeply touched by this man.

"We have to go Meolmordha. Can you supply us with horses?"

"I surely can. And you must take this with you too." He lifted my hand and placed a heavy pouch of silver into it. "The Four Tribes of Tara will forever be in your debt. You will always be welcomed here with the honours of a Chieftain."

"Chieftain. You must come! I cannot stop them!" Donoch had come running up to us in some state of frustration. Seeing my face, he smiled and shook my hand. "John!"

"We have to go. Is everything alright with the battle?" I asked him.

"Except the Tower will be destroyed!"

"I thought that was the point!"

"Yes, but have you seen it! It has wonders within. Now, the Chieftain wants to take it in one piece."

"It doesn't matter Donoch," Meolmordha said. "The men are probably right!"

"You should see it!" he said to me. "When we manage to set fire to part of it, water gushes from openings near the top of the tower. It is a wonder!"

I laughed.

"Where will you go?" asked Meolmordha.

"To the coast and then, eventually, overseas to Frankish lands. And from there back to my own time."

"That I do not understand, but there is no time for explanations now. We will keep your Sorceress from pursuing you."

"She is badly wounded if not dead. I cut her open across the belly. But if she's not dead, you will find her hard to contain. I ask you, if you can, to stop her leaving this land until at least a month has passed."

"Well, if the tower burns, she will burn inside it!"

"Even so … "

"Don't worry. You are always welcome in our tribe."

"Cairbre's allies won't give up that easily. Another army will probably be here soon Meolmordha. Perhaps tonight!"

"Yes. As you will see as you leave the battleground, we are already repairing the defences. Only this time, we will be inside them! I think there is some room for improvement too. The main thing is that we have the Abbey and College. I will find somebody worthy of Cathal's memory to be the new Abbot."

"Take good care!" I said.

With that, we were escorted from the field. Clothes from the battlefield were given to me. I put them on, finishing with a cape. I glanced over my shoulder once. The Tower burned now like a new torch. We could still see its flickering red light until dawn. With fresh horses, taken from the Abbey stable, and myself dressed again appropriately, we were at Dubh Linn by midday.

***

At Dubh Linn, we took passage on one of the only two boats that could take us from 'Iwernia,' the ancient name for Ireland, to 'Cymru,' Wales. We used a substantial amount of silver coins to enlist the help of the only captain willing to take us to sea so quickly.

Our ship, named the Sea Dragon, was perhaps forty feet long, shaped not unlike a Viking ship. It had a single mast and a furled sail at the top, hanging from a single spar, and a long oar on the right side for a rudder. The bow and stern ended in sharp wooden points, aimed straight up at the sky. Its captain, an enormous, cheerful fellow without any hair, was called Hadwyn. The sea would prove rough, but the voyage passed uneventfully until the second day:

"Storm brewing!" said Adalmand, the first mate, from his position at the oars. Ahead of the limp sail, he faced the stern and looked to the south west as he spoke. An enormous bank of black clouds had been building up there. I looked up at the plain-coloured linen sail, crisscrossed by leather bands for strength. I saw no sign of life in the sail just yet. The Sea Dragon moved slowly west, dragged by the effort of the four oarsmen and steered by the great bulk of Hadwyn on the right side at the stern. We passengers sat behind the sail and ahead of the captain, huddled together for warmth. One could see the reflection of the whole ship in the inky green sea. Only wave-lets stirred by the oars disturbed by the image. Even the sky and pale sun were reflected in the water.

"I never knew this sea could be so calm!" I said, turning, to Hadwyn.

I had picked up enough of Old English to understand and communicate with the crew by now. With few distractions, one learns fast.

"It can be for weeks!"

We had been becalmed, not far out from the Iwernian coast. Our journey wasn't often interrupted by small-talk. We were too weary. Moreover, Rose had been very cool toward me. The sight of me when I entered the Tower's chamber had shocked her. This produced an air of tension.

The only notable conversation, a short one, came when I found Rose sitting at the bow.

I put my arm around her, but she didn't yield to me.

"You look so … so young. As young as Edward! Is it really you, John?"

"Yes, it's me. My age right now is just an illusion. Don't worry. You actually look just as young as I. Haven't you seen yourself? Your hair is spectacularly brown again!"

"Really? I wondered about the hair. I haven't seen myself in a mirror!"

After nearly a day of rowing, only tiny wave-lets and the gentle eddies around the oars disturbed the sea's calm surface.

"I thought the difficulty would be with winds blowing the wrong way!" I shouted to Hadwyn

"That way!" he suddenly shouted, ignoring me. He pointed to starboard, and the rowers changed course. They began to row strongly.

"What is it?" I asked.

"A breeze! Nothing much, but it might do," Hadwyn replied.

I scanned the sea to the north for any signs of a breeze. I could see no waves or even any clouds or birds.

"I *can't* see anything! How do you know?"

"I can smell it!"

After perhaps an hour, I felt ready to sing the praises of Hadwyn to the very heavens. The sail rippled a few times, slacked, rippled again and then bowed into that pleasing curve that accompanies an adequate wind. The exhausted rowers put down their oars to rest.

"Here it comes!" shouted Hadwyn's first mate, Adalmand.

A sudden gust of wind caught the sail, and the ship leaned to starboard. The bow tried to turn and dug into a wave. Hadwyn's whole weight came to bear on the rudder, keeping the boat pointing straight ahead.

"The sail Adalmand! We must go with it now!" he yelled.

"Look," shouted Adalmand's sons who made up the other crew members. "Land!"

"I knew it!" shouted Adalmand. "You did it, Haddy!"

Thank God!

While his oldest son let out the starboard yard, the rope which anchored the corner of the sail, Adalmand struggled to haul in the port yard so that the boat slowly turned until it pointed just west of due north. Now the sail spar and the sail itself were at only about a ten-degree angle to the ship's hull. The wind began to howl a banshee wail. Simultaneously pandemonium broke out on board. Anything left untied, tried to get out of the boat, including Rose. The forty-foot boat bucked and dived over waves which were soon big enough to foam with white crests. Before, there had only been a gentle rocking motion as we ran at right angles to little waves. Now, big ones hit us from the stern and rolled right under us and tipped the boat up. At other times we slammed into the side of a wave.

We were all drenched with cold water in a matter of minutes, but Hadwyn looked pleased with it all. His serene, smiling face, stared at the coast far ahead of us.

Then the heavens opened!

"This is unbearable!" Gerard cried, in a weak voice. "Never again! Never! We'll all die!"

He clung, white-knuckled, to the gun whale, and at one point he seemed to be praying.

"Bail!" shouted Adalmand at the top of his lungs. He threw us wooden buckets. Gerard had to forget her suffering and bail water from the bottom of the hull as fast as he could with the rest of us. Even Rose had to join in. Her condition had worsened over the last few days, and I watched her efforts, biting my lip.

The boat surfed along at a terrific pace, and I felt sure we were going to escape from Georgina now. Faster and faster it went as the waves grew bigger, and the rain lashed our faces. Sometimes we seemed to surf down the side of a wave, and then shortly after, the bow would point to the black heavens. The boat leaned right over, and the lowest corner of the sail often dipped into the water.

For perhaps four hours we continued on, with the land out of sight now because of the rain. Then, Adalmand, on lookout in the bow, shouted "Land! Too close! Rocks!"

"Where?" shouted the captain. But Adalmand couldn't hear him.

"He said; 'Where?'" I repeated.

"Ahead. To port!"

I passed his message on against the howling wind and Hadwyn steered us deftly around the spikes of insolent Welsh stone.

Land appeared through the murk about five hundred yards to port. As we moved quickly past this flattish foreland, it quickly became apparent as a peninsula. Behind it calmer water ran up to gravely beaches and yellow lights.

We landed at Fiskigarðr, ancient Fishguard. At the end of the dock, sat a rather louche looking man. He swayed one leg from his perch on a large tied package and sipping from a stoneware jar, muttered:

"Ah! swiþe æþelne monnan comon mid scipum on þære stowe þe is gecueden Fiskigarðr!"

"What did he say?" asked Rose.

I had become more adept at understanding old French, which included a lot of Frankish words and Latin. One of those I recognised was 'scipum' for 'ship.' I could make a rough guess at what he'd said.

"I think he's being sarcastic! He said something like, 'Ah! A very noble man come by ship to Britain to a place called Fiskigarðr.'"

"So this is the port we wanted then?"

"Yes. Come on! Let's hurry! We have another sea voyage ahead of us."

"Oh no!" exclaimed Gerard.

We had passed the louche gentleman, but just before we were out of ear-shot, his rantings rising in volume until I heard three words which chilled me; 'moon,' 'lone' and 'wulf.' I put them out of my mind.

From Fiskigarðr, we took a ship to Juxta-Mare. From there, we took a wagon across Sumorsæte, and by Christmas, Crīstesmæsse to the people at the time, we passed Hampton, called Southampton in modern times.

In Salesberie, we met Henri le Tanner who found us lodgings until the Gate which would take us back to the

13th Century opened. He told us news of ships pursuing us, but they were wrecked on the coast of Cymru. More came later but were sailing around the south coast.

A few days later, I tried to make Rose drink blood. She refused, and so when we passed through the Gate, she was very sick and disorientated.

***

So now we were back in 13th Century France, once more just outside Paris but to the east this time.

I could hardly believe our luck. But then this came with a hint of sadness. If Georgina hadn't pursued us she must be dead. Only later, would I would learn just how lucky we had been.

By now, Rose had become very ill. I didn't understand her illness. Listless and pale, she barely ate. Although I longed to seek out Gerard and Uduward, we had to head west for Grestain.

We reached Grestain in late October and by this time Rose and I just wanted to be home. Rose wasn't eating properly, and then several times she fainted. Clearly something was very wrong! She showed me a small cut Georgina has made on her back. There were many small wounds from cuts the young Sorceress had made while taunting my wife. It seemed the young Frenchwoman could not control her jealousy, and this had seeped out in forms of cruelty – sadism even. But this wound in particular had turned slightly green.

Gangrene? Surely Georgina must have infected it?

Whether deliberate or not, time was running out. The infection had spread despite my attempts to cut out the infection and even cauterise the wound.

When we arrived at the Manor, Herleva wasn't there.

"She's been gone for nearly three weeks and won't be back until December the twelfth!" little Arlette said, taking my hand and pronouncing her words carefully.

"She left you a message though. The maid will bring it to you!"

Sure enough, the maid brought me a small roll of parchment, and I hurriedly opened it.

> Jean,
> When you receive this, if you are still alive,
> I will be away on an important errand. My
> heart tells you that you are alive but that
> some ill has come over you and your wife. I
> do not think this is the work of Georgiana
> but something more powerful, more
> malevolent. Take the road to Amiens, and
> on the other side you will find a Gate in a
> field near two burned twin oak trees before
> you reach Corbie. The trees are famous
> locally, but nobody knows about the Gate. It
> is one of the lesser-known ones. I chose it
> specifically for you to escape. It will open
> on the 3rd November at 3 pm. It will take
> you to your city of London but in the 19th
> Century. The year will be 1812. Gerard will
> give you a little more silver to help you on
> your way. Only seven days after you arrive,
> on the 10th November, you will find another
> Gate opening in the garden behind the small
> chapel in Blackfriars. I could not find a
> Gate to take you all the way back to your
> century so soon. I can tell you that
> Georgiana still pursues you. I perceive this
> clearly. Also, she is in love with you John.
> That much is clear to me now. She has sent
> many men after you, some of them shape-
> changers, while she herself has been called
> to account by the Serpents.

Your Herleva

I felt mixed emotions at the news about Georgina. Relief, mixed with dread, washed over me in alternate waves. We had to get away from here as soon as possible, not only in order to reach the Gate in time but to escape pursuit.

***

We made plans to leave in three days for Corbie.

Only the day before we left, Robertus came galloping into the courtyard at full pelt.

"Am I in time?" he asked Gerard, not noticing or recognising me. I had been sitting with Rose in the parlour.

"In time for what, Monsieur?"

"I have news and a letter for Monsieur John Rezor."

"I'm here," I said turning around.

"I rode like the wind!" he said. "Men are only a day or so from here. They come in pursuit of you."

"Is she with them?"

"She? You mean the Sorceress?"

"Yes. Georgiana?"

"No."

"But I do have news of her. She pursued you, once she had recovered from her wound. She was only one day behind you in Salisberie. As you may know she has now been called to account by others, those more powerful than herself."

"Yes. Herleva told me in a letter."

"I have one other thing for you, a written message."

"Who from?"

"I don't know his name, but if you asked me, I wouldn't advise opening it. He looked very strange to me and left me feeling uneasy."

I took the roll of parchment and turned it over in my hands. I saw no writing on the outside, and it had a blank seal.

"I will read it later, in private." I said.

Later, alone, I opened the roll.

Monsieur Jean
It has been most difficult to find out where you went. None knew, but Robertus the Scribe is said to know most things, and he assured me this message would find you. I have bad news for you. I tell you this, only as a friend and not as a servant of those whose name I dare not speak here.
Your mistress, Georgiana, has been cast through a Gate as punishment for failing. I know not what exactly in what task she has failed, but I presume her task must have been to corrupt your soul in some way because this is usually their way. All I know is that she has been sent back to the 1st Century and is unlikely to escape.
Of course, I have been given this information freely to pass on to you, but I would not pass it on if I felt it could only harm you. It is only, because I am unclear about your feelings for Georgiana that I do tell you this. The spirit world and alliances within it are even harder to discern to one who is confused and lost, as I was. I can only thank you from the bottom of my heart for the loyalty you gave my Lord and I. I have released your friend Guillaume, from the dungeon. He has gone north and wishes you a good future.

I have been told to inform you that there is a Gate which will take you back to the 1st century from 1810. If you should wish to use it, talk to a Yohannes Brieghoffer at 18 Hanbury Street. Ask him about the bright lights he sees every year on 22nd November.

I am ever your friend, Raul.

Raul! Who would ever have thought he would thank me! And Guillaume free! I am glad he isn't going anywhere near Monségur Castle.
But then thought sadly of Georgina.
The 1st Century! She won't survive long there! Herleva told me it's perilous to go so far back! Still, I can do nothing. I must ignore it.

***

I took Gerard aside as soon as I could.
"Gerard. What are we going to do about Uduward. I can't take him with me."
"No. I have given that some thought. He can stay here with me. I'll look after him."
"You would do that? I would be so grateful. I really feel bad, leaving him here."
"He'll be fine. I just hope, one day, you'll come back and visit us!"
"I just don't know how I'm going to tell him!"
The following morning, I could no longer delay. I called Gerard and Uduward to meet with me away from Rose, in the little room in which I used to sleep.
"I have to leave you both. Gerard, you know I am going tomorrow. Uduward, we didn't tell you, because I wasn't sure what to say. The thing about the future is that it's not *here*! It's where I belong, but you don't belong there. I can't take you with me. Even if I wanted

to, I'm not sure what would happen to you. Most probably you would grow old and die very quickly."

"It's alright. Gerard has already explained to me," he said, with a tear rolling down his cheek. He smiled.

"I have to take Rose back anyway. She is very ill now and won't survive if we stay here any longer. That really would mean that everything had been a waste of time, wouldn't it?" I joked.

"Yes. You might come back though, one day?"

"I don't know. It's possible. You never can tell with these things." Thoughts of Georgina ran unbidden through my mind.

Gerard seemed much more resigned about our departure when Rose and I mounted our horses to ride for Corbie. The route had not been planned, and I intended leaving no trace as we went. All those who knew where we were going, knew they had to keep our destination a strict secret.

"Good luck Monsieur Jean! It's been a great adventure with you!" the old knight called out, as we rode off.

"Adieu Monsieur!" shouted Uduward.

A tear rolled down my cheek as I called my farewells.

***

Taking a random course, we reached Corbie in time although I had to hire a wagon along the way to carry Rose. Her back had become completely inflamed now. I worried continually about her. Although feverish, she somehow managed to keep her spirits up. She smiled and often told me everything would be alright.

Only one thing of note happened on our journey. Under a warm, noon sun, I noticed something unusual next to the road.

"Well, I'm damned! Look at this Rose!"

She looked where I pointed.

To the left of the track, separated from it by an overgrown grass verge, I saw an unmistakable type of wall, still with the faint trace of a blue-painted, decorative line running along its width.

"It's Roman. Actually, if I'm not mistaken, this is the last remains of a Roman Villa!"

"Are you sure?" she asked.

"A large house like this… like a palace…? And with that construction and decoration…?"

Nowhere, in all of northern Europe did any part of an original Roman Villa still stand in my time. They had all crumbled to dust or been carried away for stone, long ago. But here, the last remains of one still stood. There were only a few courses of great whitish stone – a few more at the only remaining corner, but to the eyes of a historian, they were a wondrous sight.

"In the 20th Century, there are none of these left!"

Indeed, it didn't look as if this one would last more than another few generations. Some stone blocks had been eased away from their mortar and stacked in a neat pile a little further on up the road.

"Let's stop here for lunch. I need to look at this."

After hastily eating some bread and salted lamb, I took a walk around the ruins. There wasn't much left to see. Several old oak trees grew where the inner courtyard might have once stood, indicating that the villa had been ruined for at least a few hundred years. I found a few beggars sleeping behind the wall. They were confused when I bade them stay where they were; there were at least two children and a woman among the little bundles of rags.

I would have loved to sketch the ruin, but there wasn't any time. I could try to memorise everything about the location and make a note of it later. Perhaps one day, back in the 20th Century, I would be able to locate it. Maybe it wasn't even known about then.

When I had made the best mental notes I could, I returned to the wagon. Just as we left, another wagon, hauled by an old, mangy mule, pulled up. Its rotund, whistling occupant proceeded to winch one of the blocks from the pile, up a wooden ramp and onto the wagon using a primitive winch. The mule stretched out its scrawny neck so that it could reach a few blades of succulent grass.

We found the two oak trees, just as Herleva had described them, and I carried Rose into the white beam of light that seemed to reach up to the stars. This time she had taken a little blood, either too weak to resist or simply wishing to avoid any more suffering.

We found ourselves lying in a cobbled yard in the old City of London. I took lodgings in a garret room and immediately fetched a doctor. He seemed somewhat shocked by our clothes and even more shocked by the ancient silver coins I offered for his services. But silver is silver, and he did his best. The laudanum at least eased Rose's suffering.

***

Thus, I found I had time on my hands and so started writing up this tale. Though I have yet to write the battle scenes in any detail, staying up night and day as I have been, I have had time to add to my journal so that I have nearly completed the story.

The piece about the animal state and many other details were jotted down in what I call a journal; a large piece of vellum which I folded up and carried around with me once we returned to the 13th Century from the 7th. This I added to until by the time we arrived in this garret room, it had become almost a book in itself. Together, the journal and my scribblings in this garret, will form the whole tale I present to you, dear reader.

***

As you can imagine, the thoughts that have most often distracted from my writing have been of Rose … and Georgina.

Most taxing of all have been thoughts about the Gate that might take me back to Georgina in the 1st Century. Of course, I am still furious with her for what has befallen Rose, and I can't but help remembering what Georgina said to me in the Tower when I thought she might have sacrificed my wife.

"I tried to do it. I want the eternal life which your friend Herleva enjoys so much, but to take your wife would make you hate me forever. I just couldn't do it. You see, I still love you."

That is the problem; she loves me, and I still love her. I want to forget her, forget her plight, but I just cannot. Even now, I am contemplating placing Rose in the Gate to her own century and using the Gate on the 22nd November myself to take me back to the age of Christ. I just *might* do it. I have already met Yohannes Brieghoffer. I am sure Rose would be alright.

And now the blood is taking effect, and the time to use the final Gate has come. I have to leave you for a while. I have to carry Rose downstairs to the waiting cab which will take us to Blackfriars Chapel and, from there, through the Gate and back to the 20th Century.

***

As I write this, I am looking out over the garden from our flat in Highgate. Rose is asleep now. It's her first night away from the hospital. The infection was almost fatal and only constant medication with the strongest antibiotics saved her. The cause was never explained.

Rose and I arrived together on the shores of Lake Coniston, Cumbria, in the late afternoon of 4th September, 1997, more than a year after the skiing holiday in the Pyrenees. It was typical of Herleva to be so thoughtful as to get us home so close to the time we left. Dressed in 13th Century clothes, covered with overcoats from the 19th Century, we must have looked like refugees from some bizarre fancy-dress party. I asked some tourists to fetch the police who took us straight to the nearest hospital. I made up a story about having woken up with no memory by the lake. We said that the last we remembered was the avalanche in the Pyrenees. A few phone calls corroborated our story, and we were driven all the way home in a police Jaguar.

***

The single sheet of parchment, which I gave to Rose for safekeeping, turned out to be the original from which document BC 10 had been copied, in fact, copied by Bernard of Clairvaux. This leaf, however, unlike the torn one, was complete. It did, indeed, list the Royal line, descending from Dagobert II in the 7th Century, but the entry for Dagobert II's issue caught my eye. Next to his name I saw that of a wife, Mechthilde and two daughters, one of which was Hermine!

Immediately I remembered the young prisoners in the Tower. Could they possibly be one and the same? The Dagobert II that I knew of, famous from conspiracy theories surrounding Rennes-le-Château, had died childless. It took short work with some books on the Merovingian line of kings to discover a rumour that Dagobert II had married while studying at Slane. The rumour claimed that he'd married Mechthilde, a Saxon princess and had two daughters by her, one being named Hermine. Both daughters had become abbesses, but another rumour had it that Hermine had given birth to a son, Grimoald, quite late in life. Grimoald, for fear of his being assassinated by other claimants to the Austrian throne, had been sent south to somewhere in what is now Bulgaria to be raised in safety with a noble family.

The family's name; Raysar. From him, descendants right down to the 15th Century were listed. I had to read it about ten times before I could put the parchment down and take a deep breath. I closed my eyes, counted to ten and looked again. It still said Raysar. Could it be my family's name? I remembered seeing a genealogical list tucked into the back of the old book given to me by my grandfather, but this had run out sometime in the 15th Century. Nevertheless, the last name discovered, and the one at the top of the tree, had been Raysar. I had to dig deeper.

A friend of mine was an expert genealogist, knew about the etymology and origin of names. He confirmed that the two names were connected and went on, within two weeks, to confirm that the two trees were connected by one missing name, that of Balthasar Raysar who died in approximately 1480.

As you may know, Dagobert II's line was believed to have died with him. I now have proof that it didn't. I have even met that proof in person! I am quite sure that neither Dagobert II, nor any of his immediate descendent, were wolf-Angels or members of Ordo Lupus. However, my line of descent *is* one of Ordo Lupus; an order of wolf-Angels, winged-wolves, spirits in the fight against the Serpents – call them what you will.

This means that somewhere down the line, probably shortly after Dagobert II, the two lines merged, and I am the product of both. But, of course, Edward's son, Michael will become a member of Ordo Lupus when he grows up, and that, as I have said before, fills me with disquiet. I still do not yet fully understand what Ordo Lupus actually *is*!

***

So it seems that Georgina had been given the task of luring me to Slane, where she would sacrifice Rose. She could then prove to me that I was from the Royal blood line of Dagobert. With that firmly acknowledged by me, I would have been so enraged and filled with bitter hatred, that I would have murdered Georgina. This would have damned me forever and, given who I really am, would have made a great coup for the Serpents and Satan. This reminded me of something Cathal had once said to me when I talked about my strange talent of perception and how often I felt tempted by the Devil.

"Yes, that *is* a bit unusual, but don't you know Satan spends more time trying to tempt angels than he ever does bothering the world of men?"

Too bad, then, that Georgina couldn't do it. Too bad, also, that I did not know in time who I am really descended from. Perhaps Georgina would have told me and then shown me the prisoners as proof if she had been able to carry out the Serpent's plans.

***

Rose remained distant from me. Only one year later, on holiday, did she finally relent.

I sat beside her and put my hand gently on her shoulder. Her hand slowly reached out, and I took it.

"I missed you so, darling," I said into her ear. "I thought you would never let me touch you again."

"That thing! That thing that walked into the tower. It – you, were hideous; a cross between a wolf and a man! I don't understand any of this John. I thought I knew you, but I don't know *anything about* you! I don't understand it. But don't ever explain it to me. I don't want to understand it. You promise?"

"Okay. I do."

She turned her head and our lips met. We kissed for a long moment.

"One thing I *do* want to know," she said, as our lips parted, and she nestled her head into my shoulder.

"What's that?"

"Who is this Herleva?"

***

The End

Bibliography

Holy Entrepreneurs: Cistercians, Knights, and Economic Exchange in Twelfth-Century Burgundy by Constance Brittain Bouchard.

"Strong of Body, Brave and Noble": Chivalry and Society in Medieval France by Constance Brittain Bouchard.

Heresy in Medieval France: Dualism in Aquitaine and the Agenais, 1000-1249 by Claire Taylor.

Hugh of Poitiers: *The Vezelay Chronicle: And Other Documents from Ms. Auxerre 227 and Elsewhere, Translated into English With Notes, Introduction, and Accompanying Materials* by John Scott and John O. Ward.

The account of the Battle of Bouvines is as historically accurate as I could make it, and the following references were used.

The Legend of Bouvines: War, Religion and Culture in the Middle Ages, by Georges Duby, translated by Catherine Tihanyi.

The Battle of Bouvines according to William the Breton (prose account).

The Battle of Bouvines according to the Anonymous of Bethune.

The Battle of Bouvines according to Roger of
  Wendover:

"But since this day was a Sunday, the wisest in the
army, and particularly Renaud, formerly Count of
Boulogne, stated that it would not be very honorable to
wage a battle on such a solemn day and to sully this day
with homicide and the spilling of human blood. The
Emperor Otto went along with this viewpoint and said
that if he fought on such a day, he could never boast of
a joyous triumph. At these words, Hugh of Boves lost
his temper and, cursing, called the Count Renand a
despicable traitor, and reproached him for the lands and
the large possessions that he had received from the
King of England's generosity. He added that the
postponement of the battle to another day would bring
irreparable damage which would harm King John and
that one always has cause to repent when one has not
grasped a favorable opportunity. Renaud answered
Hugh with indignation: "This day will prove that it is I
who is loyal and you who are a traitor; because on this
Sunday I will, if need be, fight to the death for the King
while you, as usual, on this same day, you will show to
all by running away that you are the evil traitor." These
insulting words provoked by Hugh of Boves' similar
words, soured everyone's spirits and made the battle
unavoidable."

* * *

Biography of Lazlo Ferran

Lazlo Ferran: Exploring the Landscapes of Truth.

Educated near Oxford, during English author Lazlo Ferran's extraordinary life, he has been an aeronautical engineering student, dispatch rider, graphic designer, full-time busker, guitarist and singer, recording two albums. Having grown up in rural Buckinghamshire Lazlo says:

"The beautiful Chiltern Hills offered the ideal playground for a child's mind, in contrast to the ultra-strict education system of Bucks."

Brought up as a Buddhist, he has travelled widely, surviving a student uprising in Athens and living for a while in Cairo, just after Sadat's assassination. Later, he spent some time in Central Asia and was only a few blocks away from gunfire during an attempt to storm the government buildings of Bishkek in 2006. He has a keen interest in theologies and philosophies of the Far East, Middle East, Asia and Eastern Europe.

After a long and successful career within the science industry, Lazlo Ferran left to concentrate on writing, to continue exploring the landscapes of truth.

From the author:

Thank you for reading my story and I hope you liked it. I value very much feedback from people and need this if each book is to be better than the last, so if you could take the time to either post a comment on my amazon page or my blog or simply email me, I would appreciate it.

Where to find Lazlo Ferran
Blog: http://www.lazloferran.com
Email: lazloferran@gmail.com